AF172964

Mass' George
A Boy's Adventures in the Old Savannah

by

George Manville Fenn

Double 9
BOOKS

Mass' George
A Boy's Adventures in the Old Savannah
by George Manville Fenn

Copyright © 2024

All Rights reserved.

No part of this publication may be reproduced, stored in a retrieval system, or transmitted in any form or by any means, electronic, mechanical, photocopying or Otherwise, without the written permission of the publisher.
The author/editor asserts the moral right to be identified as the author/editor of this work.

ISBN: 978-93-63059-20-7

Published by

DOUBLE 9 BOOKS

2/13-B, Ansari Road
Daryaganj, New Delhi – 110002
info@double9books.com
www.double9books.com
Tel. 011-40042856

This book is under public domain

ABOUT THE AUTHOR

George Manville Fenn was a very productive author of novels, a writer, an editor, and an educator from England. He was born on January 3, 1831, in Pimlico, London. He mostly learned on his own; he taught himself Italian, French, and German. During the years 1851–1854, he went to Battersea Training College for Teachers and then became the head of a state school in Alford, Lincolnshire. In the early 1850s, Fenn started to write short stories and pieces for newspapers and magazines. The Old Forest Ranger, his first book, came out in 1856. Afterward, he wrote more than 100 books, many of them for teenagers and young adults. He was one of the most famous writers of his time, and his books were well-liked and read by many people. He also worked as a reporter and writer for Fenn. Among the newspapers and magazines, he worked for was The Boy's Own Paper, which he ran from 1866 to 1874. He worked hard to make children's books better and was a strong supporter of education and reading. The Englishman Fenn passed away on August 26, 1909, in Isleworth.

CONTENTS

Chapter One 9

Chapter Two..15

Chapter Three 18

Chapter Four 22

Chapter Five...30

Chapter Six 38

Chapter Seven..47

Chapter Eight...53

Chapter Nine..64

Chapter Ten..74

Chapter Eleven 84

Chapter Twelve...90

Chapter Thirteen...95

Chapter Fourteen..99

Chapter Fifteen 105

Chapter Sixteen...120

Chapter Seventeen...129

Chapter Eighteen...140

Chapter Nineteen 144

Chapter Twenty 151

Chapter Twenty One...160

Chapter Twenty Two 167

Chapter Twenty Three..177

Chapter Twenty Four...184

Chapter Twenty Five..187

Chapter Twenty Six..191

Chapter Twenty Seven..197

Chapter Twenty Eight...209

Chapter Twenty Nine 216

Chapter Thirty 220

Chapter Thirty One 227

Chapter Thirty Two..238

Chapter Thirty Three 245

Chapter Thirty Four...248

Chapter Thirty Five..257

Chapter Thirty Six 263

Chapter Thirty Seven 268

Chapter Thirty Eight...273

Chapter Thirty Nine..289

Chapter Forty...294

Chapter Forty One...299

Chapter Forty Two 309

Chapter Forty Three..315

Chapter Forty Four..321

Chapter Forty Five 322

Chapter Forty Six...326

Chapter Forty Seven...333

Chapter Forty Eight..339

Chapter Forty Nine 346

Chapter Fifty 350

Chapter Fifty One 353

Chapter Fifty Two 358

Chapter Fifty Three 363

Chapter Fifty Four 367

Chapter Fifty Five 372

Chapter One

Interesting? My life? Well, let me see. I suppose some people would call it so, for now I come to think of it I did go through a good deal; what with the fighting with the Spaniards, and the Indians, and the fire, and the floods, and the wild beasts, and such-like adventures. Yes; it never seemed to occur to me before, you know, me—George Bruton, son of Captain Bruton of the King's army, who went out with the General to help colonise Georgia, as they called the country after his Majesty King George the Second, and went through perils and dangers such as no one but English gentlemen and their brave followers would dare and overcome.

You'll find it all in your histories; how the General had leave to take so many followers, and carve out for themselves land and estates in the beautiful new country.

My father was one of the party. He went, for he was sick at heart and despondent. He had married a sweet English lady—my mother—and when I was about six years old she died; and after growing more and more unhappy for a couple of years, his friends told him that if he did not seek active life of some kind, he would die too, and leave me an orphan indeed.

That frightened him so that he raised himself up from his despondent state, readily embraced the opportunity offered by the General's expedition, sold his house in the country to which he had retired on leaving the army, and was going out to the southern part of North America with me only. But Sarah would not hear of parting from me, and begged my father to take her to be my attendant and his servant, just as on the same day Morgan Johns, our gardener, had volunteered to go with his master. Not that he was exactly a gardener, though he was full of gardening knowledge, and was a gardener's son; for he had been in my father's company in the old regiment, and when my father left it, followed him down and settled quite into a domestic life.

Well, as Morgan Johns volunteered to go with the expedition, and said nothing would suit him better than gardening in a new country, and doing a bit of fighting if it was wanted, and as our Sarah had volunteered too, it fell out quite as a matter of course, that one day as my father was seated in his room writing letters, and making his final preparations for his venturesome journey, and while I was seated there looking at the pictures in a book, Morgan and Sarah came in dressed in their best clothes, and stood both of them looking very red in the face.

"Well?" said my father, in the cold, stern way in which he generally spoke then; "what is it?"

"Tell him, Sarah," I heard Morgan whisper, for I had gone up to put my hand in hers.

"For shame!" she said; "it's you who ought."

"Now look you," said Morgan, who was a Welshman, and spoke very Welshy sometimes, "didn't you just go and promise to help and obey? And the first thing I tells you to do you kicks."

"I am very busy," said my father. "If you two want a holiday, say so."

"Holiday, sir? Not us," said Morgan, in a hesitating way. "We don't want no holiday, sir, only we felt like as it was our dooty to tell you what—"

"To tell me what?"

"Yes, sir; seeing as we were going out to a savage country, where you've got to do everything yourself before you can have it, and as there'd be no parsons and churches, we thought we'd get it done decent and 'spectable here first."

"My good fellow, what do you mean?" said my father.

"Why, what I've been telling of you, sir. Sarah says—"

"I did not, Morgan, and I shouldn't have thought of such a thing. It was all your doing."

"Steady in the ranks, my lass. Be fair. I'll own to half of it, but you know you were just as bad as me."

"I was not, sir, indeed," cried Sarah, beginning to sob. "He deluded me into it, and almost forced me to say yes."

"Man's dooty," said Morgan, dryly.

"What!" cried my father, smiling; "have you two gone and been married?"

"Stop there, sir, please, begging your pardon," said Morgan; "I declare to gootness, you couldn't make a better guess than that."

"I beg your pardon, sir," said Sarah, who was very red in the face before, but scarlet now; and as I sit down and write all this, as an old man, everything comes back to me as vividly as if it were only yesterday—for though I have forgotten plenty of my later life, all this is as fresh as can be—"I beg your pardon, sir, but as you know all the years I have been in your service, and with my own dear angel of a mistress—Heaven bless her!"

"Amen," said my father, and, stern soldier as he was, I saw the tears stand thick in his eyes, for poor Sarah broke down and began to sob, while Morgan turned his face and began to blow his nose like a trumpet out of tune.

"I—I beg your pardon for crying, sir, and it's very weak, I own," continued Sarah, after a few minutes' interval, during which I hurriedly put my arm round her, and she dabbed down and kissed me, leaving my face very wet; "but you know I never meant to be married, but when Morgan comes to me and talks about what I was thinking about—how you and that poor darling motherless boy was to get on in foreign abroad, all amongst wild beasts and savages, and no one to make a drop o' gruel if you had colds, or to make your beds, or sew on a button, and your poor stockings all in holes big enough to break any decent woman's heart, and to Master George's head—"

"I can wash my own head well enough now, Sarah," I said.

"Yes, my dear; but I don't believe you'd do it as well as I could, and you know I never let the soap get in your eyes. And when, sir, Morgan comes to me, and he asks me if I'd got the heart to let you both go out into the wilderness like that without a soul to look after you, and tells me as it was my dooty to marry him, and go out and look after the housekeeping for you both, while he did the garden, what could I say?"

Poor Sarah paused quite out of breath.

"Say?" said my father, smiling, but looking very much moved. "You could only say yes, like the good, true-hearted woman you are."

"Oh, sir!" exclaimed Sarah.

Mass' George: A Boy's Adventures in the Old Savannah | 11

"You have both relieved me of a great deal of care and anxiety by your faithful, friendly conduct," continued my father, "for it will make what I am going to seek in the wilderness quite a home at once. It is not the wilderness you think, for I know on very good authority that the place where we are going is a very beautiful and fertile country."

"Can't come up to Wales," said Morgan, shaking his head.

"Perhaps not," said my father, smiling; "but very beautiful all the same. I ought to warn you both, though, while there is time to draw back, that the land is entirely new."

"What, wasn't it made with the rest of the world, sir?" said Morgan, staring.

"Yes, of course," said my father; "but I mean it has never been inhabited more than by a few Indians, who passed through it when hunting. No houses; not so much as a road."

"Then there won't be no taverns, Sarah," said Morgan, giving her a nudge.

"And a very good thing too," she replied.

"So that," continued my father, "I shall have to help cut down the trees to build my own house, make my own furniture, and fence in the estate—in short, do everything."

"Well, I don't see nothing to grumble at in that, sir, so long as there's plenty of wood," said Morgan.

"There'll be too much wood, my man," said my father, smiling, "and we shall have to ply the axe hard to clear our way."

"Any stone or slate, sir?"

"Plenty of stone, but no slate that I am aware of."

"No," cried Morgan, triumphantly. "I knew there'd be no slate. That proves as it won't come up to Wales. There isn't such a country for slate anywhere as Wales. Well, sir, but even if there's no slate, we can make shift. First thing we do as soon as we get out, will be for me to rig the missus up a bit of a kitchen, and we shall take a few pots and pans in a box."

"Oh, I shall go well provided with necessaries," said my father.

"Then pray don't forget a frying-pan, sir. It's wonderful what the missus here can do with a frying-pan."

"Do be quiet, Morgan Johns," said Sarah.

"Shan't," he growled. "I'm a-telling of the truth. It's wonderful, sir, that it is. Give her a frying-pan and a bit o' fire, and we shan't never hurt for a bit o' well-cooked victuals."

"But—" began my father, when Morgan rushed in again.

"Washin', sir, I forgot all about the washing. We shall want a tub and a line. Trees 'll do for tying up to, and you'll see we shall none of us ever want for clean clothes."

"Do be quiet, Morgan."

"I shan't, Sarah. It's only fair as the master should know what you can do, look you."

"But I wish you people to think seriously now, while there is yet time," said my father.

"Seriously, sir? Oh yes, we've been thinking of it seriously enough, and—I say, missus, do try and do without flat-irons; they're very heavy kind o' traps for a man to take in his kit."

"Come, come," said my father; "you had better think better of it, and not embrace such a rough life."

"We have thought better on it, sir, and the very best too. We're coming, and if you won't take us, we'll come without. And look you, sir, of course you'll take some guns, and swords, and powder and shot."

"Of course."

"Then don't forget some tools: spades, and hoes, and seeds, and some carpenter's things and nails. You can't think what a deal can be done with a hammer, a saw, and a few nails."

"Then you mean to come?"

"Mean to come, sir?" cried Morgan, in astonishment. "Why we got married o' purpose; didn't we, Sarah?"

"Oh yes, sir; that's the very truth."

"And we shall be obliged to go now."

I did not see where the obligation came in, but I supposed it was all right.

"Then I can only say thank you heartily," cried my father, warmly; "and for my part, I'll do my duty by you both."

"Of course we know that, don't we, Sarah? Or else we shouldn't go."

"My dear master!" said Sarah, and she bent forward and kissed his hand before clapping her handkerchief to her eyes, and rushing out of the room.

"She'll be all right, sir, soon," whispered Morgan. "And look you, I'll begin getting together all sorts of little tackle, sir, as I think 'll be useful out yonder. Knives and string, and—look you, Master George, strikes me as a few hooks and lines wouldn't be amiss. A few good fish in a frying-pan, cooked as Sarah can cook 'em, arn't to be sneezed at now and then."

He gave us both a sharp nod, and hastily followed his wife, while I stayed to pester my father with endless questions about our new home.

Chapter Two

The month which followed was one scene of excitement to me. We went into lodgings in Bristol, and my father seemed to be always busy making purchases, or seeing the different gentlemen who were going out with us in the same ship.

I recollect many of their faces. There was the General, a firm, kindly-looking man, who always seemed to me as if he could not possibly be a soldier, he was too quiet. Then there was Colonel Preston, a handsome, florid gentleman, ten years older than my father, and I heard that his wife, two sons and daughter were to be of the party.

In a misty kind of way, too, I can recollect that the gentlemen who came and had long talks with my father, used to chat about the plantations in Virginia and Carolina, and about a charter from the King, and that the place we were going to was to be called Georgia, because the King's name was the same as mine.

Then, too, there was a great deal of talk about the enemy; and as I used to sit and listen, I understood that the Spaniards were the enemy, and that they lived in Florida. But every one laughed; and my father, I remember, said gravely—

"I do not fear anything that the Spaniards can do to hinder us, gentlemen, I am more disposed to dread the climate."

A great deal that followed has now, at this time of writing, become confused and mixed up; but I can remember the cheering from the wharves as our ship floated away with the tide, people talking about us as adventurers, and that soon after it came on to blow, and my next recollections are of being in a dark cabin lit by a lantern, which swung to and fro, threatening sometimes to hit the smoky ceiling. I did not pay much heed to it though, for I was too ill, and the only consolation I had was that of seeing Sarah's motherly face by the dim light, and hearing her kindly, comforting words.

Then, after a very stormy voyage, we seemed, as I recollect it, to have glided slowly out of winter into summer, and we were off a land of glorious sunshine at the mouth of a river, up which we sailed.

I know there was a great deal done afterwards in the way of formal taking possession in the name of the King, and I can recollect being delighted with the show that was made, and at seeing my father and the other gentlemen wearing gay clothes and sashes and plumes, and with swords buckled on. Even Morgan partook of the change, and I well recall how he came to me just before he landed, in a kind of grenadier uniform, with sword and musket and belts, drawing himself up very stiff and proud-looking as he let down the butt-end of his firelock with a loud bang upon the deck.

"Do I look all right and soldierly, Master George?" he whispered, after a glance round to see that he was not overheard.

"Yes," I said, "you look fine. Is your gun loaded?"

"Not yet, my lad."

"Pull out your sword and let's look at it."

"By and by, my lad," he said; "but tell me; I do look all right, don't I?"

"Yes. Why?"

"Because Sarah's got a nasty fit on this mornin'. Don't tell her I told you; but she said I looked fit to be laughed at, and that there'd be no fighting for me: Indians would all run away."

"Oh, never mind what she says," I cried. "I wish I was big enough for a soldier."

"Wait a bit, boy, you'll grow," he said, as he busily tightened a well-whitened belt. "You see it's so long since I've been soldiering, that I'm a bit out of practice."

There was no enemy, Indian or Spaniard, to oppose us, and before long the land had been roughly surveyed and portioned out, my father, as an officer of good standing, being one of the earliest to choose; and in a very short time we were preparing to go out on the beautiful little estate that had become his, for the most part forest-land, with a patch or two of rich, easily-drained marsh on both sides of a little stream which ran, not far away, into the great river up which we had sailed, and upon which, just below us, was to be formed the new city.

Then time glided on, and as I recall everything I can, I have recollections of the gentlemen of the expedition, and common men, soldiers and others, coming with their swords and guns to our place, and all working hard together, after setting sentries and scouts to give warning of danger, and cutting down trees, and using saws, and helping to roughly build a little wooden house, and put up a fence for us.

Then, after getting our things in shelter, my father and Morgan joined in helping to build and clear for some one else; and so on, week after week, all working together to begin the settlement, till we were all provided with rough huts and shelters for the valuable stores and ammunition brought out. After which people began to shift for themselves, to try and improve the rough places first built.

Chapter Three

With a new place, every touch makes a difference; and when some of those touches are given by the hand of a gardener, nature begins to help.

It was so at our Georgia home. Every bit of time my father or Morgan could find to spare, they were digging, or trimming, or planting, till Sarah would set to and grumble to me because they would not come in to their meals.

"I wouldn't care, sir," she would say, "only the supper's getting spoiled."

"But the home made more beautiful," replied my father; and then I have heard him say as he glanced through the window at flower and tree flourishing wonderfully in that beautiful climate, "If my poor wife had lived to see all this!"

Early and late worked Morgan, battling with the wild vines and beautiful growths that seemed to be always trying to make the garden we were redeeming from the wilderness come back to its former state. But he found time to gratify me, and he would screw up his dry Welsh face and beckon to me sometimes to bring a stick and hunt out squirrel, coon, or some ugly little alligator, which he knew to be hiding under the roots of a tree in some pool. Then, as much to please me as for use, a punt was bought from the owners of a brig which had sailed across from Bristol to make her last voyage, being condemned to breaking up at our infant port.

The boat, however, was nearly new, and came into my father's hands complete, with mast, sail, ropes, and oars; and it was not long before I gained the mastery over all that it was necessary to learn in the management.

Morgan's fishing-tackle came into use, and after a little instruction and help from the Welshman, I began to wage war upon the fish in our stream and in the river, catching, beside, ugly little reptiles of the tortoise or turtle family—strange objects to be hauled up from muddy depths at one end of a line, but some of them very good eating all the same.

The little settlement throve as the time went on, and though the Indians were supposed to be threatening, and to look with very little favour upon the settlement so near their hunting-grounds, all remained peaceful, and we had nothing but haughty overbearing words from our Spanish neighbours.

To a man the officers and gentlemen who had come out turned their attention to agriculture, and many were the experiments tried, and successfully too. At one estate cotton was growing; at another, where there was a lot of rich low land easily flooded, great crops of rice were raised. Here, as I walked round with my father, we passed broad fields of sugar-cane, and farther on the great crinkled-leaved Indian corn flourished wonderfully, with its flower tassels, and beautiful green and then orange-buff ears of hard, sweet, flinty corn.

Then came long talks about the want of more help, and one of the settlers braved public opinion, and every one began to talk about how shocking it was for an English gentleman to purchase slaves. But before many months had passed there was hardly a settler without slave labour, the principal exception being my father.

It is hard to paint a picture in words, but I should like those who read this to understand what my home was like when I was about twelve years old, a great strong healthy boy, with cheeks burned brown by the sun.

Our place began with one low erection, divided by a rough partition into two—our room and the Morgans'; most of our meals being eaten in the big rustic porch contrived by Morgan in what he called his spare time, and over which ran wildly the most beautiful passion-flower I had ever seen.

But then as wood was abundant, and a saw-pit had been erected, a more pretentious one-floored cottage residence was planned to join on to the first building, which before long was entirely devoted to the servants; and we soon had a very charming little home with shingle roof, over which beautiful creepers literally rioted, and hung down in festoons from our windows.

Every day seemed to mellow and beautify this place, and the wild garden dotted with lovely cypresses and flowering shrubs, mingled with every kind of fruit-tree that my father and Morgan had been able to get together. Over trellises, and on the house facing south, grape-vines flourished wonderfully. Peaches were soon in abundance, and such fruits familiar to English people at home as would bear the climate filled the garden.

My father's estate extended for a considerable distance, but the greater part remained as it had been tilled by nature, the want of assistance confining his efforts to a comparatively small garden; but he used to say to me, in his quiet, grave way—

"We might grow more useful things, George, but we could not make the place more beautiful."

And I often used to think so, as I gazed out of my window at the wild forest, and the openings leading down to the stream and away to the swamp, where I could hear the alligators barking and bellowing at night, with a feeling half dread, half curiosity, and think that some day I should live to see one that I had caught or killed myself, close at hand.

Now and then Morgan used to call me to come and see where a 'gator, as he called it, had been in the night, pointing out its track right up to the rough fence of the garden.

"You and I'll have a treat one of these days, my lad."

"Yes," I used to say; "but when?"

"Oh, one of these days when I'm not busy."

"Ah, Morgan," I used to say, impatiently, "when you're not busy: when will that be?"

"Be? One o' these days when we've cut down all the wood, and turned all that low flat swamp into plantation. You see I'm so busy just now."

"Oh, very well," I said, "I shall go by myself."

"That you won't, look you," he cried. "I heard you promise your father you wouldn't go alone. You're not much of a boy, but you're too good to feed alligators with, or let the rattlesnakes and 'cassins try their pyson on."

"But they wouldn't, I should take care."

"Take care? Do you know, there's 'gators big as trees in these swamp-holes. I shouldn't wonder if there's some of the old open-countenanced beauties big round as houses. Why, Master George, I believe there's fellows out there as old as the river, and as could take you as easy as I do a pill."

"Don't believe it."

"Ve-ry well then; only mind, if one does take you across the middle, give you a pitch up in the air, and then catch you head-first and swallow you, don't you blame me."

"Why, how could I, if he swallowed me?" I said.

"Oh, I don't know. You might holler or knock, if you had a stick in your hand."

"What stuff!"

"Oh, is it! There's plenty of room in 'em, and they're as hard as horn. But you take my advice, and don't try."

"Well, then, come with me; I know several holes where I think they live."

"How do you know that?"

"Because I've seen the footmarks leading down to them all plain in the mud."

"Then you've been going too far, and don't you run no risks again."

I walked away discontentedly, as I'd often walked away before, wishing that I had a companion of my own age.

Some of the gentlemen settled out there had sons; but they were away, and at times the place seemed very lonely; but I fancy now that was only just before a storm, or when everything felt strange and depressing. At other times I was happy enough. Every morning I had three hours' good study with my father, who very rarely let me neglect that. Then in the afternoon there was always something to do or something to see and help over. For, as far as my father's means would allow, he planned and contrived endless things to make our home more attractive and convenient.

One week it would be the contriving of rough tree-trunk steps down from the bank to the water's edge, so that the boat was easily reached, and ringbolts were driven into cut-down trees, which became natural posts for mooring the boat.

Another time during one of our walks, he stopped by a lovely pool out toward the swamp—a spot of about an acre and a half in extent, where the trees kept off the wind, and where the morning sun seemed to light up the bottom, showing every pebble and every fish as if seen through crystal glass.

"There," he said, "that will be ten times better than bathing in the river. I always feel a little nervous about you there. This shall be your own private bathing-pool, where you can learn to swim to your heart's content. That old fallen hickory will do for your dressing-room, and there are places to hang up your clothes. I don't think you can come to harm here."

Of course I was delighted, and at the same time a little disappointed; for the fact that the pool was perfectly safe took away somewhat from its attractiveness, and I began to think that there was no stream to carry one along; no very deep places to swim over and feel a thrill at the danger; no holes in the banks where an alligator might be smiling pleasantly as he thought how good a boy would be to eat.

Chapter Four

I am obliged to run quickly through my early unadventurous days, skipping, as it were, from memory to memory of things which happened before life became serious and terrible for us all at the plantation, and storms and peril followed rapidly after the first pleasant calm. For it seems to me now, as I sit and think, that nothing could have been happier than the life on the river during the first days of the settlement. Of course, everybody had to work hard, but it was in a land of constant sunshine, of endless spring and summer days—cold weather was hardly known—and when a storm came, though the thunder and lightning were terrible and the rain tremendous, everything afterwards seemed to bound into renewed life, and the scent of the virgin forest was delightful. All worked hard, but there was the certain repayment, and in what must have been a very short time, the settlers had raised a delightful home in the wilderness, where all was so dreamy and peaceful that their weapons and military stores seemed an encumbrance, and many felt that they would have done more wisely if they had brought agricultural implements instead.

Before we left England, as I have told you, the adventurers who met at my father's rooms talked of the ruthless savage—the lurking Indian of the forest and prairie, and also of our neighbours the Spaniards; but as soon as we reached the place, it seemed to all that the Indians did not exist; and as to the Spaniards, they were far south, separated by long stretches of open land, forests, river, and swamp, and might, for aught we knew, be at the other side of the world.

I was sitting indoors one bright sunny day, and I had just reached finishing distance with a Latin translation my father had left me to do, when I heard a quick "Hist!" Looking up, I saw Morgan at the window.

"'Most done?" he said.

"Yes."

"Then come along, I'll show you something."

I bounded out, to find him armed with a stick about six feet long, provided with a little fork at the end made by driving in a couple of nails and bending them out.

"What is it?" I cried, excitedly.

"Enemy. Get yourself a good stout stick."

"Rake-handle do?"

"Yes, capital."

I ran to the tool-shed and came back directly, panting.

"Now," I said, "what enemy is it—an alligator?"

"No. You said you didn't believe there were any snakes here. I've got one to show you now."

"Yes; but where?"

"Never you mind where. All you've got to do is to creep after me silent like; and when you see me pin him down with this fork, you can kill him."

"But what a cowardly way," I cried; "it isn't fair."

"Well, look you, I never did see such a boy as you are, Master George. Do you know what sort of a snake it is?"

"How should I? You wouldn't tell me."

"Well, you talk as if it was a little adder, foot and half long, or a snake at home that you might pick up in your hand. Why, it's a real rattlesnake."

"Oh!" I exclaimed, excitedly.

"Over six foot long, and as thick as my wrist."

"Pooh!" I said, with my imagination full of boa-constrictors big enough to entwine and crush us up. "That's nothing!"

"Nothing! Do you know one bite from a fellow like this will kill a man? And you talk about fighting fair. Nice lot of fairness in the way they fight. You come along, and promise to be very careful, or I shan't go."

"Oh, I'll be careful," I said.

"But if you feel afraid, say so, and I'll go alone."

"I don't feel afraid," I replied; "and if I did," I added with a laugh, "I wouldn't say I was."

"Not you," he muttered, and he held up a finger, and led the way down by the garden, and from thence into the uncleared forest, where a faint track wandered in and out among the great, tall, pillar-like trunks whose tops shut out the light of day, all but where at intervals what seemed to us like rays of golden dust, or there were silvery-looking lines of finest cobweb stretching from far on high, but which proved to be only delicate threads of sunshine which had pierced the great canopy of leaves.

Beyond this I knew that there was an opening where all was warm and glowing that was subdued and gloomy now, and it was not long before I saw, without a doubt, that Morgan was making for this clearing, and in all probability for one of the patches of stony ground that lay full in the sunshine, baked and hot.

It was very cool and silent in among the trees, whose great trunks towered up so high, and though we could hear a chirp now and then far above us in the leaves, all was as still as possible, not so much as a beetle or fly breaking the silence with its hum.

There was the opening at last, and as we neared it, the tree-trunks stood out like great black columns against the warm golden light.

Morgan held up his hand, and for the moment I felt as if we were going to do something very treacherous, till I recalled reading about some one having died twenty minutes after the bite of one of these snakes, and that made me feel more merciless, as I followed my leader, who kept picking his way, so that his feet should not light upon some dead twig which would give forth a snap.

The next minute we were out in the sunshine, and here Morgan stopped for me to overtake him, when he placed his lips close to my ear, and whispered—

"I'd been over to the bathing-pool to get some o' that white sand out of the bottom, when as I come back, I see my gentleman coiled up fast asleep. He's over yonder, just this side of the pine-trees, left of that big sugar-loaf— the light-green one."

He pointed to a tall cone-like cypress, and I felt that I knew the rough, bare, stony place exactly.

"Ready?" he whispered again.

I nodded.

"Then you must walk this time like a cat. Perhaps he's gone, but he may be fast asleep still."

He made a point with his fork to show me how he meant to fix the reptile to the ground, and I took a good grip of my rake-handle, intending to try and disable the monster by one blow.

This part of our journey was much more tedious than the other, for we were now getting close to the spot, and we knew that though sometimes it was possible to walk close by a snake without disturbing it, at other times the slightest sound would send it gliding rapidly out of sight.

We approached then in the most stealthy way, Morgan holding his fork the while as if it were a gun, and we were advancing upon the enemy.

Low growth had sprung apace about the clearing, so that we could not get a sight of the spot till we were close by, when Morgan softly parted the bush-like growth, peered out, drew back, and signed to me to advance, moving aside the while, so that I could pass him, and peer out in turn.

I was not long in availing myself of the opportunity; and there, not a dozen feet from me, lay twisted about, something like a double S, a large specimen of the serpent I had so often heard about; and a curious shrinking sensation came over me, as I noticed its broad flat head, shaped something like an old-fashioned pointed shovel, with the neck quite small behind, but rapidly increasing till the reptile was fully, as Morgan said, thick as his wrist; and then slowly tapering away for a time before rapidly running down to where I could see five curious-looking rings at the end of the dull grey tail.

"A rattlesnake," I said to myself, as with a kind of fascination I eagerly looked at the line which marked the gaping mouth showing plainly in an ugly smile; then at the dull creamy-brown and grey markings, and the scales which covered the skin, here and there looking worn and crumpled, and as if it was a trifle too big for the creature that wore it as if it were a shirt of mail.

I should have stood there staring at the repellent-looking creature for long enough, had not Morgan softly drawn me back, and then led the way round to our left, so that we could have the sun behind us, and approach the dangerous reptile without having to rustle through the bushes close at hand.

"Mind you keep back, my lad, till I've got him safe," whispered Morgan, "then hit him hard."

"Is it as dangerous as they say?" I asked.

"Worse, look you; that's why I want to pin him first. I might hit him a good crack, but snakes are hard to kill, and he might throw his head about and bite even then, though I arn't quite sure even now that they don't sting with their tails."

"I'm sure they don't," I whispered back.

"Ah, that's all very well, Master George, but I don't see as you can know much better than me. Anyhow, I'm going to risk it; so here goes, and when I say 'now,' bring down that rake-handle as big a whop as you can with both hands, right on his back."

I nodded, and we stood out now on the barren, stony patch close to the fir-trees, with the sun casting our shadows in a curious dumpy way on the earth, and our enemy about thirty feet away.

Morgan signed to me to stand still, and I obeyed trembling with excitement, and eagerly watching as he cautiously approached with his pole extended before him, ready to make a dart at the snake, whose head lay half turned for him, and its neck temptingly exposed, ready for the fork which should hold it down.

On went Morgan, inch by inch, his shadow just before him, and in spite of his injunction, I could not refrain from following, so as to get a good view of the encounter; and besides, I argued with myself, how could I be ready to help unless I was close at hand?

Consequently I stepped on nearer too, till I could see the reptile quite clearly, distinguishing every scale and noting the dull, fixed look of its eyes, which did not seem to be closed, for I was not familiar then with the organisation of snakes.

As Morgan went on the stillness of the clearing seemed terrible, and once more I could not help thinking of what a treacherous act it was to steal upon the creature like that in its sleep.

But directly after, the killing instinct toward a dangerous enemy grew strong within me, and I drew in my breath, my teeth were set fast, and my fingers tightened about the rake-handle, ready to deliver a blow.

All this took very few minutes, but it seemed to me to last a long time, and thought after thought ran through my mind, each one suggestive of danger.

"Suppose Morgan misses it," I said to myself; "it will be frightened and vicious, and strike at him, and if he is bitten I shall be obliged to attack it then, and I shall not have such a chance as he has, for the head will be darting about in all directions."

Then I began to wish I had gone first, and hit at it as it lay, with all my might.

Too late now, I knew; and as I saw in imagination Morgan lying helpless there, and myself striking hard at the snake, never taking into consideration the fact that after a deadly stroke the animal would rapidly try to escape, and glide away.

Morgan was now so near that I saw the shadow of his head begin to creep over the snake, and it loomed so black and heavy that I wondered why the reptile did not feel it and wake up.

Then I stood fast as if turned to stone, as I watched my companion softly extend the pole he carried, with the fork nearer and nearer the creature's neck, to remain perfectly motionless for a moment or two. There was a darting motion, and Morgan stood pressing the staff down as the serpent leaped into life, writhing, twining, and snapping its body in waves which ran from head to the tail which quivered in the air, sending forth a peculiar low, dull, rattling noise, and seeming to seek for something about which to curl.

"I've got him, Master George. Come along now; it's your turn."

I sprang forward to see that the evil-looking head was held down close to the ground, and that the jaws were gaping, and the eyes bright with a vindictive light, literally glittering in the sun.

"Can you hold him?" I said, hoarsely.

"Oh, yes; I've got him pretty tight. My! See that? He is strong."

For at that moment the snake's tail struck him, and twined about his left leg; untwined, and seemed to flog at him, quivering in the air the while, but only after writhing horribly, twisting round the pole which pressed it down, and forming itself into a curious moving knot.

"I can't hit at it now," I said, hoarsely; "it will strike away the pole."

"Yes; don't hit yet. Wait a bit till he untwissens himself; then give it him sharp, look you."

"You won't let it go?" I said.

"Not a bit of it, my lad. Too fond of Morgan Johns to let him stick his fangs into me. Now you've got a chance. No, you haven't; he's twisted up tighter than ever. Never mind, wait a bit; there's no hurry."

"But you are torturing it so," I cried.

"Can't help it, Master George. If I didn't, he'd torture me and you too. Well, he does twissen about. Welsh eel's nothing to him."

For the snake in its rage and pain kept twining about the pole, treating that as the cause of all its suffering. Morgan stood there full of excitement, but though longing to deliver a blow that should paralyse if it did not kill our enemy, I could not get the slightest chance.

"Ah, we ought to have had a cut at him before he twined about my pole," said Morgan, after this had been going on for some minutes; "but it wasn't your fault; there wasn't time."

"No," I said, gloomily, "there was no time. Now then, hold tight."

I made a rapid stroke at the long, lithe body which suddenly untwisted to its full length, but my rake-handle only struck the ground, for the serpent was quicker than I, and it threw itself once more in a series of quivering folds about Morgan's pole.

"Well, he is strong," cried the latter. "But I have it. I'm getting a bit 'fraid he'll work quite a hole, and get out, and I'm not at all sure that the nails arn't giving. Look here, Master George; put your hand in my pocket, and pull out and open my big knife ready for me. Then you shall hold the pole, and I'll go down and try and cut his head off."

"But will that be safe?" I said. "Hadn't we better leave go and run away?"

"What, and leave a customer like this free to hunt about our place? Now you wouldn't like to do that, I know."

"No; I shouldn't like to do that," I said; "but it would be terrible if he got away."

"Well then, out with my knife—quick! I'm beginning to wish we'd left him alone, for it'll be chizzle for both of us if he do get loose."

I hastily took his knife from his pocket, and opened it.

"That's your style, Master George. Now then, stick it across my mouth, and then take hold just under my hands. You must press it down hard, or he'll heave himself out, for he's mighty strong, I can tell you. Got hold?"

"Yes," I said, as I took hold of the pole, keeping my feet as far away as I could from the writhing knot, for fear it should suddenly untwine and embrace my legs.

"That's right, press down hard. Think you can hold him?"

"I don't know; I think so."

"Now, look ye here, my lad, thinking won't do; you've got to hold him, and if you feel as you can't you must say so. Rattlesnakes arn't garden wums."

"I'll try, and I will hold it," I said.

"There you have it, then," he said, releasing the pole, and leaving it quivering and vibrating in my hands. "Now then, I'm going to wait till he untwines again, and then I'm going to have off his head, if he don't work it out before. If he do, you've got to run as hard as you can: jump right away, my lad, never mind me."

I nodded; I could not speak, and I stood holding down the pole, seeing the snake striving to draw its head back between the little prongs of the fork, and knowing that if it did our position would be terrible.

"Now then, hold him tight," cried Morgan; "I'm going to lay hold and draw him out a bit, so as to get a cut through somewhere."

I did not speak, but pressed down with all my might, feeling my eyes strained as, with a shudder of dread, I saw Morgan stoop and boldly seize hold of the snake.

But the touch only seemed to make the great living knot tighten, and after a try Morgan ceased.

"No," he said, "it won't do. I shall only drag him out, for I'm not at all sure about those nails. I say, my lad, I really do wish we had let him alone, or had a go at him with a gun."

I tried to answer, but no words would come, and I wanted to look hopelessly at Morgan, but I could not take my eyes off the great, grey, writhing knot which was always in motion, heaving and working, now loosening, now tightening up.

"Hah!" cried Morgan, suddenly, as once more the horrible creature threw itself out to full length, and he sprang forward to seize the neck just as a wave ran along the body from tail to head; and as I pressed the pole down hard, the head rose like lightning, struck Morgan right in the face, and I saw him fall backward, rolling over and over; while, after writhing on the ground a moment or two, the snake raised its bleeding head, and I saw that it was drawing back to strike.

I don't know how it happened exactly; I only can tell that I felt horribly frightened, starting back as Morgan fell over, and that then, as the snake was preparing to strike, being naturally slow and weak from its efforts, the pole I held in both hands came down heavily, and then again and again, till our enemy lay broken and twisting weakly, its back broken in two places, and the blood flowing from its mouth.

Chapter Five

I was brought to myself again by a hearty shout just as I was trying to get rid of a shuddering sensation of fear, and wanting to go to Morgan's help—asking myself what I ought to do to any one who had been bitten by a rattlesnake.

"Brayvo! As they say, Master George. You did give it him well."

"But—Morgan—arn't you stung—bitten, I mean?" I faltered.

"Me? No, my lad. He gave me a flop on the cheek with the back of his head as he shook himself loose, and I didn't stop to give him another chance. But you did bring that down smart, and no mistake. Let's look at the end."

He took hold of the pole and examined the place where the two nails had been driven in to form the fork.

"Yes," he said, thoughtfully. "I was beginning to be afraid of that—see here. This nail's regularly bent down, and it opened the fork out so that when he snapped himself like a cart-whip he shook himself clear. Know better next time. I'll get a bit of iron or an old pitchfork, and cut the tines down short on purpose for this sort of game, Master George. Ah, would you?" he shouted, as he made a dart for where the snake was feebly writhing itself toward the undergrowth, and catching it by the tail snatched it back to lie all together, writhing slowly. "Wait till I find my knife. Oh, here it is," he said. "No. Never mind, give me yours. I'll look afterwards. Dropped it when I rolled over yonder."

I took out my knife and opened it.

"Oh, I say, my lad, don't look so white. Wern't 'fraid, were you?"

"Yes," I said, huskily. "I could not help being frightened."

"Not you," said Morgan, roughly; "you wasn't half frightened, or you wouldn't have done what you did. Now then, my gentleman, you're never going to bite and kill any one, so—there—and there!"

As he spoke he placed one foot a few inches from the rattlesnake's head, the creature opening its mouth and making a feeble attempt to bite, but the next moment my keen knife had divided the neck, and Morgan picked up the piece.

"Now look ye here, Master George, I shouldn't wonder if this gentleman's got two sharp teeth at the top here like an adder has at home. They're the poison ones, and—yes, what did I tell you?"

He laughed as he opened the creature's wide mouth with the blade of the knife, and drew forward two keen-looking fangs, to show me.

"There you are," he said. "Just like adders', only theirs is little tiny things just like a sharp bit of glass, and they lay back in the roof of their mouths so that you have to look close to see 'em."

"Throw the horrible poisonous thing away," I said.

"Yes; we'll pitch it all together in the river. Some big alligator will think it's a fine worm, and I hope he'll like it. One moment; I must find my knife."

He threw down the rattlesnake's head, and then said thoughtfully—

"No; let's take it up to the house, Master George, and let your father see the kind of game he's got on his property. I'll show it to my Sarah too, or she won't believe it was such a big one, or got such poison fangs."

"You'll have to carry it home," I said, with a shudder.

"No, I shan't, Master George, and it's of no use for you to try to make me believe you're afraid, because I shan't have it. You killed it, and I'll twist up a bit o' grass to make a rope, and you shall carry it home to show master and our Sarah. I can tie it to the end of the pole. Stop a minute; where's my knife?—must be just here."

He went straight for the low growth and bushes, and began peering about while I stood leaning on the pole and looking down at the slightly heaving form of the serpent, when my attention was taken by a hoarse cry from Morgan.

"What's the matter?" I said, as I saw that he was bending forward staring in among the bushes.

He did not reply, and feeling certain that he had found another rattlesnake, I raised the pole once more, and went to where he stood, when my lips parted, and I turned to call for help, but stopped there, for I found myself face to face with a similar object to that which had arrested Morgan. A tall, keen-faced, half-naked Indian stood before me, with his black hair gathered back and tied up so that a few eagle feathers were stuck through it; a necklace or two was about his neck and hanging down upon his breast;

a pair of fringed buckskin leggings covered his legs; and he carried a tomahawk in one hand, and a bow in the other.

Almost before I could recover from my surprise, I saw that we were completely surrounded, for at least a dozen more were dotted about the clearing.

At that moment Morgan seemed to get the better of his start, and backed to where I stood, with the Indian following him in a slow, stately manner.

"We're in for it, Master George," whispered Morgan. "What shall we do—run?"

"It would be of no use to try," I whispered.

"Not a bit, lad, they'd run us down directly. Hold up your head, lad; you arn't afraid of a rattlesnake, so you needn't be afraid of these furreners. What are they—Injuns?"

"Yes," I answered; "Red Indians," though I had never seen one before.

"Ah, well, look you, there's nothing to mind—they arn't poisonous. I shall ask them what they want. I say, what are they all coming close up to us for?"

"I don't know," I said, as I made a strong effort not to be afraid, and to keep from thinking about the stories I had heard of the Indians' cruelty, as the party came forward, evidently at a sign from the man who had faced me, and who wore more feathers than the rest.

"I say, Master George," whispered Morgan again, "hadn't I better ask 'em what they want?"

"It's of no use. I don't think they would understand."

"Well," said Morgan, coughing to clear his throat, "I'm a soldier, and I've been in a fight before now, so I know a little about it. We're surprised, Master George, by the enemy, and without arms. First dooty is to retreat, and you being my officer, you says we can't."

"I'm sure we can't," I said, talking to Morgan, but looking sharply round at the Indians, who all stood gazing at us in the sternest and most immovable way.

"Quite right, lad. Madness to talk about running, but I'd give all the wage I've got to take dooring the next ten year, look you, to be able to let the master know."

"Shall I call to him?"

"Only bring him up to be took prisoner too. Here, let's make the best of it," cried Morgan, jauntily. "How are you, gentlemen?—strangers in these parts, arn't you?"

The only man to take any notice of this easy-going address was the Indian I imagined to be the chief, and he uttered a grunt.

"Ah, I thought so. Nice country isn't it, only we've got some ugly customers here.—Sure they can't understand, Master George?"

"I feel nearly sure."

"So do I, lad.—Ugly customers, snakes—see?—snakes."

He took the pole quickly from my hand, and at the same moment I saw, as it were, a shock run through the group of Indians, each man taking tightly hold of the tomahawk he carried.

But Morgan did not notice it, and thrusting the end of the pole under the snake, he raised it up.

"See?" he cried. "We just killed it—no, we didn't, for it isn't quite dead."

The Indians looked at him and then at the snake, but in the most stolid way, and I stood wondering what was to come next.

"Know what it is, I suppose?" continued Morgan, who kept on talking in an excited way, as if to gain time while he tried to think out some plan, as was really the case; but the audience merely looked on frowningly, and I saw the chief draw back slightly as Morgan picked up the head and pointed to its fangs with his finger.

The thoughts of the risk he might be running made me forget for the moment any that was threatening us from the Indians, and I cried, in warning tones—

"Be careful; it may be dangerous though it's dead."

"Yes; this seems to be dead," replied Morgan; "but I say, Master George, I don't know whatever to do."

"Scrape a hole first, and bury that horrid thing," I said; "and then perhaps we shall see what they are going to do."

"Not to kill us, are they?" he whispered.

I could not help giving a start of horror, and looking wildly round at the Indians, who stood like so many statues looking on, as, in a hasty, excited way, Morgan roughly kicked away some of the loose gravel, and then with the rake-handle scraped out a good-sized hole, into which he threw the snake's head and dragged the body, raking the loose gravel back over them and stamping it down.

"Now then, Master George, what 'll us do next?"

"I don't know; let them take us away as prisoners, I suppose. We must not try to run away, because they would follow, and we should lead them home. Shall we run into the woods?"

"Never get there, my lad," he replied, sadly. "They'd have us before we got a hundred yards."

All doubt as to our next proceedings were put an end to at once, for the chief laid his hand upon my shoulder, and said, in a deep voice, something which was quite unintelligible to us both.

I shook my head, but he grasped my arm firmly, and pointed toward the forest.

"He means us to go," I said; and in obedience I walked toward the darkest part, but the chief checked me, and pointed toward the spot where our faint track lay which led toward the house; and feeling constrained to obey, I gave Morgan a disconsolate look, and went slowly on with the Indian walking by my side.

"We can't help it, Master George," said Morgan. "Don't be down-hearted, lad. Perhaps they don't mean any harm, and let's hope your father or my Sarah will see us in time to shut up the place, and get the guns down from the racks."

The distance was very short, but it was the most painful walk I ever had, for I felt as if I was being the guide to take the enemy right to the place my father had toiled so hard to win from the wilderness, and twice over I tried to deviate from the path, and lead the party into the forest, so as to bear right away from the house.

But it was of no use. A strong hand gripped my arm instantly; there was a stern look, a low, deep utterance, and the chief pointed again to the right track.

It was useless to try and misunderstand him, and at last, after two more feints, I felt that there was nothing else to be done but to allow myself to be forced onward.

Just before we came in sight of the house, the chief said something, and two of the men pushed Morgan forward till he was close to me, and one of the men walked on his left and the other came behind.

"See what that means, Master George?"

"No; what does it mean?"

"That Indians are clever as white men, and they've put us in the front rank to keep any one from firing at them."

I saw it plainly enough now, for as we advanced, my father appeared at the window, and I saw a gun in his hand.

He started as he caught sight of us two prisoners, but feeling, I suppose, that any attempt at defence was useless under the circumstances, he left the window for a moment or two, and I heard his voice speaking. Then he reappeared, and climbed out of the window, the door being closed and fastened.

He stepped forward boldly with the firelock resting on his arm, and walked to where the Indians had halted, holding out his hand in token of friendship, but it was not taken, the Indians' eyes running from him all over and about the place, as if they were astonished at what they saw.

"Tell me quickly," said my father, "but be cool. Everything depends upon our treating them in a friendly way, and not being afraid."

I told him how we had been surprised, and his face looked very grave as he listened.

"Well," he said, "we are in their power. If I fired it might bring help, but it would be too late to benefit us; and for aught we know, the rest of the tribe may already be up in the settlement. Stay with them and don't attempt to escape."

The Indian chief watched us curiously as my father talked to me, and two of his men half started forward as my father turned away to go back to the house.

But a word from the chief checked them, and every eye was fixed upon the returning figure, as my father walked to the door, beat upon it, called Sarah to open, and then passed in.

The faces of the Indians were a study, but they preserved their stolid looks, and uttered a sigh of satisfaction as my father appeared again with such provisions as the place afforded, and proceeded to offer them to our visitors.

I watched everything attentively, and saw the men stand fast without looking either at my father or the provisions which he placed before them, till the chief said a few words in a loud tone.

Then with an eagerness in sharp contrast to their former apathy, they seized the food and began to eat.

My father spoke to the chief again and again, and the Indian said something coldly in reply; but they were wasted words, and the rough meal was partaken of in comparative silence.

"They only mean to be friendly, father, do they?" I said at last.

"It is impossible to say; they may prove treacherous," he replied. "But don't talk, and if you grasp anything they seem to want, tell me, so that I can satisfy them. It would be terrible if they attempted to destroy all we have been at such pains to get together."

"Couldn't we all make a dart for indoors, sir?" said Morgan, in a whisper. "We have got plenty of weepons there, sir, and might manage to keep them off till help came."

"The risk is too great," said my father. "These men are as active as leopards, and before we could get within doors we should each have an axe in his brain."

"But, begging your pardon, sir, we can all run."

"As fast as a tomahawk can fly? No; they are peaceful now, and friendly; let us treat them as friends, and hope that they will soon go."

At that moment the chief made a sign with his hands to his lips, a sign that was unmistakable, and a large pail of water was fetched out by Morgan, and drunk from with avidity.

This done, the Indians sat and stood about watching everything within reach, while we were in the unpleasantly helpless state of being unable to speak, or to make them understand, and in the more unpleasant or perilous position of being unable to grasp their intentions.

As the time went on my father appeared to grow more hopeful. He had evidently come to the conclusion that it was useless to attempt resistance, and he seemed to think that our friendly treatment might win the respect of these stern, morose-looking men. Then, all at once, I saw that his hopes were dashed. He looked at me wildly, and I saw the firelock he held tremble in his hand.

"Try and be firm, George," he said, quietly, "and do not look as if I am saying anything serious to you," he continued, laughing.

"I understand, father," I said, cheerfully, though my heart kept giving great thumps against my ribs.

"Can you hear what I am saying, Morgan?" continued my father, pleasantly, and not appearing to pay the slightest attention to the Indians.

"Every word, sir; but it's hard work, for I want to run indoors to try and comfort that poor woman who is trembling there."

"So we all do," said my father, and he looked quite merry; "but don't look like that, man. It is inviting an attack if these men do mean evil."

"Right, sir; I am quite laughing now," said Morgan.

"Ah, that's worse," cried my father, "that ghastly grin will ruin us. There, listen to what I am saying. When these savages attack us, it will be in some treacherous way, so as to get the advantage of us without injury to themselves. If they do attack, never mind who goes down, the survivors must rush into the house and defend it to the last, for that poor woman's sake. Fight hopefully if I am not with you; for as soon as firing begins it may bring help from the settlement."

"Then why not fire at once, sir?" cried Morgan, earnestly.

"Because, as I intimated before, it would bring help, but help that came too late."

The calm forced way in which my father spoke seemed to be the most terrible part of the whole day's work. The inaction was bad enough, and to sit there expecting that at any moment the Indians might turn upon us and kill us with their axes, made it almost impossible to sit there as my father wished; but sit there we did, and as my eyes wandered from one to the other of the weird, fierce-looking Indians, who seemed to be doing nothing but watch us for an excuse to make an attack, it made my brain swim.

How it was all burnt into my memory, and how I can picture it all now! The bright garden, the flowers, and the promise of fruit, and the house beginning to look more lovely every month; and now in front of it Red Indians squatting about, or standing with their bows strung, arrows in a case behind them, and axes in hand, ready at the word from their chief to spring upon us.

All at once the chief uttered a peculiar sound, and the men who were seated sprang to their feet, and stood watching the tall, fierce-looking fellow.

He spoke again, and without a word they all moved off quickly toward the settlement, making straight for Colonel Preston's estate.

I sat there watching them till the last man had disappeared. Then all the bright sunshiny scene around began to swim, and wave, and grow distant, and all was blank.

Chapter Six

"Better, my boy?"

"Yes. What is it? I felt so sick and strange."

I was lying on my back looking up at my father, who was bending over me bathing my forehead with cold water.

"The sun—a little overdone. There, you are better now."

"Ah, I recollect," I said, "Where are the Indians?"

"Hush! Don't get excited. They are gone now."

"Yes, I know," I said; "gone to Colonel Preston's."

"Hist!" he cried, as I heard steps close by, and Morgan came hurrying up.

"Couldn't get far, sir. I was making haste, and getting close up to the last man as I thought, when three of the savages jumped up just in my path, and held up their bows and arrows in a way that said, plain as any tongue could speak, 'go back, or we'll send one of these through you.'"

"The chief knows what he is about," said my father, "and we cannot communicate. Now then, get inside, and we will barricade the place as well as we can, in case of their coming back. Can you walk now, George?"

"Yes, father, the giddiness has gone off now," I said; and I sprang up, but reeled and nearly fell again.

"Take my arm, boy," he said, as he helped me toward the window, and I climbed in by it, when the first thing my eyes lighted upon was the figure of our Sarah, down on her knees behind the door with her eyes shut; but a gun was leaning up against the wall; and as she heard us she sprang up, seized it, and faced round.

"Oh! I thought it was the Indians," she said, with a sigh of relief.

"Perhaps we have been frightening ourselves without cause," said my father, helping Morgan to fix up the strong shutter with which the window was provided. "The Indians are gone now."

"Yes," muttered Morgan, so that I could hear, "but they may come back again. I don't trust 'em a bit."

"Nor I, Morgan," said my father, for he had heard every word; "but a bold calm front seems to have kept them from attempting violence. If we had been shut up here, and had opened fire, not one of us would now have been alive."

"Never mind, sir," said Morgan. "If they come back let's risk it, and show a bold front here behind the shutters, with the muzzles of our guns sticking out, for I couldn't go through another hour like that again. I was beginning to turn giddy, like Master George here, and to feel as if my head was going to burst."

"Go up into the roof, and keep a good look-out from the little gratings; but keep away, so as not to show your face."

"Then you do think they'll come back, sir?"

"Yes, I feel sure of it. I am even now in doubt as to whether they are all gone. Indians are strangely furtive people, and I fully expect that a couple of them are lying down among the trees to watch us, for fear we should try to communicate with the others. I am afraid now that I made a mistake in settling down so far from the rest. Ah! Listen! A shot. Yes; there it is again."

"No, sir," said Morgan, "that wasn't a shot: it was—there it goes again!—and another."

Two distant sounds, exactly like shots, fell again upon our ears.

"Yes," cried my father, excitedly, "the fight has begun."

"Nay, sir, that was only a big 'gator threshing the water up in some corner to kill the fish," cried Morgan; and he passed up through the ceiling into the roof.

As Morgan went out of sight, and took his place in the narrow loft between the sloping rafters, my father busied himself loading guns, and placing them ready by the openings in the shutters which I had always supposed were for nothing else but to admit the light. And as he worked, Sarah stood ready to hand him powder or bullets, or a fresh weapon, behaving with such calm seriousness, and taking so much interest in the work, that my father said, gravely—

"Hardly a woman's task this, Sarah."

"Ah, sir," she replied, quietly; "it's a woman's work to help where she is wanted."

"Quite right," said my father. Then, turning to me, he went on, "I am a soldier, George, and all this is still very horrible to me, but I am making all these preparations in what I think is the right and wisest spirit; for if an enemy sees that you are well prepared, he is much less likely to attack you and cause bloodshed. We are safe all together indoors now, and with plenty of protection, so that if our Indian visitors come again, we are more upon equal terms."

"Do you really think they will come again, father?" I said.

"I'm afraid so. We have been living in too much fancied security, and ready to think there was no danger to apprehend from Indians. Now we have been rudely awakened from our dream."

"And if they come shall you shoot, father?"

"Not unless it is absolutely necessary to save our lives. I cannot help feeling that we ought to be up at the settlement, but I should have been unwilling to leave our pleasant home to the mercy of these savages; and, of course, now it is impossible to go, so we must make the best defence we can, if the enemy returns."

All this was very startling, and from time to time little shudders of dread ran through me, but at the same time there was so much novelty and excitement, that I don't think I felt very much alarmed. In fact, I found myself hoping once that the Indians would come back, so that I could see how they behaved now that we were shut up tightly in our house, all of which was very reprehensible no doubt; but I am recording here, as simply and naturally as I can, everything that I can remember of my boyish life.

The preparations for attack were at last ended, and after securing and barricading door and window in every way possible, we sat down to wait for the first sign of the enemy, and I was wondering how long it would be before we saw the Indians return, when I suddenly awoke to the fact that I was terribly hungry.

I don't suppose I should have thought of it, though, if Sarah had not made her appearance with bread and meat all ready cut for us, and very welcome it proved; Morgan, on receiving his share passed up to him in the loft, giving me a nod and a smile before he went back to continue his watch.

And this proved to be a long and weary one. The afternoon sun slowly descended; and as it sank lower, I could see that my father's face grew more and more stern.

I did not speak to him, but I knew what it meant—that he was thinking of the coming darkness, and of how terribly difficult our watch would be.

"Yes," he said, suddenly, just as if he had heard my thoughts; "they are naturally quiet, stealthy people, and the darkness will give them opportunities which would be full of risk by day. I am afraid that they are waiting in ambush for the night, and that then they will come on."

"I hope not," I thought; but I would not have let my father see how frightened I was for all the world; and trying to be as cheerful as I could under the circumstances, I went up and joined Morgan to help him watch from the latticed openings in the roof, with the garden gradually growing more gloomy, and the trees of the forest beyond rapidly becoming black.

Then darker and darker, and there was no moon that night till quite late.

Beyond the possibility of there being some reptile about that had crawled up from the river, hungry and supper-hunting, there had never seemed to be anything about home that was alarming, and night after night I had stolen out to listen to the forest sounds, and scent the cool, damp, perfumed air; but now there was a feeling of danger at hand, lurking perhaps so close that it would not have been safe to open the door; and as I watched beside Morgan from between the window-bars, we were constantly touching each other, and pointing to some tree-stump, tuft, or hillock, asking whether that was an Indian creeping cautiously toward the house.

Somehow that seemed to me the darkest night I could remember, and the various sounds, all of which were really familiar, seemed strange.

Now there was the plaintive cry of one of the goat-suckers which hawked for moths and beetles round the great trees; then, after a silence so profound that it was painful, came the deep croak of the bullfrog rising and falling and coming from a hundred different directions at once. Then all at once their deep croaking was dominated by a loud barking bellow; and as I listened with my hands feeling cold and damp, I caught hold of Morgan.

"What's that?" I whispered, excitedly.

"My arm," he replied, coolly. "Don't pinch, lad."

"No, no; I mean the sound. What noise was that?"

"Oh! Why, you know. That was a 'gator."

"Are you sure? It sounded like a man's voice."

"Not it. Who did you think could be there? Nobody likely to be out there but Indians, and they wouldn't shout; they'd whisper so that we shouldn't know they were near."

I was silent again, and sat watching and listening as sound after sound struck my ear, making it seem that the wilds had never been so full before of strange noises, though the fact was that nothing was unusual except that I did not realise that I had never been in danger before, and sat up to listen.

All at once I jumped and uttered a cry, for something had touched me.

"Hush! Don't make a noise," said a familiar voice. "I only wanted to know whether you could make out anything."

"No, father. Only the frogs and alligators are barking and bellowing."

"Can't see any sign of Indians, nor any red light from over toward the settlement?"

"No, father."

"No, sir. All's quiet," said Morgan.

"It isn't, father," I whispered. "I never heard so much noise from out by the river before. There, hark!"

We all listened in silence as a loud bellowing sound came from a distance.

"There!" I whispered, in awe-stricken tones.

"Only one of the reptiles by the stream," said my father, quietly.

"But don't you think it's because some one is there?"

"No; certainly not. Keep a sharp look-out on both sides, Morgan, and warn me if you see the slightest movement, for it may be a crawling, lurking Indian."

"We'll keep a good look-out, sir, never fear," said Morgan, and we resumed our watch—if watch it could be called, where we were more dependent upon our ears than upon our eyes.

Morgan was very silent and thoughtful till I spoke to him.

"What did my father mean about the red glare over at the settlement?"

"Hah!" he ejaculated, and he was again silent for a minute or two. Then in a quick whisper, "I was just thinking about that, Master George, when you spoke, and that it was the enemy we had to fear the most."

"What do you mean?" I asked.

"Fire, my lad, fire. I dare say that with our guns and swords we may keep them off; but that's how they'll get the better of us."

"By fire?"

"Yes; they'll get something blazing up against the house, and the moment it catches fire it's all over with us."

"What! Set fire to the house?"

"Yes, Master George, that's what your father's afraid of. No; I'm wrong there. I was at the wars with him, and I never saw him afraid—not even to-day. Takes a bold man to come out of his fort and go up to the enemy as he did—twelve to one—expecting every moment a crack from a tomahawk. He hasn't got any fear in him; but he thinks about the fire all the same. Now then, don't talk, but keep a sharp look-out, or they may steal on to us without our seeing them."

All this was said in a low whisper as we tried to keep a good look-out from the little trellised dormers; and the minutes stole on and became hours, with the darkness seeming to increase till about midnight. Then all looked darker, when Morgan pressed my arm, and I gave, a violent start.

"'Sleep, sir?"

"I? Asleep? No! Yes; I'm afraid I must have been," I said, feeling the colour come burning into my face.

"Look yonder," he whispered.

I looked from the grating and saw that, all at once, as it appeared to me, the tops of the trees were visible out to the east, and it grew plainer and plainer as I watched.

"Moon's getting very old, Master George," whispered Morgan, "but yonder she comes up."

"Then it will soon be light."

"No; but not so dark."

"Then the Indians won't come now?" I said eagerly.

"I don't know much about them, Master George, but from what I've heard say from those who do, Indians always comes when they're not expected, and if you're to be ready for them you must always be on the watch."

The overpowering sense of sleep which had made me lose consciousness for a few minutes ceased to trouble me now, and I stood watching eagerly for the time when the moon would rise above the trees, and send its light across the clearing in front of the house. I waited anxiously, for there had been the lurking dread that the Indians might creep up to the garden through the darkness, unseen, and perhaps strike at my father down below before he could be on his guard.

Once the moon was up, I felt that we should have light till daybreak, and with that light a good deal of the shivering dread caused by the darkness would pass away.

It was a long, very long while before the moon reached the tops of the trees, but when it did, the clearing and the gardens seemed to have been transformed. Long shadows, black as velvet, stretched right away, and trees were distorted so that I felt as if I was dreaming of seeing a garden upon which I had never set eyes before.

At last, almost imperceptibly, the moon, well on to its last quarter, appeared above the edge of the forest, and I was in the act of drawing myself back with a feeling of satisfaction that all was safe, when I saw something dark lying close to the shadow cast by a tree.

"Would Indians lie down and crawl?" I whispered.

"More likely to than walk, if all I hear's true, Master George."

"Then look there!" I whispered, as I pointed to the dark, shadowy figure.

"Where, lad? I can't see anything."

"There; just at the edge of that long, stretched-out shadow."

Morgan drew in his breath with a faint hiss.

"It's moving—*he's* moving," he whispered; "crawling right along to get round to the back, I should say. And look, sir, look!—another of 'em."

I just caught sight of the second figure, and then crept to the rough trap-door opening.

"Father," I whispered, "come up here. Bring a gun."

He was beneath the opening in a moment.

"Take hold of the gun," he said. "Mind!—be careful"—and he passed the heavy weapon up to me.

The next moment he was up in the rough loft, and I pointed out the figures of the Indians.

I heard him too draw in his breath with a faint hiss, as he stretched out his hand for the gun, took it, softly passed the barrel out through the open window and took aim, while I stood suffering from a nervous thrill that was painful in the extreme, for I knew that when he fired it must mean death.

I involuntarily shrank away, waiting for the heavy report which seemed as if it would never come; and at last, unable to bear the suspense longer, I pressed forward again to look hesitatingly through the window, feeling that I might have to fire a gun myself before long.

All at once, as the suspense had grown unbearable, the barrel of the firelock made a low scraping noise, for my father was drawing it back.

"A false alarm, George," he said, gently.

"No, no," I whispered; "look—look!" for I could see both figures crawling along slowly, flat on their breasts.

"Yes, I see them, my boy," he said; "and I was deceived too, for the moment, but we must not waste shot on creatures like these."

"Why, if it arn't a pair o' 'gators," said Morgan, with a suppressed laugh. "Well, they did look just like Injins, and no mistake."

I felt so vexed at making so absurd a mistake, that I remained silent till my father passed the gun to me.

"Take hold," he said, gently. "It was a mistake that deceived us all. Better be too particular than not particular enough."

He lowered himself down into the room below, and I passed him the gun before going back to where Morgan leaned against the window.

"There they go, Master George," he said, laughing. "You and me must have a new pair o' spectacles apiece from the old country if we have to do much of this sort of thing."

"I did not think I could have been so stupid," I said, angrily; and going away to the other window, so that I should not have to listen to my companion's bantering, which I felt pretty sure would come, I stood gazing at the beautiful scene without, the moon making the dark green leaves glisten like silver, while the shades grew to be of a velvety black. Every here and there patches of light shone on the great trunks of the trees, while their tops ran up like great spires into the softly-illumined sky.

The excitement had driven away all desire for sleep, and we watched on listening to every sound and cry that came from the forest surrounding, wonderfully plain in the silence of the night, which magnified croak, bellow, or faint rustling among the leaves or bushes, as some nocturnal creature made its way through the trees.

At times the watching seemed to be insufferably dreary and wearisome; then something startling would send the blood thrilling through my veins again; and so on and on, till the moon began to grow pale, the light to appear of a pearly grey in the east, golden flecks glistened high all above the trees, and once more it was new day, with the birds singing, and a feeling of wonder impressing me, it appeared so impossible that I could have been up and watching all night.

Chapter Seven

"Master George!—Master George!"

The call was repeated, for I did not answer the first, my mouth being expanded to its fullest stretch in a tremendous yawn.

"Come down, and have some breakfast. You must want it sore."

The very fact of Sarah mentioning it made me feel a horrible sinking sensation, and as soon as my father gave leave for one of us to leave the post at the window, I came down to find that, though we up in the narrow loft had heard nothing, Sarah had been for some time preparing a good meal, which, whatever might be the perils awaiting us later on, we all ate with the greatest of enjoyment.

We had hardly finished when Morgan gave the alarm, and my father hurried to his post of observation, but only to conceal his piece directly, as he uttered the word "Friend!"

For our nearest neighbour, Colonel Preston, a tall, stern, rather overbearing man, came up, followed by a couple of men.

"I've come to give you warning, Bruton," he said.

"I tried to send you warning last night," replied my father.

"What! You know?"

"Do you not see how we are barricaded?"

"Oh, I thought it was because you were just getting up. The Indians came by here then?"

"Yes," said my father; and he briefly told of our adventure, and the watch we had kept.

"Well," said the colonel, sharply, and as I thought in rather a dictatorial way; "it all goes to prove that it was a mistake for you to isolate yourself here. You must move close up to us, so that in a case of emergency we can all act together."

"It would be better," said my father, quietly.

"Then you will come?"

"No; I selected this place for its beauty, as you chose yours. I should not like to give it up."

"You'll repent it, Bruton. You must have had a narrow escape last night."

"I do not know," said my father, thoughtfully. "Of course we were very suspicious of the reason for the Indians' visit, but they did us no harm."

"Nor to us. Our numbers overawed them, I suppose."

"Our numbers did not overawe them here," said my father, smiling; but he added rather bitterly, "If they had meant mischief, we could not have counted on your help."

"Nor we on yours," said the colonel, in a rather irritable manner. "Well, of course I have no right to dictate to you; but I may as well tell you that as soon as the Indians left us, we met together, and determined to erect a block-house or fort ready to flee to in case of emergency. It is for you to chose whether you will join us in the work."

"I shall join you, of course," said my father, quietly; and, refusing any refreshment, evidently to the great disgust of his men, who exchanged glances which evidently meant breakfast, the colonel walked off.

"See those two fellows, Master George?" whispered Morgan, as my father stood gazing thoughtfully after the colonel.

"Yes; why?"

"Never see two look more hungry in my life. They'd have cleared us out, see if they wouldn't. Good job there arn't many in the settlement like 'em."

"Why?" I said.

"Because we should soon be having a famine in the land. What are you laughing at, lad?"

"You," I said, as I recalled a number of Morgan's performances with the knife and fork.

He looked at me fiercely, and as if he were terribly offended; for Morgan's Welsh blood had a way of bubbling up and frothing over like mead; but directly after there was a bit of a twitch at one corner of his mouth, then a few wrinkles started out at each side of his face about the eyes, and began to spread all over till he was showing his teeth.

"Ah, well, Master George," he said, "I can see through you. Perhaps I aren't such a very bad trencherman. Sarah says I do eat. But what's the harm? Man can't work well without; nor more can't a fire burn without you keeps on putting plenty o' wood. But I say, my lad, when those Injin fellows came down upon us, I began to think I should never be hungry again. Did I look very much frightened?"

"No; I thought you looked very brave."

"Did I? Did you think so, Master George?"

"Yes; certainly."

"Now, you're not making fun of me, are you?"

"Certainly not."

"Well, come, I'm glad of that," said Morgan, brightening up; "because do you know, Master George, 'twix' you and me, I don't think I'm quite so good that way as I ought to be. I tried hard not to seem in a fright, but I was in one all the same, and seemed to feel arrows sticking into me, and them chopping at me with tomahawks. Wasn't pleasant, look you, was it?"

"No, and it was no wonder."

"No, sir, it warn't. But I say, Master George, you didn't feel so bad as that, did you?"

I glanced round to see if my father was within hearing, and then said with a laugh—

"I'm afraid I felt ever so much worse."

"Then we'll shake hands over it," said Morgan; "but I say, Master George, I'd give everything to know whether the master felt scared too."

"I don't think he did. Oh, I'm sure he did not. See how erect and firm he was."

"Ah, that's being a soldier, sir. They drill 'em up into being as stiff as can be, and to look as if they like it when they're being shot at. That's what makes English soldiers such fine fellows in a battle."

Further discussion was put an end to by the coming up to us of my father.

"You heard what Colonel Preston said, George?"

"Yes, father."

"About being safe, and the risk of fresh attacks by the Indians?"

"Yes, father; we heard every word—didn't we, Morgan?"

"Oh yes; everything, sir."

"Well," said my father, "it is quite possible that this party came to spy out the land so as to prepare for a descent. If this is so, there is a good deal of risk in staying here. I have made up my mind what to do under the circumstances."

"Oh, master! Oh, Captain Bruton!" broke out Morgan; "don't say that after the pains we took in getting our garden in order, and in helping to build the house, and never happy unless I was going to do something to make it look pretty, you're thinking of moving and letting some one else come in?"

"I think the risk is very great in staying; and that for your wife's sake, my son's, and yours, I perhaps ought to give up this, and go and take up fresh land close to my brother settlers."

"But, begging your pardon, sir, don't you think nothing of the sort again. What do you say, Master George?"

"Oh, I shouldn't like to go away from here," I said.

"There, sir! Hear that?" cried Morgan. "Why, if you come to reckon it up, how do you know that you're going to be safer there than here? If the Injins come, that's where they'll go for first, and we're just as likely to be killed there as here."

"Possibly, Morgan."

"And then look at the place, sir, all along by the big river. It arn't half so healthy as this. I never feel well there, and I know the land arn't half so rich."

"But we must study safety, my man," said my father.

"Of course we must, sir, so what's the good of being scared about some Injins, who may never come again, and running right into where there's likely to be fevers—and if some day there don't come a big flood and half drown 'em all, I'm a Dutchman, and wasn't born in Carnarvon after all."

"But there is another consideration, Morgan; we have some one else to look after—your wife."

"Oh, don't you trouble about me, sir," cried Sarah; and we looked up in astonishment. "I came out here to look after you and Master George, not for you to look after me."

"Why, what are you doing up there?" said my father, as Sarah's nose showed between the bars of the window of the loft.

"Keeping a sharp look-out for Indians, sir."

"That's right Sarah," cried Morgan. "And, I say, you don't think we had better go, do you?"

"Certainly not," said Sarah, sharply. "Just as we're getting the place and my kitchen so snug and comfortable. I should think not indeed."

"There, sir," cried Morgan, triumphantly.

"Well," said my father, "I had made up my mind to stop, at any rate as far as I was concerned, but I wished to give you all the opportunity of going up to the settlement."

"'Tchah, sir! I don't call that a settlement. But, begging your pardon, captain, speaking *as* an old soldier *to* an old soldier," continued Morgan, "what you say is ridickerlus."

"Morgan!" cried my father, sternly.

"Can't help it, sir, even if you order me pack-drill, or even black-hole and a flogging. Why, its ridickerlus for you as an officer to tell your men to forsake you and leave you in the lurch."

"But, my good fellow—"

"Ah, I haven't done yet, captain. You've worried me and gone on till it's mutiny in the ranks, and I refuse to obey."

"Well, George," said my father, "you hear this; what do you say?"

"I say it would be a horrid pity to go away and leave the place, father. Oh, don't! I like it ever so! And we're so happy here, and I don't believe the Indians will come again."

"Then you would not be afraid to stay here and take our chance? No," he said, reverently, "place ourselves in His hands, my boy, and be content."

"Amen to all that, sir, says I," cried Morgan, taking off his hat; and then I saw him close his eyes, and his lips were moving as he turned away.

"Thank you, Morgan," said my father, quietly; "and thank you too, my boy. We will not give up our restful, beautiful home for a scare. Perhaps if the Indians find that we wish to be at peace with them, they may never attempt to molest us. We will stay."

Morgan gave his leg a slap, and turned round to me.

"There, Master George!" he cried. "Why, with all these fruit and vegetables coming on, I should have 'most broke my heart, and I know our Sarah would have broken hers."

That day was after all a nervous one, and we felt as if at any moment an Indian might appear at the edge of the wood, followed by a body perhaps a hundred strong. So our vigilance was not relaxed, neither that day nor during the next week; but nothing occurred to disturb our peace, and the regular routine went on.

From what we heard at the settlement the idea of building a block-house had been for the present given up; but Morgan came back one morning, after a visit to the colonel's man, with some news which rather disturbed my father.

"Small schooner in the river?"

"Yes, sir."

"And you say that several of the gentlemen have been buying?"

"Yes, sir; that's right," said Morgan, "and the blacks are put to work in their plantations."

My father frowned and walked away, while I eagerly turned to Morgan for an explanation.

"Oh, it's all right enough, sir, what I tell you," said Morgan; "and seems to me they're right, so long as they treat 'em well. Here's lots of land wants clearing and planting, and one pair of hands can't do it, of course, and there's no men to be hired out here, so the gentlemen have been buying slaves."

"What a shame!" I cried. "How would you like to be bought for a slave?"

Morgan looked at me, then at the sky, then down at the ground; then away straight before him, as he took off his hat and scratched one ear.

"Humph!" he ejaculated, suddenly; "that's a puzzler, Master George. Do you know I never thought of that."

"It seems to me horribly cruel."

"But then, you see, Master George, they're blacks, and that makes all the difference."

I could not see it, but I did not say so, and by degrees other things took my attention. There was so much to see, and hear, and do, that I forgot all about Indians and blacks; or if they did come to mind at all as time went on, I merely gave them a passing thought, and went off to talk to Morgan, to set a trap, to fish, or to watch the beautiful birds that came into the sunny clearing about my home.

Chapter Eight

"There," said Morgan, one day, as he gave the soil a final pat with his spade, "that job's done, and now I'm going to have a bit of a rest. Leaving-off time till the sun gets a bit down."

"What have you been planting?" I asked.

"Seeds, my lad; flower seeds, as I've picked myself. I like to keep raising the useful things, but we may as well have some bright flowers too. Where's the master?"

"Indoors, writing."

"Then what do you say to a bit of sport?"

"Another rattlesnake?" I cried.

"No, thank ye, my lad; meddling with rattlesnakes may mean bringing down the Indians, so we'll let them alone."

"Nonsense!"

"Well, perhaps it is, my lad."

"But what have you found?"

"What do you say to a 'coon?"

"Oh, they get into the hollow trees, where you can't catch them."

"Well then, a bear?"

"A bear!" I cried; "a real wild bear?"

"Ah, I thought that would set you off; but it arn't a bear; they're up among the hills."

"What is it then? How you do hang back from telling!"

"Course I do. If I let you have it all at once, you wouldn't enjoy it half so much."

"Oh, I know," I cried, "it's going to fish after those ridiculous little terrapins, and they're such horrid things to take off the hook."

"Guess again."

"Birds? An eagle?"

"No; guess again, nearly right; something as lays eggs—"

"A turtle?"

Morgan shook his head.

"Not an alligator, is it?"

He wrinkled up his face in a hearty laugh.

"Alligator it is, sir. I found a nest yesterday."

"And didn't tell me. I want to see an alligator's nest. I never could find one."

"Ah, you didn't look in the right kind of tree, Master George."

"Don't talk to me as if I were a baby, Morgan," I said; "just as if I didn't know better than that."

"Oh, but you don't know everything. I got awfully laughed at once for saying squirrels build nests in trees."

"Oh, but they do," I said; "I've seen them."

"'Course you have; but when I said so, some one laughed, and asked how many eggs you can find in a squirrel's nest.—So you don't believe the 'gators build in trees, don't you?"

"No; but I believe they lay eggs. How many are there in this?"

"Oh, it isn't that sort of nest. I mean a nest where he goes to sleep in; and you and me's going to wake him up, and try if we can't catch him and bring him home."

I could not help thinking of the Indians, as I went with Morgan to make the preparations, which were simple enough, and consisted in arming himself with a long pole and giving me one similar, after which he put a piece of rope in his pocket, and declared himself ready.

We went off in the same direction as that chosen when we killed the rattlesnake, but turned off to the left directly, and made for the bank of the river, that bore away from the landing-place, towards a low, moist part, intersected by the meandering stream which drained the marshy part.

Here we had to proceed rather cautiously, for the place was full of decayed trees covered with brilliant green and grey moss, and looking solid, but which crumbled away at a touch from the foot, and often concealed holes into which it would have been awkward to fall, since we did not know what kind of creatures lived therein.

"Seem to have lost the place," said Morgan, after we had been going along for some time pretty well parallel with the river.

"Oh, Morgan!" I exclaimed, impatiently.

"No; I have it," he cried. "I remember that tree with the long moss hanging down so far. The ground's harder here too. More to the left, Master George. There you are at last."

"But where's the nest?" I said.

"Why, there it is, my lad; can't you see?"

I looked round, but there was nothing visible but a few footprints in a muddy spot, and a hole of very moderate size, evidently going some distance down into the moist, boggy soil.

"Is this it?"

"Yes, of course."

"But you said a nest."

"Well, I meant, as I told you, his nest, his snuggery. Now I'm going to see if he's at home."

I looked on full of doubt, for the whole proceeding seemed to me to be very absurd, and I felt sure that Morgan was mistaken.

"I don't believe he knows any more about alligators than I do," I said to myself, as I saw him thrust the long pole down into the hole.

"I tried this game on yesterday, Master George, and he said he was at home."

"Nonsense!" I cried, pettishly.

"But I'm afraid he has gone out for a walk this time, and it's a case of call again to-morrow. No," he added, energetically, "it's all right. Says he's at home."

"Why, what do you mean?" I cried.

"Got a bite," said Morgan, grinning. "You try. But mind he don't come out with a rush. He might be nasty."

I hesitated for a moment, then leaning my own pole against a bush, I took hold of the one Morgan gave into my hands, and moved it slightly.

"Well?" I said. "I don't feel anything."

"Give it a bit of a stir round, my lad," he said.

I moved the pole a little, and then jumped and let go.

Mass' George: A Boy's Adventures in the Old Savannah | 55

"What's the matter?" cried Morgan, laughing.

"Something bit the pole, and made it jar right up my arm."

"That's him. I told you he was at home. Now then, you aren't afraid, are you?"

"Not a big one, is it?"

"No, not very; only tidy size; but we shall see if we get him out."

I looked rather aghast at Morgan, for the idea of getting a large alligator out there in the marshy place, and both of us unarmed, was rather startling.

"Now then, give him a good stir up."

Sooner than seem afraid, but with my heart beating heavily, I took hold of the pole, and gave it a good shake, and left go again, for it seemed as if some one had given it a good rap with a heavy stick, and a jarring sensation ran up my arm.

"No mistake about it this time," said Morgan, grinning. "Puts me in mind of sniggling for eels, and pushing a worm at the end of a willow-stick up an eel's burrow in a muddy bank. They give it a knock like that sometimes, but of course not so hard. Well, why don't you go on?"

"Go on with what?" I cried, wishing myself well out of the whole business.

"Stirring of him up, and making him savage. But stop a moment, let's have this ready."

He took out the piece of rope, and made a large noose, laying it on some thick moss, and then turning to me again.

"Now then, my lad, give him a good stir up. Don't be afraid. Make him savage, or else he won't hold on."

With a dimly defined notion of what we were aiming at, I gave the pole a good wrench round in the hole, feeling it strike against something, and almost simultaneously feeling something strike against it.

"That's the way, sir. Give it him again."

Growing reckless now, and feeling that I must not shrink, I gave the pole another twist round, with the result that it was snatched out of my hand.

"He has it," cried Morgan, excitedly. "Feel if he has got it fast, Master George."

I took hold of the pole, gazing down with no little trepidation, in the expectation of at any moment seeing some hideous monster rush out, ready to seize and devour me.

But there was no response to my touch, the pole coming loosely into my hand.

"Give him another stir up, Master George. They tell me that's the way they do it to make them savage."

"But do we want to make the creature savage?" I said.

"Course we do! There, you do as I tell you, my lad, and you'll see."

I gave the pole a good poke round in the hole again, just as if I was stirring up something in a huge pot, when almost before I had gone right round—*Whang!* The pole quivered in my hand, and a thrill ran through me as in imagination I saw a monstrous beast seize the end of the stick in its teeth and give it a savage shake.

"Hurrah!" cried Morgan. "He has got it tight now. That's right, Master George; let me come. We'll soon haul him out."

"No, no," I said, as excited now as the Welshman. "It may be dangerous."

"We'll dangerous him, my lad."

"But he may bite."

"Well, let him. 'Gators' bites arn't poisonous, like snakes. I should just like to see him bite."

"I shouldn't," I said, mentally, as Morgan pushed me a little on one side, and took hold of the pole.

"Now then, don't you be scared; I'll tackle him if he's vicious. Both pull together. He's so vexed now that he won't leave go if his teeth 'll hold."

"No," I said, setting my own teeth fast, but not in the pole. "Am I to pull?"

"To be sure. Both pull together. It's like fishing with a wooden line. Now then, haul away!"

There was a length of about ten feet of the pole down in the hole as we took hold together and began to haul, feeling something very heavy at the end, which came up in a sullen, unresisting way for some distance, giving me courage and making me nearly as eager and excited as our man.

"That's the way, sir. We'll soon— Hi! Hold tight! Wo—ho, there; wo—ho! Ah!"

For all at once the creature began to struggle furiously, shaking the pole so that we dragged at it with all our might; and then—*Whoosh!* The alligator left go, and we went backward on the soft mossy earth.

"I *am* glad!" I thought, as we struggled up.

"There, Master George, what d'yer think o' that? Can't have such games as this at home in the old country, eh?"

"No," I said. "But you're not going to try again, are you?"

"Not going to try again? I should think I am, till I get the great ugly creature here at the top. Why, you're not skeart of him, are you?"

"Wait till he's out, and then we'll see," I replied, as I thrust the pole down again, giving it a fierce twist, and felt it seized once more.

"That's the way. This is a bit of the finest sport I ever had, and it's just dangerous enough to make it exciting. Haul away, my lad."

I set my teeth and hauled, the reptile coming up quickly enough half-way, and then beginning to writhe and shake its head furiously, every movement being communicated to our arms, and giving us a good notion of the strength of the enemy we were fighting, if fighting it could be called. Up we drew it inch by inch, and I must confess that with every change of the position of my hands I hoped it would be the last, that the creature would leave go, and drop back into the hole, and that Morgan would be so disappointed that he would not try any more.

That is just how I felt, and yet, odd as it may sound, it is not as I felt, for mingled with that series of thoughts—just as a change of position shows another set of colours on a bird's back or in a piece of silk—there was another, in which I was hoping the alligator would hold on tightly, so that we might get it right out of the hole, and I could attack and kill it with the pole, so that I could show Morgan and—much more important—myself that I was not afraid to behave as boldly as the man who had hold with his hands touching mine.

My last ideas were gratified, for as we hauled together there was another savage shaking of the pole, which quivered in our grasp; then a strong drag or two, and we knew by the length of the pole that we must have the reptile within a yard of the surface, when Morgan looked down where a bright gleam of the sunlight shot from above.

"All right, Master George," he cried; "this way—over with you!" and setting the example, he dragged the pole over in the opposite direction to that in which we had it bent, when I perforce followed with him, and the next moment we were dragging a great alligator through the wet moss and black mud, the creature making very little resistance, for it was on its back, this being the result of Morgan's last movement when he dragged the pole across the hole.

The shape of the reptile's head and back made our task the more easy, and we had run with it a good fifty feet before it recovered from its surprise, loosened its hold of the pole, and began to writhe and thrash about with its tail as it twisted itself over into its proper position, in a way that was startling.

"Now, Master George, we've got him. I'll keep him from running back into his hole; you go and get the rope."

I could not stir for a few moments, but stood watching, as I saw Morgan raise up the pole, and bring it down bang across the alligator's back, but without doing it the slightest injury, for the end struck a half-rotten log, and the pole snapped off a yard above Morgan's hands.

"Never mind! I'll keep him back," roared Morgan, as the reptile kept facing him, and half turning to strike at him with its tail. "Quick, lad! The rope—the rope!"

I started off at once, and picked up the rope with its noose all ready, and then seized my pole as well, too much excited now to think of being afraid. Then I trotted back to Morgan just as he was having a fierce fight with the creature, which kept on snapping and turning at him in a way that, to say the least, was alarming.

"Ah, would you!" Morgan kept crying, as the brute snapped at him, and he presented the broken pole, upon which the reptile's teeth closed, giving the wood a savage shake which nearly wrenched it out of Morgan's hands; but he held on, and had all his work to do to avoid the tangled growth and the blows of the creature's tail.

"That's it, Master George. Now quick: drop that rope, and next time he opens his pretty mouth give him the pole. Aren't afraid of him, are you?"

I did not answer.

I did not want to answer just then, but I did exactly as I was told, dropping the rope and standing ready with my pole on one side, so as to thrust it into the brute's mouth.

I did not have long to wait for my opportunity, and it was not the alligator's fault that he did not get right hold, for through nervousness, I suppose, I thrust short, and the jaws came together with an ugly snap that was startling.

"Never mind; try again; quick, my lad, or he'll get away back to the hole."

To prevent this Morgan made a rush, and gave the brute a sounding thwack with his broken pole, sufficiently hard to make it turn in another direction, when, thoroughly excited now, I made a poke at it with the pole, and it snapped at it viciously.

I made another and another, and then the teeth closed upon the end, and the pole quivered in my grasp.

"Well done! Brave lad!" shouted Morgan, for he did not know I was all of a tremble. "That's the way; hold on, and keep him thinking about you just a moment. Pull! Let go! Pull again!"

As he gave me these directions, he got the end of the pole from me for a moment so as to pass the noose of the rope he had picked up over it, and then once more shouting to me to pull, he boldly ran the wide noose down over the pole; and as the brute saw him so near, it loosed its hold to make a fierce snap; but Morgan was too quick for the creature, and leaped away with a shout of triumph, tightening the rope, which was right round the reptile's neck, and running and passing the other end about a tree.

"Got him now," panted Morgan, as the alligator thrashed at the rope with its tail, and tugged and strained with all its might, but of course only tightening the noose with every effort.

"Yes," I said, breathlessly, as I stood now well out of danger; "we've got him now."

"Yes, we've got him now," said Morgan again, as we made the end of the rope fast to a branch. "That would hold one twice as big. Let's see; 'bout how long is he?"

"Seven feet," I said, making a rapid guess.

"Well," said Morgan, in a slow, hesitating way; "here, hi! Keep your tail still, will you, while you're being measured."

But the reptile seemed to thrash all the harder, dragging the noose tight, and flogging at the rope in a way which promised, if time enough was given, to wear it through.

"Oh, well, if you won't, I must guess. Yes, sir, he's quite seven feet long—nearer eight; but he must be pretty young, for he's a lean, lizardly-looking brute. Not nice things to tackle, are they? Look ye here at the marks of his teeth."

As he said this, Morgan held up his broken pole, first one piece then the other. "I say, Master George, he can nip. If that had been your leg or my arm, we should have wanted a bit or two of sticking-plaster, even if we hadn't had the bone cracked in two."

"It's a horribly ugly brute," I said, as I approached it a little nearer, and examined it by the warm ruddy glow which shone down here and there into the gloomy swamp forest.

"Yes; his mother ought to be very proud of him," said Morgan, laughing; "wonder what his brothers and sisters are like. Ha! Ha! Ha!"

"What are you laughing at?" I said.

"I was only thinking, Master George. The idea of me coming out of Carnarvonshire across the sea to find things like that!"

"Yes; it's different to home," I said.

"This is home," replied Morgan, stolidly—"home now. I've set and tended many a lot of eggs; but I say, Master George, only think of a thing like that coming out of a new-laid egg. Do rattlesnakes!"

I could not help smiling at the idea, but my face felt strange, and there was a twitching about my temples as the last words fell upon my ears.

"Halloa! What's the matter, lad?"

"You—you said rattlesnakes," I whispered hoarsely.

"Well, what of it? This is 'gator country. Rattlesnakes, they tell me, likes the high, dry, hot, stony places."

"Yes—father said so," I replied in a whisper, as I looked cautiously round.

"Well then, what are you looking for?"

"Indians," I whispered, for I had recalled how the savages had surrounded us while our attention was taken up by the last noxious creature we had attacked.

At my words Morgan made a bound, and then began to move past a tree. But he stopped short, and returned to my side, looking wildly round the while.

"See 'em—see any of 'em?" he whispered.

"No; but suppose they have stolen upon us again as they did before!"

"Yah! What do you mean by frightening a man? I teclare to cootness it's too bad of you, Master George."

I smiled once more, for Morgan's speech had sounded very droll and Welsh, as it often was when he grew excited.

"You tit it to scare me," he said, angrily.

"Indeed, no."

"Yes, inteet," he said; "and look you—I say, Master George, was it meant for a choke?"

"Indeed, no, Morgan; I really felt startled."

"Then it's all right," he said. "There's none of 'em here, so let's get home."

"But what are you going to do with the alligator?"

"Eh? Oh, I never thought of that. I wanted to catch him so that you might have a bit of fun."

"But now we have caught him?"

"Well, dunno, my lad. Might take him home and chain him up. Turn down a barrel to make him a kennel; he can bark."

"Oh, nonsense! We can't do that."

"He's no good to eat, though they say the savages eat 'em. Here, I know; let's take him home, and ask master what's to be done with him."

"Take him home?" I faltered.

"Ay, to be sure. I'll lead him by the string, and you can come behind and give him a poke with the pole when he won't go. Ought by rights to have two ropes, like they do at home with a vicious cow; then when he ran at me, you could pull; and when he ran at you, I could pull him back."

"But we haven't two ropes. That isn't long enough to cut, and I can't stop him if he runs at you."

"Might pull his tail," said Morgan.

"Ugh!" I ejaculated, as I recalled the use the creature could make of it, giving blows that I knew would knock me off my feet.

"Well then, I tell you what; let's leave him tied up as he is, and get back. The master will be wondering where we are, and fancying all sorts of trouble."

"Seems cruel," I said. "The creature will be strangled."

"Not he. If he does, he'll strangle himself. I never feel very merciful to things that go about doing all the harm they can as long as they live. Say, shall I kill him at once?"

"No; let's leave him, and see what my father says."

Morgan examined the knot he had made, and then started away, for the reptile made a lash at him with its tail, and in retort he took out his big-bladed knife, opened it, and held it out threateningly.

"It's all very well, look you," he said; "but if you'd hit me with that tail of yours, I'd have had it off as sure as you're alive."

It was Morgan's farewell to the alligator as we turned off with our poles, broken and sound, and hurried back to find my father with a gun over his arm, fast coming in search of us.

Chapter Nine

"I was afraid something was wrong," he said. "And look here, Morgan, I want to live at peace with all the world, but self-preservation is the first law of nature, and I would rather you did not leave the place again unarmed.— Well, George," he continued, turning to me, "where have you been?"

I told him of our adventure, and he was thoughtful for a few moments.

"You must go together in the morning and kill the thing," he said. "I don't like destroying life, but these wild creatures of the forest and swamp must give way to man. If they do not they must perish. All deadly creatures must be killed without mercy. There is not room in the parts of the earth we chose to live in for both."

Consequently, after making our arrangements, I called Morgan at daybreak, and we took a gun and ammunition to execute the alligator.

"Be a lesson for you in the use of a firelock, Master George," said Morgan, as we travelled on across our clearing, and paused at the edge of the forest. "Now then, my lad," he cried, giving his orders in a military way, and bidding me load.

I had seen the charging of a gun often enough to be able to go through the task sufficiently well to get a few words of commendation, but a good many of blame.

"Ram well home, my lad. I like to see the rod hop again, and the powder solid."

"What difference does it make?" I asked.

"All the difference in the world, my lad. Powder's rum stuff, and good loading makes it do its work well. Bad loading makes it do its work anyhow."

"I don't understand you," I said.

"It's easy enough, sir. S'pose I take a charge of powder, and lay it loose on a stone. If I set light to it there's a puff and some smoke, and that's all, because it has plenty of room. But if I shut it up tight in a gun-barrel rammed down hard, it goes off with a loud bang, because it has to burst its way out.

If you ram lightly, the bullet will go only a little way. If you ram hard, your bullet will go straight to the mark."

"There it is then, rammed hard," I said, as I made the ramrod ring.

"That's right. Now you shall shoot the 'gator. Some folks say their skin's too hard for the bullet to go through. We shall see."

We went on together toward our landing-place, and then on and away to the left, following our previous day's trail more and more into the swamp, beside the river, talking about the fight we had had with the reptile, Morgan laughingly saying that he should like to have another with one twice as big, while I thought I should not, but did not say so.

The morning was delightful, with the birds piping and singing, and in the open sunny parts we caught sight of the lovely orange orioles, and those all yellow and black—birds which took the place of our thrushes and blackbirds of the old country. Every now and then a tall crane would fly up from where he had been prodding about with his sharp bill in some mossy pool, his long legs trailing out behind him as if he had been dancing on stilts.

It had all grown familiar to me now, but I was never tired of gazing at the dark, shadowy places where the cypresses rose right out of the black water, and the great trailing moss, ten and fifteen feet long, hung down from the boughs like ragged veils. The place looked as if it might be the haunt of large, water-loving serpents, or strange beasts which lurked in waiting for the unwary traveller; but we heard nothing but the cries of birds and the rustling and beating of wings, or the hum of insect life, save now and then when there was a splash from the river away to our right, or from a black pool hidden from us by the dense growth.

"Make some of 'em stare over at home, Master George," said Morgan.

"What at?"

"Place like this. Miles and miles of it, and no use made of it. Round here! That's right. Remember that old rotten tree?"

"Yes," I said; "we must be close to the place now. How near shall I stand to the alligator when I shoot?"

"Oh, just as near as you like. Mind that hole; I shouldn't wonder if another one lived there."

I stepped quickly aside from the ugly-looking spot, and felt so vexed on seeing my companion smile, that I turned back and stood looking down into the place, forcing myself to do so quietly, and then following in a deliberate way, though all the time I could not help feeling a kind of shuddering sensation run over me, as if I had suddenly stepped out of the hot woodland into a current of fresh cool air.

I glanced at Morgan as I overtook him, but he did not say anything, only trudged on till, suddenly laying his hand upon my arm, he pointed to a tree dimly-seen through the overhung shades.

"That's the one I tied the line to," he said; "now I shouldn't wonder if we find he has scratched himself a hole in the soft earth. It's nearly half water, and I dare say he could easy."

"And if he has, what then?"

"Why, we must pull him back by the rope. He won't make much of a struggle; it will be too tight round his neck, and choke him so. There, what did I tell you!"

He pointed to where the rope ran down from the tree apparently into the ground.

"But if he had scratched a hole," I said, "he would have made a heap."

"Oh no; it's all so soft as soon as you get through the roots. He'd worm himself down right out of sight in no time, and— Well, I am took aback."

Morgan had stooped down and picked up the noose. The alligator had gone.

"Somebody must have set him free, Morgan."

"Somebody? What somebody would do that? There arn't no monkeys about here as I know of, or it might have been one of them. Nobody else would do it. Ah, I see."

He pointed to the noose, and showed me how the rope was frayed and teazled out, as if by the application of claws.

"That's it, plain enough. He's had all night to do it in, and there he has been scrat, scrat, scrat, scrat at his neck with those fore-paws of his, till he got it loose and pushed it over his head."

"Nonsense!" I said; "a thing like that wouldn't be clever enough."

"I don't know," said Morgan. "They're clever enough to hunt and catch dinners by slapping the water with their tails till the fish are stunned; they're clever enough to make nests and lay eggs; and this one was clever enough to try and cut me down with his tail, and I don't see that it was so very wonderful for him to try and scratch off anything that hurt his neck. Mind that gun, my lad; you don't want to shoot me, I know."

I coloured, and felt vexed at my clumsiness in the way of carrying the loaded piece, and stood watching while Morgan untied the rope from the tree, rolled it up in a ring, fastened it, and put his arm through before turning back.

"Never mind," he said, cheerily, "better luck next time. Now let's get home to breakfast. I dare say he has gone down to the river and got his long enough ago."

We walked back to find a couple of men from the settlement—which promised some day to be a town—and as I caught sight of them, I felt sure that it was bad news which they had brought, and my father's serious face confirmed the idea as he spoke to one of the men.

"Yes; tell the General I will be there in good time," my father was saying, as we came within earshot; and the men saluted and went off in regular military style, for many of them who had now turned settlers and farmers had served in the army with the leaders of the expedition. And often, on thinking it over since, I have felt how wise a selection of men there was; for, as you have yet to learn, it was highly necessary to have folk who could turn their swords and spears into ploughshares and sickles; but who, when it was necessary, could turn them back and use them in the defence of their new homes.

"Have the Indians come back, father?" I asked, eagerly.

He looked round quickly, starting slightly, for he had not seen me approach, and he was deep in thought.

"No, boy," he said, sighing, "but it seems we are not to enjoy our homes in peace; a new enemy is in the field."

I looked at him, waiting to hear more, but he was silent, and began walking slowly to and fro till breakfast was ready.

During the meal he said suddenly—

"Put on the best things you have, my boy. I am going up to the settlement this morning. I thought you would like to go."

I was not long in getting ready as soon as the meal was ended, and, to my surprise, I found my father in uniform, and with his sword by his side; but he looked so quiet and stern that I did not like to question him, and walked on steadily by his side, as he drew himself up and marched forward, just as if his clothes had brought back old days, and made him the stern, firm soldier once more.

It was a glorious walk. The sun was scorchingly hot, but our whole way was between the great sweet-scented pines, whose needle-like leaves glistened like silver as they reflected back the sun's beams, and shaded our way. After a time we began to have glimpses of the big river, and at last as we approached an opening I caught sight of a large ship, and uttered an exclamation.

"Yes," said my father, as he saw what had taken my attention; "it is a fine ship, but unfortunately she is not a friend."

I looked up at him inquiringly.

"Spaniard," he said, laconically. "The Spaniards have a settlement down in the south, and they have taken it into their heads that we are trespassers. I am going to be one of those who meet the officers this morning."

Our walk was soon at an end, and my eyes were busy noting the way in which houses had sprung up in large patches of land, spread along at a short distance from the bank of the broad river into which our stream ran, and evidently marked out regularly and running for some distance back.

It was the beginning of a town, but as I saw it then, it was a collection of houses and goodly gardens, with plantations of corn, sugar-cane, and cotton, all growing luxuriantly among the trees, which had been left standing here and there.

The scene was as animated as it was beautiful. Boats lay at anchor, dotted about in the glistening river, and right out, a quarter of a mile from the shore, lay the Spanish vessel with her colours flying, and a large boat lying alongside; while on shore I could see several of the gentlemen I knew by sight, dressed like my father in uniform, and mostly walking two and two in deep converse.

I had eyes for everything, and the picture I saw was soon printed vividly in my imagination; one object that I remember well being the English flag, which was blowing out from the top of a pole, which I soon saw was not planted by man, being a tall straight pine which had been lopped and smoothed down till it was exactly suited for the purpose to which it was put.

Another thing too struck me, and that was the fact that though the greater part of the men I saw about, standing idling and evidently watching the ship with its boat alongside, were familiar to me, there was quite a number of black faces, whose owners were loosely clad in white cotton shirt and breeches, talking together, showing their white teeth, and basking in the sun.

"Yes," said my father, as I looked inquiringly at him, "and it has been in opposition to my wishes; but I am only one against many—they are slaves."

Directly after, Colonel Preston came out of the largest of the wooden houses in company with another officer, and as they caught sight of my father, they hastened their pace and came towards him.

"Ah, Bruton," said the colonel, "you have come."

"Yes," said my father, smiling, as he shook hands with both; "and you had been thinking that as I was such an opponent of many of your measures, and held myself so much aloof, I should stay away."

"Well," said the colonel, who seemed startled by my father's words, "I must confess I—"

"Had not much faith in me, Preston. But I hope that in any emergency where my help is required, I shall not be found wanting."

"I am sure of it. I beg your pardon for my ungenerous thoughts," said the colonel, warmly; "and I am sorry that you and I do not always think the same."

"Whatever we may think, Preston," said my father, warmly, "I hope we shall always hold each other in esteem."

"I know we shall," cried the colonel; and he shook hands warmly with me. "Glad to see you, youngster," he said; "but be quick and grow into a man. We want sturdy fellows who can handle a sword, and fight for their land."

"Then they are aggressive, Preston?" said my father.

"Aggressive! You never heard such overbearing insolence."

"Yes, insolence," said the other officer. "Would you believe it, Captain Bruton; they demand that we shall immediately give up this land—this settlement which we have taken in the name and by permission of his Majesty the King—and go."

"Where?" said my father, gravely.

"Ah, that they do not say," cried Colonel Preston. "An officer has come with this command from the governor of their settlement, and, in the customary haughty style of the overbearing Spaniard, the message has been delivered, and the ambassador is coming to meet us at the General's in about an hour for our reply as to how soon we shall be gone."

"That sounds Spanish," said my father. "Then they do not propose to reimburse us for all that we have done, or to find us another settlement?"

"No, no, no," cried the colonel, angrily; "our orders are to go—to evacuate the settlement at once."

"That would be a painful task if we had to submit."

"Submit!" said the colonel, angrily. "Surely, Bruton, you would not advocate such a plan after all that we have done?"

My father made no reply, but turned to look thoughtfully at the Spanish ship, while the colonel seemed to be raging with anger.

"You will be present at the meeting, of course?" he said.

"Yes," said my father, quickly; "I have come on purpose. We must have this peaceably settled if possible."

"Good heavens!" cried the colonel. "Ah, here is the General," he cried, as the quiet, grave, benevolent man came up, dressed in a very shabby uniform, whose gold lace was sadly frayed and tarnished. "Hark here, sir; Captain Bruton talks of a peaceful settlement of this difficulty."

"Indeed!" said the General, frowning; and I looked at him eagerly, as I recalled that he it was who had been spoken of as the leader of our expedition. "Well, we shall see."

"And very shortly too," said Colonel Preston, warmly, "for here they come."

All eyes were directed toward the large boat which had just pushed away from the Spaniard, and which was now running rapidly toward the shore, with the blades of the oars flashing, the flag in the stern-sheets trailing in the water, and the glint of weapons seen now and then, showing that those on board were well-armed. Then the General spoke.

"Preston and Crayford, have the goodness to receive these Spanish gentlemen, and bring them up to my house. The rest, I hope, will assemble quickly there, so that I can hear what they have to say."

This had evidently all been planned over night, for the officers in uniform all seemed to be making fast for the house out of which I had seen the General come, and before many minutes had elapsed the room was thronged, and I was standing behind my father, who was close to where the General stood.

Not a word was spoken, and in the silence I could hear plainly the noise made by the sailors in laying in their oars, after which there was a pause, and then plainly heard there were the tramp of men, the buzz of voices. About a dozen soldiers halted outside, and four tall, dark, handsome-looking Spanish officers were ushered in by Colonel Preston and Mr Crayford.

Seats were proffered, but declined, and all remained standing, while the Spanish officers conferred together for a few moments before one, who seemed the youngest and lowest in rank, stepped forward, and in fair English said haughtily—

"Gentlemen, I have come for your answer to the communication brought to you last night from the governor of his most sacred Majesty's possessions here in America. What is it to be?"

"Let me say first, sir," said the General, quietly, "that we do not recognise the authority here of the King of Spain. We are on ground belonging to his Majesty the King of England."

"You are interlopers, sir, on the colonial possessions of his Majesty the King of Spain," said the young officer, coldly. "When will you have evacuated this land?"

"What is to be our reply, gentlemen?" said the General, looking round. "Am I to send word back that you will give up tamely, and submit to this demand?"

"No, no, no," rose in an angry roar throughout the room.

"You alone were silent, Captain Bruton," said the General, sternly. "Have you nothing to say?"

"Yes," said my father, who turned very white; and he took a step forward. "Sir," he said to the Spanish officer, "is the governor of your settlement aware that we are no trespassers here, but that we came under the authority of his Majesty King George?"

"I believe all that has been discussed, sir," said the officer, coldly. "Again I ask, how soon will you evacuate this place?"

"You are hasty, sir," said my father; and a murmur arose in the room. "Gentlemen," he continued, turning towards his brother officers and members of the expedition, "bear with me for a few moments."

There was another murmur and then silence, with every eye fixed angrily upon my father's face, as he turned once more to the Spanish officers.

"Gentlemen," he said, "all of us who are here consider that we are acting within our rights in taking and holding this land, which you see we have turned from a wilderness into a smiling home. The question of right seems to be in dispute. Cannot it be peacefully settled, for the sake of all? I think we can convince your governor that we are only acting within our rights."

The Spanish officer who was evidently the leader said a few words angrily to the interpreter, who nodded shortly.

"Your answer?" he said, haughtily.

"That we demand a peaceable solution of this difficulty, and that there be no bloodshed."

"When will you go?" cried the young Spaniard aggressively, and amidst a low angry murmur I saw my father's face flush, as he took another step forward, and raising his sword with his left hand he clapped his right down upon the hilt.

A silence fell upon all, and his words rang out loudly and clearly as he exclaimed with his eyes flashing and his brows knit—

"When our hands have no longer strength to draw our swords, sir— when the last man has been beaten down in our struggle for liberty and life—when we have again taught haughty, overbearing Spain that the English race is not one to draw back—when—I beg your pardon, General," said my father, stopping short.

"Go on, sir," said the General, sternly. "I would not wish for a better exponent of my views."

"Then go, sir," continued my father, "and tell the man who sent you that we are, all whom you see here, Englishmen who have made this our home—men who mean to keep what we have won in defiance of Spain and all her hosts."

"Is this your answer?" said the Spanish officer, sternly, as soon as silence came after a tremendous cheer.

"Yes," cried the General, "that is our answer, gentlemen, so go in peace."

"Yes, sir," said the Spaniard, after a few muttered words with his companions, "to return in war."

His defiance was received in calm silence, and he and his companions were led out again by Colonel Preston and Mr Crayford, not a word being spoken till they had been seen to march down to the rough quay, embark, and row off to their ship.

It was not till Colonel Preston and Mr Crayford had returned, full of excitement, that the silence was broken by the General.

"Well, gentlemen," he said, "what have you to say?"

"God save the King!" said my father, enthusiastically.

"Then you will all fight in defence of your hearths and homes?"

A tremendous cheer was the answer.

"Well, then," said the General, "we must be prepared. I look upon it all as an empty, insolent piece of bombast; but whatever it is, we must not be taken unawares. Help shall be at once asked from England, and meantime we must do all we can to place ourselves in a state of defence."

"Well, George," said my father, as we walked back home, seeing the sails of the Spaniard set, and that she was gliding slowly down the river, "what have you to say to all this?"

"I should like to know whether the Spaniards will come back."

"Ah, that remains to be proved, my boy. We shall see."

"Not they," said Morgan, when I told him, and he was listening eagerly to my account of what had taken place. "If we were Indians perhaps they would; but we're Englishmen and Welshmen, look you. No, my lad, we're more likely to see those Indians. Depend upon it, all that Spaniel said was a bit of bounce."

Chapter Ten

Those were busy times at the settlement, where the crops and everything else were neglected so that all hands might work at the block-house, or fort, it was determined to build, so as to have a place to flee to in case of attack, and the fight going against us.

Wood was plentiful enough, and the *chip-chop* of the axes was heard all day long, willing hands toiling hard, so that at the end of a week a strong wooden breastwork was contrived; and this, as the time went by, was gradually improved, sheds and huts being run up within for shelter from the dews and rain, and for store-places in case we were besieged.

But the weeks went by, and the Spaniards made no sign, and as far as we could tell were not likely to. Still the General did not relax his efforts; outposts and guards did duty; a well was dug inside the fort, and stores were gathered in, but no enemies came, and their visit began to seem like a bit of history.

My father and Morgan had walked over with me to the fort every morning, and there gentlemen toiled beside the ordinary labourers and the slaves; but no fresh alarm came, and at last we were back at the house regularly, and time was devoted to making up for the past neglect, Morgan bemoaning the state of the garden most piteously.

I suppose I must have been about fifteen years old then, but cannot be sure. All I know is that the whole business stands out vividly in my mind, as if it had taken place yesterday. In fact I can sit down, close my eyes, and recall nearly the whole of my boyish life on the river, with the scenes coloured by memory till they seem to grow. At such times it seems to me that I can actually breathe in the sweet lemony odour of the great laurel-leaved flowers borne on what, there, were often great trees dotted with blossoms which looked like gigantic creamy-white tulips, one of which great magnolias flourished at the end of our house.

On the day of which I am speaking, Morgan Johns, our serving-man and general hand, for there was nothing he was not ready to do, came and told my father that there was a schooner in the river, adding something which my father shook his head over and groaned. This, of course, made me open my ears and take an interest in the matter at once.

"Well, sir, look you," said Morgan, "I'll do as much as I can, but you keep on fencing in more and more land, and planting more and more trees."

"Yes, I do, Morgan," said my father, apologetically; "but see how different it is to cold, mountainous North Wales."

"North Wales is a very coot country, sir," said Morgan, severely. "No man should look down on the place of his birth."

"Nobody does, Morgan. I often long to see Snowdon, and the great ridge of blue mountains growing less and less till they sink into the sea."

"Ah," said Morgan, enthusiastically, and speaking more broadly, "it's a fery coot country is Wales. Where are your mountains here?"

"Ah, where are they, Morgan? The place is flat enough, but see how rich and fat the soil is."

"Yes, it's fery good," said Morgan, growing more English.

"And see how things grow."

"Yes; that's the worst of them, sir; they grow while you're looking at them; and how can one man fight against the weeds, which grow so fast they lift your coat off the ground?"

"In time, Morgan, in time," said my father. "Yes, sir, in time. Ah, well, I'll work till I die, and I can't do any more."

"No, Morgan," said my father, quietly, "you cannot do any more."

"The other gentlemen who came out don't mind doing it, and their little estates are in better order than ours."

"No, Morgan," said my father, decisively, "I will not have that. Nobody had such fruit as we did last year."

"Well, master," said our old servant, with his hard, dry face brightening up into a smile, "I think we can beat them all round; but if you are going on enclosing fresh clearings from the forest, I must have more help." My father shook his head and Morgan went on, "The other gentlemen are going aboard, one after another; why don't you go too, sir?"

"If I went, it would be to try to put a stop to it, Morgan, and cry shame on my neighbours for what they are doing."

"Ah, well, master, I've done," said Morgan. "I'll work till I drop, and I can do no more."

My father turned to the old-fashioned desk he had brought from home, and went on writing a letter, while, after giving him a look full of vexation, our man gave his straw hat a flop against his side, and went out.

I was not long in following and overtaking him by the rough fence which enclosed our garden.

"Morgan! Morgan!" I cried.

"Well, Master George, boy, what is it?"

"What did you want father to do?"

"Go and ask him."

"No, I shan't; I shall ask you. Did you want him to buy something to help in the garden?"

Morgan looked at me quietly and nodded.

"What was it?—a new spade?"

"Nay, boy; but people to use spades and hoes—'specially the last."

"But you can't buy people."

"Can't you, boy?"

"Only slaves. Oh, I say, Morgan! I know; you wanted father to buy some slaves."

"Ay, boy, that's it. Every one else here's doing it, so why shouldn't we?"

"I don't know," I said, thoughtfully. "I know this," I cried; "that schooner that came into the river has got slaves on board."

"That's right, Master George, boy. Cargo of blacks from the Guinea coast, and our neighbours are buying 'em so fast that there won't be one left if we want any."

"We don't want any," I said, indignantly.

"No, Master George, boy, so your father said; and I'm going to ask him to graft me."

"To graft you?"

"Ay, my lad, with a row of extra arms all down each side, like that picture of the Injin idol in your book."

"What nonsense, Morgan!"

"Oh, I don't know, Master George. One pair of hands can't do the work here. Wants a dozen pair, seems to me. Well, I've done my dooty. I told master there was a chance to get some slaves."

"And of course my father would not buy slaves," I said, indignantly.

"No, sir; and the house and plantations I've took such pride in will all go to ruin now."

"Morgan!"

We both started and looked round to see my father standing in the rough porch of rugged oak-wood.

The man went up to him.

"You have made me uneasy about all this," he said, thoughtfully. "I will go on board the schooner, and see who is there among my neighbours. I should like to interfere if I could."

"Better not, sir. May make bad blood after."

"Morgan!" cried my father, so sternly that the man drew himself up as if he were on parade, and his old officer were in uniform. "Do not forget yourself, sir. Go and unloose the boat. You can row me on board."

Morgan saluted and went away, while my father began to walk up and down the sandy path among his flowers. I waited a bit, and then went hesitatingly up to him. For a few minutes he did not notice me, and I saw that his lips were pressed close together, and his brow wrinkled.

"Ah, George," he said at last, and he laid his hand upon my shoulder.

"Going out in the boat, father?"

"Yes, my boy."

"Take me too."

He looked at me quickly, and shook his head.

"But I should like to go, father."

"My boy," he said, "I am going on board a ship lying in the river—a vessel used by cruel-hearted men for trafficking in their fellow-creatures."

"Yes, I know, father," I said; "a slaver."

He frowned a little, but went on.

"I am going to see if I can do any good among my friends and neighbours. It would be no proper sight for you."

I felt disappointed, but when my father spoke in that firm, quiet way, I knew that he meant every word he said, and I remained silent, but followed him as he took his hat and stick and walked slowly down to the little landing-place, where Morgan was already seated in the boat with the painter held in one hand, passed just round the trunk of the nearest tree, and ready to slip as soon as my father stepped on board.

A slight motion of an oar sent the stern of the boat close in to the bank, my father stepped in, the painter was slipped, and the boat yielded to the quick current, and began to glide away.

But just then my father raised his head, saw me standing there disconsolate, and said aloud—

"Would you very much like to come, George?"

"Oh, yes, father," I shouted; and he made a sign. Morgan pulled his left-hand oar, and I forced my way through the dense undergrowth to reach the spot where the boat was being pulled in, fifty yards down stream.

It was hard work, and I had not gone far through the dense leafage, and over the soft, spongy, river-soaked bank, before there was a rush and a scuffle, followed by a splash, and though I saw nothing, I knew that it was a small alligator, taking refuge in the water after a night's wandering ashore.

I had heard these sounds so often, and was so accustomed to the dread shown by the reptiles, that I did not hesitate to go on, and soon after reached the place where Morgan was holding on by the overhanging bushes, drawing the boat so close in that I easily stepped down on to one of the thwarts, giving my father a bright, eager look, but he did not see it; so taking one of the oars, I sat down behind our man, and rowed hard till our boat glided out of the mouth of the stream which ran through my father's property, and reached the turbid waters of the great river.

As we passed out of the mouth of our stream, and round the bushes on the point, there lay the schooner a couple of hundred yards away, anchored in the middle, with her long raking masts tapering in the sunshine, and the great spars glistening and bright as if freshly greased.

She was low in the water, and as I looked over my shoulder, I caught sight of a boat just pushing off to go down stream, and noted that she was rowed by some of our neighbours, and had black men on board.

I saw my father give a quick look in the direction of the boat, and frown, but he did not speak, and we rowed on.

As we neared the schooner I more than once became conscious of a peculiar offensive odour, that I thought must be something coming up with the tide; but I was too much interested in the slaver to give more than a passing thought to such a matter, and my eagerness and excitement increased as we drew near. For I heard loud voices, and saw our nearest neighbour close to the side, talking to a hard-looking, deeply-bronzed man.

Then one of the sailors threw us a rope; we made fast, my father stepped on board, and I followed.

"Better take the other two I've got, colonel, and clear me out," said the bronzed man.

"No, I think not," said Colonel Preston, who had exchanged a short nod with my father, and he turned to where a dejected-looking group of negroes, both men and women, were standing on the deck close to the open hold.

"Better alter your mind; make your black hay while the sun shines. I may never come up your river again. I'll throw in the other two dirt cheap."

I felt the colour come into my cheeks, and then felt how pitiful it was for the miserable, drooping, nearly nude creatures to be sold like that; but my attention was taken up directly by my father's looks and the colonel's words as he said, sternly—

"No; six are all I want, and it seems to me that half of these will die before I have had them long ashore."

"No; they'll soon pick up. We've had a rough crossing," said the slaver captain, "and the quarters are a bit close. We ran short of water too, and a tidy lot died, and made the others bad. You give 'em time, and that lot 'll turn out as cheap as anything you ever bought. You should have seen them when they first came aboard—lively and spry as could be. Have the other two. Hi! Below there!" he continued, as he went to the open hold, and boy-like I stepped forward, full of curiosity, to look down too.

But I started back in horror, as a hot puff of the revolting odour I had previously noticed came up from below.

"Ah, not very sweet, youngster," said the slaver captain, with a laugh. "Going to brimstone it out well as soon as I've made a clearance. Got two more, haven't you?"

"Ay," came up in a growl.

"Man and woman, eh?"

"Boy and a man," came up.

"Send 'em on deck."

There was a pause, during which I heard from below—"Now then! Up with you!" and the sound of blows, which made me draw a long breath, and I was going back once more to the hold when I felt my father's hand upon my shoulder, and saw as I looked up that he was deadly pale.

"Hoist 'em up there!" shouted the captain, and a rope rove through a block was lowered down.

"How can you join in this cursed business, Preston?" said my father in a low tone to our neighbour.

"I was going to ask you that," said the colonel, coldly.

"Me? Ask me?"

"Yes, sir; you have come on board to buy slaves, I suppose, with the rest of us?"

"I deny it," said my father, flashing out, as he drew himself up. "I came on board, too late it seems, to try and prevail upon my brother emigrants— English gentlemen of birth and position—to discountenance this hateful traffic in the bodies of our fellow-creatures."

"We must have men to work if our colony is to succeed, Captain Bruton."

"Oh!" ejaculated my father, and then in a low voice, as his eyes rested on the group of poor black wretches huddled together, I heard him say, "It is monstrous!"

At that moment a couple of sailors began to haul at the rope run through the block; it tightened, and with a cheery "Yo-ho!" they ran up what seemed to be the dead body of a big negro, whose head and arms hung down inert as he was hoisted on high; the spar to which the block was fastened swung round, the rope slackened, and the poor wretch plumped down on the deck, to lie motionless all of a heap.

"Not in very good fettle," said the slave captain, curtly; "but he'll come round."

The rope was cast loose from the negro's chest, lowered down again, and I gazed from the poor wretch lying half or quite dead on the deck, to my father, and back again, noting that he was very pale, biting his lower lip, and frowning in a way that I knew of old meant a storm.

"Now then, up with him!" shouted the captain.

"Ay, ay, but look out, or he'll be overboard. He's lively as an eel," came from below.

"Right!" said the captain; and he took up a small line and held it ready in both hands.

The rope tightened; there was a cheery "Yo-ho!" and up came a black, impish-looking boy of about my own age, kicking, struggling, and tearing at the rope round his chest.

But it was all in vain; he was swung round, held suspended with his feet just clear of the deck, and his wrists were caught in a loop of the line bound together, his ankles were served the same, and the lad was dropped on the deck to lie writhing like some wild animal, showing his teeth, and watching us all in turn with his rolling eyes.

"Come," said the slave captain, laughingly turning to Colonel Preston; "he's lively enough to make up for the other. Better have 'em. I'll throw them in for next to nothing."

"No," said our neighbour, coldly. "That man is dying, and the boy would be of no use to me."

"The man is not dying," said the slave captain roughly, "but he soon will be if you don't have him. As for this shaver, he's about as near being an imp as we can find. Keep away, my lad, or he may bite you."

This was to me, as I approached the boy, who showed his teeth at me like a vicious dog.

"Going to have 'em, colonel?"

"No; once more, no," said the colonel, sternly. "I am only waiting for my boat."

"All right, sir, I don't go begging. What do you say?" he continued, turning to my father. "Will you buy those two?"

"I?" cried my father, angrily; "buy my fellow-creatures for slaves?"

"Oh, no, of course not," said the slave captain. And then to himself, but I heard him, "Too good a man, I suppose.—Sorry you won't have 'em, colonel.—Heave 'em down."

The men on deck advanced to the insensible negro, and were in the act of stooping to pass the rope once more about his chest, when my father, who could bear the scene no longer, said quietly—

"Do you not see that man is dying?"

"Yes, sir. Altered your mind? You can have the two a bargain."

"Bah!" exclaimed my father, fiercely. "Man, have you no heart, no feeling?"

"Not that I know of, sir. This trade would take it out of any one."

"But the poor creature's lips are dried up. He wants water."

"He'll have plenty to-night, sir," said the slave captain, with a laugh. "Down with him, my lads."

"Ay, ay, sir," said the men; the rope was passed round the negro, and the men seized the end to haul.

"I can't bear it," I heard my father say in a whisper; and then aloud— "Stop!"

"Eh? What for?"

"I will buy the man," said my father.

"And the boy?"

"N—"

"Yes, yes," I shouted, excitedly.

My father turned upon me with an angry look, but he seemed to read mine, and his face changed.

"Yes," he said, quietly.

"Right, and a good riddance," said the captain, laughing, as he held out his hand for the money my father began to count out. "I don't mind telling you now, sir; if you hadn't bought him, he'd have been dead enough to-night; but you get him ashore and take care of him, and he'll come round— he will indeed; I'm not tricking you. It's wonderful what a deal these niggers will bear. There, I like to deal square," he added, as he thrust the money in his pocket. "Smithers, shove a chain on that boy's legs, and another on the man's."

"Ay, ay, sir."

"No, no, for Heaven's sake, no," cried my father.

"Oh, just as you like," said the slave captain. "I was going to give you the shackles; only I warn you, if you don't have them on, that man as soon as you revive him will make for the river and drown himself, and the boy will be off into the woods."

"Do what is best," said my father, and the shackles were put on.

"Shall we hoist them into the boat for you?"

"If you please," said my father, coldly.

"Heave ahead, my lads," cried the slave captain; "and below there, get those brimstone-pans going at once."

"Ay, ay," came from below, and I saw a lighted lanthorn passed down as my father's two slaves were hoisted over the side, and lowered into the boat, where Morgan stood ready with a grim smile upon his lip.

"You'll get yours home first, Bruton," said Colonel Preston, coming to my father's side; "my boat's all behind. I say, neighbour, don't preach at me any more. You're as bad as any of us, and I'm glad you've come to your senses at last."

My father gave him a peculiar look, and then glanced at the group of slaves destined for the Preston property, where they stood huddled together quite apathetic and hopeless-looking.

The next minute we were at the gangway, and as I passed down, I saw three rough-looking men coming up out of the hold, and a thin bluish vapour began to curl up before they smothered it down by rapidly covering the opening and drawing over it a well-tarred canvas.

Very soon after I was in the boat, stooping to take an oar, and gazing at the stern, where the man lay as if dead, and the boy, whose bonds had been secured to the thwart, lay glaring at me viciously, and had taken hold of the edge of the boat in his white teeth; and directly after, as we rowed away from the floating horror upon whose deck we had so lately stood, there came the regular beat of oars, and I saw Colonel Preston's boat, which had evidently been ashore with one load, coming back for the other poor wretches and their owner.

"Why, hang me!" said a voice, evidently not intended for our ears, "if that puritanical Captain Bruton hasn't been buying niggers too."

The calm water bears sound to a great distance.

I saw my father wince a little, and he turned to me bending down, so that his lips were pretty close to my ear.

"Yes," he said, "Captain Bruton has been buying niggers too."

"No, no, father," I said, looking up; "one of them is mine."

"And what are you going to do with him?" he said, slowly, as his eyes seemed to search mine.

"Do with him, father?" I said, promptly. "Let him go."

Chapter Eleven

Our first task on getting out of the main river and up our stream to the landing-place where the boat was made fast, was to get the boy ashore, and it proved to be no light task; coaxing and threats were received in the same spirit—for of course he could not comprehend a word. All he seemed to realise was that he was in the hands of his enemies; and that if he could get a chance, he ought to bite those hands.

"You'll have to be careful, Morgan," I said, as our man stooped down to unfasten the rope which held the boy to the thwart.

"Careful? What for, Master George? Think I should break him?"

"No; he bites."

"Oh, he won't bite me," said Morgan, confidently. "Like to catch him at it."

He had his wish, for the boy swung himself round and set his teeth hard in Morgan's leg.

"Oh! Well, he is hungry, and no mistake," said Morgan, freeing himself by giving the boy's head a sharp thrust.

"Has he bitten you?" said my father.

"Well, he have, and he haven't, sir. Breeches was a bit too tough for him, but he has nipped me finely. Wonderful power in his jaw. No, no, Master George, don't you touch him; he'll have to go in the copper first. Ah, would you! Why, he's like a fish, only he arn't hooked."

For the boy had made a dash for liberty, and it was only after a severe struggle that he was held down, and this time I was the sufferer; for, as I helped to keep him from springing overboard, he swung his head round and fixed his teeth in my left arm in a pinch that seemed to be scooping out a circular piece of flesh.

"Well, he is a warmint, and no mistake. Let go, will you, sir?"

"Don't strike the boy," said my father. "Let me get hold of his jaw."

The boy saw the hand coming and wrenched himself away, seeming to take a piece of my arm with him, and leaving me throbbing with agonising pain, and feeling as if I must yell out and sob and cry.

"Well done, George!" said my father, pressing my shoulder in a firm grip. "That's brave; always try and bear pain like a man."

"But it hurts horribly," I said, with my eyes full of tears.

"I know it does, my lad, but noise will not ease the pang.—Now, Morgan, you had better fetch another rope and bind him well."

"S'pose I had, sir. I'd take hold of him and carry him ashore, but he'd have his teeth into me directly. S'pose people don't go mad after being bit by boys? On'y feel mad, eh, Master George?"

I nodded, for I could not trust myself to speak, and I stood looking on as the boy was held back in the bottom of the boat, with my father's foot upon his breast.

"Shall I fetch a rope, sir? Can you hold him?"

"Yes, I think so. We can manage him between us."

Morgan leaped ashore, and he was about to go up to the house, when a rush and scramble brought him back, for the boy was struggling like an eel; and how he managed I do not know, but he wriggled from beneath my father's foot, passed under the thwart, and, as I tried to stop him, threw me backwards, and was over the side with a splash and beneath the stream.

As I uttered a cry of horror I saw the boy's woolly head appear for a moment above the surface, and then go down, weighted as he was by the shackles on his ankles; and, as I gazed, I nearly went after him, the boat gave such a lunge, but I saved myself, and found that it was caused by Morgan leaping back rope in hand, after unfastening the moorings, and it was well he did so, sending the boat well off into the stream, floating after our purchase.

"See him?" cried my father, eagerly, as he threw off hat and coat ready to dive in.

"Not yet, sir," said Morgan, standing ready with the boat-hook.

"I would not have him drowned for five hundred pounds," cried my father. "No, no, George, my boy, you must not go after him; his struggles would drown you both."

"Don't see him, sir. Big alligator hasn't got him, has it?"

"Don't talk like that, man," cried my father, with a shudder; "but you ought to be able to see him in this clear water."

"I see him!" I cried, excitedly; "give me the boat-hook."

It was passed to me, and after a couple of misses, I felt the hook take hold, drew up gently, and as I hauled in, we found that the boy was coming up feet first, the iron having passed between the ring of the shackle and the boy's ankle.

"Steady, my lad, steady!" cried Morgan, as I drew the boy nearer, and the next minute he was seized and drawn into the boat, feeble and helpless now, half dead, and making no further attempt to escape as the boat was paddled back toward the landing-place.

"That's quieted him a bit anyhow, sir," said Morgan. "Won't take his clothes long to dry, Master George, will it?"

"Poor fellow! He has been so ill-used," said my father, "that he thinks we mean to do him harm."

"Oh, we'll soon teach him better, sir," replied Morgan, as I laid my hand on the boy's side to feel if his heart was beating. "Oh, he arn't drowned, sir, and the wash 'll do him no end of good. Here we are!"

He leaped out, made the boat fast, and then, coming back, was about to carry the boy ashore; but my father had forestalled him, and stepped out with the boy in his arms, laying him gently down on the grass, and then looking wonderingly at Morgan, who had followed, and knelt down to pass a rope through the shackle and make it fast to a ring-bolt used for mooring the boat, and driven into one of the tree-trunks close to the water.

"Not necessary," said my father.

"Begging your pardon, sir, he'll come to and be off while we're busy perhaps. Now about the man; I'm rather 'fraid about him."

"We must get him ashore," said my father; and after securing the boat parallel with the log which formed the bottom of the landing-place, they managed to get the poor creature, who was quite an inert mass, out upon the bank, and then, after placing one of the bottom-boards of the boat under his back, I joined in, and we dragged him right up to where the boy lay insensible.

"I'm afraid we are too late," said my father, as he felt the black's pulse.

"Yes, sir, you've threw good money away here," said Morgan; "he'll never do a stroke of work for us, but thank you kindly for meaning help all the same, and I must try what I can do with the boy."

"Is he dead, father?" I whispered, in an awe-stricken tone.

"No, but dying, I am afraid. He has been starved and suffocated in that vile schooner. Good heavens! How can men be such fiends?"

"Ay, that can't do no harm," said Morgan, as I filled the boat's baler with water, and knelt down by the negro's side to begin trickling a few drops from time to time between his cracked lips, and sprinkling his face.

"I will fetch a few drops of spirit," said my father. "Keep on giving him a little water."

He went away toward the house while I continued my task, and Morgan kept up a running commentary upon the man's appearance.

"Pity, too," he said. "Master oughtn't to have let them cheat him though, like this. Fine working chap. See what a broad, deep chest he's got, Master George. Don't think much of his legs, but he's got wonderful arms. My! What a sight of hoeing I could have got him to do, but it's a case of hoe dear me! With him, I'm afraid."

"You don't think he'll die, Morgan, do you?" I said, piteously.

"Ay, but I do, my dear lad. They've 'bout killed him. We want help, but I'm 'fraid all that slave-dealing's 'bout as bad as bad can be. Give him a few more drops o' water; those others trickled down."

I gave the man a few more drops, pouring them from my fingers almost at minute intervals, but he made no sign. Then, all at once, I felt half startled, for a pair of eyes were watching me, and I saw that the boy had recovered sufficiently to be noticing everything that was going on.

As our eyes met, he looked at me like a fierce dog who was watching for an opportunity to make a successful snap; but as he saw me trickle a few more drops of water between the man's lips, his face suddenly grew eager, and he looked at me, found my eyes fixed upon him, and slowly opened his mouth widely.

"Want some water?" I said; and I was going to him when he jerked himself fiercely away, and showed his beautiful white teeth at me.

"Wo ho!" cried Morgan. "Mind, lad, or he'll have his teeth in you."

"He's thirsty," I said; and I held the tin baler half full of water to him.

He looked at me, then at the water, and I could see his lips move and his teeth part, showing his dry tongue quivering like that of a dog. Then he fixed his eyes upon me again fiercely.

"Let me give it him," said Morgan, as the boy's mouth opened widely again, and there was a pitiful, imploring look in his eyes.

Mass' George: A Boy's Adventures in the Old Savannah | 87

Now I could not understand all that when I was so young, but I've often thought about it since, and seemed to read it all, and how nature was making him beg for water for his parched tongue, while his education forced upon him the desire to fight me as a cruel enemy.

"There," I said, going a little nearer, pushing the baler close to his hands, and drawing back.

He looked at me, then at the water, and back at me, fixing me with his eyes, as one hand stole slowly from his side towards the baler, drawing it nearer and nearer stealthily, as if in dread of my snatching it away; and then it was at his lips, and he gulped down the contents.

"There, I'm not going to hurt you," I said, stretching out my hand for the baler, and getting it, meaning to go and fill it once more; and as I returned I saw that he was watching me so wildly that I walked up, with him shrinking away as far as he could go, and offered the tin to him again.

He took it in the same shrinking way, evidently expecting a blow, and drank heavily once more.

"Well, he couldn't ha' swallowed much, Master George, else he wouldn't be so thirsty," said Morgan. "Now give this here one a dose, though it seems to me labour in vain; only it may make him go off a bit easy."

He filled the baler, and I knelt down again to sprinkle the poor fellow's temples, and trickle a few drops once more between his lips, the boy watching me the while, and then giving me the first notice of my father's return by shuffling away in another direction.

"Poor wretch!" I heard my father mutter, as he gave me a piece of bread-cake, and pointed to the boy, before taking the cork from a bottle, and slowly dropping a spoonful or two of spirit between the man's teeth.

After this he waited, and I saw that the boy was watching him wildly. Then he poured in a little more, without apparently the slightest effect, and after looking on for a few minutes, I advanced toward the boy, holding out the cake. But I stopped short, with my hand extended, looking at him, and then, as he took no notice of the cake, but stared wildly at me, I broke off a few crumbs, and began to eat before him, treating him as I would have treated some savage creature I wished to tame, and breaking off a piece and throwing it within his reach.

Then I went on eating again, and after a time I saw his hand steal slowly to the bread, his eyes fixed on mine, and he snatched the piece and conveyed it to his mouth with a motion that was wonderful from its rapidity.

This I repeated two or three times before feeling that I ought now to have won his confidence a little, when I went close to him, put down the cake, and went back to kneel by my father, whose hand was upon the man's throat.

"Is he getting better?" I said.

There was a shake of the head, and I looked then with a feeling of awe at the black face before me, with the eyes so close that there was just a gleam of the white eyeballs visible; but as I gazed, I fancied I saw a jerking motion in the throat, and I whispered to my father to look.

"A good sign, or a bad one, my boy," he whispered. "You had better go now, back to the house."

"Yes, father," I said, unwillingly; "but don't you think you can cure him like you did me when I was so ill?"

"I would to heaven I could, boy!" he said, so earnestly that I was startled, and the more so that at the same moment the man slowly opened his eyes, and stared at us vacantly.

"It is a hopeful sign," said my father, and he took the baler, poured out all but a few drops of water, added some spirit, and placed it to the man's lips, with the result that he managed to drink a little, and then lay perfectly still, gazing at my father with a strange look which I know now was one full of vindictive hate, for the poor wretch must have read all this attention to mean an attempt to keep him alive for more ill-treatment, or until he was sold.

"Take a little more," said my father, offering the vessel again, and the man drank and once more lay still, glaring at us all in turn.

"Why, you'll save him after all, sir," said Morgan, eagerly. "Hurrah!"

But no one paid heed to his remark, for at that moment there was a sort of bound, and we saw that the boy had contrived to force himself so near that he could lay his hand on the man's cheek, uttering as he did so a few words incomprehensible to us, but their effect on the man was magical: his features softened, and two great tears stole slowly from his eyes as we watched the pair, the boy glaring at us defiantly, as if to protect his companion, and I heard my father say softly—

"Thank God!"

Chapter Twelve

After a time, with the boy seeming to watch defiantly beside the great fellow, the black revived sufficiently to swallow some bread soaked in wine-and-water; the dull, filmy look left his eyes; and at last he dropped off into a heavy sleep.

"Shall we try and carry him up to one of the sheds, sir?" said Morgan.

"No; the poor fellow has had a very narrow escape from death," replied my father; "and I do not know even now that he will recover. Fetch a few boards to lay against that bough, and tie the boat-mast up there, and fasten the sail against it, so as to act as a bit of shelter to keep off the sun. George, put some dry grass in a sack, and it will do for a pillow."

We set about our task at once.

"Lor' ha' mussy!" grumbled Morgan, "what a fuss we are making about a nigger. Pillows for him! Why don't master say, 'Get the best bedroom ready, and put on clean sheets'? I say, Master George, think he'd come off black?"

But all the same Morgan worked hard, with the great drops of perspiration running off his face, till he had rigged up the shelter, the black sleeping heavily the while, but the boy watching every act of ours in a suspicious way, his eyes rolling about, and his lips twitching as if he were ready to fly at us and bite.

"I know," said Morgan, all at once with a broad grin, as he was sloping some boards lately cut from a tree over the sleeping negro.

"Know what?" I said.

"What young sooty's a thinking. He's a young canny ball, and he believes we're going to make a fire and roast 'em for a feast."

Whatever the boy thought, he had ceased to struggle to get away, but lay quite still with his arm stretched-out, so that he could touch the big negro, and he was in this attitude when my father came back from the house.

"Yes, that will do," he said, approvingly.

"Yes, sir, there won't be no sun get at him now. Think he'll come right?"

"Yes, I hope so. Poor fellow!—if he has managed to live through the horrors of that slaver's hold, now that he has taken a turn for the better he may recover. He must have been a splendidly healthy fellow, and—"

"Well, he arn't now, sir, anyhow," said Morgan. "What'll I do with young coal-box, sir? Better chain him up in the shed, hadn't I, or he'll be off?"

My father did not reply for some moments, but stood watching the boy, as he lay with his bright eyes fixed on first one and then the other, like a wild creature ready to act on its defence.

"He must have known a good deal of this negro," said my father, thoughtfully. "Go and slacken that rope."

"If I do, sir, he'll go off like a 'coon, and we shall never see him again," said Morgan.

"Did you hear my orders?" said my father, in the sharp military way in which he spoke sometimes.

Morgan went to the ring-bolt, and began to unfasten the rope, when at the first quiver the boy half started up and remained crouching, ready to spring away.

"Shall I go on, sir?" said Morgan.

"Yes; slacken the rope sufficiently to let him reach the man."

"He'll make a dash for it, Master George," grumbled Morgan.

He was right, for the boy did make a dash as soon as he saw that the rope which tethered him to the tree was loosened, but only to creep close up to the negro, thrust his arm under his neck, and press close to his side.

"I thought so," said my father. "Draw that rope from the shackles."

"What, undo him altogether, sir?"

"Yes."

"Oh, all right, Master George," grumbled Morgan to me. "I could have leathered the young imp into shape, and made a labourer of him in time; but if your father likes to waste his money it is no business of mine."

My father's back was towards us, and he was standing at some little distance so as not to startle the boy, who rose again, crouched, and looked wildly at us, as the rope which had been simply passed through the iron shackles began to run through a link till the end was drawn out, and run over the ground to where Morgan stood grumbling and coiling up the rope.

"No, he will not," said my father, gravely. "There is something stronger than hempen rope to hold him, George, evidently. Unless I am much mistaken, he will not leave the poor fellow's side."

"Ah, well, sir," said Morgan, as he hung the rope on the stump of a branch, "they're your niggers, and niggers *is* niggers. I shouldn't trust 'em, and they'll cut and run."

"If they do, my man, I shall be sorry," said my father, gravely, "for they may fall into worse hands than ours. We have no key to those shackles; could you turn them with a file?"

"Little screwdriver may do it, sir?" said Morgan, thoughtfully.

"Fetch it from the tool-chest," said my father, shortly; and Morgan went off grumbling something about waste of money.

He was back in a short time, during which the black still slept, and the boy crouched by him watching us eagerly.

"Now," said my father, "see if you can open those ankle-rings. No, no; I mean the man's."

"But s'pose he's only shamming, sir, and jumps up, half kills me, and runs?"

"I'll forgive him if he does," said my father, dryly, "for you are getting to be a very dictatorial, meddling, insolent servant, Morgan."

"Well!" exclaimed Morgan. "Hear that, Master George, and after me following faithful all the way to these here wild shores. Ah, master, I didn't think you'd ha' said— Hi! Keep back, you young warmint!"

For at the first movement of Morgan toward the sleeping black's feet, the boy sprang up and showed his teeth like a dog.

"Stop! Keep back," said my father, and Morgan drew away, muttering something about a savage young tom wolf.

"It is quite natural," said my father, "and strengthens my ideas. He thought his companion was going to be hurt." As my father spoke, he moved toward the boy.

"Don't go anigh him without a stick, sir," said Morgan, hastily.

My father did not notice the remark, but turned to me.

"Be on your guard, George," he said; "but be firm, and I think the poor fellow will understand what you are going to do. Take the screwdriver, and try if you can unfasten the boy's anklets first."

I obeyed, and advanced to the boy, whose aspect was rather startling; but I went down on my knees, and before he could fly at me I caught quickly hold of the chain which connected his legs.

That made him pause for a moment, and look down sharply to see what I was going to do. He seemed to have some idea directly; and as luck would have it, the little square hole that was used to turn the screw was toward me, the screwdriver went in, and it turned so easily that I was able to open the filthy, rusty shackle, and set one leg free.

The boy's head moved like that of a bird, as he looked first at his foot and then at me, and he stood quite still now, as I unscrewed the second anklet and took it off.

"Throw the chains into the river," said my father.

"No, no," cried Morgan; "they may come in handy."

"For you?" said my father, with a curious smile.

Splash! Went the iron rings and links, and the boy looked puzzled, but made no opposition as I knelt down hard by the sleeping negro's feet, and using the screwdriver as a key, opened both the anklets in turn, and pointed to them as they lay on the grass, looking hard at the lad the while.

He stared at me stupidly for a few moments, and then in a curiously sullen manner stooped down, knelt down, and began to replace them on the sleeping man's legs.

"No, no," I shouted; and the boy started away, flinching as if expecting a blow; but as I stood pointing down at the irons, he stooped once more and picked them up, looking at me wonderingly again, but as I pointed to the river a flash of intelligence came from his eyes, and he whisked the irons over his head, and cast them right out into the stream.

"Now fetch him something to eat," said my father, as the boy crouched down by the man's head again under the shelter.

I went for some bread, and after a long time managed to make the boy take it; but he only snatched it up after the fashion of a wild animal, and ate it voraciously.

"There," said my father at last; "leave them now. I dare say the poor fellow will sleep for hours, and it will be the best thing for him. Don't go far away, George; and if you find that he wakes, try and give him some bread soaked in that thin French wine."

"Well," said Morgan, as soon as my father had gone back into the house, "you don't catch me saying any more about it; but your father gave a lot o' money for them two, and they might ha' been useful on the plantation; but you mark my word, Master George, that there big nigger 'll begin to open first one eye and then the other when we aren't looking; then him and the boy 'll slip into the boat, and a'most afore we know it, look you, they'll be gone."

"Nonsense, Morgan!" I said.

"Nonsense! Why, no, my boy, I reckon it's madness. If master didn't mean to have slaves why did he buy them?"

"To save them from being ill-treated."

"Ill-treated?" said Morgan, scornfully; "why, they're only niggers."

"Well, they're men, Morgan."

"Dunno so much about that, Master George. They're blacks, that's what they are, and everybody but master buys 'em to work on the plantations. I did think master was going to be sensible at last. Only slaves!"

"How would you like to be a slave, Morgan?"

"Me, Master George? Well, you see I couldn't be. I aren't a black. There, I've got lots to do, and can't stand talking here. These weeds 'll be all over my garden again directly. You're going to stop, I s'pose?"

"Yes."

"Well, call me if they seize the boat. We can't let 'em have that. When they do go, they'll have to swim."

So Morgan went off to his hoeing, and I stopped under the shade of the big magnolia to keep my long watch.

Chapter Thirteen

I kept about near the rough shelter rigged up for the two blacks, wondering how my father would set about giving them their freedom, for I seemed fully to understand that this was what he intended to do. Every now and then I glanced toward the place, where everything was wonderfully still, and at such times I found myself thinking about Morgan's words; and it appeared only natural that the poor fellows should try to escape, being quite in ignorance of the hands into which they had fallen; but if they did, I was fully determined to put a stop to their taking our boat, for I did not mean to lose that, and have my fishing expeditions spoiled.

After a time my task began to grow tedious, and I wanted to go and peep in to see if they were asleep; but somehow I shrank from doing this, and I began to wander about, now up to the house, and now back to the river, thinking, as I stood there gazing down into the clear water, that it would not be safe for the two blacks to lie there after dark, when the great alligators came crawling out of the pools in search of food. For there were plenty of accounts current among the settlers of how people had been attacked by the great reptiles, and I meant to suggest to my father that the two should be sheltered in the great shed, which had a strong door.

I glanced toward the canvas which hung from the spar, and suddenly awoke to the fact that there was something black at one end; seeing directly after that a bright eye was watching me, but only to be carefully withdrawn as soon as its owner realised that he was seen.

I smiled to myself at this, and went off into the garden, where I could hear Morgan's great hoe with its regular chop-chop, as he battled away with the weeds which refused to acknowledge the difference between wild waste and cultivated ground.

"Hullo!" cried Morgan, as soon as he saw me. "What, have they slipped off?"

"Slipped off? No," I said, indignantly. "I want a peach."

"Right, my lad," said Morgan; "and, look you, get one off the further tree; they're not the best to look at, but they're the sweetest and the best to taste, I can tell you."

Peaches grew easily and plentifully in the hot sunshine of our garden, and securing a sample of the best, I went back toward the landing-place, where I saw the boy's head pop back out of sight as soon as I appeared. Then laying down the fruit just within reach of the corner from which I had seen the boy watching me, I was in the act of turning away, when I saw that I was being watched from the other side.

"Hullo, Morgan!" I said. "You there?"

"Yes, Master George, I'm here, and it's time I was," he cried, sourly. "Do you think your father and me grafted them peach trees, and coaxed 'em on into bearing, for you to feed niggers with them?"

"I've a right to do what I like with the fruit, if I don't eat it," I said, angrily.

"Oh, very well; I've done. Seems to me that if master's to be always bullying me on one side, and you on the other, the sooner I make up my bundle and go home to Carnarvon, the better."

"That's what you always say, Morgan," I replied, laughing; "but you never do go."

"Ah, but you'll see some day; and then you'll be sorry," he grumbled, and away he went.

"I don't want to hurt his feelings," I thought; "but he needn't be so disagreeable about the poor black fellows."

After a time I went to the shelter and looked in, to see that the man was lying with his eyes opened; and, recalling what my father had said, I gave him some bread and wine, which he ate as it was put to his lips, in a dull, forbidding way which took all the pleasure out of what I had thought was an act of kindness.

The peaches had disappeared, and I was saying to myself, "You might have given him one!" when I found that both of them were lying close to the black's head untouched.

About sunset my father came and looked at his purchase in a very grave way, and then apparently satisfied he drew back.

"The man is recovering," he said. "We saved his life, my boy, but they must not stay there to-night. I hardly believe that an alligator would attack them; but one great fellow has been travelling through the garden in the night, and if he came near them, there would be a terrible scare if nothing worse."

"Where are they to go then, father?"

"In the large shed. There are plenty of bundles of corn straw, and they must make shift with that until we can build them a hut."

"Build them a hut?" I said, in wondering tones. "Are they going to stop?"

"Stop? Where else can they go, my lad?"

"I did not think of that, father," I said.

"No, poor fellows, when they have been sold into slavery, there is no going back. Even if we could put them ashore in Africa, it would only be for them to be slain or sold again."

"Then—" I stopped short, afraid to finish my speech.

"Well, what were you going to say?"

"I was going to ask you if—if—"

"I was going to keep slaves like my neighbours, eh?"

"Yes, father," I said, bluntly.

"Yes, my boy. It is forced upon me to do so; but it will be an easy slavery, George. We have thrown their chains away, and they are free to go wherever they like. Now call Morgan, and let's have them up here."

I called our man, and the sail was dragged aside, for the boy to crouch menacingly by the man, who lay gazing at us in a dull, heavy way.

"How are we to make them understand?" said my father, who advanced, bent down, and took hold of the negro's wrist and felt his pulse.

The boy bared his teeth, but the man said a word or two in his own language, and the boy drew back.

"Stronger, decidedly," said my father; and he stood watching his patient, while I fetched some more bread and soaked it in wine.

He ate it slowly and mechanically, like some beast of burden, and when it was finished my father signed to him to get up, saying the words at the same time.

He evidently understood, and tried to raise himself, nearly reaching to a sitting position, but falling back from sheer weakness, and gazing shrinkingly at us as if expecting a blow.

But as no blow came he spoke to the boy, who at once took his hands and pulled him into a sitting position, but the man could do no more, and uttered a low groan in his abject weakness as he gazed up in his eyes.

My father thought for a moment and then turned to Morgan.

"Get the sail," he said; and the triangular piece of canvas was spread beside the man on the ground.

"Now," said my father, "creep on to that, and we'll carry you."

The man looked up at him with his brow puckered over with lines, but he did not comprehend.

"Show him what I mean," said my father; and I lay down on the canvas, and then rose up, and my father pointed.

The negro understood him, spoke to the boy, and with his help and Morgan's half rolled, half dragged himself on to the sail.

"Now," said my father; "he's big and heavy; Morgan and I will take the top, you take the bottom, George. If you could get that boy to understand, it would be easy."

I took hold of the bottom of the sail and made signs to the boy, but he could not or would not understand, till the black uttered a guttural word or two, when he came shrinkingly to my side, and took hold, watching me the while as if to be aware of danger.

"Now then," said my father, "I don't suppose you two can lift; but if you ease the load up a little from the ground, that will be all that is necessary. Now together, Morgan."

They turned their backs on us as they took a good hold of the sail, and began to drag our load toward the great barn-like shed at the end of the house, reaching it without much difficulty, and drawing the sail right over a quantity of dry corn-stalks.

Here, after giving them some food to eat if they desired it, we left them and closed the door.

"There, Morgan," said my father, with a smile, as we crossed the garden, "I am a slave-owner now like my neighbours, and as soon as that man is well and strong, you will have no excuse for grumbling about the want of help."

Chapter Fourteen

I was so curious the next morning to see whether the slaves had run away, that I crept down soon after daybreak, and a curious feeling of vexation came over me as I saw that the door of the big shed was open.

"They're gone," I said, and ran back and down to the landing-place, to see if they had taken to the boat.

But there it was, all safe, and I drew back and stood watching as I caught sight of a droll-looking object, so busy that he had not noticed me; for about forty yards away there was the boy, coating himself all over with the soft yellow mud he scooped up from the stream, where he stood about up to his knees, rubbing it well, and not forgetting his woolly head, just as I might have used soap.

The appearance of the boy was so comical that I could hardly keep back a laugh. But I refrained, and watched him earnestly at work for a few minutes, before throwing himself down, and sluicing off the thin mud, his black skin appearing once more, and ending by diving out into deep water, and beginning to swim with an ease that I envied.

This went on for about ten minutes, when he came out dripping, gave himself a shake, and then catching sight of me, ran up the bank and as hard as he could go for the shed.

I followed, and on reaching it found that the boy was not visible, having probably hidden himself among the corn-stalks, while his companion lay sleeping heavily — a great savage-looking black.

I came away without closing the door, thinking of my father's words; and I'm afraid with something of the same thoughts as I should have had about some of the wild creatures I had before tried to tame, I began to long for the coming down of Mrs Morgan to prepare breakfast, meaning to get from her a good bowl of the Indian corn porridge that she regularly prepared.

As it happened she was extra early that morning; and as soon as I had proffered my request, she informed me rather tartly that she knew all about it, for the master had given her orders the night before.

By the time it was ready and cooling, my father was down.

"That for the blacks?" he said, as he saw the bowl I was taking to the shed.

"Yes," I said; and I told him about what I had seen.

"Poor fellow! I am not surprised," he said. "What can be more horrible than the way in which they were confined?"

The man was awake, and on our entering the dim shed he made an effort to rise, but fell back helplessly, and lay gazing at us in a half fierce, half sullen way, not changing his aspect as my father felt his pulse, and laid his hand upon his head.

"Hah! That's better," said my father; "less fever. If he can eat, it is only a question of time. Where is the boy?"

We looked round, but he was invisible.

"Call the boy," said my father, looking hard at the man, and pointing to the food; but there was no sign of being understood, and my father turned to me. "Set the bowl down," he said. "They will get used to us in time."

I followed him out, and we went in to our breakfast, where the position was pretty well discussed.

"Let them be, poor wretches," said my father at last. "By and by, perhaps, they will find out that all white people do not mean evil by them. It is very unfortunate, and I had made a vow that I would never have a slave, and here I am with two of my own purchasing."

As soon as I could get away, I hurried off to the shed to hear a quick rustling sound as I neared the door, and I got to the opening time enough to see some of the corn-stalks in motion, betraying where the boy had rushed off to on hearing my steps.

I did not make a rush after him, for fear of making him more wild, but took up the bowl to find it empty, and I looked at our invalid and laughed. But he made no sign, only gazed at me with the same weary sullen look, and I went away feeling a little disheartened.

"Hullo, Master George, been to see my deppyties?" said Morgan. "I was just going to look at 'em. That big black isn't going to die, is he?"

I turned back with him to the door of the shed, and he stood gazing in.

"No; he won't die this time. But I don't much like his looks, Master George. Seems the sort of fellow to turn ugly and knock me down with the big hoe, and I shan't like that, nor my wife neither. Where's young smutty?"

"Under the corn-stalks in the corner."

"What, hiding?"

"Yes."

"Here, stop a minute till I get the pitchfork; I'll soon turn him out."

"No, no," I cried; "they're to be treated gently."

"And as if they were human beings," said my father's stern voice, for he had come silently behind us. "Have the goodness to remember that, Morgan. If I am to be a slave-owner, my people shall meet with consideration, and not be treated as if they were the beasts of the field. Do you understand?"

"Oh yes, sir, I understand," said Morgan, good-humouredly; "you can count on me doing what's right by them. They can't help the colour of their skins."

"I am satisfied," said my father, quietly, and he left us staring in that heavy, sombre face before us—a face full of despair, but one to which we could not address words of sympathy.

The change that took place in the man day by day was wonderful, as far as health was concerned. In three days he was walking slowly about; in a week he was ready to take the tool in hand which Morgan gave him, and he went on clumsily with the work he was set to do, but displaying strength that was the admiration of us all. But he was moody, shrinking, and suspicious, and the boy was precisely the same. For it always seemed to me that the boy was constantly on the look-out to avoid a blow or some ill-usage on my part, and his companion to be expecting it from my father. The treatment they had been receiving for months had utterly cowed them, but when they began to realise that they had fallen among friends, the change was rapid indeed.

Of course they could not understand us, and when they spoke, which was very seldom, their language was utterly beyond our comprehension; but we got on pretty well by signs, after a few weeks when the change came.

It was one glorious afternoon, when, after worrying Morgan into getting me some bait, I prepared my rough lines for fishing, and while I was disentangling the hooks which had been thrown carelessly together, the boy who was passing nodded and looked on.

"Going fishing," I said. "Come with me?"

He looked at me without comprehension, and when I took hold of him by the arm, he shrank away.

"Oh, I say," I said, "I wish you wouldn't. Who's going to hit you? Carry this basket."

I placed one in his hand, and gave him the pot containing the bait in the other, signed to him to follow, and in a dull, sad way he came behind to where the boat was moored; but as soon as he saw me step in, he began to look wildly out into the stream, and to shrink away.

"It's all right," I said, "there's no slaver out there. Come along."

But he shrank away more and more, with his eyes dilating, and he said a few words quite fiercely in his own tongue.

"Don't be so stupid," I said, jumping out and securing him just in time to stop him from running off with my bait and lines.

He struggled for a moment, but ceased, and in a drooping, dejected way allowed me to lead him to the boat, into which he stepped sadly, and dropped down in a sitting position, with his legs under him, and his head bent upon his breast.

"Oh, I say," I cried, "don't do that. Look here; we are going fishing. Here, take an oar and row."

I had cast off the boat, and we were floating down the stream as I placed the oar in his hands, took the other, and in a sad, depressed, obedient way, he clumsily imitated my actions, rowing steadily if not ably on.

"There," I said, when we were as far out as I wished to be; "that will do. Lay your oar in like that," and I laid down my own.

He obeyed me, and then sat looking at me as mournfully as if I were going to drown him.

"Oh, I do wish you'd try and take it differently," I said, looking pleasantly at him the while. "Now, look here, I'm going to catch a fish."

As I spoke, I put a large bait on the strong hook I had ready, threw it over the side, and twisted the stout cord round my hand, while the boy sat watching me.

"Well, you have got a bit better," I said to him; "the other day you always wanted to bite. Do try and come round, because you're not a slave, after all. Oh!"

I uttered a yell, as I started up to pay out line, for, as we floated gently down stream, there was a tremendous tug which cut my hand, and seemed ready to jerk my arm from out its socket.

But I had so twisted the line that I could not pay it out, and as I stood, there came another so fierce a tug that I lost my balance, caught at the boy to save myself, and the light boat careened over, and seemed to shoot us both out into the river.

For a few moments the water thundered in my ears; the great fish, which must have been a gar pike, tugged at my hand, broke away, and I was swimming with the black head of the boy close by me, as we struggled as quickly as we could to the bank, reached it together, climbed out, and I dropped down into a sitting position, with my companion staring wonderingly at me.

His aspect was so comical, and his eyes sought mine in such a wondering way, as if asking me whether this was the way I went fishing, that I burst out into an uncontrollable roar of laughter, when, to my utter astonishment, the sad black face before me began to expand, the eyes to twinkle, the white teeth to show, and for the first time perhaps for months the boy laughed as merrily as I did.

Then, all at once, I remembered the boat, which was floating steadily away down stream toward the big river, and pointing to it, I ran as far as I could along the bank, and plunged in to swim out and secure it.

There was another plunge and the boy was by my side, and we swam on, he being ready to leave me behind, being far more active in the water than I. But he kept waiting for me, till I pointed on at the boat, and he seemed to understand, and went on.

The boat had gone into a swift current, and it was a long way from where I swam, and by degrees I began to find that I had rather miscalculated my strength. I was only lightly clad, but my clothes began to feel heavy, the banks to look a long way off, and the boat as far; while all at once the thought struck me, after I had been swimming some time, that I should never be able to reach the boat or the shore.

I tried to get rid of the fancy, but it would not go, and one effect of that thought was to make me swim more quickly than I should have done, or, as I should express it, use my limbs more rapidly than I ought, so that I was quickly growing tired, and at last so utterly worn out that a cold chill came over me. I looked despairingly to right and left at the beautiful tree-hung river-side, and then forward to where the boy had just reached the boat, and saw him climb in, the sun shining upon his wet back.

"Hi! Boy!" I shouted, "take the oars, and row."

I might as well have held my tongue, for he could not understand a word; and as I shouted again and again I looked at him despairingly, for he was sitting on the thwart laughing, with the boat gliding downstream faster than I seemed to be able to swim, while I knew that I should never be able to overtake it, and that I was getting deeper in the water.

"Oh, if I could only make him understand!—if I could only make him understand!" I kept thinking, as I shouted again hoarsely; and this time he did seem to comprehend that something was wrong, for I saw him jump up and begin making signs to me. Then he shouted something, and I saw that he was about to jump in again as if to come to me.

But he stopped, and took up one of the oars, to begin rowing, but of course only to send the boat round. Then, as if puzzled, he put the oar over the other side, and rowed hard like that, to send the boat's head in the other direction, repeating this again and again, and now standing up to shout to me.

I could not shout in return, only stare at him wildly, as he kept on making ineffective efforts to row to me, till all seemed to be over; the bright water and the beautiful green banks began to grow misty; and I knew that though I might keep struggling on for a few minutes, I should never reach the boat, and that he would never be able to row it to me.

I did not feel in much trouble nor get in any great alarm, for I suppose the severe exertion dulled everything, and robbed my sufferings of their poignancy as I still swam on more and more slowly, with my starting eyes fixed upon the boat still many yards away from me, and growing more and more dim as the water began to bubble about my lips.

All at once in front of me I saw the boy's black figure rise up in the boat like a shadow. Then there was a splash and the water flashed up, and I knew he must be swimming toward me to help me; but I could not see that he had taken the rope in his teeth, after finding himself unable to row in my direction, and had essayed to swim to me and tug the boat in his wake.

This in so swift a stream was impossible, but his brave act saved my life, for he was able to hold his own by swimming hard till the current bore me down to him just as I was sinking; and my next recollection is of feeling myself clutched and my hand being raised to the edge of the boat, while one arm was about my waist.

The feeling of comparative security brought back my fleeting senses, and I made a convulsive clutch with the other hand at the gunwale; while the next thing I remember is feeling myself helped over the side by the boy, who had climbed in, and lying in the bottom with the sun beating down upon me—sick almost to death.

Chapter Fifteen

By a wonderfully kindly arrangement of nature we recover very rapidly when we are young; and before half an hour had passed I was seated on the thwart, using one of the oars, while the boy was using the other, but he kept leaving off rowing to gaze earnestly in my face; and when I smiled at him to show him that I was better, he showed his white teeth, and even then I could not help thinking what a bright, chubby-looking face he had, as he plunged his oar in again, and tugged at it, rowing very clumsily, of course, but helping me to get the boat along till we reached the rough logs and the stumps which formed our landing-place, where I was very glad to get ashore and make the boat fast.

"Well, George, how many fish?" cried my father, as I went up to the house, to find him in the garden trying to direct the big black how to use his hoe.

"None, father," I said, half hysterically, for I was quite broken down.

"Why, what's the matter?" he said. "Hallo! Been in?"

"Yes—been drowned—that boy."

"What!" cried my father, furiously.

"No, no! He jumped in—saved me—I was going down."

I saw my father close his eyes, and his lips moved as he stood holding my hand in his, evidently struggling with his emotion. Then he said quietly—

"Better go in and get some dry clothes, and—"

He stopped and stood listening and gazing in wonder at the great negro and my companion, for the boy had gone up to him, and gesticulating rapidly and with animated face he seemed to be relating what had passed.

The change that came over the big fellow's face was wonderful. The minute before it wore its old, hard, darkening look of misery, with the eyes wild and the forehead all wrinkled and creased; but now as he stood listening, his eyes lit up, his forehead grew smooth, and his face seemed to have grown younger; his tightly-drawn-together lips parted, showing his white teeth. So that as my father took a step or two forward, seized the boy's arm, and then laid his hand upon his head, it was a completely transformed countenance that looked in my father's. For the man caught his hand, bent down and held it against his forehead, saying a few words in a low tone, and then drew respectfully away.

"You have had a narrow escape, my boy," said my father, huskily; "but out of evil sometimes comes good; and it looks as if your accident has broken the ice. Those two are completely transformed. It is just as if we had been doing them good, instead of their doing good to us. But there, get in. I don't want to have you down with a fever."

My father was right; our two servants—I will not call them slaves, for they never were that to us—appeared indeed to be quite transformed, and from that day they always greeted me with a smile, and seemed to be struggling hard to pick up the words of our language, making, too, the most rapid progress. The heavy, hard look had gone from the black's face, and the boy was always showing his white teeth, and on the look-out either to do something for me, or to go with me on my excursions.

In a week it was "Mass' George," and in a month, in a blundering way, he could begin to express what he had to say, but only to break down and stamp, ending by bursting into a hearty laugh.

It was my doing that the pair were called Pompey and Hannibal, and day after day, as I used to be out in the garden, watching the big black, who had entirely recovered his strength, display how great that strength was, I wondered how it was possible that the great happy-looking fellow could be the same dull, morose savage that we had brought dying ashore.

At the end of another couple of months, I went in one day full of a new discovery.

"Do you know who Pomp is, father?" I exclaimed.

"Yes; an unfortunate young negro from the west coast of Africa."

"Yes, father, but more than that. Hannibal has been telling me, and I think I understand him, though it's rather hard. They lived in a village up the country, and the enemy came in the night, and killed some, and took the rest prisoners to march them down to the coast, and sell them for slaves. Pomp's mother was one of them, and she fell down and died on the march."

"Did Hannibal tell you this?"

"Yes, father, and sat and cried as he told me; and Pompey's his son."

"Are you sure?"

"Oh, yes. He always calls Pompey 'my boy,' and Pomp called him 'fader' to-day."

"Ah, but that may merely be imitation."

"I don't think it is," I said, eagerly; and I proved to be right, for they certainly were father and son.

The winter came and passed rapidly away, and it was never cold to signify, and with the coming spring all thoughts of the Indians and the Spaniards died away.

My father would talk about the Indians' visitation sometimes, but he considered that it was only to see if we were disposed to be enemies, and likely to attack them; but finding we did not interfere in the least, and were the most peaceable of neighbours, they were content to leave us alone.

"And the Spaniards only tried to frighten us away, Morgan," I said one day.

"Well, I s'pose so, Master George; but you see we're so shut up here we never know what's going to take place unless a ship puts in. It's a very beautiful place, but there isn't a road, you see, that's worth calling a road. Ah, there were roads in Carnarvon!"

"I don't believe you'd care to go back to them though, Morgan," I said.

"Well, I hardly know, Master George; you see this place don't 'pear to agree with our Sarah's temper. It gets very trying sometimes when it's hot. It was very hot this morning, and she was so put out that when young Pomp put his black head in at the door she threw the big wooden shovel at him."

"But what for?"

"That's what I said to her, Master George. 'Sarah,' I says, 'what had the poor black boy done to make you throw things at him?'

"'Done,' she says; 'didn't you see him put his head round the door and grin at me?'

"'Well,' I says, 'Sarah, my girl, that's only his way of showing that he likes you.'

"'Then I don't want him to like me, and he's more trouble than he's worth.' And there's a lot of truth in that, Master George."

"Why he works hard, Morgan," I said.

"Yes, just so long as you are watching him. Then he's off to play some prank or another. That boy always seems to me as if he must be doing something he ought not to do."

"Oh, he's a very good boy."

"Never make such a man as his father, my lad. Humph! Here he is."

I turned, and there, sure enough, was Pomp making a large display of his white teeth, and holding something behind so that we should not see.

"What have you got?" I said.

He drew a basket forward and displayed four good-sized terrapins, and offered them to Morgan for a present.

"No, no," grumbled the man, "I don't want them, and I'm sure that the missus would find fault if I took them in. She hates them; besides, I'm not going to be sugared over like that, to keep me from speaking out. Now, look here, you've been fishing."

"Yes, sah. Kedge de terrupum."

"And I told you to hoe down between those yams, didn't I?"

"Yes, Mass' Morgan, I going to hoe down de yam-yam."

"But why isn't it done?"

"I d'know," said Pomp, innocently.

"You don't know?"

"No, sah, don't know 'tall."

"But I told you to do them," said Morgan, angrily. "Didn't I?"

"Yes, sah."

"Then why didn't you do them?"

"Wanted to go and kedge terrupum."

"Now, look here, sir, you've got to do what you're told."

"What you tell me, den?"

"I told you to go and hoe those yams, and you neglected the duty to go fishing."

"Yes, sir, go fishing; kedge terrupum."

"Instead of doing your work."

"Mass' Morgan, sah," began Pomp, in a tone of protest, but Morgan interrupted him.

"Now then, how is it those yams are not hoed?"

"Don't know, sah. Tell Hannibal hoe them."

"You told Hannibal to hoe them—your father?"

"Yes, tell um fader hoe um; Mass' Morgan want um done."

"Yes, but I wanted you to do them."

"Yes, sah, and I want um fader to hoe um yam while I go kedge terrupum. You make big holler at um for not do um."

"Now then, look you, Master George, oughtn't this fellow to be flogged?"

"You say no, Mass' George, and—"

Morgan darted out a hand to catch Pomp's arm, but the boy was too quick, and dodged behind me.

"Let him be," I said; "he doesn't know any better."

"But I want to teach him better," grumbled Morgan.

"Hist! Mass' George. I find great 'gator."

"Where?" I asked, eagerly, for I had long had an idea that I should like to see another of the monsters.

"Down by de ribber. All lay long so, out in de hot sun."

Pomp threw himself on the ground, and wallowed along a little way. "All along so, sah, while I done kedge de terrupum, and then all along tell Mass' George come and shoot um."

"How big was it?" I said, eagerly.

"Big as ebber so much. Come on, see um, Mass' George."

"It's only some little one, half as big as the one we pulled out of the hole," said Morgan. "You never want to go on them games now you've got that black chap."

"Oh, I'll go with you any time, if you'll come."

"Too busy, sir, too busy. Going to get a gun?"

"Yes, I'll go and see. It may be a big one. Colonel Preston's man told me there are some very big ones up the river on the mud-banks."

"Yes, sir, but nobody ever sees them."

"Well, I'll try this time, and if my father asks for me, say where I've gone."

I heard Morgan mutter something, but paid no heed, knowing that it was something about being careful with the gun, for I was not without my share of conceit and belief in my capacity of taking care of a gun. For my father had rather encouraged me to practise with his fowling-piece, as also with one of the heavy fire-locks we had in the house.

"An emergency might come," he said; and what with his instructions and those of Morgan, I was, if not a good marksman, as fairly expert as could be expected from a boy of my years.

I soon had the gun from its slings, and, providing myself with powder and ball, rejoined Pomp, whose eyes rolled with excitement at the sight of the piece.

"Me carry de powder shot bag," he cried, eagerly; and I let him sling the pouches over his shoulder, and followed behind him, as he marched off with head erect, and a look of pride that was ludicrous. He was, as a rule, a creature apparently made up of springs, which were always setting him in motion; but when bound upon any shooting or fishing excursion the natural pride in his brain rose above everything else, and I was often turned into quite a secondary personage, and had to obey.

It was so upon this occasion, for just as we reached the edge of the forest he stopped short, and in a stern whisper said—

"'Top here and load um gun, or wake ole 'gator where um sleep."

I obeyed, of course, ramming home a bullet, and as I was in the act of removing the rod from the barrel, Pomp suddenly exclaimed—

"Top um bit."

He ran off at full speed, and came back with his eyes flashing, and flourishing a small axe which he had fetched from the shed. This he directly after thrust into his belt, and holding up his hand, whispered—

"Now, no make noise. I go first."

He went on, leading me through the drier part of the swamp, and right away from the river, to my great wonderment; but after walking silently about half an hour he stopped, again held up his hand, and then with the greatest of caution crept on through the bushes, and in and out among the swamp-trees, never making the slightest sound, and I followed as well as I could for about a quarter of an hour, when he signed to me to stop, and I knew by the bright light a little farther on that the river was pretty near.

The next moment he was down flat, crawling slowly over the mossy ground, looking back to see if I was watching him, and pausing at last close to a gnarled old tree, which he tried to keep between him and the water.

I had been watching him lying there for about five minutes, when I became aware of the fact that he was returning as silently as he had gone, and as he reached me he put his lips to my ear.

"'Gator sleep in de mud. Mass' George, crawl up to de big tree, look 'long gun, and shoot um."

I was skilled enough then in the huntsman's craft to know what to do, and divesting myself of hat and boots, I went down and crawled cautiously in the trail made by the boy, trying hard to go as silently and with as little effort, but the nervous excitement set my heart beating, and by the time I reached the great gnarled tree I felt breathless, and my hands trembled exceedingly.

I lay quite still for a few minutes before venturing to do more, and then inch by inch I drew myself sidewise, and peered round the rugged trunk of the tree.

The next moment I was quite paralysed by the surprise I felt, for there, not twenty feet away from the spot where I lay, was a monstrous alligator, evidently fast asleep on a glistening mud-bank, his trail from the water being distinctly marked in the soft mud. There were the prints of his paws, and of his long tapering tail, and I could do nothing but gaze at his great proportions.

As far as I could judge he was about fourteen feet long, but evidently of great age, from his bulk, his horny hide banded and barred and corrugated, while the strength of such a beast must be, I knew, tremendous.

How long I watched the sleeping monster I cannot tell, but it was some time before I woke up to the fact that I had come on purpose to put an end to its destructive career, and that I had a gun ready charged in my hand lying close alongside.

Then with my heart beating fast I slowly pushed the barrel forward, resting it upon one of the mossy buttresses at the tree-trunk, my eyes fixed all the time upon the great closed and smiling mouth, and the peculiar heavily-browed eyes.

As if I were moved by something that was not myself, I gradually got the gun into position, grasping it firmly and pressing the butt home, while I carefully sighted the monster, wondering a little what the consequences would be if I missed, whether I should be attacked, and whether I should have time to get away. But directly after every sense was concentrated upon the task I had in hand, and just as I was about to draw trigger the creature quickly raised its head, as if suspecting the nearness of danger.

I was well ready though now, and raised the barrel of my gun slightly, pressed it against the tree, and fired.

There was the roar of the gun, a tremendous kick on the shoulder, and beyond the heavy sour-smelling smoke by which I was surrounded I heard a tremendous splashing and thrashing noise, accompanied by heavy blows, as if the monster was striking hard at something near.

But I lay perfectly still, feeling that the wounded monster would on seeing me make a spring, and if it did I knew that my life was at an end.

The splashings and the dull beating sound continued, but I kept behind the sheltering tree, now wondering whether the creature would have strength to get back into the river, or whether it would be there waiting for its assailant. At last, fascinated as it were by the desire to peep round the tree-trunk which sheltered me from my victim, I gently peered out, and stared in astonishment, for there was Pomp busy at work with his axe cutting off the reptile's head, while the tail kept writhing and lashing the stream, alongside which it had nearly crawled.

"Dat's got um," cried Pomp. "Hi! Ohey! Mass' George."

I was already on my legs, and, gun in hand, I parted the bushes, and joined the boy just as the monster gave a tremendous heave and a writhe, and rolled off the bank with a tremendous splash in the water.

"Ah, you no kedge fish and eat um no more, eh, Mass' George?" he cried. "'Gator no good widout um head, eh?"

I looked down on the mud, and there, sure enough, lay the creature's head.

"Why, Pomp!" I exclaimed; "what have you been doing?"

"Cut off um head, Mass' George. He no like dat."

Pomp broke out with one of his laughs, hooked hold of the grinning head, and dragged it out of the mud up to the side of a clear pool, a little way back in the swamp.

"Stop a bit," I said; "I want to have a good look at it."

"Wait till I wash um, Mass' George. No; must wash umself fus. Here a mess."

Pomp was about to jump into the pool to wash the mud from his legs, when he suddenly clapped his hands.

"Oh, here's game, Mass' George; only look. Dat's ole 'gator's house a water, where he keep all 'um lil pickaninny. Look at 'um."

Sure enough, there were five or six small alligators at the far end—little fellows not very long out of the shell.

"Oh dear!" cried Pomp, "I very sorry for you poor fellows. Poor old fader got um head cut off. What, you no b'lieve um? Den look dah."

He threw the great head into the pool with a splash, and then jumped in to stand up to his knees, washing it about till it was free from mud, and his legs too, when he dragged it out again on to the green moss, and we proceeded to examine the horrible jaws.

"Him much worse den Pomp."

"What do you mean?"

"Mass' Morgan and de capen say Pomp do lot o' mischuff. Dat do more mischuff den Pomp."

"Yes, I should think so," I said, as I examined the dripping head, and saw plainly that my bullet must have gone right through the monster's brain, probably only stunning it for the time being, and enough to give the boy time to hack off its head. For these creatures have an amount of vitality that is wonderful, and after injuries that are certain in the end to prove fatal, contrive to get back into the water and swim away.

It was a long time before I was satisfied with gazing at the grinning head, with its great teeth and holes in the upper jaw into which they seemed to fit as into a sheath. At last though I turned to the boy.

"We must take it home, Pomp," I said.

"No," he said, with a look of disgust. "Um quite dead now. Frow um into de ribber."

"Oh no! I want my father to see it, and Morgan."

"We go an' fess um den."

"No, no. You must carry it home."

"No, too heaby, Mass' George, and um begin to 'tink."

I laughed, for Pomp was beginning to show his natural disinclination for work, though certainly the hideous head did send forth an unpleasant, musky odour. So long as an exciting task was on hand which interested him, Pomp would work most industriously; but over anything plodding and approaching drudgery he was laziness itself.

"I frow um in de ribber, or you frow um in, Mass' George."

"Neither," I said. "It must be carried home."

"What, dat great heaby head?"

"Yes."

"What, all de way fro' de tree?"

"Yes."

"No, no, Mass' George, um too heaby. Dat kill a poor nigger all dead, oh!"

"Nonsense! It is not so heavy as all that."

"Oh, yes; um drefful heaby. Frow um in."

"But I want my father to see it, and Morgan would like to."

"Eh? I see."

He ducked down quickly, and lifted the head on to an old stump. Then, breaking off a bough of dead wood, he chopped a short piece off and propped open the huge jaws.

"Dah!" he exclaimed, gleefully. "Dat make um laugh, and de fly come in an' out, an' um no snap at um no more."

"But don't I tell you that I want them to see it at home. Sarah would like to see it too."

"Eh? Oh, no, Mass' George," cried Pomp, excitedly, and beginning to imitate poor Sarah's sharp acid way so accurately that I roared with laughter. For every tone of her voice—every gesticulation—was exactly true to nature.

"'What!'" he cried; "'what you mean, you nast' black young rascal, bring dat ting in my clean kitchun? I get hold ob you, I box your ears. How dah you—how dah you! Take um away—take um away!' Dat what Misses Sarah say."

"But we will not take it into her clean kitchen, Pomp. We'll put it on that pine-stump at the bottom of the garden."

"Oh, no, Mass' George. Sun shine on um, and de fly come on. Make um 'mell horrid."

"Oh, that will soon go off," I said. "Come, let's get back. Wait till I've loaded again though. Here, give me the powder and a bullet. We might see something else."

"Eh?"

"I said give me the powder and a bullet. Halloa! Where's the ammunition?"

"Eh? Now where I put dat amnisham, Mass' George? I dunno."

"Why, you must have laid it down on the ground when we came after the alligator."

"Sure I did, Mass' George. Ah, you are clebber boy. Come 'long, we find um we go back."

"No, no, stop. I want that head carried home."

"But um so heaby, Mass' George, and poor Pomp dreffel hot an' tire."

"Dreadful lazy you mean," I cried, angrily. "Come, sir."

"Now, Mass' George cross again, and goin' break poor lil nigger heart," he whimpered.

"Stuff! Sham! Lay hold of that head."

"Break um back den, carry dat great heaby thing."

"It will not. You didn't think it heavy when you dragged it along with the axe."

"Head all hot den, Mass' George; got cold now."

"Why, you lazy, cunning young rascal!" I cried; "if you don't pick that head up directly, and bring it along!"

"Ugh!" ejaculated Pomp, with a shudder; "um so dreffel ugly, Pomp frighten to deff."

I could not help laughing heartily at his faces, and the excuses he kept inventing, and he went on—

"Pomp wouldn't mind a bit if de head dry, but um so dreffel wet an' nasty. An' you come close here, Mass' George, an' 'mell um. Ugh!"

He pinched his nose between his fingers, and turned his back on the monster.

"Now, no nonsense, sir," I said, severely. "I will have that carried home."

"For de massa see um, an' Mass' Morgan?"

"Yes," I said.

"Oh!" exclaimed the boy, in a tone which suggested that he at last understood me; "for de massa and Mass' Morgan see um. I run home fess um here."

He was off like a shot, but my voice checked him.

"Stop, sir."

"You call, Mass' George?"

Mass' George: A Boy's Adventures in the Old Savannah | 115

"Come here, you young rascal!"

"Come dah, Mass' George? No fess um here?" he said, coming slowly cringing up.

"No, sir. Now then, no nonsense; take hold of that head."

Pomp stuck the handle of the axe into the band of his short cotton drawers, wiped a tear out of each eye, and took the hideous great head off the stump, looking at me reproachfully, as he bent with its weight.

"Is it very heavy?" I said.

"Kill poor boy carry um all dat way, Mass' George."

I stood the gun up against the nearest tree, and went to him and lifted the head, to find that it really was a pretty good weight.

"Yes," I said, replacing it on the stump; "it is heavy, Pomp."

"Den I go fess Mass' Bruton here," he cried, joyfully.

"No. Give me that axe."

He took the little chopper out of his belt, and slowly and shrinkingly gave me the handle; then dropped on his knees, crossed his hands on his breast, and lowered his head.

"Don' kill um dis time, Mass' George. Pomp berry sorry such a lazy rascal."

"Get up, and don't to stupid," I said, roughly. "Who's going to kill you?" and looking round, I had soon found and cut down a stout young sapling, which I trimmed into a pole, Pomp watching me the while with a piteous expression on his countenance.

"There," I said, when I had done, and provided myself with a stout pole about ten feet long.

"Oh! Ow!" burst forth Pomp in a terrified howl.

"What's the matter now?" I cried in astonishment.

"Nebber tink Mass' George such coward."

"Eh? What do you mean?"

"Lil bit do, Mass' George."

"No, it wouldn't."

"Off!"

"Here, what's the matter? What do you mean?" I cried, as he threw himself down on the moss, and kept on drawing up his legs as if in agony, and kicking them out again like a frog.

"Nebber tink Mass' George such coward."

"I'm not, sir. Why?"

"Cut great big 'tick like dat to beat poor lil nigger like Pomp."

"Lil nigger like Pomp!" I cried, mockingly; "why, you're as big as I am. Get up, you great tar-coloured stupid."

"No, no, Mass' George; hit um lyem down, please; not hurt so much."

"Get up!" I shouted; and I poked him in the ribs with the end of the pole.

"Ow! Ow!" yelled Pomp at every touch, and the more he shouted the more I laughed and stirred him up, till he suddenly sat up, drew his knees to his chest, put his arms round them, and wrinkling his forehead into lines, he looked up at me pitifully.

"Arn't done nuff yet, Mass' George?" he whimpered.

"Enough?" I cried. "Did you think I cut this great pole to whop you?"

"Yes, Mass' George."

"Why, it was to carry the head on, one at each end."

"Oh!" cried Pomp, jumping up as if made of springs, and showing his teeth; "I knew dat a hall de time."

"You wicked young story-teller," I cried, raising the pole quarter-staff fashion, and making an offer at him, when Pomp dropped on his knees again, and raised his hands for mercy.

"Ah, you deserve it," I said; "telling a fib like that."

"Was dat a fib, Mass' George?"

"Yes; you didn't know it all the time."

"No, Mass' George; not till you tell um. I tought you cut de big 'tick to whop poor nigger all black and blue."

"Why, how could I?" and I roared with laughter as I looked at his shiny, ebony skin.

"Dunno, Mass' George. Hit berry hard, make um bruisum all ober de body, same as you say when you tumble down—you say make um all black and blue."

Mass' George: A Boy's Adventures in the Old Savannah | 117

"There, come along," I said; "let's get the thing home. Phew! Look at the flies already."

"Whish—whoosh—whoosh!" cried Pomp, breaking off a bough and sweeping it round. "Nebber mind, Mass' George; fly keep on eat lit bit all de way home; not hab so much a carry."

"But how are we to manage? Here, you must find some tough cane to lay the head on."

"I know now," cried Pomp, taking the pole.

"What are you going to do?" I said.

"Put um down um troat. So."

As he spoke, he ran the pole through the open jaws and out at the neck, so that the head was safely swinging in the middle.

"Dah," he said, "now you carry dat end, I carry dis end. Dat end nice an' tin for Mass' George."

"Why, you cunning young rascal," I said, "you want me to carry the dirty wet end, do you?"

Pomp grinned, and broke off some thick leaves to carefully clean the sullied end, chuckling merrily the while.

"Um was horrid nassy, Mass' George," he said. "Now all right."

I took up and shouldered the gun, and then seizing one end of the pole, we marched triumphantly back with our grisly trophy, accompanied by quite a cloud of flies which kept up a tremendous humming noise.

I went first, and easily found the spot where the ammunition had been set down by Pomp in his excitement; and after he had thrown the pouch-straps over his shoulder and I had decided not to load again, as we were going straight home, we prepared for a fresh start.

"Mass' George like to come dis end?" said Pomp.

"No," I said; "I'll go first;" and we went on till Pomp began to grunt and shudder.

"What's the matter?" I said, looking back.

"Poor Pomp get all de 'mell ob de head dis end."

"All right," I said; "it won't hurt you."

"But um do 'tink horrid, Mass' George."

"We'll carry it the other way, side by side, as soon as we get out of the trees," I said; and we went on a little further, when the boy uttered a shout.

"What's the matter now?" I said.

"De fly, Mass' George."

"Never mind the flies," I said; "they will not hurt you."

"But dey do, Mass' George. Dey keep tink Pomp am de head, and sit on um and bite lil bit out ob um arm and neck. Poor nigger hardly got a bit ob clothes on."

"And a good job too, Pomp," I cried. "I wish I hadn't. Phew! It is hot!"

After divers changes about, in which I got my fair share of the nuisance, we reached the house, to find my father at home; and he, Morgan, and Hannibal came on to meet our triumphant procession.

"Bravo, George!" said my father; "why, that's quite a patriarch. How did you manage to kill him?"

"Mass' George shoot um, and Pomp cut um head off," cried the boy, proudly.

"Yes," I said; "Pomp found him asleep, and fetched me. Morgan, I want it on that stump."

"No, no, sir," said Morgan. "I'll get the hammer and a big spike-nail, and drive it through the back of the skin into that big tree at the bottom."

"Capital!" I cried.

"But it will be a nuisance," said my father.

"Oh no, sir. It's full in the hot sun, and the flies will clean it. Before a week's out it will be dry."

Hannibal fetched the short ladder, and held the head, while Morgan drove in the nail so that the great head with its propped open jaws hung there grinning at the bottom of the garden; the skin soon shrinking away so that the head hung as it were by a skin loop; and before a month was past it was perfectly inoffensive, and had preserved in drying its natural appearance in a wonderful way.

Chapter Sixteen

Recollections of sunny days in the cotton-fields, with the men and women cramming the white bursting pods into baskets as they laughed and chattered together, and every now and then burst into some song or chorus, their natural light-heartedness making them, if well treated, forget the bonds from which they suffered. Of those many days in the hot glow, where the men were busy with great chopping-knives cutting down the tall, towering canes ready to be piled high in the mule-carts and borne off to the crushing-mills.

For as time went on the visit of the slave schooner was repeated again and again, and the settlers brought more land under cultivation, and the place grew more busy week by week.

But at home all remained the same, only that by the help of Hannibal our garden increased in beauty and productiveness to a wonderful extent, and Pomp and I revelled in the abundance of the fruit.

I used to look at the boy and his father, and wonder how it was possible for them to have settled down so contentedly. But they had, and it did not seem to me that they had a single thought of the past, so light and easy-going they were.

But I misjudged them, as time proved.

I was merry and lively enough in those days, never happier than when playing Morgan some trick to arouse his wrath; but I was the perfection of quietness compared to Pomp, who was more like a monkey in his antics than a boy; and his father, the morose-looking, gloomy slave that he had been, seemed to have grown as full of life and fun as his son.

I don't think that there was anything I could have asked that pair that they would not have done. If I expressed a wish to have a pair of young squirrels for pets, they were sure to be obtained, just as the raccoon was, and the woodchuck. If I wished to fish, the baits were ready and the boat cleaned out; while if I told Hannibal I wanted him to come and row for me, his black face shone with pleasure, and he would toil on in the hot sun, hour after hour, with the oars, evidently sharing my delight whenever I caught a fish.

I remember one day when my father had gone across to the settlement on some business, taking Morgan with him—I think it was to see and select from some fruit-trees and seeds which had been brought over from the old country—that I sat in our room, busy over the study which I had promised to have done by the time of my father's return.

As I sat there I glanced out of the window from time to time to see Hannibal toiling away with his hoe, in a great perspiration which glistened in the sun, but evidently supremely happy, as he chattered away to Pomp, who was also supposed to be working hard, but only at preserving his position as he squatted on the top of a post with his arms about his knees, and his hoe laid across his head, perfectly balanced.

I laughed to myself, and then went on with my work, a piece of Latin translation, for my father used to say, "There is nothing to prevent you being a gentleman, my boy, even if we do live out in the wilds."

All at once I heard Sarah's quick step, as she went out of the place, and directly after she was busy over something.

Carelessly enough I looked up, and saw that she was beating and brushing my father's uniform, previous to hanging it over a rail, so as to guard it from decay by exposure to the sun.

I sat looking at the bright scarlet and gold lace, and saw that she had brought out the cap too. Then I went on with my work again, finished it, and with a sigh of satisfaction put all away, thinking that I would go down to the pool and have a bathe.

The idea seemed good, and I stepped out, thinking what a patient, industrious, careful woman Sarah was, and seeing that she must have fetched is the uniform again, and put it away.

I went through the fence into the garden, meaning to make Pomp go with me, but he was no longer perched on the stump, one of the many left when the garden was made; and on looking round for Hannibal to ask where the boy had gone, I found he too had left his work.

"Hasn't finished," I said to myself, for the man's hoe was leaning against the tree.

Carelessly enough, I strolled on down to the bottom of the garden, looking at the alligator's great grinning jaws as I went by, and out at the end, to see if the pair were in the little hut that had been built for their use, and a laugh which I heard as I drew nearer told me that I was right as far as Hannibal was concerned, while a few excited words which I could not make out proved that Pomp was there as well.

"What are they doing?" I thought to myself; and with the idea of giving them a surprise, I did not go up to the door, but turned off, walked round to the back, and parting the trees by whose leaves the place was shadowed, I reached the little square window at the rear of the house, and stood looking in, hardly knowing which to do—be furiously angry, or burst out laughing.

For the moment I did neither, but stood gazing in unseen. There to my left was Pomp, both his eyes twinkling with delight, squatting on the floor, and holding his knees, his favourite attitude, while his thick lips were drawn back from his milky-white teeth, from between which came a low, half-hissing, half-humming noise evidently indicative of his satisfaction, and in its way resembling the purring of a cat.

To my right, slowly walking up and down, with a grave display of dignity that was most ludicrous, was Hannibal, his head erect, eyes very wide open, and arms held firmly to his sides, a position that he must have imitated from seeing some of the drilling preparations going on at the settlement, and kept up ever since the scare produced by the coming of the Indians and the Spaniards.

The reason for this attitudinising and parading was plain the moment I appeared at the window and grasped the situation; for it was clear enough—Pomp had seen the gay uniform airing upon the rail, had annexed it, and carried it off to the hut, probably with his father as an abettor, in what could only have been meant for a loan; and he had followed the boy in, and possibly with his assistance put on the clothes, which fitted him fairly well; but his appearance was not perfect.

For there over the white-faced scarlet coat was the shiny black face, surmounted by the military cap worn wrong way foremost, while the breeches were unbuttoned at the knee, and the leggings were not there, only Hannibal's black legs, and below them his dusty toes, which spread out far from each other, and worked about in a way most absurd.

But the most absurd thing of all was the aspect of satisfied dignity in the man's countenance. It was as if he were supremely happy and contented with himself, the clothes having evidently raised him enormously in his own estimation.

"Now what shall I do?" I thought; "go in and scold them both, or wait and see if they put the things back?"

I was still hesitating and thinking how angry my father would be, when I found suddenly that there would be no need for me to speak and upset the equanimity of the happy pair, for all at once I heard a loud exclamation from the direction of the house, where Sarah had just come out to fetch in the uniform; and directly after, she jumped at the right conclusion, and made the place echo with the cry of "Pompey!"

The effect was wondrous.

The boy seemed for the moment turned to stone; his jaw fell, and he stared at his father, whose face seemed to grow ashy, and from whose aspect all the dignity had vanished in an instant.

Then, quick as some wild animal, Pomp sprang at his father, the shock with which he struck him in the chest causing the hat to fall off back on to the floor as he tore at the buttons to get the coat off.

Hannibal, with his fingers shaking and twitching, helped all he could, and hindered more, while I stood smothering my laughter and waiting to see the end of the comedy.

Those garments were dragged off doubtlessly much more quickly than they were put on, and as soon as they were huddled together, father and son stood listening to Sarah's voice, their eyes starting, and the perspiration standing in great drops upon their faces.

"What will they do next?" I said to myself.

Apparently they had no plans, for Hannibal looked reproachfully at his son and shook his head at him, his lips moving, and in a low, husky voice he said—

"Whatebber will I do!"

A way out of the difficulty seemed to come to the younger black, for he suddenly darted at the hat, picked it up, and dabbed it down on the bundle of white and scarlet clothes. Then, whispering a few words to his father— who seemed to be hanging back but to give way at last—the boy ran to the door, dropped down on all fours so as to be hidden by the trees from the house, and glided off almost as rapidly as some four-legged animal.

"The young coward, to run away like that," I said to myself, as another loud cry of "Pompey, Pompey! Where are you?" came from the front of the house.

"Poor old Hannibal!" I thought to myself, as I saw the utterly cowed object before me, so strangely contrasted with the dignified being a short time back in uniform, that I could hardly restrain my merriment.

But I did not laugh out, for I was sorry for the poor fellow, and tried to think of some way of extricating him from his difficulty, as he stood there with the uniform huddled up in his arms.

Somehow no idea came, only a feeling of anger against the cowardly young scoundrel of a boy, who had left his father in the lurch.

"If it was only he," I said to myself, "I'd glory in seeing old Sarah pull his ears, a mischievous young dog!"

But there was Hannibal before me, and whenever I looked in the poor fellow's face I never could help a feeling of respectful liking for the unhappy slave whom I had seen lying half dead upon the bank of the stream when we first brought him ashore.

Then with Sarah's voice still heard at intervals raging and storming, I strove to think of a plan to get the poor fellow out of his hobble, while at the same time, in a confused way, the scene on the bank kept coming back, and with it thoughts of how the boy had been ready to fight for his father then, while now he had taken to his heels and fled.

"I don't know what to do," I said at last to myself, as I felt that our civilising had spoiled Pomp. "To go and talk to her, and tell her not to make a fuss."

"Pompey! Pompey!" rang out from close by now, and Hannibal let fall the uniform, and clasped his hands.

It was evident that Sarah was coming to see if the boy was in the hut, and there was nothing for it but to bear the blame.

"Pompey! Do you hear me?"

"A—y—ou," came from right the other side of the house. "You call a me, missie Sarah?"

"Oh, there you are, are you?" she cried; and as I peeped through the trees, I saw her turn sharply round and hurry back, talking volubly the while. Then she called again—

"Pompey!"

"Yes, missie."

"Come here, sir."

"You call a me, missie?"

"Yes, you know I called you. Where are you?"

"Hey—oh—hi—ho! Hey oh—hi oh! Ally olly hi—oh—olly olly hi!" came in musical tones from the other side of the house; and as I peeped once more through the windows I saw Hannibal's bent back, as he stooped and picked up the clothes, brushed off some dust, and then with them held all ready and his face working with excitement, he crept to the door.

"Pompey, do you hear me?" cried Sarah, who was gone up now to the house.

"Hey—oh—hi—oh! Yes, missie, you call a me?" came from a little farther away.

"Do you hear what I say, sir?"

"Yes, missie."

"Then come here directly."

"Ole massa go along, an' Massa George a 'top alonga."

"Pompey!"

"Yes, missie; you call a me?"

"Oh!" cried Sarah, fiercely, "just wait till I get hold of you, sir;" and she ran off down the path at the other side of the house, shouting for the boy, who kept on answering, and, as I realised now, purposely leading her farther and farther away to give his father time.

For, stooping low down, and with wonderful speed and agility, Hannibal, who had crept out of the hut, suddenly darted into and down the garden, and as I followed, keeping well hidden among the trees, I saw him reach the front of the house, shake out the uniform, hang coat and breeches on the rail, stick the cap on the end, and dart off away in another direction, so to reach the path leading into the forest on the way to the stream.

I ached with my efforts to keep down my laughter, as I saw him scud off, glad at heart though, all the same, for, poor fellow, he had escaped. Then all at once my admiration for Pomp increased to a wonderful degree, for I heard a howl from the other side of the house, the sound of blows, heavy ones too; and as Pomp shrieked and howled, it was evident that Sarah was cuffing him tremendously.

Her voice grew louder every moment, so did Pomp's cries and protestations, till I could hear every word from my hiding-place, thoroughly enjoying of course the punishment that had fallen on the boy, while delighted by his ruse to get the clothes back and save his father.

"Oh don't, missie; don't whop a poor lil nigger," came loudly.

"You mischievous—(*bang!*)—young—(*bang!*)—Where are those clothes?"

"No, haven't got 'em, missie; no, haven't got 'em. Oh! *oh!* Oh!"

"Don't tell me your wicked stories, sir. Tell me this moment, or master shall know, and you shall be flogged. You have stolen them away."

"No, no, missie, Pompey nebber 'teal, no, nebber; wouldn't 'teal notin'."

"You—(*bang!*)—have taken—(*bang!*)—those clothes away. Where are they, sir?"

"Oh, don't whip lil nigger, missie. No got no clothes on'y lil cotton drawers, an' lil shirtums," howled Pomp, as he was dragged into sight now, Sarah holding on tightly by one of his ears.

"And I say you have got them, sir. Nobody else could have taken them," cried Sarah. "You wicked black magpie, you! Show me this instant where you have put them, or I don't know what I won't do."

I knew what was coming; it was all plain enough. But no, not quite all; but I did see the *dénouement* to some extent, for, as Sarah dragged the boy forward, I could contain myself no longer.

"Oh don't, missie!" howled the young dog.

"Oh, but I will," cried Sarah. "I put poor master's uniform on that rail to air, and—*Well!*"

"Ha—ha—ha—ha—ha!"

I never laughed louder in my life, as I burst forth into quite a yell, for there stood poor Sarah, with her mouth wide open, staring at the uniform hanging on the rail, and then at Pomp, who looked up at her with his face screwed up in mock agony, but his eyes twinkling with delight.

"Was dem a clothes you gone lose, missie?" he said, innocently; and Sarah panted and looked is my direction. "Dat Massa George brass out alarfin for you whip poor lil nigger nuffin tall."

"Oh—oh—oh!" burst forth Sarah at last, hysterically; "it's a shame—a cruel shame, Master George, to play me such a good-for-nothing trick."

I ceased laughing directly, and my mouth opened now with astonishment at the turn things had taken.

"You ought to be ashamed of yourself, sir," cried Sarah; "and here have I been ill-using this poor boy because— Oh, Pompey, Pompey, Pompey!"

She caught him in her arms and gave him a motherly hug, while I stood amongst the trees speechless.

"Missie cry her eyes cos she whip Pompey?"

"Yes, my poor boy," cried Sarah. "But his father shall know. Ah, you may well stop in hiding, sir; it's a shame." Then, ever so much louder, "It's a shame!"

"Don't 'cold Massa George, missie," said Pompey. "Him nebber do nuffin."

"Do nothing, indeed!" cried Sarah. "You come along in with me, and I'm very, very sorry I whipped you."

"Pompey done mind, missie," said the boy, showing his teeth.

"There, you're a very good, forgiving boy," said Sarah, as she caught up the uniform to take it in; "and I wish I could forgive myself."

Then, catching Pomp by the arm, she led him into the house, from which he soon after returned with a corn-cake and half a pot of prime jam of Sarah's own make.

And there I stood all the time thinking seriously among the trees, and unable to make up my mind what to do. If I did not speak, I should bear the blame, and Sarah would remain angry with me. If I told all, poor Hannibal, who had been led into the indulgence in a bit of vanity by his boy, would be in disgrace, and I knew that the poor fellow would feel it keenly. If I did not tell all, that young rascal would triumph in his cunning and deceit, and enjoy letting me have the credit of playing the trick on Sarah.

"I will tell," I said, sharply, as I saw Pomp come out licking his thick lips, and enjoying the jam.

Then I thought of how patiently he had borne Sarah's blows, so as to save his father from getting into disgrace, and that disarmed me again; so that my mind see-sawed about in the most tiresome way, till I gave up in despair, coming to no conclusion, and leaving the matter to settle itself, but determined to give Master Pomp a good thrashing soon, so as to get some satisfaction out of the affair.

"Pomp," I said, half aloud, "Pomp. Yes, I called him Pomp; and after what I saw in the hut I ought to call old Hannibal Vanity. So I will—Pomp and Vanity. I wish I could make up my mind what to do."

I had something else to think of the next moment, for I heard a shout, and Hannibal himself came running along the path from the stream.

"Hi—hi—Mass' George!" he shouted, breathlessly.

"What's the matter?" I said, running towards the house to get a gun. "Here, quick, come in here."

I strained my eyes as I ran, expecting to see Indians in pursuit of him, but he alone was visible, and he pointed, breathless and panting, in the direction from which he came.

"What is it?" I cried. "What's the matter?"

The answer came in a peculiar, low, hissing, rushing sound, as if a storm were coming through the forest. It ceased directly, and died away in a low, dull roar.

Chapter Seventeen

"Here, what's the matter?" I cried; and at that moment Sarah came running out again, looking inquiringly from one to the other.

"What was that noise?" she said.

"De ribber—de ribber," panted Hannibal. Then he tried to say more, but he was so excited that his command of English failed him, and he turned to Pomp, who had just come back from the hut, and said something to him volubly in his own tongue. Pomp's mouth opened wide, and he stared wildly at his father. Then turning to me, he caught hold of my arm.

"Come, get up the tree, Mass' George. Pull missie up the tree."

"What for? What's the matter?" I said, as the dull roaring seemed to be coming back.

"Ribber run all ober; water take away de boat, and all gone."

"River running over? What do you mean—a flood?"

"Yes, dat's flood. Come, get up a tree."

"Oh, nonsense! Come and see."

"No, no, Mass' George, mustn't go," cried Pomp, seizing my arm, and I was making for the path leading to the stream. "Hark! Hear dat?"

I certainly did hear a low, ominous roar rising and falling in the air, but it sounded like distant thunder dying away. I began to be startled now, for the look of dread in Hannibal's features was not without its effect upon me. Just then Pomp began to drag Sarah toward the biggest cypress about the place, chattering to her excitedly the while.

"No, no, I can't; my good boy, no," she cried. "What! Get up the tree? Oh, nonsense! Here, Master George, my dear boy, what does it all mean?"

"I don't know. I'm as puzzled as you are, but it means that we're going to have a flood. I wish my father was here."

"Look here, Pomp," I said; "we need not climb a tree; it's a great chance if the water reaches as high as the garden;" and I looked round, thinking how wise my father had been to select this spot, which was the only rising bit of ground near, though he had not chosen it on account of fears of flood, but so as to be well above the swamp damp and mists.

Hannibal said something excitedly to his son.

"Yes; climb up a tree, Mass' George. Big water come roll down, wash um all away. Ah! Make um hase, Mass' George." He seized me by the arm, and pushed me toward the tree, which was about a hundred feet away down the slope at the back, but almost instantaneously a wave of water came washing and sighing through the forest slowly but surely, and lapped onward as it swept out from the forest line at a rate which, deliberate as it seemed, was sufficient for it to reach the big cypress before we could; and I stopped short appalled and looked round for a place of refuge.

The water came on, and in another minute would have been up to where we stood, but it shrank back again toward the forest, and I felt that the danger was over, when to my great delight I heard a shout, the splashing of some one running through water, and my father came into sight to run up the slope to the place where we stood, closely followed by Morgan, and both at first too much exhausted to speak.

"Thank God!" he cried at last. "Don't speak. Flood. The settlement deep in water. Rising fast. The boat?"

"Wash away, massa," cried Pomp.

"Ah!" cried my father, despairingly. "Quick, all of you. It is coming now."

As he spoke I heard the deep roar increasing, and after a glance round, my father pointed to the tree.

"We must get up into that. No: too late."

For the flood came in a great, smooth, swelling wave out from the edge of the forest, and then glided toward us, rising rapidly up the slope.

"I'm with you," cried my father, and catching Sarah by the hand, he dragged her into the house, seized the rough ladder, and made her climb up silent and trembling into the loft, where, before we could join her, the water was over the doorsteps and had risen to our knees.

But the moment Sarah was in the loft, my father ordered Pomp and me to follow, then Hannibal and Morgan, coming up last himself, by which time the water was up to his waist.

As soon as he was in the little low loft, my father forced out the wooden bars across one of the windows and looked out, to take in the extent of our danger, and I pressed close to his side.

"Is there any danger?" I said, rather huskily.

"I hope not, my boy," he said, sadly. "The question is whether the house will be swept right away. Everything depends upon whether it comes with a fierce rash, or rises slowly."

I looked round and could see that the flood kept coming in little swells or waves from the edge of the forest, the water rushing out from among the tall trunks, and then seeming to undulate gently toward the house. The garden was covered deeply, and where I had been accustomed to look at the pleasant sand-walks, and the young fruit-trees, all was now water, out of which rose the tops of trees here and there.

The thatched roof of the blacks' hut was just visible as a grey point seen amongst the tree-tops, and all at once I saw it rise up high out of the water and then settle down again and float slowly away.

At that moment my father uttered a low sigh, and then there was another loud dull roar, and a great wave came rolling out of the edge of the forest, swelling onward, the tops of the trees bending towards us as it came on and on slowly, but with a force that bore all before it, and I felt my father's hand clasp mine in his.

"Quick!" he whispered; "climb out, and get on the ridge of the roof."

"Are you coming too, father?" I said.

"Out, quick!" he answered, but before I was clear of the window, he had hold of me and half drew me back, holding to me tightly, and not without need, for there was a dull thud, the house quivered from the tremendous blow, and I felt the water leap over me, deluging me from head to foot, and making me gasp for breath as I struggled to get back.

"Quiet!" said my father, sternly, and I remained still, expecting to feel the house swept away, to go floating like the roof of the hut, right away.

But it stood firm, the wave gliding off, but leaving the water now rippling up between the boards, telling that the lower floor was filled, and the flood rising through the ceiling.

An anxious ten minutes ensued, during which wave after wave came rolling out of the forest, each to deliver a heavy blow at our house, making the roof crack, but never yield, and with the last came so great an influx of water that our position rapidly began to grow untenable.

My father made no effort to induce me to climb up after the first wave struck us, till the water had risen well up into the loft, when he said quietly—

"Up with you, Morgan, on to the ridge."

"Begging your pardon, sir, I—"

"Silence, sir! Out and up with you, and be ready to take your wife's hands."

It was the officer spoke then, and Morgan crept out through the rough dormer window, and directly after shouted briefly—

"Ready."

"Now, Sarah, my good woman, be brave and firm; creep out here," said my father. "Don't think about the water, and grasp your husband's hands at once."

I heard Sarah give a deep sigh, and she caught at and pressed my shoulder as she passed; then with an activity I should not have expected of her, she crept out of the window, my father holding her dress tightly; there was a loud scrambling sound heard above the hissing and roaring of the water, and my father spoke again.

"Safe!" he muttered. Then aloud, "Now, boys—both of you—up, and on to the ridge."

"You first, Pomp," I said; and the boy scrambled out, and I followed, the task being, of course, mere play to us as we crept up the well-timbered roof, and got outside of the ridge-pole.

We had not been there a minute before Hannibal and my father were beside us, and the waste of water all around.

"Not much too soon," said my father, cheerfully. "Do you see, George?"

"Yes, father," I said, feeling rather white, or as I suppose any one would feel if he were white, for the water was level now with the bottom of the window; "will it rise higher?"

"I am afraid so," he said, gravely, as he looked sharply round at the various trees standing out of the water. "Yes," he continued, with the firmness of one who has made his decision; "Morgan, you swim well, and the current sets in the right direction. If the house gives way—"

"Oh, but it won't, sir; we made it too strong for that."

"Then if the water compels us to leave here, do you think you can support your wife to that tree, if I swim beside and help you?"

"I will support her there, sir," said Morgan, firmly.

"That's right. Hannibal, you can easily reach there?"

"Yes, sah."

"And you boys can, of course. We may have to take to that tree, for I think it will stand."

We all declared our ability to reach the new refuge, and Pomp gave me a nod and a smile, for it was the tree we had before meant to reach; and then we sat there awe-struck, and wondering whether the house would give way, and be swept from its position.

But now no fresh waves came rolling out of the forest, only a current swept gently past, and after a long silence my father said—

"Yes, that must be it. A terrible series of storms must have been occurring, hundreds, perhaps a thousand miles away up in the highlands and mountains, gathering force, till a flood has swept down to here like a series of huge waves passing down the rivers, and flooding all their banks. The first violence has passed, and I think we may hope that the waters will go down as rapidly as they rose."

But his words did not seem likely to prove correct, for as we sat there, with evening creeping on, it was plain to see that the water was still rising— very slowly, but creeping steadily on. At first it was only level with the dormer window; then by slow degrees it was half way up; and as darkness was coming on, the top of the window was nearly reached.

The roof was high in pitch, so that we were well out of the reach of the cold current as yet; but calculating by the rate of advance, it was plain that before many hours had passed the water would have risen to us; and the question my father had to ask us all was, whether we should stay there in the hope that at any time the highest point of the flood might have been reached, or try and swim at once to the great cypress, and take refuge among its boughs.

"What do you say, Morgan?" said my father at last. "Shall we go or stay?"

"Don't know what to say, sir. We are dry now, but if we swim to the tree we shall all be drenched, except these two blacks, and they can easily wring out their things. Then it means sitting in our wet clothes half perished through the night. I don't so much mind, but it would be terrible for her."

"Don't study me, sir, please," said Sarah, firmly. "Do what is for the best."

"I think what you say is right, Morgan. We can but swim to the tree when the water rises too high for us to stay here longer."

"But you don't really think it'll get any higher, sir, do you?"

Mass' George: A Boy's Adventures in the Old Savannah | 133

"I am afraid to say what I think," replied my father. "We are in a vast continent whose rivers are enormous. You see the water is still rising."

"Oh yes, sir, it's still rising," grumbled Morgan; "but I wish it would keep still. Going to stop or go, sir? If we go it had better be at once."

"We will stay," said my father; and as terrible a vigil as ever poor creatures kept commenced.

Fortunately for us the night was glorious, and as the last gleam of daylight passed away, the great stars came out rapidly, till the darkened heavens were one blaze of splendour, while the scene was made more grand by the glittering being reflected from the calm surface of the waters all around, till we seemed to be sitting there in the midst of a sea of gold, with blackened figures standing up dotted here and there, and beyond them the dark line of the forest.

The silence for a time was awful, for the current now ran very slowly, and the rise of the water was so insidious that it could hardly be perceived.

From time to time my father tried to raise our spirits by speaking hopefully and prayerfully of our position, but it was hard work to raise the spirits of poor creatures in so perilous a strait, and after a time he became silent, and we all sat wondering, and bending down to feel if the water was still rising.

Then all at once a curious thrill of horror ran through me, for the hideous bellow of an alligator was heard, and Morgan's hand went involuntarily to his pocket.

"Got knives, everybody?" he said. "Don't want them cowardly beasts to tackle us now."

"It is hardly likely," said my father, but at that moment as he spoke Pomp touched my arm.

"Dah 'gator!" he said, pointing.

I could see nothing, only that there was a broken lustre of the stars reflected on the water; and if it was one of the monsters it slowly glided away.

Then it began to grow colder and colder, and as I sat and gazed before me, the dark trees standing above the flood grew misty, and a pleasant sensation was stealing over me, when I felt my arm grasped tightly, and I gave quite a jump.

"No, no, my boy!" said my father, sternly. "You must not give way to that."

"I—I—" I faltered.

"You were dropping off to sleep," said my father, firmly. "You must master the desire. Hannibal, take care that Pomp does not go to sleep."

"Him sleep long time, sah," said the black. "Wake um up?"

"No; let him sleep; only keep watch over him, or he may slide into the water."

There was silence again, only broken by a low sigh or two from Sarah, to whom Morgan muttered something again and again as the time crawled slowly on and the waters still rose higher and higher toward our feet.

Never did the night seem so long before, and the only relief I had in my wearisome position was derived from the efforts I had to make from time to time to master the terrible feeling of drowsiness which would keep coming on.

Every now and then there was a little buzz of conversation, and I made out that my father asked every one's opinion, and made all try to make out how much higher the water had risen, so as to excite their interest, though it was all plain enough.

And so the night wore on, with the flood gliding up and up, and strange splashings and bellowings heard from time to time, now far off, now nearer, and every eye was strained to see if the creatures that made these noises were appearing.

Then all was silent again, and we waited, with the water still rising.

All at once I caught at my father's arm.

"What's that?" I whispered, in awe-stricken tones, for there was a curious quivering thrill in the timbers of the house, and it felt to me as if it was at last yielding to the presence of the water, and preparing to break up and float away.

My father did not answer for a few moments, and I knew that he was listening intently.

"I am not sure," he said at last. "I think—and hope—that it was something heavy swept against the house, and that it has passed on."

The alarm died out, and we sat either in silence or talking together of the state of affairs at the settlement, and the possibility of help coming in the shape of boats at daybreak, when Pomp's sharp voice suddenly rang out—

"Hi! Who did dat? Who pour cole water on nigger leg?"

In spite of the cold and misery and peril of my position, I could not help laughing heartily as I heard Hannibal speaking angrily.

Pomp retorted just as sharply, but though his father spoke in their West African tongue the boy replied in his broken English, to which he was daily becoming more accustomed, while his father acquired it far more slowly.

"How I know?" cried Pomp, irritably. "I tought Mass' George play trick. Hi! Mass' George, you dah?"

"Yes," I said. "What is it?"

"You got anyfing to eat? I so dreffle hungry."

"No, Pomp," I replied, sadly; "nothing at all."

"You been sleep, sah?" he continued, turning to my father.

"No, my lad, no," replied my father, good-humouredly, and I heard the boy yawn loudly.

There was no need to measure the water now, or to be in doubt as to whether it was rising, for it had wetted our feet as we sat astride, or eased the position by sitting in the ordinary way. But the stars still shone, and the night dragged its slow way on.

"Will morning never come?" I said, despairingly to my father at last. "Oh, I am so—so sleepy."

He took my hand and pressed it. "Try and bear it all like a man, my boy," he whispered. "There is a woman with us, and you have not heard her make a single complaint."

"No; it was very selfish and cowardly of me, father," I whispered back, "and I will try."

I did, and I conquered, for I know that not a single complaint afterwards escaped my lips.

And higher still rose the black, gold-spangled water over our ankles, creeping chilly and numbing up our legs, and we knew that before long the effort would have to be made to reach the great black mound of boughs which we could dimly see a short distance away.

"How far do you think it is from daybreak, Morgan?" said my father suddenly, after what seemed to me a terrible time of suspense.

"Don't know, sir. Daren't guess at it," said Morgan, despondently. "Time has gone so slowly that it may be hours off yet."

"No," said my father, "it cannot be very far away. If I could feel sure I would still wait before making our attempt, but I am afraid to wait long. We are getting chilled and numb."

"Just so, sir," said Morgan, sadly. "You think for us all, sir, and give your orders. I'll do my best."

There was another pause, and I heard my father draw a deep breath, and then speak sharply—

"Well, George," he said; "how do you feel for your swim?"

I tried to answer, but a feeling of despair choked me, as I looked across at the dark boughs, thought of the depth of water between, and that I could not swim there now.

"Oh, come, come, lad, pick up," cried my father. "The distance is nothing. I shall want you to help me."

"Yes, father," I said, despondently; and I heard him draw a deep, catching breath.

But he knew that on him lay the task of saving us all, and he said cheerfully—

"You can easily swim that, Hannibal?"

"Yes, sah," said the black, quietly.

"And you, Pompey?"

"Eh, massa? Swim dat? Yes, Pomp swim all dat, sah."

"We shall be forced to start directly," said my father. "Do you hear, Morgan? We must not wait to be floated off."

"No, sir," replied Morgan; and his voice sounded sad and grave, and a low sigh came from by his side. Then arose in a low voice—

"Master George, dear, could you get here?"

"Yes," I said, trying to stir myself; and, catching hold of my father's hand, I stood up with a foot on each side of the ridge, stiff, cramped, and with the water streaming from me.

"That's right," said my father, cheerfully. "Mind how you go, my lad. It will stretch your legs. Take hold of Hannibal; don't slip and get a ducking."

He said all this cheerily, and I knew it was to encourage us all; but as I passed by him, stepping right over his legs, he whispered, "Speak cheerily to the poor woman."

"Yes, father," I whispered back.

"Don't keep him, Sarah," said my father. "I want to come there myself; I shall swim by your other side."

She did not answer, and I crept by Hannibal and then over Pomp, who gave me a hug, his teeth chattering as he said—

"Oh, I say, Mass' George, I so dreffle cold. Water right up a-top."

The next moment I was seated again on the ridge, feeling that the water really was right up to the top, as Sarah's cold arms closed round me, and her wet face was pressed to mine as she kissed me.

"Good-bye; God bless you, my darling!"

"Don't, don't talk like that," I said. "We'll all mount the tree, and the water will go down."

A piteous, despairing sigh came into my ear, and I felt Morgan's hand seek mine, and give me what I knew was meant for a farewell grip.

A bad preparation for a swim to save one's life, and the chill of the rising water began now to increase as I fancied it made a leap at us, as if to snatch us off and bear us away to the far-off dark shores beyond which there was a newer life.

"Come, George, my lad. Back with you," cried my father; "I want to come there. Be ready every one; we must start in a few minutes."

"Yes, father," I said; and I was on my way back, passing Pomp, who began to follow me, and together we crept, splashing through the water, holding tight by Hannibal, and then by my father.

"You too, my lad?" he said, kindly.

"Yes, massa," replied Pomp.

"Swim steadily, both of you. The distance is very short, and there is nothing to mind." Then as if to himself— "Oh, if I could only tell when morning would come!"

"Massa want know when time to get up to go to work?" said Pomp, sharply.

"Yes."

"Oh, quite soon, sah. Sun come up dreckly, and warm poor little nigger; I so dreffle cold."

"How do you know?" cried my father, clinging as it were like a drowning man to a straw of hope.

"Oh, Pomp know, sah. Dah! You ope bofe ear, and listum to lil bird. Dat him. Lil blackum yellow bird, go *pinkum-winkum-wee.*"

A dead silence fell upon us, and what had been inaudible to me, but quite plain to the boy, came faintly from the distance—the twittering cry of a bird in one of the trees at the edge of the forest; and directly after it was answered from far away, and I felt my father's cold wet hand grasp mine as he exclaimed hoarsely—"Thank God."

I could hear him breathing hard, and the tears ran down my cheeks as my head rested on his breast, and I clung to him for a few seconds.

Then he drew another deep breath, and his voice and manner were entirely changed, as he cried out—

"Do you hear, Morgan? Daybreak in a few minutes, and the sun before long. I think we could hold out here for an hour at a pinch. We shall have our swim long before that, and with heaven's good light to help us safely there."

"Hurrah!" shouted Morgan, hoarsely. And then we all joined in a hearty cheer, while the cry of the bird rang out directly after from close at hand.

Chapter Eighteen

Black night comes quickly down there in the south, with but little of the twilight of the north, and after the night's dark reign there is but a short dawn before the sun springs up to shed hope and light, and the bright thoughts of a new day.

And now, with the blood seeming to flow more swiftly through our chilled frames, came the pipings and twitterings of the birds at the edge of the forest; there was a misty light, then a roseate flush overhead which rapidly changed to orange above and below. The black mirror spangled with diamonds and gold had gone, and as we sat there with the water lapping now over the ridge, which was quite invisible, the sun's edge rose over the forest, glorifying the tops of the trees, and the great green cypress stood up with golden gleams darting through it, and offering us an inviting refuge from the peril in which we were placed.

"Now, Morgan, ready?" said my father, as he stood up and shook his limbs.

"Yes, sir, ready. Cheer up, old lass; we'll soon get you there."

I caught a glimpse of Sarah's white despairing face, but my attention was taken up directly by my father's words.

"Come, Pompey, brave lad, jump in and swim across to the big tree, and show us the way."

"Iss, massa," cried the boy; and he started up and dived in plump, to disappear, and then his black head popped up. "Come 'long, Mass' George," he cried; "so lubbly warm."

"Yes; in with you!" cried my father; and I rose, hesitated a moment, and then plunged in, to find that by comparison with the air the water was quite warm.

"I dab fuss," cried Pompey, and he swam on to soon reach one of the boughs, and turn round to wait for me.

I did not keep him long; and as soon as we had seated ourselves astride of the great branch just level with the water, we stayed to watch the coming of the rest.

That little swim after the effort required to make the first plunge was simplicity itself to us boys; and consequently I looked almost wonderingly at the effort it caused my father and Morgan to get across with Sarah, whom they supported between them.

They started well, swimming of course abreast, and with Hannibal coming behind, but after a time they began to get deeper in the water, and to be swimming with more effort, fighting so fiercely at last that if it had not been for Hannibal lending them a helping hand, they would have been swept away.

I could not understand the reason for some time, but at last made out that they had drifted into a spot where two little currents met, and were striving against a force which I had not encountered, and were being carried away.

At last, by making a desperate effort, they swam on up the swift little current, and were nearing the tree fast, getting well toward the bough on which we two boys were seated, when all at once they stopped and began struggling again.

They were so near the end of the bough, that had we been there I could almost have reached them, and yet, so close to safety, they were, as I at last realised, completely helpless.

"What is it? What's the matter, father?" I cried, excitedly.

"Caught—caught among the boughs underneath," he panted, hoarsely; and I knew now that they had swum into and become entangled among the submerged boughs.

Just then I heard Sarah say piteously—

"It's of no use. Try and save yourselves."

I looked at Pomp, and he nodded his head, as if he fully comprehended me, beginning at once to creep along the bough we were on, like a monkey, and I followed as well as I could, pretty quickly, but not with his agility.

The bough was thick where we sat, about a couple of feet above the water, and rose up at the end to about ten feet above. But as I hoped, when we were some distance along, it began to bend more and more, and the thinner branch we now reached bent so rapidly that we were soon only five feet, after climbing to six, then four, three—two—then one, and then touching the water into which we sank now, going along hand over hand, making the rough bough act as a natural rope, till Pomp was at the full extent of the thinnest twigs and nearly within reach of the helpless group.

"Now, Mass' George, come," he said.

Mass' George: A Boy's Adventures in the Old Savannah | 141

I grasped his meaning and passed on abreast of him, took a good hold with one hand grasping quite a bunch of twigs, while the boy took the other and reached out toward where Morgan was just able to keep himself afloat, with the others beyond him, and all growing weaker minute by minute.

Pomp got out as far as he could and stretched out his hand, but he was a full yard off still, and in a despairing way I looked at Morgan's upturned face.

"No catch hold, massa?" cried Pomp; and then he said something in his own tongue, whose effect was to make Hannibal swim rapidly towards him from where he had been supporting my father, he being the only one not entangled by the boughs.

The peril taught the man how to act, and catching his son's hand, he bridged the space and extended his other hand to Morgan, so that we formed a human chain in the water, dependent upon the strength of my wrist and the bunch of twigs and leaves I held.

"Now, father," I said; "can you get clear?"

He struggled feebly, and I began to tremble for my hold.

"No," he said; "my foot is caught in a fork among the boughs, and if you draw, it only tightens it."

A dead silence ensued. What was to be done? I could not answer the question, and I knew that everything depended upon how long I could hold on. Was all our effort to result in failure after all? It seemed so, and I tried to say something about kicking free, but no words would come, and once more I began to feel a horrible sensation of fear. The difficulty was solved by my father, who roused himself to a final effort just in the height of our despair.

"Get her into the tree," he said, hoarsely. "Never mind me."

What followed seems to me now like part of a confused dream. Nearly all my early adventures stand out, when I go back, brightly vivid and distinct, but a mist comes over my brain when I try to recall that scene.

I can remember though how Pomp changed his grasp of my hand after a struggle, by getting his teeth well into the skirt of the loose black garment I wore, thus setting both my hands at liberty, so that I was able to get a double hold upon the boughs, and drag and draw with such good effect that Pomp was soon within reach of another.

He seized this, and together we managed to draw Hannibal and then Morgan within reach, so that they too got a good grip of the bended twigs, and were in comparative safety.

But my father?

I looked from where I held on, up to my chin in the water, outward toward the spot in which I had seen him last. But he was not there. He had really been the only one entangled, and as soon as he had loosened his hold of poor Sarah, a good struggle in the outward direction had set him free, and I saw him now striking out feebly and floating helplessly away.

My first thought was to swim to his help, but I was utterly unnerved and overdone. A few strokes would have been all that I could have taken, and then I might have gone down, but a hand was stretched-out and caught me by the collar, and Morgan's voice whispered—

"No, no, my lad, leave it to them."

And now for the first time, in a confused way, I understood that Hannibal and Pompey were swimming to my father's help, while I remained clinging there.

More misty than ever all that follows seems, but I have a recollection of seeing the two black heads nearing where my father was still struggling to keep afloat, drifting farther and farther away, and next of his being close up to the great fork of the tree some dozen yards from where we clung.

It was no easy task to join them, but the danger was past now, and after a rest we three—Morgan, Sarah, and myself—managed to get along the bough to where we could reach another, lower down, and level with the water.

The rest was simple, and before many more minutes had elapsed, we were all gathered together in the great fork among the huge branches, wringing away part of the water that drenched us, and mentally thankful for our narrow escape from death as we revelled in the warm beams of the sun.

Chapter Nineteen

Very little was said for some time, every one being glad of the calm and silence, and drawing in the genial warmth which was delicious to our cramped and thoroughly weary limbs.

And as I sat there, gazing out over the waters at what seemed to be a vast lake, it did not appear like a scene of desolation, for the sunbeams danced on the rippled water, or turned it to a glittering mirror, where it flowed calm and still; the trees stood out at intervals all green and beautiful; and the forest beyond the clearings, though dwarfed, was unchanged. Now and then a fish flashed out like a bar of silver, and the birds twittered, piped, and sang as if nothing had happened. It was only the poor human beings who were helpless, and beginning to feel, now that the excitement had passed, the pangs of a trouble that it was impossible to meet.

One of my first acts, as soon as I began to grow dry and warm, was to take my knife from my pocket and cut a notch in the tree just on a level with the water.

Pomp looked at me and then shook his head.

"No," he said; "no, Mass' George, no get sug gum dah, an' Pomp dreffle hungry."

"I know that," I said, rather surlily, for my notch was not meant for the purpose he thought, and I knew the difference between a cypress and a sugar maple.

"Den what for cut um tree?"

"To see whether the water is rising or going down."

"Not do nuffum," said the boy, eagerly. "'Top so."

"Yes, he is right," said my father, who had been higher up the tree, trying to get a glimpse in the direction of the settlement, in the hope of help in the shape of a boat being on the way. "The flood seems to have reached its highest point, and we may begin to hope that it will go down now."

But the hours glided by and there was no help, and no sign of the flood sinking. Pomp was quite right; it did "'top so," and we began to suffer keenly from hunger.

We had long got well warm in the sunshine, and the thirst we felt was easily assuaged, though there was very little temptation to partake of the turbid water; but our sensations of hunger grew apace, and I saw that while we white people sat there about the fork of the tree, trying to bear our sufferings stoically, both the blacks were in constant movement, and they had always something to say, Hannibal confining his remarks however to his son.

"Look, look!" cried Pomp, excitedly; "dah um fis. No got hookum line, no got net."

He shook his head despondently, evidently quite oblivious of the fact that even with hook and line he had no bait, and that it was impossible to use a net.

Then he was off up the tree, first ascending one great bough and then another, to lean out, staring away between the twigs in search of something, but he always came down again looking quite disconsolate.

"What have you been looking for?" I said on one of these occasions.

"Simmon tree, Mass' George. No see one nowhere 'bout."

"But you couldn't get there if you could see them."

"No get um?" he said with a laugh. "Pomp no get um? Wait a bit."

"Why, how could you manage?"

"No manage 'tall. 'Wim dah, and 'wim back."

Then we scanned the waste of waters in the hope that we might see something, even if it was only some drowned animal, but nothing came in sight till well on in the afternoon, when Hannibal made some remark which sent Pompey into a tremendous state of excitement.

"What is it?" I cried, eagerly rising from where I had been down to examine my notch, to find that the water remained nearly unchanged.

"Pomp and um fader see some fis' good to eat," said the boy. "Come see."

I climbed up to where he was, and he pointed; but for some time I could make out nothing but driftwood, a tree floating roots upward, and some great patches of grass that seemed to have been scooped out of a bank, roots and all.

Mass' George: A Boy's Adventures in the Old Savannah | 145

"I can't see anything," I said at last.

"What, not dah?" cried Pomp.

"No."

"All 'long side dat tree?"

"Oh, yes," I cried; "what is it—a big fish?"

"No; dat nice lil 'gator, sah."

"What? Why, we couldn't eat alligator."

"Oh, yes; eat um, got nuffum else," cried Pomp, to my great disgust.

"But even if you would eat the nasty wretch, you can't catch it."

"No," said Pomp. "Tell um fader can't catch. Pomp wish dat, but lil 'gator, see um come on, cock um tail up and go right to de bottom. Oh, oh, Mass' George, I so dreffle hungry. Feel as if um eatum own fader."

There was something so comic in the poor fellow's trouble that I could not forbear smiling as I went along to where Morgan was seated quietly enough by Sarah, and I felt something like anger and disgust as I saw that the former was eating something.

"Oh, Morgan!" I said, sharply; "if I had had something to eat I would have shared it."

"Isn't much, but you shall have some if you like, sir. Sarah here won't touch it."

He took a flat brass box out of his pocket, opened it, and held it to me.

"Tobacco!" I said, looking with disgust at the black, twisted leaf.

"Yes, sir, 'bacco keeps off the hunger."

"I'd rather have the hunger," I said; and he shut the box with a snap.

Restless as Pomp now, and growing more and more miserable, I climbed to where my father was sitting watching one break among the trees in the direction of the settlement, and he turned to me with a smile.

"Tired and hungry?" he said. "Yes, I know. But patience, my boy, patience. Our lives have been spared, and help may come at any moment."

"But do you think we shall escape?"

"Why not?" he said, calmly. "We were in much greater peril last night."

"Yes, father," I said; "but we weren't half so hungry."

My remark brought the first smile I had seen to his lip for hours.

"Yes, yes; I know," he said; "but patience. I think we shall soon see the water begin to fall, for when I was at the settlement yesterday, the tide was turning and going down about this time. If it does not take with it the inundation, we must divide ourselves into two parties, one to sit and watch while the other sleeps. By to-morrow the flood will either have fallen, or help will have come."

"Sleep, father!" I said, dolefully; "who can sleep at a time like this?"

"All of us, I hope," he said. "We shall easily drop off after our past night's watch."

"But who could go to sleep feeling so hungry as this?" I protested.

"You," he said, smiling; "and recollect the French proverb, *Qui dort dine*. You know what that means."

"No, father," I said, dolefully.

"Shame! You should not forget your French. He who sleeps dines, my boy."

"Perhaps that's so in France, father, but it isn't so here, in the midst of a flood, and I don't think any Frenchman would say so if he were up in this tree like we are now."

I climbed down again to look at the notch I had made, and see if there was any difference, then sent up a shout of delight, for the water had sunk a foot, and was going down so rapidly that I could almost trace its descent.

It was as my father had hoped; the flood was running out with the tide; and as the cause was over we had every prospect of being set at liberty before many hours had passed.

It was the apparent certainty of this hope which enabled us to bear patiently the rest of our imprisonment, and the pangs of hunger. For night came with the water still falling; but the fact was plainly before us—we should have to pass one night in the tree.

I looked forward to the long, dreary hours with horror, but after getting astride of one branch, and putting my arms round another, feeling half ready to groan with misery, the present dropped away all at once, and I was conscious of nothing till the sun was brightly shining again, when I awoke to find that my wrists were tightly bound together on the other side of the great bough I had embraced; and on recovering my senses sufficiently to look down, I saw that the water had not all drained away, there being several feet in the lower part of the clearings, but the house was so nearly standing out clear that there could not have been more than a couple of feet in depth on the floor.

Morgan and Hannibal were already down, wading breast-high towards the house; and as my father set free my hands, we prepared to follow.

It was no easy task, for the branches were far apart, and covered with slimy mud, but we descended cautiously, promising to come back with ropes to lower poor Sarah and Pomp.

The latter looked gloomy and discontented on being told that he was to stay and keep Sarah company; but he proceeded to walk along to her as we lowered ourselves down, and then contrived to be first, for his bare feet slipped on the muddy bough, and he went headlong down splash into five feet of water and mud, to rise again looking the most pitiable object imaginable.

"Pomp come up again?" he asked, dolefully.

"No; go and have a good wash," said my father, and as the boy went off swimming and wading, we two descended into the thin mud and water, and made our way toward the house.

I looked up at my father to see what he would say to the desolation, as I saw the change that had taken place in so short a time, and then, miserably weak and half-hysterical as I was—perhaps that was the cause—I burst into an uncontrollable fit of laughter. For Pomp had come close up behind us, after an expedition to the hut that had been made for his home, and his sharp voice rose suddenly just in the midst of our sad thoughts, with—

"Oh! Here a mess!"

Even my father could not help laughing as he looked at the boy.

But there was nothing humorous in the scene to Pomp, who looked up at my father with his brow knit, and continued—

"Place all gone—wash away, and can't find my tick."

"The hut washed away?" asked my father.

"Iss; all agone."

"Never mind! We must build another. Well, Morgan, can you find anything to eat?"

For Morgan had just waded out of the house again with a basket in his hand, and he hastened to open it and produce a couple of roast fowls and a couple of loaves of bread, the latter all swollen up into a great sop, while the former were covered with a thin coating of mud.

"Quick!" said my father, seizing one of the fowls and cutting it in two; "get a rope from the shed, and the little ladder. Take this to your wife at once. No; stop a minute. Here, you go, George; there is some wine in the cupboard."

I went splashing through the door, and fetched the bottle, for I knew exactly where it stood; and on my return this was given to Morgan, who was sent at once to the tree, while we four stood there in the water eating the remains of the fowls ravenously, both Hannibal and Pomp evidently enjoying the well-soaked bread, which was not bad to one so hungry as I, after I had cut away the muddy outside.

"Yes," said my father, smiling at Pomp, after we had relieved the terrible cravings of hunger from which we had suffered; "it is a mess. But look, George, the water is still sinking fast."

That was plain enough to see now, and as it went lower and lower, the damage done, though of course great, was not what might have been expected. We had been saved from utter destruction by the fact that only a moderate-sized clearing had been made in the virgin forest, whose mighty trunks had formed a natural fence round our house, and checked the rush of the flood, which, instead of reaching us in an overwhelming wave, had been broken up, and its force destroyed before it could reach us.

Even the open fences about the garden had escaped, the water having played freely in and out; and though Hannibal's hut had been lifted up and floated right away, the fence-top was now appearing above the water, and seemed to be quite unharmed.

The water sank so fast now that my father shouted to Morgan to let Sarah stay where she was till there was solid earth for her to descend to, and consequently he came down to see what he could do to help. That amounted to nothing, for until the water had passed away nothing could be done, save splash here and there, looking at the fruit-trees bestrewed with moss and muddy reeds and grass, while Morgan uttered groan after groan, as he at last saw the bushes and the tops of his vegetables appear covered with slime.

"The place is ruined, sir," he groaned. "Whatever is to be done? Go back to the old country?"

"Get to work as soon as the place is dry," replied my father. "A few showers of rain after the sun has dried and cracked the mud will soon wash your garden clean."

Morgan shook his head. "And I don't know what my poor wife will say to her kitchen."

"Ah, now you are touching upon the more serious part, my man," said my father. "Come, Morgan, you and I have got the better of worse troubles than this, so set to work, and by some means contrive to get fires going in each of the rooms."

"With wet wood," said Morgan, grumpily.

"Why, it's only wet outside," I cried. "Here, Pomp, try and find the little chopper. Know where it is?"

"Ise know where chopper, but de hut all gone away."

The wood-shed was standing though, and before very long, with Hannibal's help, a good basketful of dry wood was cut; and after a long struggle and several dryings in the hot sun, the tinder and matches acted, and big fires were blazing in the house, whose floors were now only covered with mud.

Already the thatch and shingle roof had ceased to drip, and was rapidly drying, while by midday Sarah was busy at work with brush and pail cleansing the floors, and keeping the two blacks and myself busy bringing things out to dry, while Morgan was removing mud from the various objects within the house.

The main difficulty we had to encounter was how to find a dry resting-place for the night. Sheets and blankets promised to be quite fit for use by sundown, but the question was where to lay them. Every one naturally objected to the trees, and the ridge of the roof was no more inviting than on the first night. But a little ingenuity soon put all right. Timber was so plentiful with us that poles and planks lay piled up at the back of the house, and after a number of these had been hunted up, from where they had floated among the trees, and laid in the full sunshine, a platform was built up high above the muddy earth, and then another upon which pine boughs were laid, and good, dry resting-places contrived for our weary bones.

Chapter Twenty

It is needless to relate the shifts and plans adopted to restore the place to its former state, but we were favoured by the weather, a long spell of hot sunshine working wonders, and the rapid drying and the work of many hands soon produced a change. In two days we could go about on dry ground. In four, mud was scaling over everything in cakes, and being cracked into dust it regularly powdered off the trees, and a couple of tremendous tropical showers sufficed to clear off the remainder from twig and leaf, so that what with the rapid vegetation, and the clearing effects of rain and dew, a month had hardly passed before the place began to look very much as it did before the misfortune, Morgan informing me smilingly that the soft mud was as good for the garden as a great dressing of manure.

Our furniture in the house was of the simplest, and though Sarah declared that the place would never be the same again, I very soon began to forget all about our trouble, and was only reminded of it by the wisps of dry grass and muddy, woody twigs that clung here and there among some of the trees.

On one occasion I found Pomp busy with a bucket of water and a brush down at the bottom of the garden, where he was scrubbing away at something black.

"Hallo!" I exclaimed. "What's that?"

"'Gator head, Mass' George. Pomp find um 'tuck in dah 'tween um two trees."

He illustrated his meaning by showing me how the head had been washed from its place, and swept between a couple of tree-stumps, where it had remained covered with mud and rubbish, till it had caught his eye, such a trophy being too valuable to lie there in neglect.

I stopped till he had done, and then, all wet and glistening, the great dried head with its gaping jaws was replaced on the spike-nail Morgan had driven in the tree.

"Dah, you 'top till water come and wash um down again, and den Pomp come and wash um up."

These words of the boy set me thinking; and that night I asked my father about the probabilities of another flood.

"It is impossible to say how long it may be before we have another visitation," he replied. "From what I can gather, it seems that they are so rare that a generation may go by without such a flood occurring, and I hardly like to give up so satisfactory a home on the chance of a fresh one coming during our lives."

"Oh no, father, don't give it up," I said. "Everything at the settlement seems to be straight again."

"They suffered more than we did too," he continued.

"But don't you think some one ought to have come in a boat to help us?"

"Yes, if the poor things had thought of it; but I fully believe that in their trouble and excitement, trying to save life as they were, they did not even give a thought to us."

Then the flood was set aside with the troubles from the Indians and the Spaniards, my father saying quietly enough that people who came out to an entirely new country must do so bearing in mind that they have to take the risks with the pleasures. Some of which Sarah heard, for she took up the subject next time I saw her alone, and she shook her head at me as she said—

"Yes, my dear, there's a lot to put up with for those who come to live in new lands, and a couple more of my chickens gone; but I don't know what you and your poor father would have done if me and Morgan had not made up our minds to come too."

I'm afraid I was playing the impostor a little, for I said to her, "We couldn't have got on at all without you, Sarah;" but all the time I was thinking how much more easily we could have managed during the night of peril if we had not had Sarah with us, and how it was in trying to save her that my father nearly lost his life.

But I did not let her see it, and said quietly—

"Lost two more of the chickens?"

"Yes, my dear; and it seems so strange that the birds that could take such care of themselves all through that dreadful flood should be lost now."

"It does seem strange," I said, as my thoughts went back to the flood, and I recalled how the fowls took refuge in the pine-trees, and kept going higher and higher as the water rose, hopping calmly enough from branch to branch, and roosting high up at the top, to stop picking about till the flood was sinking, and then slowly descend with the falling waters, to find quite a feast in the mud.

"You don't think, do you, that those two blacks, Master George—"

"What, like chickens?"

"Yes, my dear."

"The people up at the settlement say they do, and that they can't keep any fowls at all."

"Then that's it," cried Sarah, triumphantly; "and I was right about that smell a few nights ago."

"What smell?"

"Of something roasting in the lean-to shed where those two sleep."

"Nonsense, Sarah! It was squirrel or something of that kind that they had knocked down and cooked."

"No, my dear; it was exactly like roast chicken, and I'm very much afraid—"

"So am I, Sarah, that you are going to make a mistake. I don't believe either of them would steal. Ah! Here comes Pomp all in a hurry about something.—What is it?"

"Hi! Find um, Mass' George," cried the boy, who was in a high state of excitement.

"Find what?" I cried.

"Oh, yes, Pomp find um; come and see."

"Yes, I'll come," I said. "But, I say, Pomp, there are two chickens gone. Do you know anything about them?"

"Yes. Such big bird come and take um, Mass' George. Big bird fly ober de tree, *whish—whoosh*! And 'tick um foot into de chickum."

Sarah shook her head in a peculiar severe way; but I guessed that she had the question of the uniform upon her mind, and she held her tongue, while Pomp dragged me off to see his discovery.

He led me into a part of the forest where I had not been since the flood, and there, sure enough, twenty feet above the ground, and preserving its perpendicular position, was the greater part of the hut, Pomp climbing up to it in triumph, and then on to the top, with the result that his weight was just sufficient to dislodge it, and the whole affair came down with a crash, and with the boy seated in the ruins.

"What do dat for?" he cried in a whimpering tone as he sat rubbing himself.

"Do what?" I cried, laughing.

"Pull um down down an' break up. How we get um back now?"

"I didn't touch it."

"Not touch um! How um tumble down den? Oh my leg—my leg!"

"No, no; you're not hurt much, Pomp. There, get up, we can't get the hut back; and you know father said a new and better one was to be built. We'll set this one up here and make a summer-house of it, to come to when I'm shooting."

"Eh! What a summer-house?"

"That will be."

"No; dat hut; massa say dat hut."

"But we'll make it into a summer-house."

Pomp shook his head and looked puzzled.

"Pomp find de hut, and Massa George say um summer-house. 'Pose um find de boat 'ticking in tree, dat be summer-house too?"

"No, no, you old stupid," I cried. "But, I say, Pomp," I continued, as the thought occurred to me that this might be possible, and that the boat had not gone down the stream to the river, and from thence out to sea.

"What Mass' George say?" cried the boy, for I had stopped to think.

"Wait a minute," I cried. Then, after a few moments' thought—

"Why, yes, it is possible; the flood came from the big river, up ours, and the boat must be somewhere in the forest after all."

Pomp shook his head.

"Done know what um mean," he said.

"I mean that perhaps our boat was washed up somewhere."

"Iss, Pomp wash um up two-tree-day 'fore took away wif de mop."

"I mean the flood carried the boat up into the forest among the trees, like it did the hut."

"Mass' George fink so?"

"Yes."

"Come 'long find um."

Willingly enough I started with the boy, but stopped directly, for I remembered that Hannibal had come running up to announce the loss of the boat, and that he might have some recollection of the direction in which it was carried.

"Let's ask your father," I said; and we went to where he was in the garden.

To my great delight, his description tallied with my idea. The boat had been carried up stream, and full of eagerness we set out, but it was too late to do much that day, and we soon returned, after planning to start at daybreak the next morning, Pomp having undertaken to awaken me, while I arranged with Sarah for a basketful of provisions, so that we might be able to spend a good long day.

In the course of the evening I related the finding of the hut to my father, and my hope that the boat might be discovered too, but he shook his head.

"Extremely doubtful, my boy. But wait a bit and then go and search, though, if you like; and even if you do not find it, you will have a glorious ramble along the river-bank."

"Will you come too, father?" I said.

"I should like to, but I have promised for several days to go over to the settlement to meet the General and Colonel Preston. Take Morgan or Hannibal with you, if you like."

"Oh no, father," I said, "Pomp will be guide enough; I believe he often steals off to go long distances into the forest after woodchucks and squirrels."

"You will take a gun, I suppose. Any game will be welcome."

"Yes, father."

"And take care not to get into danger."

"What danger?"

"Snakes and other reptiles may be in abundance."

"I'll take care."

"And for aught we know Indians may be hunting in the neighbourhood."

"Should not we have heard them or seen them, if they were?" I said, for I did not like the idea of giving up my trip.

"Well, perhaps so," said my father. "There, I will not stop you; I only say again, be careful when you do go."

"Can't I go to-morrow?" I said.

"No, I would rather that you did not go right away while I am from home. Wait a few days, and then have your trip."

I said no more, but of course felt disappointed, and a strange temptation came over me next day, on finding how bright it was, to go and explore a little, the more especially that Pomp came up with his face shining and full of excitement.

"Now," he cried, "go and find summer-house."

"No, no," I said; "the boat."

"Mass' George call him summer-house yesterday."

"We'll go soon," I said, "but not for a few days."

"What Mass' George going do, then?"

"Stop about at home and take care of the house."

"Mass' George tink water come 'gain, wash um away?"

"No, no, I hope not," I said, laughing. "But I'm not going far away."

"Mass' George come fish terrapum?"

"No, Pomp, I'm going to stop about here. Perhaps I shall go and have a bathe at the pool by and by, but I'm not sure."

"Pomp go wif Mass' George have 'wim."

"No, no," I said, pettishly, for I was out of temper, hot and disappointed at not being able to go and hunt for the boat. Then I felt annoyed at having to stop at home when my father had gone to the settlement, and somehow that place had never seemed to attract me so much before.

"Father might have taken me," I said to myself, as I thought of how beautiful the sugar-canes must be now, after the soaking and dressing they had had with the mud. Then, too, the Indian corn must be waving gloriously, and I longed to see slaves at work in the cotton-field.

"Father will be seeing all that," I thought, "and it's all nonsense about stopping and taking care of the place. I couldn't do anything if there was a flood, or if the Indians came. I should have liked to go."

All of which was very absurd and stupid, but I have known other boys think and talk in a similar way.

I went to the fence, and stood leaning over it, feeling more out of humour than ever, and I hit viciously at a fly or two which settled upon me.

Pomp was watching me all the time in a half puzzled way, and at last he broke out with—

"Mass' George."

"Don't bother!"

Pomp drew back, took out the knife I had given him, picked up a piece of wood and began to cut it, while I stood kicking at the fence, and watching Morgan and old Vanity, as I mentally called him, busy at work cutting down the former's deadly enemies, the weeds.

"Say, Mass' George."

"Don't bother, I tell you," I cried viciously; and there was another pause, during which Pomp made a low whistling noise, which was not such a very bad imitation of the bobolink.

But Pomp could not be quiet long, and he broke out again with—

"Mass' George."

I turned fiercely round to see that his black face was full of animation, and eyes and lips bright with mischievous glee, all of which annoyed me the more, for what business had he to be happy when I was so disappointed, out of humour, and miserable?

"Be off! Why don't you go to work, sir?"

"Won't Mass' George come in de wood?"

"No. Be off!"

"Pomp come and have a 'wim 'long o' Mass' George?"

"No, you won't. Be off; I don't want you."

The boy looked at me aghast, and his thick lower lip worked.

"Mass' George get tire poor old Pomp?"

"Yes. Be off!"

"Mass' George send poor old Pomp 'way?"

"Yes. Don't bother. Can't you see I don't want you?"

"Wugh!" Pomp threw himself down on his face, and rested his forehead on his crossed arms.

"Don't do that," I said. "Get up, and be off, or I shall kick you."

The boy sprang up with his eyes flashing, but they were full of tears, and this gave me satisfaction, for I was in that absurd state of mind when one likes to make others feel as uncomfortable as oneself.

"Mass' George want poor ole Pomp to go away?"

"Yes," I cried; "and don't be so idiotic, you miserable little nigger, calling yourself 'poor ole Pomp!'"

"Mass' George break poor ole Pomp heart."

"I'll break poor ole Pomp's head if he bothers me any more," I cried, sulkily, as I once more leaned over the fence and began kicking off some of the dry mud which still adhered, though the leafage above it was clear and green.

I heard Pomp draw in his breath hard, and he gave his bare foot a stamp on the ground.

"You want poor ole Pomp go drown self?"

"Yes," I said, sourly.

"Pomp go jump in de ribber."

"Go on then."

"You nebber see poor ole Pomp, nebber no more."

"Don't want to."

"Oh, Mass' George!—oh, Mass' George!"

These words came so piteously that all my ill-humour gave way to pity for the boy, who was as affectionate as he was passionate by nature; but his next words hardened me, and I stood fast, trying to hide my mirth as he broke out in a lachrymose way, pitying himself.

"Poor lil nigger! Oh dear, dear, poor lil black nigger slave! Nobody care dump poor ole Pomp!"

Then there was a long pause.

"You want Pomp go drown self, Mass' George?"

"Yes," I said. "Mind you don't get wet."

"Eh?"

"I say, go and have a good dry drown."

"How you do dat all?"

"I don't know. Be off."

"Poor ole Pomp! De 'gators eat um all up like lil yam."

"Ha—ha—ha—ha—ha!" I burst out, for I could contain myself no longer. The comparison to the "lil yam" was too much for me, and as I faced round, good-humoured once more, and ready to go and bathe or do anything with the boy who was my only companion, he showed his teeth at me fiercely, made a run, jumped over the fence into the garden, and I saw him dash down the middle path toward the forest as hard as he could go.

I stood looking in the direction he had taken for a minute or two, and felt disposed to go after him; but I had seen him get into a temper before, and get out of it again, and I knew that next time we met all this would have passed away from both of us like a cloud.

"No, I won't go after him," I said to myself; "it will make him vain and conceited, and he's bad enough as it is. Poor ole Pomp! Poor lil nigger! What a rum fellow he can be when he likes!"

This little episode had quite carried off the sour feeling from which I had suffered, and I began to look about me, enjoying the beauty of the morning, forgetting all about Pomp, who had, no doubt, I thought, found out a nice sunny spot and gone off to sleep.

Chapter Twenty One

No one would have thought there had been a flood to have seen the garden and plantation so soon after the waters had gone down; for where the slimy mud had lain in pools, it had cracked all over till it was creased and marked like an alligator's back, through which cracks the tender green growth soon thrust itself, to spring up at a wondrous rate, as if glad to be fertilised by the soft alluvial soil.

Wherever the mud had lain thick on broad leaf or grass, it had, as I have said, cracked and fallen off, or been washed away by the heavy rains and dews, and our grounds and the country round were as beautiful as ever— more beautiful, I ought to say, for everything was fresher and greener, and where the swamps had been muddy and parched, and overhung with dry growth, all was bright and glorious, with the pools full up, and the water-ways overhung with mossy drapery, glittering and flashing back the sun's rays wherever the sun pierced the trees.

"Going for a walk, Master George?" said Morgan that morning, as I sauntered down the garden in the hot sunshine, wondering what I should do with myself.

"Yes," I said, eagerly, for the question had given me the idea I wanted. Yes, I would go for a walk.

"Better be careful, my lad. I would not overheat myself. After all this flooding there may be fever in the air. But there, you will take care of yourself."

"Yes, Morgan," I said, "I'll try. Seen Pomp anywhere?"

"No; not since breakfast. A lazy young dog. Make his father do all the work. What's that, sir?"

We both looked sharply round toward the forest, for there was the faint rustle of something moving, but the sound ceased as he spoke.

"Only a squirrel," I said, at a guess. "I think I shall go and have a bathe."

"Where?" said Morgan; "not in the river; the stream is too swift, sir, yet."

"No; in our big pool."

"Better take a pole and prod about well first. After all this water there may be a young alligator or two crept in."

"Oh, I'm not afraid of them," I said, laughing; and I listened again, for there was another faint rustle among the leaves, but it ceased, and I stood watching as Morgan tied up two or three of the great succulent vine-shoots which were trailing over one of the trees, luxuriating in the glowing sunshine, and showing goodly-sized bunches of grapes, such as would in another two months be so many little amber bags of luscious sweetness.

"Yes, I haven't had a swim since the flood," I thought to myself, as I went on, leaped over the rough, moss-grown fence, and was soon after making my way along past the edge of the sugar-cane plantation, where the weeds were growing like mad, and then through the great, tall-leaved rows of tobacco in the new clearing, where the stumps of the trees so laboriously cut down still stood.

In another ten minutes I was out of the glowing sunshine beneath the oaks with their flowing drapery of moss, now peering up to see if anything alive was moving among the branches, now noticing how far up the flood had risen, as shown by the mark of dried mud and the patches of withered reed, which still clung here and there.

But there was no sign of living thing, and I walked on for a time in and out among the great trunks in the deep shade towards where there was a broad patch of sunshine, and all therein looked to be of green and gold. It was the clearing where the trees had been cut down for building and fencing when we first came.

I was not long in placing myself upon a stump out here in the broad sunshine, to watch what was going on, for this was a favourite old place of mine, where I generally found something to interest me.

So it was on this day, for a great crane flew up and went off with a great deal of wing-flapping before it was clear of the trees; and as I was eagerly watching the spot where it had disappeared, there was one bright flash, and one only, as a humming-bird darted across the sunny clearing, to poise itself first here and then there, before the open flowers of the great creepers, its wings vibrating so rapidly that they were invisible, and the lovely little creature looked more like some great moth than a bird.

I knew him and his kind well enough, and that if I had had it in my hand, I should have seen his head and crest all of a bright ruby tint, and the scale-like feathers of its throat glowing almost like fire; but as it flew rapidly here and there, it seemed all of a dull, warm brown, surrounded by a transparency formed by its rapidly-beating wings.

I sat watching the humming-bird till another and another came to disturb the first, and begin chasing it, darting here and there like dragon-flies, now up, and now down; round and round, and sometimes coming so close that I could have beaten one to the ground with a bough. Then, all at once, they soared up and up, passed over the trees, and were gone, leaving me swinging my legs and whistling softly, as my eyes now wandered about in search of something else.

Oaks draped with moss, a great cypress at the edge of the clearing, which had grown up and up till it was higher than some of the trees, and spread its boughs over them like an umbrella to keep off the rain, and keeping off the sunshine as well, so that they had grown up so many tall, thin trunks, with tops quite hidden by the dark green cypress, and looking like upright props to keep its great top spread.

I knew that in all probability there was more than one 'possum in the great trees surrounding the opening, but Pomp was not there to find them, and I had no dog. I felt, too, that in all probability more than one bright pair of eyes were watching me from some bough, and their owners' bushy tails twitching and whisking about; but I could see nothing, and after a time, as a sudden thought struck me, I got down softly, and looked round for a stick. This was soon found, for whenever I cut one I generally left it thrust in somewhere among the dense growth.

Thus armed, I went cautiously across the clearing toward the farther side, where the gravelly bank was crowned by a tuft of pines, beneath which, in the full sunshine, the ground was almost bare, and dotted with stones, ashy, and dark, and dull, and grey.

I had committed more than one murder there, but they were murders in which I exulted, for they meant death to the horrible rattlesnake or deadly moccasin, as they lay sunning their cold blood in the hot rays, ready to deal death to the passer-by, whose inadvertent foot should disturb their sleep.

I went very cautiously, with my eyes scanning the spot eagerly, for at very little distance the reptiles would be invisible from the way in which their scales assimilated with the earth. But, though I used every caution, I saw no wavy or coiled up serpent asleep, nor caught sight of a tail rapidly following its owner in amongst the stunted herbage and stones.

"Getting scarcer," I said to myself, as I turned off again, and made for a faint track between the trees—a seldom-used path, leading on to the edge of the swamp that bordered the little river running down to the great tidal stream, which came from far away to the north-west among the mountains.

For a time, as I went on peering here and there, I forgot all about my first intention, but it came back strongly as I reached a natural opening, and once more passed out of the shade, which seemed streaked with threads of silver where the sun-rays darted through, and stood looking down at the broad, glistening, shallow pool, where we boys had often bathed.

The place looked beautiful as ever; the water wonderfully clear. Small fish darted away at my approach, and took refuge in the reeds and grass at the side, or in the broad patch of water-growth in one corner some twenty yards across.

There was the dead tree on my side of the pool, which was about sixty yards in length, and looked as tempting a spot for a bath as can be imagined.

The heat was growing oppressive, but the air was beautifully pure and clear; and the insects which darted about flashed in the sunshine, and kept up a continuous hum that was soothing and pleasant, as I began to take off my clothes, enjoying the sensation of the hot sun pouring its heat down upon my skin.

"I wish Pomp was here," I said to myself; and as I said those words, I burst out into a hearty fit of laughter, as in imagination I saw his black face shining in the water, and the great drops standing like pearls in his woolly head.

My thoughts did not promise him much enjoyment in his bath, for divers ideas connected with ducking, splashing, and the like occurred to me, the more forcibly from the fact, that though Pomp swam admirably, it was after the fashion of a duck, and not of a fish, for he never, if he could possibly help it, put his head under water.

I was half undressed, when I caught a glimpse of a good-sized pike, slowly rising to the surface to bask, and stooping down, and picking up the stick I had brought with me—a good stout piece of hickory nearly six feet long—I drew back a little, stole gently along the edge of the pool till I deemed myself about opposite, and then raising the stick with both hands, stole forward, to deal a heavy blow at the fish, trusting that if I missed it the stroke on the water might paralyse it, until I had had time to hook it ashore.

"Don't see why a crack with a stick should not do as well as an alligator's tail," I said to myself.

That blow was not delivered, for before I could gather myself up and bring my muscles to bear, the water flashed as a little wave rose, and the fish was far out of reach.

"Better luck next time," I said, as I went back to the tree, finished undressing, stood for a moment or two on the edge of the pool, and then dived in, sending the water flying up sparkling in the light.

It was deliciously invigorating, though the water was too much warmed by the sun to give me a swift electric shock; and as I rose to the surface, shook the drops from my eyes, and began to swim slowly along, I felt as if I had never enjoyed a bath so well before. For the water felt soft, and yielding, and elastic, and as if no effort was required to keep myself afloat.

"Pity old Pomp isn't here," I said, as I lazily swam to one end, where there were tufts of water weeds, and a kind of natural ditch took off the surplus water into a pool of similar size, a hundred yards away among the trees—a black-looking, overhung place, suggestive of reptiles, and depth, and dead tree-trunks with snaggy boughs ready to remove a swimmer's skin, though possibly if the trees had all been cleared away, and the bright sunshine had flooded it with light, it might have looked attractive enough.

As it was, I should have thought it madness to venture into such a spot, not knowing what danger might lurk therein, and I turned and swam back toward the other end, but stopped in the middle opposite my clothes lying on the fallen tree, and turned over to float and gaze up at the blue sky and the glorious hues of green upon the trees which surrounded the pool.

"I wonder where Pomp is," I said to myself, and then, satisfied that if he saw Morgan he would learn where I had gone, and follow, I turned over on my breast and began to swim lazily toward the end where the reeds grew.

"I dare say all the fish have taken refuge in there," I said to myself. "If one had a net to spread round, and then send Pomp in there with a pole to beat and thrash about, one might get, a good haul."

I swam on, driven by I don't know what attraction toward the great patch of reeds standing up out of the clear water, when all at once Morgan's words concerning alligators came to my mind, and for a moment I hesitated and ceased swimming, gazing straight before me at the large patch of aquatic growth, and then at another, a dozen yards away to my right.

"They'd only he little ones and scuttle off as hard as they could," I thought directly, and continued swimming toward the great patch before me, when, just as I was about a dozen feet from the thickest part, I felt a chill of horror run through me, paralysing every nerve, and my lips parted to utter a cry, for the reeds were suddenly agitated as by the passage of something forcing its way out, and to my horror the hideous open-mouthed snout of a great alligator was thrust forth, and from its wide jaws there came a horrible bellowing roar which sounded to me at the moment as if the monster had uttered the word *Houk*!

I could not for the moment stir nor utter a cry for help. Then as the reeds were more roughly agitated, and I saw that the brute was struggling out from the tangle of matted roots below the surface, I threw myself back, and splashing and beating the water with all my might to scare the reptile, I made for the shore.

The distance was only short, but to me then it seemed interminable.

I had only glanced over my shoulder once, to see that the alligator was in full pursuit, with its open jaws well above the surface, and evidently gaining upon me fast, as I tore through the water, sending all I could back over the monster's muzzle; but in those agonised moments all seemed in vain, as in imagination I felt myself seized, dragged under, and drowned.

The thought was far too horrible to bear; and, in spite of myself, I felt that I must turn round and face the brute, to make one brave struggle for life, and not let it seize me by the leg and drag me down, when just as I was about to yield to this feeling, and in the act of turning, my horror culminated, for there was a rush, and a great wave of water rose from the open patch of reeds on my left, and I knew that a second enemy had rushed out from its lair and was making for me.

I uttered a hoarse gasp, and began swimming again toward the shore, when once more a strange sensation ran through me, mingled of horror, despair, and wonder, as I heard in a hoarse, hollow voice I well knew, though it sounded strange—

"Oh, oh, Mass' George! Help! Great 'gator, Mass' George—help!"

The cry did not come from the bank, nor from among the trees, but from close behind me where the first alligator was in full pursuit, and as I once more ceased swimming, paralysed by wonder, I saw my first pursuer rise up in a peculiar way in the water, raise its two black paws to its head, take it off, and dash it at the second alligator, which seized it on the instant, a second head appearing just above the surface, closing upon the first with a snap, and then there was a tremendous swirl in the water, a tail appeared above the surface as the brute dived down, and as I swam on panting, the surface of the water behind grew calm.

But I was not swimming alone. Pomp's black head was close by me, and his voice rose in a sobbing howl as, shivering with horror, he kept on—

"Oh, swim fass, Mass' George; swim fass, Mass' George, 'fore de 'gator catch us. Oh, swim fass, Mass' George; swim fass, Mass' George! 'Fore de 'gator catch us," till we reached the shore and scrambled out, white and black, in the blazing sun, the water streaming down us, and both panting hard and trembling in every limb.

Chapter Twenty Two

"Oh—ho—ho—ho—ho! What a lubbly bit fun!" cried Pomp, as soon as the danger had passed away.

"Why, Pomp!" I cried at last, fiercely, for I was too much astonished to speak at first.

But he was off along the bank, to stop opposite the smaller batch of reeds, where he stood with both his fists doubled, stamping his bare feet, and shouting a perfect torrent of abuse at the invisible enemy.

I caught a word here and there, words full of threats of what he would do to the "ugly 'gator, nex' time." But I was too much upset to shout till I had scrambled into my clothes, when I went sharply along the edge of the pool to where the boy was still shaking his fists, and abusing the reptile which had nearly scared him to death.

But there was another scare ready for Pomp. Indignation was hot within me, and I made my presence known by a smart kick with my bare foot which nearly sent him into the pool again, and a cuff on the side of the head which knocked him back.

"Oh—oh—oh! Don't, Mass' George," he bellowed, as he dropped on his knees and held up his hands; "don't flog um, Mass' George. I nebber, nebber do so no more."

"You rascal!" I cried, catching him by the ear. "How came you to play me that trick?"

"On'y for bit ob fun, Mass' George; on'y for bit ob fun."

"You dog!" I cried, shaking him.

"On'y lil bit o' fun, Mass' George; got de 'gator's head on to frighten um. Nebber tink no 'gator dah, or not nebber done it."

"No, I suppose not," I cried. "How dare you try to frighten me like that!"

"Say, Mass' George, you pull dat ear right off."

"Serve you right too, sir. You insolent rascal. But I'll tell my father, and you shall be flogged."

"Oh no, don't do dat ah, Mass' George. Kick um again and pull um oder ear. Pomp won't holler much. Don't tell de massa."

"A blackguardly, cowardly trick with that nasty old alligator's head."

"But, Mass' George," cried Pomp, suddenly jumping up, "you no business beat kick a boy."

"What, sir!"

"Why, if I no do dat, an de ole 'gator get hold ob de head, he get hold ob you, an where you be now?"

My hand dropped to my side, and I stared in a puzzled way at Pomp, who began to show his white teeth, as it seemed to me that what he said was true, and that if the reptile had not dashed at the boy, and seized the old head thrown at him, he might have seized me and dragged me down.

"Tink I sabe you, Mass' George, and you hab berry narrow scrape; and den you say you tell de massa, and hab me flog."

"Yes," I said, half aloud, "he might have seized me."

"Oh, he hab you, sure 'nuff, Mass' George, and um be pickin' you bone now down in de mud—iyah—iyah—iyah!" he roared, in a great burst of laughter as he turned round to the water, rested his hands on his knees, and shouted—

"How you like big 'gator head, eh? You find um berry hard? Hope you like um, sah."

He faced round to me again, showing his teeth, and with his eyes twinkling with merriment.

"Don't tell a massa," he said, pleadingly.

I was conquered, for it was clear enough to me now that the boy's prank had in all probability saved my life. But I still hesitated as I seized him by both ears now, and gently swayed his head to and fro.

"Dat's right, Mass' George, pull um hard. I no mine a bit."

"You rascal!" I cried; "will you promise never to do it again?"

"Can't do it again, Mass' George; ugly great 'gator got de head."

"But will you play me such a trick again?"

"Dunno, Mass' George. You pull hard bofe ears togedder, and kick um."

"Where are your clothes?" I said, quite disarmed now.

"In de tree, Mass' George. Hab noder pull."

"No," I said. "Put on your clothes."

Pomp threw himself on the ground and began to howl.

"What's that for, sir?"

"You go tell de capen, and hab poor nigger flog. Ah, Mass' George, you bery cruel young massa."

"Get up, Pomp. I'm not going to tell father, but you shouldn't have played me such a trick."

The boy seemed as if made of india-rubber, for he sprang up, ducked down, stood on his head, and then went over and over head over heels three or four times before leaping up with a loud shout.

"Oh, Mass' George, pull um out; got big forn in um back."

It was quite true, and after I had relieved him of the spine, he ran to the biggest tree near, climbed up into the fork, and descended directly with his clothes, into which he slipped—not a long job, for he was by this time dry, and his garments consisted only of a short-sleeved shirt and a pair of cotton drawers, which came down to mid thigh.

"Now, look here, Mass' George," he cried, excitedly; "you'n me got to kill dat 'gator."

"Yes," I said, "I must lie in wait and shoot him."

"I tink so. What did he come in young mass' bath for? I go fetch um gun now."

"No, no," I said. "It would be no use."

"No," said Pomp, thoughtfully, and then showing his teeth; "too busy fryin' um dinner. Oh, Mass' George, what a bit ob fun!"

Pompey threw himself down, and laughed till the tears rolled down his cheeks.

"I ten times—hund times more frightum than you, Mass' George. I tought um catch dis nigger for sartum, an' I felt so sorry for you, Mass' George, dat I holler out loud."

"Sorry for me?"

"Yes, sah. What you do widout Pomp?"

"Come along," I said, half surlily, half amused at the easy-going, light-hearted way in which the boy could forget the horrible peril in which he had placed himself.

"You berry sorry too, Mass' George.—I know."

"Know what?"

"How catch um 'gator?"

"How?"

"Pompey know. Show um a morrow. Good-bye, sah. Bring you 'noder dinner morrow morning."

He made a mock salutation in the direction he believed the reptile to have taken, and then together we began to thread our way through the trees, back toward the clearing, and then after another cautious look round for snakes made for the garden. But before we were within a hundred yards, Pomp stopped.

"Ole massa in big garden, Mass' George?"

"I don't know," I said. "He was going to be back to dinner."

"I go round de oder way. Mass' say I chop wood, and I was going to chop wood till I hear you say Morgan you go for walk, and I know you go for 'wim."

"Well?"

"Pomp very hurt upon Mass' George."

"Oh, were you?" I said.

"Mass' George say cruel fing to Pomp, so um go an' fess de ole 'gator head, and undress umself, an' get in de water firs, an' fright um."

"Ah, well, you'll be flogged one of these days, Master Pomp, without my telling tales of you."

"I 'pose I will," he said, thoughtfully. "No like for Mass' George tell, dough."

"Why not?"

"Cos dat hurt Pomp more dan de floggum."

"Nonsense!"

"Eh? Dat nonsense, Mass' George? I don't know. If Mass' Morgan tell and get Pomp flog, Pomp holler, 'Oh don't, oh don't!' an' fro himself on de ground, an' squiggle an' kick. But soon as done flog um, Pomp rub um back up gen tree, an' nebber mine a bit."

"I suppose so," I said.

"But if Mass' George tell an' get Pomp flog, dunno why, but no use rub back gen de tree. Hurt Pomp all de same."

So Pomp ran off to get round to the wood-shed, where I heard him as I reached the house chopping away as hard as he could, and making the wood fly; and I need hardly say I did not tell any tales about the boy's trick, though I thought about it a great deal.

My ideas of punishment were not of the flogging kind, but connected with some way of giving Master Pomp tit for tat by means of a scare; but my invention was rather at fault, and idea after idea was dismissed as soon as formed. They were not pleasant ideas, some of them, and they were all wanting in the element I wished to impart.

One of Sarah's wild-plum jam puffs, with a dose of medicine concealed therein, was dismissed at once. So was a snake in his bed, because there were objections to the trick. In all probability the snake would not stop there; and if it did, as it must necessarily be a harmless one, it would not frighten Pomp a bit, and might suggest the idea of playing a similar trick on me.

I could push him into the water first time we were on the river-bank, but he would only laugh and swim out.

I might lasso him suddenly some day, and tie him up to a tree, and leave him in the forest without anything to eat for a few hours; but I knew that I couldn't find the heart to torture the poor fellow like that; and if I could, no knots that I contrived would ever hold him very long.

"Bah! It's waste of time!" I said; and I gave it up, not knowing that I should soon have something far more serious to think about. For just as I was deep in my cogitations I heard a step, and my father came into sight, looking very hot and tired.

That evening, as we sat together by the light of a candle, with the forest insects humming round, he said suddenly—

"I'm afraid our troubles with the Spaniards are not over, George. These people are threatening again."

"But that does not matter, does it, father?"

"I don't know yet, my boy. There is a great deal of braggadocio and pride in your Spanish don, and they have plenty of enterprise and fight in them sometimes, as we know by what they have done."

"But will they come and fight against us, father?" I said, eagerly.

"I don't know that they will come and fight against *us*," he replied, dryly.

I felt the blood come up into my temples, and I spoke quickly—

"I know I'm only a boy, father, and not big enough to fight for you, or by your side like a soldier, but I could load."

He smiled and leaned toward me, and patted my shoulder.

"I beg your pardon, George," he said, kindly. "I ought not to have spoken as I did. You are only a boy, and while you are a boy I pray heaven that you may enjoy a boy's happy life, and that we may be free from all the troubles that are threatening. I am a soldier, and I have fought in the service of my country."

"Yes," I said, proudly, "I know. Morgan has often told me."

"Morgan ought to hold his tongue, and not put vain notions into your head."

"But he said it was glorious, father."

He looked at me sadly, and sighed.

"I am a soldier, George," he said; "but I am afraid that I have very little belief in what people call glory. In too many cases the brilliancy of the glory is dulled with blood and horror too terrible to be spoken of without a shudder. It is glorious to fight in defence of your country, its women and children, or to fight here for our homes; and while I have strength to lift a sword, or voice and knowledge to lead and direct others in such a cause, I will, if it is necessary, fight again. But after what I have been through and seen, I am ready to go down on my knees and pray the God of love and peace and mercy that neither I nor you may ever see sword flashed or shot fired in anger while we live."

He was silent for a few moments, and then he said, cheerfully—

"Come, what did the Latin writer say about a man defending his own country?"

"'*Dulce et decorum est*—'" I said, promptly, and then stopped short. "I forget the rest, father."

He laughed.

"Our life out here, as the pioneers of a new civilisation, is not conducive to the study of the classics, my boy. It's a rough school, where we have to take care to avoid fevers, and meet Indians, and are threatened with Spanish aggression, and have to fight for our lives against a flood. But there, we have drifted into a very serious talk."

"But I like it, father," I said eagerly, "though I am ashamed to have forgotten my Latin."

"Ah, well, you will look that passage up in your Horace, and I venture to say that it will be so impressed now upon your memory that it will never slip away. There, I mentioned the flood. Flood suggests boat. You said you thought the boat might have been carried up the stream into the woods somewhere."

"Yes," I said; "the water did come out of the big river and rush up ours."

"It is quite probable. You may find it as you say you did the hut. When are you going to search for it?"

"When you give me leave."

"Go when you like. I did think I should have to go again to-morrow to the settlement to confer with the General and the others, but messages have again been sent back to the Spanish Governor of Florida, and it must be many days, perhaps weeks, before we hear again, so you can go to-morrow if you will."

I leaped up from my seat excitedly.

"Where are you going now?"

"To tell Pomp to call me, and ask Sarah to prepare a basket of something to eat."

He nodded and took up a book, while after telling our housekeeper of my wants, I ran across the clearing to the edge of the forest to call the boy to get ready.

As I drew near I found Hannibal seated on a stump left by the cutting down of one of the trees to make room for the new hut, with his chin resting in his hands.

"Hallo, Han," I said; "anything the matter?"

"No, Mass' George," he said. "I only look up at de 'tars and tink."

"What about?"

"I wonder wedder dey de 'tars I see in my own country."

"Yes," I said; "I do know that. Do you ever want to go back again?"

"Back again, sah?"

"Yes—to your own country."

He shook his head. "No, Mass' George. Too much fight—too much kill—too much sell for slave; nebber go back again."

"Then you are happy here?"

"Yes, sah. Happy here wif Mass' George and de capen. Can't talk. Understand?"

"Oh, yes," I said; "I understand. Where's Pomp?"

"Sleep. Dah! I call um."

"No, no; let me," I said, laughing.

I went into the hut, and there on the blanket in a corner, with his mouth wide open, lay the boy fast asleep.

It was so dark inside that I should not have been able to make him out but for the gleam of light from the window, which made his teeth just visible.

I stood looking down at him and listening to his breathing for a few moments, before slipping out of the hut, taking my knife from my pocket, and cutting a long twig which I stripped, all but a few leaves at the end. As I came back, Hannibal rose.

"Don't whip, Mass' George," he said in a pleading whisper, as he laid his hand upon my arm.

"I was not going to," I said, laughing, "only to tickle him."

I saw the big African's teeth gleam, and I stole back into the hut on tip-toe, thinking the while how marvellous it was that a great fellow like the black, who could have almost crushed me with one hand, should be so patiently submissive, and give up to me as he did.

But that thought passed away as I stood over Pomp and gently tickled him on one cheek. He moved restlessly, and I tickled the other with the leaves. He turned back again, and the end of the twig began to play about his neck. There was a quick rustle, one hand struck at the twig and Pomp rolled over upon his face. This gave me a good opportunity to titillate both sides of his neck, and he sprang round again.

"Bodder!" I heard him mutter; but I persevered, making the twig play well about him.

"Bodder de fly!" he cried, viciously; but the twig tickled away, and Pomp's eyes were so tightly closed that he contented himself with twisting and rubbing himself.

"Wait I get up, I mash all de ole fly eberywhere," he muttered.

Tickle—tickle—tickle.

Slip slap. Pomp's hands delivered a couple of blows on his bare skin.

Tickle—tickle—tickle.

"You no like me come mash you, eh?"

Tickle—tickle—tickle.

"Yah! You great ugly skeeter, you leave lil nigger go sleep."

"*Buzz—buzz—hum.*" Tickle—tickle—tickle. I made as good an imitation as I could of a gnat's hum, and kept up the tickling till he made two or three vicious lounges out at where I stood in the darkness, and this time he got hold of the twig.

"Eh?" he exclaimed. "Dat not skeeter fly. Dat you, fader? You let lil nigger go sleep. Keep a 'tick 'till."

"Eh? Who dat? Ah, yah! It you, Mass' George. I know all de time."

"No, you didn't, old sleepy head."

"Eh? Well, what head for at night but sleep um? You want Pomp go after 'coon?"

"No; look here, Pomp; we're to go and try to find the boat in the morning. Come and call me as soon as it's day."

"Eh? Why not go now, Mass' George?"

"No, no; I want to go and have a good sleep first. Mind, as soon as it's light; I'll take the gun."

"I call you, Mass' George, widout come an' ticklum wif lil 'tick, ha—ha—ha! I know."

"Good-night."

"Good-night, Mass' George; I come and climb up your window; and you look out."

"I will," I said to myself as I went away, said good-night to Hannibal, and hurried back to bed, but not till I had carefully fastened my window ajar, so that Pomp could not get it open in the morning. And there I was, too much excited by the ideas of the trip to get to sleep. For as I lay there I could picture the little river winding in and out among the great trees of the primeval forest, and see it here black as night flowing sluggishly beneath the drooping moss-hung trees, there dancing in the sunshine that rained down from above, and then on and on in amongst the mysterious shades where in all probability the foot of man had never trod.

"Oh," I said to myself at last, as I lay listening to the monotonous piping insect hum, and the bellowings and croakings from the wood, "how hot it is! I do wish it was day."

But it seemed that many hours must elapse before day could come, and in a curious dreamy way I was wandering on and on through the tangled wood close to the river-bank, when Pomp said in a whisper—

"Hi! Mass' George, you go 'top seep all day?"

I started up to find that I had slept for hours, and light in the shape of the morning was at the window, in company with darkness in the form of Pomp's black face.

Chapter Twenty Three

I lost no time in dressing after opening my window wide, there being no fear now of Pomp getting at me to have his revenge while I was asleep for the tricks I had played upon him.

The boy thrust in his legs with an easy motion, as soon as the window was thrown open, raising himself and dropping gently into a sitting position to watch me wash and dress.

"Well, why are you looking on in that contemptuous way?" I said at last, as I noted the play of his face.

"Dat not temshus, Mass' George," he said. "I only sit and fink what long time you are wash and dress."

"That's not long," I said; "why, how long are you?"

"No time, Mass' George. I go bed like am now, and get up like am now, and come on."

"But do you mean to say you haven't washed this morning?"

"How I 'top go to ribber an' wash, when Mass' George wait to be called? Hab good 'wim when we get to ribber."

I finished dressing, and took Pomp into Sarah's kitchen, where we both made a hearty meal, which was interrupted by Pomp insisting upon having the shot and powder pouches buckled on him at once, so that he might make sure of them, and not be defrauded of the honour of carrying them by any tricks on my part.

He did not look so pleased at having to carry the wallet which had been well stored ready for our use, but he submitted to have the strap thrown over his head, and passed one arm through. Then full of eagerness I shouldered the gun, and we started off into the forest, passing the clearing where the rattlesnake had been killed, and next passing on to the little river, up whose course we were to make our way, keeping a good look-out for the boat the while.

The morning was glorious, the sun piercing the low-lying mist, which rapidly grew more transparent, broke up, and seemed to dissolve away. The birds were piping and screaming in the trees, and as we reached the river, where all was light and sunshine, we started first a great white crane, which rose from the shallows and flew off, then a kingfisher with dazzling coat, and soon after came in sight of a little flock of rosy-winged flamingoes, with their curious, long, snaky, writhing necks, and quaintly-shaped bills, which always looked to me as if they were made to use upside down.

"Well, I nebber see!" cried Pomp at last, after stepping back, and preserving the most profound silence time after time.

"What's the matter?"

"Why Mass' George no shoot?"

"Because we don't want the birds. You don't care to have to carry them, do you?"

"No; dis wallet um so dreffle heabby."

We tramped on a little farther, now in the deep shade, now in the golden sunshine when we could get close to the stream, and then Pomp sighed.

"Mass' George like to carry de walletum now?"

"No; I'm carrying the gun."

"Pomp carry de gun."

"Oh, no," I said, "I'll manage that;" and we went slowly on again. There was no track, and near the river where the light and sunshine played there was plenty of thick undergrowth, while a short distance back in the forest the walking was easy among the trees, where scarcely anything clothed the ground in the deep shadow.

Pomp kept trudging away toward the dark, shadowy forest, and I had to stop him again and again, for the boat was not likely to be in there. On the last occasion he said—

"Walletum dreffle heabby, Mass' George. Don't think better carry um inside?"

"What do you mean?"

"Mass' George eat half, and Pomp eat half. Den we hab nuffum to carry."

I naturally enough burst out laughing.

"Why, we've only just had a good breakfast, and couldn't eat any more."

"Oh yes, Pomp could, big lots."

"And what are we to have to eat by and by, when we get hungry?"

"Mass' George shoot ducks; Pomp make fire an' roace um."

"No, no, no," I cried. "Here, pass me the wallet, and I'll give you a rest."

"And Pomp carry de gun," he cried, eagerly.

"No, sir. If you can carry the gun, you can carry the wallet. Here, give me hold."

Pomp looked disappointed as he handed over the wallet very slowly, and after slinging it on we once more progressed, looking carefully in all directions in search of the lost boat, but seeing nothing; and I soon had to come to the conclusion that the chances were very greatly against our finding the object of our search.

It was slow work, but for some miles the place was familiar, my father having brought me as far exploring, and Pomp and I having several times over boated through the dark forest along that bright, winding highway— the river; generally with some difficulty, on account of the fallen trees, and snags, and dense overgrowth, beneath which we often had to force our way, while at other times we had almost to cut a channel through the lilies and other water plants which choked the stream.

It was plain enough to see though, now, how comparatively easy a journey would have been in a boat, for the large flood-waves which had swept up the river had scoured out its bed, throwing vast rotting heaps of the succulent water-growths ashore to rot, fester, and dry in the hot sun.

High up too I could see the traces where the flood had reached, well marked by the dry grass hanging among the boughs.

But we kept on forcing our way slowly, soon getting into a part of the river that was entirely new, and growing more and more fascinating to me at every step.

For there was, in addition to the glorious beauty of the bright, sunny river, with its banks where in places the trees drooped down and dipped their boughs in the smooth water, and the various growths were of the most dazzling green, always something new—bird, quadruped, insect, or fish taking my attention to such a degree that I often forgot the boat and the object of our journey.

Pomp was just as excited as I, touching my arm every now and then to point with a black finger at some grey heron standing thigh-deep, watching for the fish that nearly made the waters alive; and perhaps just as we were waiting to see him make the next dart with his beak at some shoal of unfortunate fry, there would be what seemed to be a great curved bar of silver flash out of the water, to plunge in again, giving us just a glimpse of the fierce fish's glittering scales. Every now and then some big fellow would leap right out, to come down again with a heavy splash, and send a whole shoal of tiny fish, invisible to us before, flying out of the water to avoid their enemy, the river shark.

A little farther, and Pomp's lips would be close to my ear imploring me to shoot as he indicated a bit of sandy or muddy shore where, just clear of the water and looking like a piece of tree-stump, a great alligator would lie basking in the hot sunshine.

But I invariably resisted his prayers, and as we went on, the reptile would suddenly hear our coming and scuffle rapidly out of sight, making a great swirl in the water as he disappeared.

"No, Pomp," I would say, "the first 'gator I shoot must be that one in the bathing-pool. Come along."

On we went, with the river winding in and out through the forest, and there was always something fresh to see: humming-birds that were not so big as some of the butterflies and beetles that swarmed in the sunshiny parts; great lagoon-like pools where the running of the stream became invisible, and we could see far down in the deep water where fish were slowly gliding in and out among the roots of the trees, which in many places clothed the bottom with masses of fibre. Now Pomp's eyes would be ready to start out of his head as we neared a corner, or starting off into the forest to avoid some wild or swampy patch, we crept out to the river's bank again, to startle a little flock of ducks which had been preening themselves, and sent feathers like tiny boats floating down the stream.

"Plenty of time," I would keep saying. "We don't want them yet, and I'll shoot them when we do."

"But 'pose dey not dah to shoot when you want um, Mass' George. I dreffle hungry now."

"Ah," I said at last, "our wallet is getting heavy. Let's pick out a place, and have some lunch."

Pomp pricked up his ears, as he generally did when he heard a new word, and this was one ready for him to adopt.

"Iss," he said, eagerly, "I berry fond o' lunch. I fought smell um yesday when missie cook um."

"Cook what?" I said.

"Dat lunch, Mass' George."

I laughed, and pressed on to look for a good spot, and soon found one where a great tree, whose roots had been undermined by the river, had fallen diagonally with its branches half in the water, and offering us a good seat just nicely shaded from the burning sun, while we had only to lie out on its great trunk and reach down to be able to fill the tin can I had with the clear water.

The gun was leaned up against the tree-roots; we each sat astride facing each other, the bigness of the tree making it rather an uneasy seat; I slung the wallet round and placed it between us, and had just thrust in my hand, while Pomp wrenched himself round to hang the ammunition pouches close to the gun on a ragged root behind him, when, all at once, the boy's left leg flew over and kicked the wallet out of my hands, and he bounded a couple of yards away to stand grinning angrily and rubbing himself.

"Too bad, Mass' George. What do dat for?"

"Do what?" I cried, roaring with laughter, as I stooped down and picked up the wallet, out of which fortunately nothing had fallen.

"'Tick um pin in poor lil nigger."

"I didn't," I said; "and see what you've done."

"Yes, Mass' George did. Pomp felt um. You wait bit, I serb you out."

"But I tell you I did not, Pomp," I cried, as I wiped my eyes. "Oh, you ridiculous-looking little chap! Come and sit down."

"No, won't. You 'tick um pin in poor lil nigger behind leg 'gain."

"I will not, 'pon my honour," I cried. "Oh, you did look comic."

"Made um feel comic dicklus," cried Pomp, catching up the two words I had used. "Did hurt."

"Come and sit down."

"You no 'tick um pin in 'gain?"

"I haven't got a pin," I said.

"Den I know; it was um big forn."

"It wasn't, Pomp. Come and sit down and have some lunch."

"No. Won't come. Don't want no lunchum. Hurt poor Pomp dreffle. You alway play um trick."

"I tell you I didn't do anything, Pomp. There, come along."

He caught sight of the food I brought now from the wallet, and it was irresistible.

"You no 'tick pin in nigger 'gain?"

"No."

"Nor yet um forn?"

"No. Come along, you little unbeliever. Come along."

"I serb you out fo dat, Mass' George, you see," he said, sidling back to the tree, watching me cautiously the while.

"Oh, very well, I'll forgive you," I said, as he retook his place. "I say, Pomp, I am thirsty."

"So 'm I, Mass' George. Dat lunchum?"

"Yes; that's lunch," I said, as I laid the neatly-done-up napkin containing provision of some kind on the tree-trunk between us, and taking out the tin can I leaned right back, gripping the tree with both legs, and lowering my hand I dipped the vessel full of water.

I was just in the act of rising cautiously and very slowly, when a sharp pain in the fleshy part of my leg made me spring forward in agony, dashing the water in Pomp's face, knocking the wallet and its contents over sidewise, and in my pain and rage I seized the boy to begin cuffing him, while he wrestled with me to get away, as we hugged and struggled like two fighting men in a *mêlée* on the same horse.

"How dare you!" I panted; "that was the point of your knife. I'll teach you to—Oh, murder!"

"Oh, Mass' George, don't! *Oh!* Oh! Oh!"

We both made a bound together, went off the trunk sidewise, and Pomp struggled up, tore off his shirt and drawers, and began to beat and shake them, and then peep inside, pausing every moment to have a rub; while I, without going to his extreme, was doing the best I could to rid myself of my pain.

"Nas' lil fing!" cried Pomp, stamping on something in the grass. "Look, look, Mass' George, make hase; dey eat all de lunchum."

The mystery was out. We had seated ourselves upon the home of a vicious kind of ant, whose nest was under the rotten bark of the tree, and as soon as Pomp realised the truth he danced about with delight.

"I fought you 'tick pin in lil nigger. You fought I 'tick um knife in Mass' George! You catch um, too."

"Yes," I said, wriggling under my clothes, and rubbing myself. "Oh! Quick! Back of my neck, Pomp, look. Biting."

Pomp sprang to me in an instant.

"I got um, Mass' George. Dah!" he cried, as he placed the vicious little insect between his teeth, and bit it in two. "You no bite young massa 'gain. How you like be bite, sah? Make you feel dicklus, eh? Oh! Ugh! Tiff! Tiff! Tiff! Oh, um do tase nasty."

Pomp spat and shuddered and ended by washing out his mouth by running a little way, lying flat with his head over the bank, and scooping up some water with his hand.

Meanwhile I cautiously picked up the provisions, the napkin and wallet, and carefully shook them clear of the vicious little things—no easy job, by the way; after which, stinging and smarting still, I sought another place where we could eat our meal in peace.

Chapter Twenty Four

"No, no, Pomp," I said, after a time, during which we had been thoroughly enjoying our food, "you've had quite enough. We shall want to make this last till night."

"Mass' George no want to finish um all up?"

"No."

"So not hav' to carry walletum."

"Of course not. We shall soon be hungry again."

"Catch fis; shoot de duck; Pomp fine plenty 'tick; and make a fire."

"I wish you'd find the boat," I said, packing up the remains of the meal the while. "Think it's any use to go any farther?"

"Yes; go right on, Mass' George; plenty time."

"Yes, we'll go on," I said, for I felt refreshed and rested, and as if I should like to go journeying on for days—the beauty of the river and the various things we saw exciting a desire to continue our trip. "I don't suppose any one ever came here before, but we mustn't lose our way."

"Couldn't lose way, Mass' George. Ony got to keep by ribber, and he show de way back."

"Of course," I said; "I forgot that."

"No walk back."

"I hope not," I said. "We are going to find the boat."

Pomp made a grimace and looked round, as if to say, "Not likely."

"No find a boat, put lot ob 'tick togedder and float down de ribber home."

"Ah, well, we'll see," I said; and we continued our journey for hour after hour, always finding some fresh beauty to entice me, or living object for Pomp to stalk and beg me to shoot. But though we looked here and there as well as we could, there was no sign of the object of our search; in fact, I soon began to feel that I had embarked upon an enterprise that was almost an impossibility.

The river had now grown a little swifter, and though there was plenty of swampy land down by its banks, it seemed as if we were getting into a more elevated region, the margin being higher, and here and there quite precipitous, but it was always more beautiful, and the objects of natural history grew frequent every hour.

Now it was a squirrel, of which there seemed to be great numbers; then all at once, as we were threading our way through the low bushes, something sprang up from its lair and went bounding off among the trees, giving me just a glimpse of a pretty head with large eyes and small horns, before it was gone.

"Oh, Mass' George, you ought shoot dat," said Pomp, reproachfully. "Dat berry good to eat."

"If I had been on the look-out, I could not have hit it," I said. "But I say, Pomp," I continued, looking round as we came upon a high sandy bluff through which the river had cut its way, and whose dry, sun-bathed sides offered a pleasant resting-place, "aren't you tired?"

"No," said the boy, thoughtfully, "Pomp not bit tired, only one leg."

"Well, are you hungry then?"

"Dreffle, Mass' George. You like emp de walletum now?"

"Yes, we'll sit down and have a good meal, and then we shall have to make haste back."

"Top lil bit, Mass' George," said the boy, cautiously.

"Oh no, there are no pins and forns there to 'tick in us," I said.

"No, Mass' George, but dat sort o' place for rattle tailum 'nake. I go look fust."

I felt a shudder run through me at the mention of the noxious creature, and brought the gun to bear as we advanced.

"No; no shoot," whispered the boy. "Big 'tick bess for 'nake."

We advanced very cautiously, with our eyes searching the ground, but there was nothing in sight, and after selecting a comfortable place where the sand had slowly been washed down from the bluff till it lay thick and dry as when it is drifted on the seashore, we sat down, the fine grains feeling delightful to our limbs, and made a hearty meal of the remains left in the wallet.

It was wonderfully still there, the trees being quite motionless, and the only sounds heard being the hum of some insect and the ripple of the water a dozen yards away. High above us through the thin tracery of an overhanging tree the sky looked of a brilliant blue, and away to left and right extended the forest.

Pomp was lying face downwards, lazily scooping a hole in the sand, and watching it trickle back as fast as he scraped it away, just as if it were so much dry water in grains. I was lying on my back where the sand sloped up to the bank; and as I gazed at the trees, half expecting to see our boat sticking somewhere up among the branches, it seemed to me as if I had never felt so happy and contented before. Perhaps it was the soft, clear atmosphere, or the fact that I was resting, or that I had just partaken of a pleasant meal. I don't know. All I can say is that everything felt peaceful and restful; even Pomp, who as a rule was like a piece of spring in motion. There was a lovely pale blue haze in the distance, and a warm golden glow nearer at hand; the sun was getting well to the west; and I knew that we must soon start and walk fast, so as to get back, but I did not feel disposed to move for a few minutes.

We should be able to walk so much better after a rest, I thought, and we should not stop to look for the boat, or at anything, but keep steadily walking on, so that it would not take us a quarter of the time; and if night did come on, the moon would rise early, and we could easily get to the house.

How deliriously faint and blue that looked right away there in the distance, and how still it all was! Even Pomp enjoyed the silence, and I would not disturb him yet, but let him rest too. No fear of any snakes coming if we were there, and in a few minutes I'd jump up, tell Pomp, and we'd go and have a delicious bathe, and dry ourselves in the warm sand; that would make us walk splendidly. But I would not wake him yet—not just yet—I'd wake him presently, for he was so still that he must have gone to sleep. There he lay with his face to the sand, and his fingers half buried in the hole he had been scraping.

"What a fellow he is to snooze!" I thought to myself. "Lucky I'm not so ready to go to sleep. How—how long shall I wait before I wake him?—How long—how long—how—"

Chapter Twenty Five

A jerk! Then a hasty movement. I must have left the window open, and a fly or a beetle had got in and was tickling my ear. Now it was on my cheek—then on the other cheek—my neck again—my ear—my eyes—and now—

"Ertchsshaw—ertchsshaw!" It was right on my nose, and I start up to brush it away, and in the gloom recognise the figure of Pomp, who burst into a roar of laughter.

"Mass' George tiddle lil nigger; now lil nigger tiddle Mass' George."

"Why, Pomp," I said, sitting up and staring, "I—I thought I was at home."

"No, Mass' George. Home long a way. Been sleep, and Pomp been sleep."

I shivered, got up, and stamped about.

"Yes, Mass' George, um dreffle cole."

"Here, get the powder and shot, and let's go back."

Pomp shook his head.

"No good go now. Get 'tuck in de forn, or tumble in de ribber."

"But we must go."

"No see de way; an' all de big 'gator go out for walk now, Mass' George."

"What time can it be?"

"Dunno, Mass' George, o'ny know not morrow mornin' yet."

I looked about me, and tried to make out the forest path by which we should have to go; but all was dark as night could be, except overhead where a faint gleam showed where the moon should have been giving her light, had not the clouds and mist interposed.

I did not like the look of it, but on the other hand I was afraid to give up; I knew that my father would be anxious, perhaps setting out in search of me.

That last thought fixed me in my determination, and taking up the gun, I said firmly—

"Come along."

"Mass' George go shoot somefin?"

"No; let's get back home."

"No get home now. Too dark."

"But we must get home."

"Mass' George say muss get home, but de dark night say he no get home."

"Let's try," I said.

Pomp was obedience itself, and he followed me as I strode back to the edge of the forest, entered the dense thicket close to the river, and had not gone a hundred yards before just in front of me there was a crashing, rustling noise, and a dull sullen plunge.

"I yah, ugly ole 'gator. Take care, Mass' George, he don't hab you."

I felt my heart beat fast, but I tried to fix it upon my mind in the foremost place that the reptiles fled from me, and were perhaps more alarmed than I was; but as I pressed forward, Pomp suddenly said, piteously—

"No got shoe like Mass' George. Poor Pomp put him foot in 'gator mouf. Oh!"

Pomp caught hold of me tightly, for from somewhere in front there came a low snarling roar, which I had never before heard; but report had told of different savage creatures which came down from the hills sometimes, mountain lions, as the settlers called them, and to face one of these creatures in the dark was too much for my nerves.

"It's unlucky," I said to Pomp; "but we can't get back to-night. We had better get out from among the trees."

Pomp wanted no second hint; he was behind, and he turned at once, and led the way back to the sandy bluff, where he stood shivering.

"What was dat, Mass' George?"

"I don't know," I said. "Some kind of great cat, I suppose."

"Pomp tink he know. It great big monkey like in him country. Great big as fader, and big long arm, an um shout *ooooor*! Like dat."

He uttered as deep-toned a roar as he could, and made a snatch at me directly and held on, for from out of the forest came an answering roar that sounded terrific to us, as we stood there shivering with cold and fear.

"Mass' George! Mass' George!" whispered Pomp, with his lips close to my ear, "tell um I berry sorry. I no do um no more."

"Hush!" I said, and I stood ready with the gun presented, fully expecting to see a dark shadowy form crawling over the light-coloured sand, and trying to get within range for a spring.

But all was still once more, and we waited in expectancy for some minutes before there was a great floundering splash in the water to our right; and then away to the left where the river ran black and mysterious in the night—where all was bright and beautiful by day—there came evidently from three different parts as many bellows, such as must have been given by alligators of great size.

"Come 'long, Mass' George," whispered Pomp.

"No," I said, "we must wait till day."

"Dey come and hab us bofe, Mass' George, we 'top here. Come 'long."

"But it is impossible."

"Yes, Mass' George, um possible; come and get up dat big tree."

The proposition seemed so much in unison with my feelings that I followed my companion at once, and he paused under a great oak a little farther from the river, and beyond the bluff.

"Dah, Mass' George, make base up an' let me come. I dreffle frighten."

"Then go first."

"No, Mass' George, you go firs', you de mas'r."

"Then I order you to go first, Pomp," I said.

"Den we bofe clime up togedder, Mass' George. You go one way, and Pomp go oder way."

There seemed to be no time for discussion on questions of precedent, so we began to climb together, reaching a great branch about twenty feet from the ground, no easy task for me, encumbered as I was by the gun.

"Ha ha!" cried Pomp, who seemed to have recovered his courage as soon as he was up in the tree; "no 'gator catch um up here, Mass' George. Nebber see 'gator, no, not eben lil 'gator, climb up tree."

"No," I said in a low tone, which impressed the boy so that he sat speechless for some time; "no, but the panthers can, more easily than we do, Pomp."

I don't know what sort of a shot I should have made; probably I should have been too nervous to take good aim up there in the dark; but for what seemed a terrible length of time I sat there gun in hand, ready to fire at the first savage creature I could see, and a dozen times over I conjured up something stealthily approaching. But it was not until we had been up there about an hour that I felt quite certain of some great cat-like creature being beneath the tree.

It was not creeping forward, but crouched down as if watching us, ready at our first movement to change its waiting attitude into one of offence.

Pomp made no sign, but he was so still that I felt sure he could see it too, and I was afraid to call his attention to it, lest it should bring the creature on me so suddenly that it might disorder my aim. So I sat on with the piece directed at the object, my finger on the trigger, hesitating, then determined to fire, when all at once it seemed to me that the animal had grown plainer.

This, though I had not detected the movement, must mean that it was getting nearer and about to spring, so casting all hesitancy to the winds, I raised the gun to my shoulder, and then quite started, for Pomp said aloud—

"Mass' George going shoot?"

"Yes," I said, in a husky whisper. "Keep still; do you see it?"

"No. Where be um?"

"There, there," I whispered; "down straight before us."

"What, dat?"

"Yes. Be still, or you'll make it leap at us."

"Why, dat lil tree."

There was a tone of such astonishment in the boy's voice that I bent lower and lower down, knowing how much better Pomp's eyes were than mine; and as I looked, I saw that the object was clear, and that it was indeed a low patch of shrub getting plainer and plainer rapidly now, for it was morning once more.

Chapter Twenty Six

"Now, Mass' George," said Pomp, as we stood at the foot of the tree, and stamped about to get rid of the stiffness, and cold brought on by our cramped position on the branch, "de fuss ting am breckfuss. I so dreffle hungry."

"But we ate everything last night," I said.

"Neb mind; plenty duck in de ribber. You go shoot four lil duck, dat two piece, while Pomp make fire to roace um."

"But how are we to get a light?"

"You see," he said, as he busily began to get together all the loose sticks he could find lying about, at the same time showing me a stone and his knife with a little bag full of tinder. "I soon get light, Mass' George; I get big fire much soon you get de duck."

The proposition was so sensible that I went off with the gun, and following the course of the river beyond the bluff, I was not long before I heard a familiar noise, and creeping forward in the grey dawn, I was soon crouching behind the low growth by a wide pool of the river, where quite a flock of ducks were disporting themselves, preening their feathers, diving, making the bright drops run over their backs like pearls, and ending by flapping and beating the water heavily with their wings, exactly as I had seen them perform in the pond at home.

I waited my opportunity, lying flat now on my chest, and at last, after nearly firing three or four times and always waiting for a better chance, I drew trigger upon a knot of the ducks after getting several well in a line. There was a deafening report, a sensation as if my shoulder was broken, and a thick film of smoke hid everything from my sight. But as the shot went echoing along the side of the forest, I could hear the whistling and whirring of wings where the ducks flapped along the water, rose, and swept away over the trees. Then the smoke rose, and to my great delight there lay five of the unfortunate ducks; three perfectly still, and floating slowly to the shallow below the pool, the other two flapping wildly and trying to reach the farther shore.

To get the three was easy. I had but to wait and then wade in over the shallow to where I could see the sandy and pebbly bottom quite plain. To get the wounded ducks meant a swim, and perhaps a long hunt.

"Better shoot at them again," I thought, when I shuddered, for something dark appeared behind one; there was a snap, and it disappeared, while almost at the same moment the other, which must have been nearly twenty yards away, was suddenly struck down beneath the water by something which puzzled me at first, but which the next minute I knew to be an alligator's tail.

I turned to my three, now well over the shallows, and hesitated as to whether I dared risk going after them, not knowing but that an alligator might make a rush out of the deep black pool and seize them first, or failing them perhaps seize me.

But I was hungry too, and leaping in, I secured all three birds after splashing through the water a bit, and reached the shore again in safety, but not without many an excited look round at the deep place where I knew the monsters were lurking; and as I shook the water from my legs, and stamped about on the bank, I found myself thinking what a pity it was such a lovely country should be marred by dangerous beasts and horrible reptiles like the rattlesnakes and alligators.

Then I thought of the ducks, and as I held them all three by their orange legs, and looked down at their beautifully-coloured plumage, all soft browns and chestnuts, and with wing-spots of lovely green, and having a head of the same colour, my conscience smote me, and I found myself wondering what the ducks thought that beautiful morning when they were having their baths and preening themselves ready for a long flight or a good swim. And I seemed to see them all again playing about, and passing their heads over their backs, and rubbing the points of their beaks in the oil-gland to make their plumage keep off the water. And how soft and close it was!

"What must they have thought," I said to myself, "about a monster who came with a horrible, fire-dealing weapon that strikes them down like a flash of lightning? Not much room for me to complain about the alligators!" I exclaimed. "But if I had not killed the ducks they would have killed all kinds of insects and little fishes, and if they did not kill the insects and fishes, the insects and fishes would have killed smaller ones. Everything seems to be killing everything else, and I suppose it's because we are all hungry, as I am now."

I walked sharply back along the river-bank with the sun now well up, and before long came in sight of a little cloud of smoke rising softly above the trees, and soon after I could hear the crackling of wood, and as I drew near, there was Pomp dodging about in the smoke, piling up pieces of dried stick, and making a roaring fire.

The sight of this took away all my feelings of compunction, and in imagination I began to see the brown sides of the well-roasted ducks, to smell their appetising odour, and to taste the juicy, tender bits about the bones.

"I heard you shoot um, Mass' George," cried Pomp, excitedly. "Got lubbly fire. How many?"

"Three," I said.

"Oh!"

"What's the matter?"

"On'y got flee. Dat two Mass' George, and on'y one for Pomp, an' I so dreffle hungly, I mose eat bit a 'gator."

"There'll be plenty," I said. "I shall only eat one."

"Eh? Mass' George on'y eat one duck-bird?"

"That's all."

"Mass' George sure?"

"Yes. Let's cook them."

"But is Mass' George quite sure?"

"Yes—yes—yes!"

"Oh! Den Mass' George hab dis bewfler one wid um green head. Dat's biggess and bess."

"Here, what are you going to do?" I cried, as Pomp suddenly seized the three ducks and threw them into the fire. "That's not the way to roast ducks."

"Pomp know dat, Mass' George," cried the boy, poking the birds about with a long, sharp-pointed stick, one of several which he had cut ready. "Pomp fader show um how to do ober dah."

"Ober dah" evidently meant Africa.

"Dat a way to get all de fedder off fuss. Dah, see dat?" he cried, as he turned one out scorched brown. "Now Mass' George see."

As I watched him, he cleverly ran his sharp-pointed stick through this first duck, stuck the point down into the sand, so that the bird was close in to the glowing embers, and then deftly served the others the same.

"Mass' George shoot um duck, Pomp cook um; same Pomp cook and make de cake at home. Pomp fader nebber cook. Pomp cook de fis, and de yam, and make um hominy. Pomp berry clebber 'deed, Mass' George. Ah, you try burn you 'tick an' tummle in de fire, would you, sah? No, you don't! You 'top dah an' get rock nice for Mass' George."

As he spoke he made a snatch at one of the sticks, and turned the bird, as he stuck it afresh in the sand, closer to the glowing embers, for the flame and smoke had nearly gone now, and the ducks were sputtering, browning, and beginning to give forth a tempting odour.

As the boy was evidently, as he modestly said, so "clebber," I did not interfere, but took off my shoes and stockings, wrung the latter well out, and laid them and the shoes in the warm glow to dry, a little rubbing about in the hot dry sand from the bluff soon drying my feet. Then I carefully reloaded the gun, in accordance with Morgan's instructions, making the ramrod leap well on the powder charge and wad, while Pomp looked on eagerly, his fingers working, his lips moving, and his eyes seeming to devour everything that was done.

"Pomp load um gun," he said all at once.

"You go on with your cooking," I replied; "that one's 'burning um 'tick.'"

Pomp darted at the wooden spit, and drawing it out replaced it in a better position.

"Dat duck lil rarksle," he said, showing his teeth. "Dat free time try to burn um 'tick and tummle in de fire, rock umself. Dah, you 'tan 'till, will you? Oh, I say, Mass' George, done um 'mell good?"

"Yes; they begin to smell nice."

"Dat de one hab green head. He berry juicy 'deed; dat one for Mass' George. What Mass' George going to do?"

"Put the gun and powder and shot farther away from the fire."

"What for?"

"A spark might set the powder off."

"Oh!" ejaculated Pomp. Then, "What powder do if 'park send um off?"

"Blow the fire out and send the ducks into the river."

"What? An' de 'gator get um? Pomp not cook de duck for 'gator. 'Gator eat de duck raw, and no pick um fedder. Take de gun away."

I was already doing so, and standing it up behind us against a patch of low bushes, I hung the powder and shot pouches by their straps to the iron ramrod. Then going back to my place I sat watching the cooking, as the boy turned and re-turned the birds, which grew browner and more appetising every moment.

There were faults in that cooking, no doubt. There was neither plate nor dish, no bread, no salt or pepper, and no table-cloth. But there was something else—young, healthy appetite, as we sat at last in the bright morning sunshine, drawn back now from the fire, Pomp and I, each with a roasting-stick in one hand, his knife in the other, cutting off the juicy brown bits, and eating them with the greatest of gusto, after an incision had been made, and the whole of the hardened interior had been allowed to fall out into the fire.

We hardly spoke, but went on eating, Pomp watching me and cutting the bird exactly as I did mine; then picking each bone as it was detached from the stick, and so on and on, till we had each finished his duck. Our hands were not very clean, and we had no table napkins for our lips; but as we ate that meal, I can safely say for myself that it was the most delicious repast I ever had.

Then we sat perfectly still, after throwing our sticks into the remains of the fire, reduced now to a few glowing embers.

But there is one thing more of which I must speak, that is the third duck, which, certainly the best cooked and least burned of the three, had been served to table; that is to say, its burnt stick had been stuck in the sand between us, and there it was, nicely cooling down, and looking tempting in the extreme.

Pomp looked at me, and I looked at Pomp.

"I dreffle glad we come an' 'top out all night," he said, showing his white teeth. "Mass' George, go an' shoot more duck, an' Pomp cook um."

"We haven't finished that one," I said.

"No, Mass' George, no hab finish dat oder duck."

"Well, go on; I've had quite enough."

"Pomp had quite nuff too."

"Then we'll wrap it up in the napkin, and we'll eat it by and by for lunch."

"Yes; wrap um up an' eat um bime by."

I drew out the napkin, and Pomp shot the duck off the wooden spit on to the cloth, which, with due care to avoid the addition of sand, was folded up, and then I said —

"Now, Pomp, we must find the boat as we go back."

"Mass' George go back?" he said.

"Yes, of course; and get there as soon as we can."

"Yes, Mass' George," he said, sadly. "Pomp wouldn't mind 'top if Mass' George say 'top here."

"We'll come again," I said, laughing. "Let's find the boat if we can, but we must make haste back."

"Hi! Ohey!" he shouted.

"What's the matter?" I said.

"Wha dat all gun?"

Chapter Twenty Seven

I looked sharply round at the bush, hardly comprehending my black companion's remark.

"What?" I said, in a confused way.

"Wha dat gun?"

"I stood it up against that bush," I said; and then, shaking off the dull stupid feeling which troubled me, darted to the bush, expecting to see that it had slipped down among the little branches.

The gun was gone, and I looked round at the other bushes dotted about.

"I put it here, didn't I?"

"Yes; Mass' George put um gun dah. Pomp know," he cried, running to me, and dropping on his knees as he pointed to the impression left in the dry sand by the butt. "Gun gone down dah."

He began scratching up the sand for a few moments, and I watched him, half hoping and believing that he might be right.

But the boy ceased as quickly as he had begun.

"I know, Mass' George," he cried, starting up and gazing toward the river. "'Gator 'fraid we come shoot um, and come out of de ribber and 'teal a gun."

"Nonsense! An alligator wouldn't do that."

"Oh, I done know. 'Gator berry wicked ole rarksle."

"Where are the marks then?" I said.

"Ah, Pomp find um foots and de mark of de tail."

He looked sharply round, so did I; but as he searched the sand I examined the bushes, feeling that I must be mistaken, and that I must have laid the gun somewhere else.

It was very stupid, but I knew people did make such mistakes sometimes; and quite convinced now that this was a lapse of memory, began to cudgel my brains to try and recall the last thing I had done with the gun.

Pomp settled that, for he came back to me suddenly, and said—

"See Mass' George put de gun dah!"

"You are sure, Pomp?" I said, as he stood pointing his black finger at the bush.

"Yes, Pomp ebber so sure."

"Did you find any alligator marks?"

"No, Mass' George, nowhere."

"Then some one must have come and stolen it while we were eating."

"How people come 'teal a gun wif Pomp and Mass' George eatin' um breakfast here?"

"I don't know. Come and look for footsteps."

"Did; and de 'gator not been."

"No, but perhaps a man has."

"Man? No man lib here."

"Let's look," I whispered—"look for men's footsteps."

The boy glanced at me wonderingly for a moment or two, then nodded his head and began to search.

Where we stood by the bush, saving that the ground had been trampled by my feet, the task would have been easy enough, for everything showed in the soft dry sand; but the bush was at the edge where the sand began running from the foot of the bluff to the river, and everywhere on the other side was dense growth; patches of shrubs, grass, dry reed and rush, where hundreds of feet might have passed, and, save to the carefully-trained eye of an Indian, nothing would have been seen.

Certainly nothing was visible to me, but the fact that it was quite possible for a man to have crawled from the forest, keeping the patches of shrubby growth between him and us, till he reached the bushes, through which he could have cautiously stolen, and passing a hand over softly, lifted the gun and its pouches from where I had stood them, and then stolen away as he had come.

One thing was evident, we had an enemy not far away; and, unarmed as we were, saving that we had our knives, the sooner we took flight the better.

All this was plain to me, but as I gazed in Pomp's face I found it was not so clear to him; there was a strange look in his eyes, his skin did not seem so black as usual, and he was certainly trembling.

"Why, Pomp," I said, "don't look like that." For though I felt a little nervous, I saw no cause for the boy's abject dread, having yet to learn that anything not comprehensible to the savage mind is set down at once as being the work of some evil spirit.

He caught my arm and looked round, the whites of his eyes showing strangely, and his thick lips seemed drawn in as if to make a thin line.

"Come 'way," he whispered. "Run, Mass' George, run, 'fore um come and cotch us."

"Who? What?" I said, half angrily, though amused.

"Hush! Done holler, Mass' George, fear um hear. Come take us bofe, like um took de gun."

"I have it," I said suddenly. "Your father has come up the river after us, and he has taken the gun to tease us. Hi! Hannibal—Vanity—Van!"

"Oh, Mass' George! Oh, Mass' George, done, done holler. Not fader. Oh, no. It somefing dreffle. Let run."

"Why isn't it your father playing a trick?"

"Him couldn't play um trick if him try. No, Mass' George, him nebber play trick. It somefing dreffle. Come 'way."

"Well, we were going back," I said, feeling rather ashamed of my eagerness to get away, and still half uneasy about the gun, as I looked up at the tree where we had slept to see if I had left it there.

No; that was impossible, because I had had it to shoot the ducks. But still I might have put it somewhere else, and forgotten what I had done.

I turned away unwillingly, and yet glad, if that can be understood, and with Pomp leading first, we began our retreat as nearly as possible over the ground by which we had come.

For some little distance we went on in silence, totally forgetting the object of our journey; but as we got more distant from the scene of our last adventure, Pomp left off running into bushes and against trees in spite of my warnings, for he had been progressing with his head screwed round first on one side then on the other to look behind him, doing so much to drive away such terror as I felt by his comical aspect, that I ended by roaring with laughter.

"Oh, Mass' George," he said, reproachfully, "you great big foolish boy, or you no laugh like dat all. You done know what am after us."

"No," I said; "but I know we lost one of our guns, and father will be very cross. There, don't walk quite so fast."

"But Pomp want to run," he said, pitifully.

"And we can't run, because of the bushes and trees. I don't think there was anything to be afraid of, after all."

"Oh! Run, Mass' George, run!" yelled Pomp; and instead of running I stood paralysed for an instant at the scene before me.

We were pretty close to the river-bank, and forcing our way through a cane brake which looked just as if it must be the home of alligators, when a man suddenly stood in the boy's path.

Quick as thought the brave little fellow sprang at him, seeing in him an enemy, and called to me to run, which of course I did not do, but, as soon as I recovered from my surprise, ran on to his help. As I did so the path seemed darkened behind me, I heard a quick rustling, my arms were seized, and the next moment I was thrown down and a knee was on my chest.

"Oh, Mass' George, why didn't you run?"

Poor Pomp's voice rang out from close beside me in despairing tones, and I wrenched my head round, just catching a glimpse of him through the canes. Then I looked up in the stern faces of my captors, thinking that I had seen them before, though no doubt it was only a similarity of aspect that struck me, as I realised that we had fallen into the hands of the Indians once more.

They did not give us much time to think, but after taking away our knives twisted up some lithe canes and secured our wrists and arms behind us, two holding each of us upright, while another fastened our hands.

Then they drew back from us, and stood round looking at us as if we were two curiosities.

"Well, this is a nice game, Pomp," I said at last.

"Yes, dis nice game, Mass' George. Why you no run away?"

"How could I?"

"How you could? You ought run, jump in libber and go 'cross. Wish I run and tell de capen an' Mass' Morgan."

"Ah!" I ejaculated.

"You tie too tight, Mass' George?"

"Yes, but I was thinking of something else. Pomp, those Indians are going to attack our place and the settlement, and no one will know they are coming."

"Pomp hope so," he said, sulkily, and screwing himself about with the pain caused by his tight bonds.

"What?"

"Den de capen an' Mass' Morgan shoot um, an' Serb um right."

"But they will take them by surprise."

"Wait bit. We soon get dese off, and go down tell 'em Injum come."

"I'm afraid we shall not have the chance."

Just then a firm brown hand was clapped on my shoulder, and a stalwart Indian signed to me to go on through the canes.

I obeyed mechanically, seeing the while that the half-dozen Indians who had captured us had silently increased to over a dozen quietly-moving, stealthy-looking fellows, who passed through the dense thicket, almost without a sound, and with their eyes watchfully turned in every direction, as if they were always on the look-out for danger. And so I walked awkwardly on, feeling, now that my arms were bound behind me, as if at any moment I should stumble and fall.

The mystery of the gun's disappearance was clear enough now, without the proof which came later on. It was quite plain to me that some of these strange, furtive-looking savages had crawled up behind the bush and carried off the piece, after which they had lain in ambush waiting for us to retrace our steps along the track we had broken down the previous day, and then pounced upon us and made us prisoners.

At my last encounter they had contented themselves with following us home, but now everything seemed to betoken mischief. They seemed to me to be better armed, and had begun to treat us roughly by binding our arms, and this it struck me could only mean one thing—to keep us from getting away and giving the alarm.

I felt too now—for thoughts came quickly—that the report of the gun that morning had guided them to our temporary camp, that and the smoke of the fire; and as I felt how unlucky all this was, I found that we were getting farther and farther from the river, and in a few minutes more we were in an open portion of the wood, where about fifty more Indians were seated about a fire.

A shout from our party made them all start to their feet and come to meet us, surrounding and staring at us in a fierce, stolid way that sent a chill through me as the question rose— Would they kill us both?

In a dull, despondent way the answer seemed to me—*yes*; not just then, for we were both placed back against a young tree, and hide ropes being produced, we were tightly bound to the trunks and left, while the Indians all gathered together in a group, squatted down, and sat in silence for a time smoking.

Then all at once I saw one jump up, axe in hand, to begin talking loudly, gesticulating, waving his axe, and making quite a long address, to which the others listened attentively, grunting a little now and then, and evidently being a good deal influenced by his words.

At last he sat down and another took his place, to dance about, talking volubly the while, and waving his axe too, and evidently saying threatening things, which, as he pointed at us now and then, and also in the direction of the settlement, I felt certain must relate to their expedition.

In spite of my anxiety about my fate, I could not help feeling interested in these people, for everything was so new and strange. But other thoughts soon forced themselves upon me. They must, I felt, be going on to the settlement, and it was my duty at any cost to get away, and give the alarm. But how?

"Pomp," I said, after a time, "do you think we could get loose and run back home?"

The boy looked at me with his face screwed up.

"Pomp done know," he said.

"Could you get the knots undone?"

"Pomp 'fraid try. Come and hit um. Going to kill us, Mass' George?"

"Oh, no; I don't think there's any fear of that."

"Then why they tie us up?"

"Don't talk so loud. It makes them look round."

"Look dah!"

"What at?"

"Dah de gun. Dat big ugly Injum got um. Him fief."

"Never mind the gun," I said. "Let's think about getting away."

"Yes; dat's what Pomp do fink about, Mass' George."

"If they had not taken our knives, I might perhaps have cut ourselves free. Oh, I'd give anything to let them know at home. Look here; if you can get loose, never mind about me; run back home, and warn my father to escape to the settlement."

"You tell um," said Pomp, shortly.

"But I mean if you can get free without me."

"What, you fink Pomp run 'way and leab Mass' George all 'lone?"

"Yes; it is to save those at home."

"Capen flog um for going."

"No, no; he would not."

"Fader knock um down an' kick um."

"I tell you he would not. Try all you can to get loose and creep away when they are not looking."

"Always looking," said Pomp, shortly; and it was quite true, for some one or other of the Indians always seemed to be on the watch, and after trying to wrench myself clear, I stood resting my aching legs by hanging a little on the rope, for the hours were slowly gliding by, and afternoon came without relief.

At last a couple of the men brought us some water and a piece each of badly-roasted and burned deer-flesh, setting our hands at liberty so that we could eat and drink, but leaving the hide ropes holding us tightly to the trees, and sitting down to watch us, listening intently as we spoke, but evidently not understanding a word.

"Well," I said, after a few minutes, during which I had been eating with very poor appetite, "why don't you eat, Pomp?"

"Done like um. 'Mell nasty."

"It's only burnt," I said.

"How Mass' George know what um eat?"

"What?" I said, looking curiously at the meat.

"Pomp fink it poor lil nigger been kill and cook um."

"Nonsense; it's deer's flesh."

"Mass' George sewer?"

"Yes, quite."

"Oh!"

That was all the boy said, for he set to work directly and soon finished his portion, taking a good deep drink afterward; and as soon as he had done one of the Indians secured his hands again, a task which necessitated a loosening of the hide rope, Pomp submitting with a very good grace.

Then came my turn, and as soon as I was secured, the Indians went slowly back to where the others were grouped, and squatted down to listen to the talking going on.

It was a weary, weary time; the sun was getting lower, and birds came and chirped about in the dense branches of the trees to which we were bound, and I felt a strange feeling of envy as I looked up from time to time and thought of their being at liberty to come and go. And all through those painfully long hours the talking went on constantly about the fire, which one or the other of the Indians made up by throwing on some branches of wood.

As I watched them, I saw that they kept going and coming in different directions, so that the number in the camp did not vary much, and though the day wore on, there was no cessation of the talking, for there was always a fresh Indian ready to leap to his feet, and begin relating something with the greatest vehemence, to which the rest listened attentively.

"They must be going on to the settlement to-night," I thought; and as I noted their bows, arrows, axes, and knives, I conjured up horrors that I felt would be sure to take place if we could not get free and give the alarm.

All sorts of plans occurred to me. The forest would, I felt, be full of the enemy, and if we could get loose there would be no chance of our stealing away without being captured. But could we get across the river in safety, and make our way along the farther bank; or could we swim down? I shuddered as I thought of what would be the consequences of trying such a feat.

Then my ponderings were interrupted by the coming of a couple more of the Indians, who examined our fastenings and then went back.

"Mass' George 'leep?" said Pomp suddenly, in a low voice.

"Asleep? No. Who could go to sleep like this?"

"No, not nice go 'leep 'tanning up," said Pomp, coolly; and there was a long pause, with the monotonous talking of the Indians still going on.

All at once one of the Indians who had last examined our bonds came back, peeping about him inquiringly, examining our ropes, and looking about our feet for some minutes before going back, carefully scanning the ground and bushes as he went, and after a good deal of hesitation reseating himself.

By this time I was utterly wearied out, and hung forward from the rope with my head upon my chest, gazing down hopelessly at the thick moss and other growth at our feet.

"Mass' George 'leep?" whispered Pomp again.

"No, no," I said, sadly; "I could not sleep at a time like this."

"'Cause Mass' George no go to sleep."

I looked at him despondently, and saw that he was amusing himself by picking the moss and leaves with his toes, getting a tuft together, snatching it off, and dropping it again, almost as cleverly as a monkey would have done the same thing.

Then I ceased to notice it, for I saw a couple of the Indians get up from the fireside, and come to examine us again. They felt all the knots, and appeared satisfied, going back to the fire as before, while others threw on fresh sticks. Then the smoking and talking went on, and the flames cast their shadows about, and on the trees now in a peculiarly weird way.

We were almost in darkness, but they were in what seemed to be a circle or great halo of red light, which shone upon their copper-coloured skins, and from the axes and the hilts of the knives they had stuck in the bands of their deer-skin leggings.

"Soon be quite dark now, Mass' George," whispered Pomp; "den you see."

"See? See what? Their fire?"

"Wait bit—you see."

My heart gave a great throb, and I wanted to speak, but the words in my agitation would not come. It was evident that the boy had some plan afoot, and as I waited for him to speak again, feeling ashamed that this poor black savage lad should be keener of intellect than I, he suddenly began to laugh.

"Pomp," I whispered, "what is it?"

"You mose ready, Mass' George?"

"Ready? What for?"

"You see dreckerly. You know what dat Injum look about for?"

"No."

"Lose um knife."

"Well?"

"Pomp got um."

"You have? Where?"

"Down dah," he said, making a sign with one foot toward the loose moss and leaves he had picked.

"Why, Pomp," I whispered, joyfully, "how did you manage that?"

"Ciss! Coming."

Two of the Indians had risen again from the fire, and once more approached, feeling the knots, and to my despair, binding us more securely with a couple of fresh ropes of hide.

Then I saw their dark figures go half way to the fire, return and pass near us, and out along the banks of the river toward the settlement.

Then six more rose and went slowly out of sight among the trees, and I felt that these must be going to form outposts to guard the little camp from attack.

"Now, Mass' George," whispered Pomp—"ah, look dah."

I was already looking, and saw that about a dozen more left the fireside to go out in different directions, their tall dark figures passing out of sight among the trees.

"What are you going to do with the knife?" I whispered softly.

"'Top; you see," said the boy.

"But how did you get it?"

"You see dat Injum come feel de rope. He 'tuck Pomp head down under um arm while he tie de knot hurt um, so Pomp mean to bite um; but Pomp see de handle ob de knife 'tick up close to um mouf, and um take hold wid um teef, pull um out, and let um fall and put um foot ober um."

"Oh, Pomp!" I said.

"Den he gone, Pomp push um out ob sight and put um foot ober um again, and now I juss pick um up wid Pomp toe."

I heard a faint rustle, and then he whispered after a faint grunting sound—

"Got um."

I stared sidewise at where he was—only about six feet away—and half fancied that I could see him pick up the knife with his toes, and bend his foot up till he could pass the blade into his hand.

"Hff!"

"What's the matter?" I whispered, as I heard a faint ejaculation.

"Pomp cut umself."

Then I heard a curious sawing sound, which seemed to be loud enough to reach the Indians' ears, but as I looked, they were all talking, and I turned my eyes again in the direction of my companion, whose black body and light drawers had stood out plainly in the faint glow of the fire a minute before, and I could only just restrain an exclamation, for he was not there.

At the same moment his lips were at my ear—

"'Tan 'till."

I obeyed, and felt the tension and loosening as he rapidly cut through the hide rope and the cane bonds which held me; but I was so stiff, and my wrists were so numbed, that the feeling had gone from my hands.

"Mass' George ready?"

"No; yes," I said, as I gazed wildly at the group about the fire, and felt that our movements must be seen. But the Indians made no sign, and Pomp went on—

"Injum ebberywhere now. Can't run away."

"But we must," I whispered.

"Catchum gain, dreckerly. Dis here tree. Mass' George go up fuss."

"Up the tree!" I faltered.

Then grasping the cleverness of the boy's idea, I stretched out my arms, seized a branch overhead, and in spite of my numbness, swung myself up and stood on it, holding by the branch of the great pine close behind the two small trees to which we had been bound.

Pomp was beside me directly. "Up!" he whispered; and as silently as I could, I crept on toward the dense crown, the many horizontal branches giving good foot-hold, and the fire gleaming among the needle-like foliage as I went higher, with Pomp always ready to touch me and try to guide.

It was a huge tree, quite a cone of dense foliage, after we were some distance up, and we had just reached the part where great, flat, heavily-laden boughs spread between us and the ground, when Pomp drew himself quickly to my side, and laid his hand on my mouth.

It was not necessary, for at the same moment as he I had noted the danger, just catching sight of two black shadows on the ground, which I knew were those of a couple of the Indians approaching our trees from the fire.

Then we could see no more, but remained there clinging to the boughs as if part of the tree itself, wondering what was to come.

It seemed quite a space of time before from just below I heard a discordant yell which thrilled through me, and actually for the moment made me loose my hold. But I was clinging fast again directly, as the yell was answered by a couple of score of throats; there was the rapid beat of feet, the crunching of dead sticks and crushing of bushes, and I clung there with closed eyes, listening to a confused gabble of excited voices, and waiting for what I seemed to know would come next.

For in my excitement I could in fancy picture the Indians examining the cut thongs lying where they had dropped by the trees, and then one great stalwart fellow took a step out from the rest and pointed up to where we two clung forty feet from the ground, and I saw a score of arrows fitted to the bow-strings, and their owners prepare to shoot and bring us down.

I cannot attempt to describe the sensation that thrilled through me in what was almost momentary, nor the wild thoughts flashing in my brain. I only know that I wondered whether the arrow which pierced me would hurt much, and thought what a pity it was that the tree we were in did not hang over the stream, so that we might have fallen in the water.

But no flight of arrows rattled among the boughs, and all we heard was the gabble of excited voices. Then came yell after yell from a little distance farther away from the settlement, and from the excited questioning which seemed to follow, I knew that a number of the Indians had returned to the camp to talk hurriedly to those beneath the tree.

Then there were a couple of yells given in a peculiar tone, and a faint series of sounds reached us, suggesting to me that the whole party had spread out, and were quickly and cautiously creeping along through the forest from the edge of the stream for some distance in, and then all was still.

Chapter Twenty Eight

A pair of warm lips at my ear made me start again.

"Dey all 'tupid, dem Injum. I know dey nebber tink we get up tree. Think we run home. All gone. Come down."

"No, no; it is not safe," I whispered.

"Yes; all gone dat way. We go oder."

He was already descending almost as rapidly as a monkey, and I followed as fast as I could, fully expecting to be seized; but all was silent, and the fire had sunk quite low as we bent down and crept along by the edge of the opening, and directly after were well in the shelter and darkness of the trees, with the fire behind only making its presence known by a dull glow.

"Where are you going?" I whispered at last.

"Get away from Injum. Come!"

He said this shortly, and I began thinking that it was our wisest course to get right away, and, as soon as we could find a spot at daybreak, cross to the other side, and then try to thread our way back home. But a curiously dull, deadening feeling came over me, as I felt that the Indians must now get there first, and that we should be too late to give the alarm.

I was just thinking this when Pomp stopped short.

"Mass' George take off um shoes," he whispered. "Carry um. Injum no see footmarks a-morrow."

I hurriedly did as he suggested, for there was wisdom in what he said, and I hoped that the print of my stockinged feet, if our trail was found and followed, might pass for the impressions made by moccasins.

I did not know much then about such matters, but still I had heard a good deal of talk about the skill of the Indians in tracking, and naturally felt nervous as I immediately began magnifying their powers, and fancied that as soon as it was day they would take up our trail like a pack of hounds, and follow it step by step, first my clumsy shoe-prints, then Pomp's bare feet, with the great toe spreading wide out from the others, which all seemed long and loose, as I had often noticed and laughed at when I had seen them in the mud or sand. In fact, I had more than once followed him by his footprints, and as I recalled all this, I seemed to see the fierce-looking savages coming on swiftly, and urged Pomp to make haste, though my heart sank as I felt that every step took us farther into the wilderness, and with the exception of the knife the boy had secured, we were without arms.

"Can't go no fasser, Mass' George," he said; "so dark. But done you be 'fraid. Dem on'y 'tupid savage. Pomp too clebber let um cotch him 'gain."

In spite of my anxiety I could not help smiling at my companion's conceit, and his reference to "'tupid" savages. Pomp's connection with civilisation was making its mark upon him in other ways beside the rapid manner in which he had acquired our tongue.

And so we tramped on hour after hour, going, as I knew by the stars whenever we got a glimpse of them, nearly due west, and trying to avoid breaking branch or trampling down thick patches of growth by making a detour.

Of course this hindered us a good deal, but still it was the surest way of avoiding recapture; and at last, after our long, weary walk, whose monotony I had relieved by softly chafing my arms and wrists to get rid of the remains of the numbness produced by the bonds, there came a familiar note or two from the trees overhead, and I knew that in a very short time it would be light.

"Tired, Pomp?" I said.

"No, Mass' George, but I dreffle hungly 'gain. Oh! Dem ugly tief 'teal de gun. No get duck for breakfass, eh?"

"Let's think about escaping and getting back to the house before these savages.—Ah, it's getting light."

I remember how eagerly I said this, as I saw the pale grey appearing through the leaves, and making the tall, gloomy-looking trunks stand up like great columns in all directions.

"Now," I said, "where do you think the river is?"

"Ober dah," said Pomp, without a moment's hesitation; and he pointed to the left.

"Is it far?"

"No, not far."

"Let's get to it at once then."

We struck off again, bearing to the left, and just at sunrise found that we were at the edge of the forest once more, with a well-defined track, showing where the river ran. Where we stood we were under the shade of the great trees, where scarcely anything grew beneath the spreading, tangled branches, while just beyond them there was a dense thicket of succulent growth glittering in the sunshine, where the leaves were still moist with dew, and some hundred or a hundred and fifty yards away there once more was the other edge of the forest, rising up over a rich band of growth similar to that which was close to where we stood.

The river lay between, I knew, though invisible from where we stood; and for the moment I felt more hopeful, for, after the long, dark tramp through the wilderness, we seemed to be now on the broad high-road which led straight past home.

Then my heart sank again, as I felt that perhaps the Indians were already on our track, and that even if they were not, they were between us and safety.

My reverie was interrupted by Pomp, who said briskly—

"Now, Mass' George, what you tink?"

"We must get across the river at once."

Pomp made a grimace.

"How we 'wim ober dah wid de 'gator all awaiting to hab us for breakfass, Mass' George?"

I shuddered as I thought of the task, but it seemed as if that was the only thing to do, and then tramp along the opposite bank downward.

"What are you doing?" I said, as the boy began to step about, cautiously penetrating once more into the forest, and stopping at last beside a moderate-sized pine, whose trunk was dotted with the stumps of dead branches, till about fifty feet from the ground, where it formed a pretty dense tuft, whose top was well in the sunlight.

"Now we go up dah and hide, and rest a bit."

"But why not try that tree, or that, or that?" I said; and I pointed rapidly to three or four more, all far more thickly clothed with branch and foliage.

"If Injum come he fink p'raps we hide in dah, an' look. No fink we get up dat oder tree. Injum berry 'tupid."

"But hadn't we better try and get across or down the stream?"

Pomp shook his head.

"See Injum, and dey dreffle cross dat we run 'way. Wait a bit, Mass' George."

"But my father—yours—and Morgan?"

"Well, what 'bout um, Mass' George?"

"We ought to warn them."

"Dey must take care ob demself. No good to go and be caught. Dat not help um fader."

There was so much truth in this that I did not oppose Pomp's plan of getting up in the tree, and hiding until the pursuit was over. For it was only reasonable to suppose that after a thorough hunt in one direction, the Indians would come in the other. Besides, I was utterly wearied out the previous evening, and glad to rest my tired limbs by hanging against the rope, and taking the weight off my feet. Since then we had tramped through the night many dreary miles, made more painful by the constant stress of avoiding obstacles, and the sensation of being hunted by a pack of savages whose cries might at any moment rise upon the ear.

It was not a comfortable resting-place for one who felt as if he would give anything to throw himself down and lie at full length, but it promised to be safe, and following Pomp's lead, I climbed steadily up the tree to where the dense head formed quite a scaffolding of crossing boughs, and here, after getting well out of sight of any one who might be passing below, we seated ourselves as securely as possible, and waited for what was to come next.

"Wait Injum gone, and we kedge fis' and roast um for dinner," said Pomp; and then we sat for some little time in silence, listening for the slightest sound.

Birds we heard from time to time, and now and then the rustle of a squirrel as it leaped from bough to bough, but nothing else till there were, one after the other, four ominous splashings in the river, which gave me a very uncomfortable feeling with regard to crossing to the other side, and I looked at Pomp.

"Dat 'gators," he said shortly. "No 'wim cross de ribber."

Then quite a couple of hours must have passed, and Pomp began to fidget about terribly, making so much noise that if the Indians had been anywhere at hand, they must have heard.

"Hush!" I said; "sit still."

"Can't, Mass' George," he said sharply. "I so dreffle hungly."

"Yes, so am I. What are you going to do?"

"Get down again. Injum no come now."

I hesitated; and as I was heartily sick of waiting, and famished, I made myself believe that our enemies were not pursuing us, and descended quickly to look at my companion.

"What we do now, Mass' George—kedge fis?"

"If we can," I said; "but how?"

"Pomp show Mass' George."

He led on through the thick growth just outside the forest edge, and looking sharply from side to side, soon pitched upon a couple of long, thin, tapering canes, which he hacked off and trimmed neatly, so that they formed a pair of very decent fishing-rods, and he looked at me triumphantly.

"Dah!" he said.

"But where are the hooks and lines?"

Pomp's face was wonderful in its change.

"Wha de hookum line?" he said.

"Yes, you can't catch fish like that."

Scratching the head when puzzled must be a natural act common to all peoples, for the boy gave his woolly sconce a good scratch with first one hand and then the other.

"Dat berry 'tupid," he said at last; "Pomp no 'tink of dat. What we do now?"

I stood musing for a few minutes as puzzled as he was. Then the bright thought came, and I took the lighter of the two canes, cut off the most pliant part, and then tearing my silk neckerchief in thin strips, I split the end of the cane, thrust in the haft of the knife, so that it was held as by a fork, and bound the cane tightly down the length of the knife-handle, and also below, so that the wood should split no farther; and as the knife was narrow in blade, and ran to a sharp point, we now had a formidable lance, with shaft fully twelve feet long.

"There!" I said triumphantly in turn, as I looked at Pomp.

"'Tick um froo de fis?" he said.

"Yes. We must find some deep pool, and see if we cannot spear something, so as to be food for the day."

"Mass' George 'tick um fis, Pomp find um."

I nodded, eager enough to try and get something in the way of food, so that we might be better able to bear our day's journey, for I felt that somehow we must get back; but I always hesitated from starting, lest we should be seen by pursuing Indians, and being recaptured, have no chance of giving the alarm at home.

Pomp was not long in finding a deep hole close under the bank, in whose clear, tree-shaded water I could see about a dozen fish slowly gliding about. They were only small, but anything was food for us then; and introducing my lance cautiously, I waited my opportunity, and then struck rapidly at a fish.

Vain effort! The fish was out of reach before the point of the knife could reach him; and a few more such strokes emptied the hole, but not in the way I intended.

"Find another," I said; and Pomp crept along, and soon signed to me to come.

As he made way for me, and I crept to the edge, I felt a thrill of pleasure, for there, close under the bank, just balanced over some water-weed, was a fine fish about a foot and a half long.

"If I can get you," I thought, "we shall do."

Carefully getting my spear-shaft upright, I lowered the point, and aiming carefully, I struck.

Whether I aimed badly, or the refraction of the water was not allowed for, I cannot say, but there was no result. I only saw a quivering of the surface and the fish was off into the river.

The same result for a dozen more tries, and then Pomp said protestingly—

"I nebber tink dat ob any good."

"But it is good if I could strike one," I said, testily.

"Um on'y tummle off 'gain, Mass' George."

"Never mind; try and find another good hole, I'll do it yet."

He gave his head a rub and went on along the river-side, peering among the overhanging bushes, and one way and another we made a trail that any one could have followed; but likely holes and pools were scarce now, and I was getting hot, faint, and weary, when, after creeping close to the edge of the stream again, Pomp signed to me to give him the lance.

I hesitated for a moment, not liking to give up, but ended by passing the spear; and, taking it, Pomp lay flat down, crept to the edge where the bank overhung the river, as it proved, very gently thrust his eyes beyond, drew back, and quickly picked a good-sized bunch of long grass, which he bound at one end, opened the bunch at the other, and put it on like a cap, the result being that the long grassy strands hung right over his face loosely.

He laughed at me, and crept back again, moving his head slowly to and fro for a few moments, as if to get the occupants of the pool used to his presence.

Then very slowly and cautiously he manipulated the lance shaft, so that it was upright, and holding it with both hands lowered the point down and down till six feet had disappeared, then seven, eight, nine at least; and as I was thinking how deep it must be down there, the long cane became stationary, with the boy's hands holding it above his head.

I stood leaning forward, wondering what luck he would have, and full of hope, for I was too hungry to feel envious and hope that he would miss. But still he did not strike, and the moments glided on till I was getting quite out of patience, and about to creep forward and look down to see how big the fish might be, when, quick as thought, down went the shaft with a tremendous dig, and then, with the cane quivering exceedingly, Pomp seemed to be holding something he had pinned tightly down against the bottom, till its first fierce struggles were at an end.

"Got him?" I exclaimed, joyfully.

"Pomp 'tick knife right froo um," he panted; and then springing up, he rapidly drew the shaft from the water, hand over hand, till, to my intense astonishment, he raised to the bank, muddy, dripping, and flapping heavily, the largest terrapin I had seen, and putting his foot upon it, he drew out the spear, which had transfixed it right in the middle of the back.

"Dah!" he exclaimed; and seizing his capture, he led the way into the forest, where, risking discovery, we soon had a fire of dead sticks and pine-needles blazing merrily over the shell of our terrapin, off which we made at last, if not a good meal, a sufficiently satisfying one to give us spirit for trying to get back home.

Chapter Twenty Nine

"Now, Pomp," I said, after we had each lain down and had a good hearty drink of clear water, "the way to get home is to make a raft and float down the river."

"Don't want raft—want um boat," he said.

"Do you know what a raft is?" I said.

"No, Mass' George."

I explained to him, and he shook his head.

"'Gator come and pick Pomp and Mass' George off."

"We must make it so big that they could not."

"How make big raft?—no chopper to cut down tree."

"We must cut down and tie together bundles of canes," I said, after a long pause, well occupied by thinking. "They will bear us if we lie down upon them. We have a knife; let's try."

It was no easy task to get the knife free, for the threads by which it was bound into the split end of the cane had swollen; but it was clear at last, and selecting a suitable spot where the shore was quite a cane brake, we toiled away cutting and tying together bundle after bundle of canes, till we had six which roughly resembled as many big trusses of straw. These we secured to four of the stoutest canes we could find, passing them through the bands crosswise, and after a good deal of difficulty, and at the risk of undoing our work, we managed to thrust it off the bank into the river, where, to my great delight, upon trying it, the buoyancy far exceeded my expectations. In fact, though we could not have stood upon it, lying down it supported us well, and without any hesitation, after cutting a couple of light poles for steering or directing, we thrust off from the side, and began gliding down the stream.

From that moment it seemed as if our troubles were over, for we had little difficulty in keeping well out from the overhanging boughs, while a thrust or two with our poles enabled us to avoid fallen trees and patches of growth rising from the river shallows.

I soon felt convinced that if the bands we had made would hold out, we should have no difficulty in floating down, for I could recall no rapids or falls likely to give us trouble. Certainly we had seen nor heard neither. Our risks were from the collapse of our raft, from the reptiles that we kept seeing from time to time as we glided slowly on, and from the Indians, whom, as I scanned the bank, I expected moment by moment to see start from the dense growth which fringed the sides with a yell.

If we could have felt secure, the ride down the river would have been delightful, for it was all in the bright sunshine, with a wall of the loveliest verdure on either side. Flowers hung in clusters, or sprang from the moist banks; birds flitted here and there, and every now and then some great heron or crane sprang up with flapping wings and harsh cry at being disturbed while fishing.

But every now and then an excited movement on the part of Pomp told me that an alligator was in sight, sunning himself on a shoal, or where he had beaten down the reedy growth as he had crawled out upon the bank.

Such movements on the boy's part were perilous, the side of the raft going down slowly and steadily, till I forced him to lie still.

"They will not touch us," I said, "unless we are struggling in the water. Do you want to fall in or upset the raft?"

He shuddered, and his eyes rolled a little, but he lay still, and we glided on till we must have gone down a couple of miles, when all at once Pomp uttered a cry.

"Hush!" I said, despairingly. "You will be heard."

"Nebber mind. Quick, Mass' George! Push! Push!"

I could not understand what he meant, but it was evident that something was wrong, and there was no time to ask for an explanation; so I helped all I could to push the raft toward the farther shore, convinced that the Indians were upon us, and that we must seek safety in the forest once again.

It was easy enough to float with the stream, but hard work to make the raft to move as we wished, and we must have gone down fully a hundred yards farther before there was a chance to seize an overhanging branch, and tow the raft to a clear piece of the farther bank, on to which Pomp scrambled at once.

"Quick, Mass' George, quick!" he cried; and leaving me to follow, he disappeared at once in the dense cane and bush.

I was not long in following; and as I got ashore I saw the raft caught by an eddy, as it rose relieved from my weight, and as I plunged into the thicket I had a glimpse of it being carried out into the swift stream.

I was too much excited and hurried to follow Pomp, whom I heard crashing on before me, to pause to think about our retreat being now cut off by water, unless we made a new raft. The Indians must be there within view, I felt; but why did no arrows come; and why did not my companion plunge at once into the forest?

The explanation came directly, as I struggled on, seeing my route marked by trampled down reed and broken twig, for Pomp suddenly shouted—

"I got um, Mass' George."

What had he got? Something eatable, I felt, for he was always hungry; and to obtain this we had lost our raft, and should have all the work to do over again.

"Hush!" I whispered, angrily; "you will be heard."

"Done matter now," came from close at hand, though I could see nothing yet. "Pomp fine um."

I struggled out of the low brushwood, and came into a more open part of the bank, and there stood in astonishment, to find my companion dancing with delight, and pointing to where, six feet above my head, just as it had been left by the subsiding of the water, and on a nearly even keel, was the lost boat, perched among the bushes, and apparently none the worse for its journey.

"Oh, Pomp!" I cried, as excited now as he, "this is a find."

"See juss lit' bit ob um back up dah, Mass' George," he said. "Come try and get um down."

I beat and pressed down the bushes as much as I could, and together we reached the stern of the boat; but as I touched it a fresh thought arose to damp my spirits.

There was the boat, but in what condition was it? It did not seem possible that it could have been drifting about in that flood and left here without damage—a hole made by some jagged projecting tree branch, or a plank started.

"Now den, Mass' George, pull."

I dragged at the stem, and then uttered a warning cry and threw myself back, for the boat was so lightly perched on the bushes that it came down with a rush, and as we started up again, and examined it, as far as I could see it was completely uninjured, and even the oars were in their places beneath the thwarts.

The rest of the journey toward the water was not quite so easy, but we tugged and lifted, and by degrees got it on the few yards farther, and at last had the satisfaction of sending it crashing down into a bed of reedy growth, and springing in to push it onward into the stream, where, once clear of the dense water grasses, it began to glide down easily and well.

Now that the excitement of the discovery and launching of the boat was over, it all seemed to have been a kind of day-dream; and though I took my seat on a thwart, and got an oar over the side, I could hardly believe it real till I recalled that it was possible that our actions had all been watched, and that amongst the trees and bushes of the other side dozens of keen eyes might be aiming arrows at us, and the oar almost dropped from my hand.

Pomp was thinking of our enemies too, for, as he got his oar over the side, and was looking down stream, he exclaimed suddenly—

"Yah! Who 'fraid now? Look, Mass' George, dat big ugly ole 'gator, dah."

"Pomp!" I cried, in an excited whisper; and I half rose to fling myself down, to lie in shelter of the boat's side.

For at that moment, from some distance off, came a cry that I recognised as an Indian yell.

Chapter Thirty

I do not suppose that many who read this have ever heard a Red Indian's cry, and I hope those who have not never will. It was no doubt invented on purpose to scare an enemy, and it answers its purpose thoroughly.

To me it sounded blood-curdling, and a curious sensation ran through me, as if the blood was chilling in my veins. But on thinking of it afterwards, I did not believe that it curdled, and on talking the matter over just before sitting down to write this narrative of my boyish adventures, my doctor said it was all nonsense; that the sensation was produced by the nerves, and that if a body's blood curdled there would be an end of him at once.

Of course the doctor was right, for the effect of that cry was to make me drop down in the boat again, whisper to Pomp to pull, and row with all my might.

Then another yell came from our right, and was answered from the forest, the Indian who shouted evidently being not very far away.

"Hear dat, Mass' George?" said Pomp.

"Yes; pull hard. It is the Indians."

"Well, who car' for old Injum? Dey can't cotch us now."

"Don't be too sure," I whispered. "There may be some of them waiting to shoot at us with their bows and arrows."

Pomp turned his head quickly over his right shoulder to look at the low bushes and reedy plants by the river-bank, and in doing so thrust his oar too deeply down, with the result that he received a blow in the chest, his legs rose up in the air, and his head went down between my legs.

He lay on his back for a moment staring wildly up at me over his forehead, his eyes rolling and his mouth wide.

"Why Mass' George do dat?" he cried.

"I didn't, you stupid little nigger," I cried, angrily. "Get up and mind your oar. You caught a crab. Pull!"

Pomp scrambled back in his place, and began to pull again as hard as he could, for my voice had rather startled him.

"What Mass' George say?" he whispered.

"Pull!"

"Yes, I pull; but what Mass' George say 'fore dat?"

"I said you caught a crab."

"Didn't! It was great big terrapum."

"I mean you put your oar in too deep."

"Den what for say catch um crab? Mass' George say Injum in de bush shootin' at Pomp, and den he look round an' no Injum dah; Mass' George play trick to fright um, and den call poor Pomp 'tupid lil nigger."

"Will you hold your tongue and row?" I whispered fiercely.

"Pomp can't hold um tongue and pull de oar bofe togedder."

"Hush!"

Pow—ow—ow—ow—ow—ow! Came faintly from among the trees, and Pomp turned sharply round, with circles of white showing round the dark part of his eyes; but this time he kept his oar out of the water, and the boat instead of turning toward the side continued to glide swiftly down the stream.

"Dat de Injum?" he whispered.

"Yes. Pull—hard!"

He swung round in his place, and began to row again so sturdily that I had to work hard to keep the boat's head straight; and the stream favouring us, we went on down at a rapid rate, though every now and then I was obliged to whisper to him to easy as we neared some sharp curve or sandbank, to avoid which obstacles I had to keep turning round to look ahead.

We had been rowing steadily like this for some time now without hearing the cries of the Indians, but I did not feel any the more confident, for I knew enough of their habits to think that when they were most silent the greatest danger might be near. The banks glided slowly by us, and we had this great advantage, that even if we slackened speed the boat still travelled fast. But Pomp worked hard, and evidently believing that the danger was entirely past, his spirits rose again and he began to laugh.

"Poor ole Injum," he said; "I berry sorry for um. Poor ole Injum lose um knife. Pomp wonner what um say. How soon we get home now, Mass' George?"

"Oh, it will take hours yet," I replied; and just then I turned my head to see that we were rapidly approaching a ridge of sand right in the middle of the river. I was about to give my oar a vigorous tug, when I noted that the stream divided, and ran in two swift currents on either side of the ridge. As we then were, I saw that the boat would go through the narrower one—the swifter evidently; and at the same moment a pile of wood and dead rubbish on the sandspit ceased to obstruct the view, and to my horror I saw that the little long islet, whose sands were only just above the level of the water, was occupied by a group of seven or eight alligators, the nearest being a monster, the rest varying to the smallest, which was not above three feet long.

I involuntarily ceased rowing and Pomp did the same, just as we were entering the narrow channel, and so close to the sandspit, that the blade of the boy's oar held ready for the next dip swept over the sand.

Pomp was gazing in the other direction, scanning the river-bank; and as I saw what was about to happen, I said in a quick whisper—

"Look out!"

Almost as I spoke, the blade of Pomp's oar swept over the rugged horny coat of the largest alligator, which, like the rest, was sleeping in the hot sunshine perfectly ignorant of our near approach.

The effect was instantaneous. As the boy turned sharply round to look out, the great reptile sprang up, opened its huge jaws, and made a snap at the oar-blade, whisked round its tail, striking the boat, and then made a series of plunges to reach the water on the other side, its actions alarming the rest, which on their retreat made the sandspit seem alive, and the water splash and foam; while Pomp uttered a yell of horror, loosed his hold of his oar, and dived down into the boat, to rise again and stare over the stern as soon as I told him the danger was past.

It was all the work of a few moments, during which I was startled enough, especially when I saw the gaping jaws of the great reptile, and heard the snap it made at the oar-blade; but we were going swiftly by, and mingled with the terror there was something so comic in Pomp's actions, that in the reaction I began to laugh.

This brought Pomp's face round directly, and his reproachful black eyes seemed to ask me what I could see to laugh at.

"Come," I said, "you can't tell me I was playing tricks then.—Why, Pomp, your oar's overboard," I cried as I realised that fact.

"Yes, Mass' George. Dat great 'gator 'wallow um."

"Nonsense!" I cried, as I tried to check the progress of the boat on catching sight of the oar gliding swiftly down stream twenty yards away. "There it is. Wait till it comes close. I'll try and manage to get you near it."

"Dah it am! Whah?"

"There, just off to your left."

"So um are, Mass' George. 'Gator no like um, an' 'pit um out 'gain."

"There: mind! Now then, quick! Catch hold."

I had managed to check the boat enough to let the oar overtake us, and Pomp made a snatch at it, but drew back sharply with a low cry of horror.

"What's the matter now?" I said. "Make haste; you'll lose it."

"Great big Injum down dah," he whispered, hoarsely. "Um want to bite off poor Pomp arm."

"Nonsense! How could an Indian be there?" I said, as we floated on side by side with the oar.

"Injum? Pomp say great big 'gator. You look, Mass' George."

"You said Indian, Pomp," I continued, as I drew in my oar, picked up the boat-hook, and went cautiously to the side to look down into the transparent water, where, sure enough, one of the reptiles was swimming along; but it was quite a small one, and a sharp dig down with the boat-hook sent it undulating away, and I recovered the oar, passing it to Pomp with a gesture, as there arose once more a cry from the forest right away back, and it was answered in two places.

Pomp took the oar and began to row again steadily, staring back at the sandspit, now fast growing distant. Then all at once, as the faint cry arose from the forest—

"Dat not Injum," he cried sharply; "dat fock."

"Fox!" I said, recalling the little jackal-like creatures, of which I had seen one or two that had been shot by Morgan.

"Yes, dat fock. Um shout like dat to noder fock in um wood when um lose umself."

"Yes, but that would be at night," I said, wondering whether he was right.

"'Pose um lose umself in de day. Make um cry?"

"No," I said, thoughtfully. "It is like the cry of the fox, Pomp, but I think it's the Indians making it."

"Why Injum cry out like fock when um can cry like Injum?"

"To deceive any one who hears them."

"What deceive?" said Pomp.

"Cheat—trick."

"Oh!" he said, and we rowed on steadily hour after hour, realising how we must have increased our distance from home in the night.

Sometimes as we swept round one of the river bends we encountered a breath of fresh air, but mostly deep down in that narrow way winding through the forest the heat was intense; and there were times when, as I paused to sweep the perspiration from my face, I felt that I must give up, and lie down at the bottom of the boat.

But almost invariably at these times I heard faintly what I believed to be the Indians calling to each other as they came on through the forest; and in the hope that perhaps after all we had got the start, and would reach home in time to give the alarm, I tugged at my oar again, and so long as I rowed Pomp never for a moment flagged.

But I could not keep his tongue quiet. Now he would be making derisively defiant remarks about the 'gators; then he had something disparaging to say about the Indians; and when I spoke to him angrily he would be quiet for a time, but only to burst out with reproaches at me for calling him a "'tupid lil nigger."

Nothing ever hurt Pomp's feelings more than that term, which seemed to him the very extreme of reviling, and always went straight to his heart.

It was getting toward evening, and a rich orange glow was beginning to glorify the long reach of the river down which we were rowing—sluggishly now, for we were both tired out—when it struck me that I had not heard the cry for some time now, and I made the remark to Pomp.

"No; fock gone asleep now till de moon get up. Den fock get up too, an' holler."

"No, Pomp," I said, "it's the Indians, and they are silent because they are getting near the house now."

"So Pomp get near de house, and don't care for de Injum. He so dreffle hungry."

So was I; but my intense anxiety drove away all that, and I tried to tug harder at the oar, for I knew that we were near home now; familiar trees and corners of the stream kept coming into view, and I was just thinking that very soon I should be able to look behind me and see our landing-place, when a faintly-heard hail came along the river.

We both turned sharply, and Pomp exclaimed in words what I only too gratefully saw—

"Dah de capen an Mass' Morgan in 'noder boat. Wha my fader too?"

I stood up for a moment and waved my hand, and then sat down, and we both pulled our best, after Pomp had grumbled a little, and wanted to let the boat float down alone.

A few minutes later I was holding on to the gunwale of the strange boat in which my father was seated, almost too much exhausted to speak.

"I was getting uneasy about you, my boy," my father said, "for there have been some fresh rumours at the settlement about Indians, and Morgan went round and borrowed this boat; we were coming on to see after you. Why, George, is anything the matter?"

"Yes, father," I panted. "The Indians—they are coming on."

"No," said Pomp sharply, and he struck his hand on the side of the boat to emphasise his words. "Mass' George hear de fock—lose him lil self an holler, and he only tink it de— Ah, look! Look, Mass' George, look! Who dat?"

He pointed back up the steam, where at the edge of the bank that the river swept round previous to passing along the straight reach, there stood two tall figures, their feathers and wild dress thrown up by the bright glare of the setting sun. They were evidently reconnoitring, and though we saw them clearly for a few seconds, the next moment they seemed to have died away.

"Indians," said my father, drawing in his breath with a low hiss; "and we must not neglect this warning. Morgan, I'll get in here with the boys; you go back, make your boat fast at the landing-place, and run up to the house, and bring your wife and Hannibal down."

"But the things in the house, sir?"

"Lives are of more importance than chattels, man," said my father, in his sternest and most military way. "Tell your wife she is to stop for nothing, but to come."

"An' s'pose she won't, sir?" said Morgan sharply.

"Carry her," said my father laconically, as he stepped into our boat and pushed the other off.

"But bring nothing else, sir?" said Morgan, piteously.

"Yes; two guns, and all the ammunition you can carry; but be quick, man, we shall be waiting at the landing-place. The Indians are coming in earnest now. We shall stop till you come, and open fire if it is necessary." My father capped the gun he had brought from the boat. "Stop. Hand me your gun and pouches."

Morgan gave a stroke or two with his oar, and brought the boats alongside of each other again, then handed the gun to me.

"Now then," said my father, "off! Remember, I shall be trying to keep the Indians at bay if they show, and delay on your part may mean the loss of our lives and—your own."

Morgan gave his head a sharp nod, bent to his oars, and my father turned to me, and cried, as if he were addressing a line of men—

"Load!"

Chapter Thirty One

I believe my hands trembled, but I stood up firmly in the boat and charged the heavy piece, making the ramrod leap, as I had been told, examined the priming, and then, in obedience to my father's sign, sat down.

Pomp had taken both oars, and was dipping them gently from time to time, to keep the boat's head straight, and after a long look up the reach, my father sat down too.

"Let's see, George," he said, "we are about a mile above the landing-place, and we must give Morgan plenty of time to get there, up to the house, and back. Hold up your gun, and let the Indians see it if they are watching, and I suppose they are. These bow-and-arrow people have a very wholesome dread of powder."

"But suppose they keep creeping near us under shelter, father," I said, "and shoot?"

"They will in all probability miss; let's hope so, at all events. Come, my lad, you have a gun, and you must play soldier now. Will you lie down under shelter of the boat's side?"

"Soldiers don't lie down," I said firmly, though I wanted to do so very badly indeed.

"Oh, yes, they do sometimes. We will as soon as it is necessary; but what I want to do now, my boy, is to gain time. If we row swiftly to the landing-place, the Indians will come on rushing from tree to tree, and be upon us in a few minutes, for I presume they are in force."

I told him quickly how many we had seen.

"It is a mercy that you went and were taken, George," he said; "it has saved our lives, no doubt. But as I was saying, we want to gain time, and while we sit here slowly drifting down, with these menacing guns pointing in their direction, they will advance very slowly, and keep under cover. If it becomes necessary, I shall have the boat turned, and advance to meet them."

"And then, father?"

"They will retire for a time, not being able to understand so bold an advance, and think that an attack is about to be made upon them from the other side. We must keep them back, and it is to be done by preserving a bold front. They are cruel and treacherous, and can fight well when they think they are in strength over a weak adversary; but from what I learned of those who have had to do with them, they are as cowardly as they are cruel. Look!"

I gazed sharply up the wooded bank of the river, but I could see nothing, and said so.

"No; they were gone directly. They were two spies who had stolen closer up. It means war in earnest now, I am afraid."

He changed his position a little, and examined his gun.

"Mass' goin' shoot dat gun?" said Pomp, excitedly, after watching and listening with all his energy.

"Yes, my lad," said my father, smiling.

"Mass' won't shoot Pomp?"

"No. Attend to the oars, and keep the boat's head straight. Don't speak."

"No, massa. Oh, look, dat dah!"

Pomp's loud exclamation was due to the fact that an arrow came flying from a low clump of bushes nearly two hundred yards away, its reed shaft glistening in the ruddy light, and its wings looking as if of fire, till it dropped without a splash into the river, far away from where we sat.

"Now I should like to return their fire," said my father, "but I am very doubtful about my gun doing any harm at this distance, so we must wait. Pull a little, boy, but very gently, so that they will hardly be able to see that we are doing anything to get away."

Pomp dipped the oars, and I sat with my heart beating, waiting to see another arrow come, but for quite a minute there was no sign.

"Good practice for one beginning a frontier life, George," said my father. "Sweep the bank well, and note the smallest movement of a bough. You see there is no wind to move them now."

"I am watching, father," I said, "but I cannot see anything."

"Pomp see lil bit o' one," came from behind us.

"Where, boy?"

"Dah by dat big tree. See um arm. Going to shoot."

Almost as the words left the boy's lips, an arrow came spinning through the air, describing a good arc, and falling in a direct line with the boat, some twenty yards short.

"That's better," said my father, coolly resting his gun on the stern, and half lying down in the boat. "Hah! I could see that."

I had also seen what appeared to be a quick movement of the bushes a short distance from the edge of the bank, a movement which seemed such as would have been made by an animal dashing through.

The waving of the foliage stopped just by a great swamp oak, and upon this tree I fancied that my father fixed his eye.

"Dah again," said Pomp, excitedly. "Going shoot um bow an' arrow."

Bang!

The boat rocked a little with the concussion, and as the smoke lifted, I saw an arrow drop into the river a long way to our left.

"I don't think I hit him," said my father; "but I disarranged his aim, and it will check him for a bit."

His words proved correct, for though he stood up in the boat to re-charge his piece, and offered a striking object for the Indian's arrows, none came; and as we floated on and on, it began to seem as if the one shot had been enough to scare the enemy. I said so, but my father shook his head.

"No such good fortune, my boy."

"What are you going to do, father?" I said, after some minutes' watching, and thinking how strange it was that my calm, quiet father, who was so fond of his studies and his garden, should in a time of emergency like this prove himself to be a firm soldier, ready to fight or scheme against our dangerous foes.

"Escape to the settlement if we can get safely away."

"But—"

I stopped short.

"Well?" he said.

"I was thinking about the house and garden, the furniture and books, and all our treasures."

"Doomed, I'm afraid, George," he said with a sigh. "We must think about saving our lives. We can build up the house again."

"Build it up again, father?"

"Yes, if it is burnt, and replace our books; but we cannot restore life, my boy. Besides, all these things that we shall lose are not worth grieving over. There, I think we have waited long enough now to give them time, and we are near the landing-place. Pull steadily now, boy, right for the posts."

Pomp obeyed, and the boat glided on, swept round a wooded point, and the landing-place with its overhanging trees was in sight.

"Are they there?" said my father, sharply.

"I can't see them, father."

A sharp stamp with his foot on the thwart of the boat told of the excitement he felt, and made me realise more than ever the peril we were in.

"Pull, boy—pull!" he said.

I sat down in front of Pomp, laid my gun across the thwarts, and placing my hands on the oars, helped with a good thrust at every tug, sending the boat well along, so that in a couple of minutes more we were at the landing-place, where I leaped out, and secured the boat by passing the rope through a ring-bolt.

"Don't fasten it tightly," said my father; "leave it so that you can slip it at a moment's notice. No, no, boy, sit still ready to row."

Pomp, who was about to spring out, plumped down again, his brow wrinkled up, and his twinkling dark eyes watching my father, of whom he stood in terrible awe.

"They ought to have been here; they ought to have been here," said my father, unfastening the other boat, and making a loop of the rope that could be just hung over one of the posts, besides bringing the boat close in.

"I cannot go, George," he said sharply. "This is our only means of escape, and it would be like throwing it away: they ought to have been here."

"Pomp hear um come," cried the boy eagerly; and we both listened, but for a few moments I could make out nothing.

Then as my father was eagerly scanning the edge of the river, gun in hand, on the look-out for the first approach of the Indians, I heard *plod—plod—plod—plod*, and directly after Morgan came into sight laden with the guns and ammunition, followed by Hannibal with a box on his shoulder; and lastly there was Sarah, red-faced and panting, as she bore a large white bundle that looked like a feather-bed tied up in a sheet.

"What madness!" cried my father, angrily stamping his foot. "Quick, Morgan! Quick!"

Morgan broke into a trot, and soon reached us, rapidly placed his load in the boat, and took up one of the pieces.

"How could you waste time by letting that woman come loaded in this ridiculous way?"

"She would bring them, sir; she wouldn't come without."

"No," said Sarah, who came up completely breathless, "I wasn't going to."

"Into the boat," cried my father, "if you value your life!"

Hannibal was already in with his box, and my father tried to drag the bundle from Sarah, but she held on with such tenacity that she was forced in bundle and all.

Hannibal placed the huge white sphere in the stern, where it rose up high and projected far over the sides. Then, in obedience to my father's orders, he seized the oars and sat down.

"Quick, Morgan!" said my father; "be ready to fire steadily as you can if I give the order. Stop!" he cried quickly, as a sudden thought struck him; "pass that box into this boat. There, across the stern, as you have placed that bundle."

The boats were drawn together, and the transfer was made, while my hands grew wet with perspiration as I scanned the edge of the forest, fancying I could hear the breaking and rustling of twigs and leaves.

"Here dey come," said Pomp, huskily, just as my father exclaimed, "Cast off!" and the boats were thrust out into the stream.

It was only just in time, for as our boat was being thrust away with the oar there was a fierce yell, and a score of savages rushed out of the edge of the forest, ran rapidly over the bushy ground between, and the two first sprang into the shallow water, one of them seizing an oar, the other coming further out, and catching at the boat's side with one hand, striking at my father with an axe at the same time.

I felt as if the blow had struck me, so keen was the agony I endured; but relief came on the instant, for the axe edge was warded off by the barrel of the piece my father held, and before the savage could strike again he received the butt of the piece full in his forehead, and dropped back into the water.

Meanwhile the other savage was trying to tear the oar from Pomp's grasp, and he would have succeeded had not the boy drawn the knife he had stuck in his waist, and given the Indian quickly a sharp cut across the hands, making him yell and loosen his hold.

The others were so near that we must have been captured had it not been for the sharp stream which had caught the boat, and was bearing us away.

In the second boat another struggle had taken place, three of the Indians, as I saw at my second glance, making for it; but they fared no better than their companions. Hannibal had already pushed off, and was standing up with one oar in his hand. This he swept round as if it were a huge two-handed sword, and one Indian went down at once; the second caught and clung to the oar, and he too struck at Hannibal with his axe; but the great black caught the handle, gave it a wrench round, tore it from the man's grasp, and I closed my eyes for a moment as I saw what was about to follow. When I opened them again the Indian was floating in the river, and a companion was drawing him to land, while another was helping the Indian who had attacked Morgan, and was struck down by a blow with the gun-barrel.

The boats were now moving fast, and as I saw the Indians all there bending their bows, my father shouted "Fire!" Our three pieces went off nearly simultaneously with a tremendous roar, and when the smoke rose I saw three men on the ground by our landing-place, and the others in full flight for the forest. I stared at these three in horror, when, to my surprise, they leaped up and ran after their companions. But three others lay where their comrades had dragged them half drowned, and stunned by the blows they had received. Those who got up and ran were no doubt knocked down by their companions in their flight and dismay, for I do not think our fire did them any harm. But I was brought to myself by a sharp command to reload.

"Quick! Crouch down!" said my father; and as he spoke a shower of arrows whistled by, fortunately without doing hurt. "Morgan," continued my father, "make a breastwork of that bundle; it will protect you. Hannibal, row straight out, so as to get that bundle between you and the enemy."

The great black's response was a pull or two with one oar, while, in obedience to my father's instructions, Pomp did the same; and I now saw the good of the box placed across the stern, behind which we two sheltered, and kept up as rapid a fire as we could, doing but little harm, for the Indians were well sheltered among the trees, and rarely showed more than a hand and arm with one side of the face, the rest of the body being always hidden behind the trunk of some great tree. But our shots did good to this extent, for whenever the enemy made a determined rush, as if to reach a spot opposite to where the boats glided down stream, a little volley invariably sent them back to cover.

Still by darting from tree to tree, or crawling under the thick bushes, they kept close in our wake, and poor Sarah's encumbrances proved invaluable, the box and huge bundle forming excellent shelter, from behind which we could fire, saving the woman too as she lay right in the bottom of the boat; for the arrows came fast—*whizz, whizz, whizz,* now sticking in the box with a hollow sounding rap, or into the big bundle in the other boat with a dull, thudding sound, till both box and bundle actually bristled with the missiles.

"Keep your head down, my boy," my father kept saying to me. "Only look up when you are going to fire."

This was good advice, but I did not see that he took it to himself, and I kept feeling a curious shrinking sensation as some better-aimed arrow than usual struck the box close to his head.

And so we went slowly on, my father dividing his time between loading, firing, and directing Pomp and Hannibal how to row, so as to keep the boats one behind the other, and diagonally across the stream, so that our sheltering defences might be presented square to the enemy, who followed us along the bank.

I'm afraid—and yet I do not know that I ought to speak like that of a set of savages who were thirsting for our blood—several of the Indians went down severely wounded, not from my firing, but from that of Morgan, for I saw them stagger and fall three times over after his shots. What happened after my father's I could not see, for we were close together, and the smoke obscured everything.

For fully ten minutes this duel between lead and arrow went on, but no one on our side was hurt, though we had some very narrow escapes. I felt one arrow give quite a twitch at my hair as it passed close to my temple, and another went through my father's hat. In the other boat too Morgan kept answering to our inquiries, and telling us that all was right, only that some of the arrows had come, as he termed it, "precious nigh, look you."

"We shall not shake them off," said my father, "till we reach the mouth and get into the big river, when I hope our firing will be heard and put them on their guard at the settlement. So don't spare your shots when we get well out. They will be doing double duty—scaring the enemy and warning our friends. That's right, Pompey, my lad, pull steadily."

"Iss, massa, pull berry 'tead'ly," said the boy, grinning.

"As soon as we get a little farther we will relieve you, my lad; and then, George," he said, turning to me, "we must row hard for the settlement, unless," he added, sadly, "the enemy are before us, and then— Hah!"

I started at the moment when my father uttered that ejaculation, for an arrow dropped between us, and stuck quivering in the thwart, standing nearly upright, as if it had fallen from the clouds.

"They have altered their tactics," said my father. "Look there."

Another arrow fell with a faint *plop* into the river close to the edge of the boat. "They find our breastwork too much for them," said my father; "and they are shooting up right over us, so as to try and hit us that way."

"Oh! Oh! Oh!" came in wild yells of pain from Pomp, as I heard a dull thud just behind me; and turning sharply, there was the boy dancing about in his agony, and tugging to free his hand from an arrow which had fallen and gone right through, pinning it to one of the oars.

"Stop! Don't struggle, boy," cried my father, laying his gun across the box.

"But um hurt dreffle, massa. Oh, Mass' George, lookye here—lookye dah."

The boat was drifting now, and turning slowly side on to the shore, when my father made a sign, and I left my gun lying across the box and crept into Pomp's place, while my father seized the boy's hand, held it tightly, detached the arrow with a tug from where it stuck in the oar, and then as I began to row he pulled Pomp down into the bottom of the boat, the boy sobbing with the pain.

Whizz! An arrow made me duck my head, and I don't know how I looked, but I felt as if I must have turned pale.

"Pull your right, George; pull your right," said my father, coolly. "Now, Pomp, my boy, let me look. Come, be a man."

My father took his hand, and the boy jumped and uttered a cry of pain, but he evidently mastered himself, and rising to his knees, he resigned himself to my father, but doubled his other fist and shook it in the direction of the shore as he shouted fiercely—

"Ah, you wait bit, great big coward—great big ugly Injum tief. You wait bit—Pomp and um fader get hold you, gib you de 'tick. Hab you flog—hab you—Oh! Oh, Mass' Capen, done, done," he cried piteously, changing his tone and appealing to my father, as he saw him take out and open his great gardening knife, which was as sharp as a razor.

"Be quiet," said my father; "I will not hurt you much."

"No, no," whimpered Pomp. "Mass' George, ask massa not cut arm off. Cut off lil toe, Massa Capen; cut off um foot. What poor lil nigger do wif ony one arm?"

"Be quiet, you cowardly little rascal," said my father, smiling, as with one sharp cut he took off the head of the arrow, and then easily drew the shaft back from where it had passed right through Pomp's black hand.

As soon as he saw the arrow-head cut off, and understood what my father meant, Pomp knelt there as coolly as could be.

"Hurt much?" said my father, pressing his finger and thumb on the wound at the back and palm of the boy's hand.

"Um tickle, sah: dat all. Pomp tought you cut um arm off. Hi! You dah," he shouted excitedly; "you wait till Pomp get lil bit of rag round um hand, you see how I serb you. Yah! You big coward Injum tief."

My father rapidly drew his handkerchief from his pocket, tore a piece off, divided it in two, and making the two pieces into little pads, applied one each to the back and front of the boy's hand before binding them securely there.

As soon as this was done, Pomp looked up at him with his eyes sparkling and showing his teeth.

"Pomp not mind a bit," he said. "Here, Mass' George, come here an' shoot um. Let Pomp hab de oars."

"No," said my father. "Sit down there in the bottom of the boat. Hah!"

He seized his gun and fired; then caught up mine, waited till the smoke had risen a little, and fired again, a shot coming almost at the same moment from the other boat.

It was quite time, for the Indians, encouraged by the cessation of the firing, and seeing that some one was wounded, were coming on well abreast of us. But the first shot warned them, and the two which followed sent them once more back under cover, leaving one of their number, to Pomp's great delight, motionless among the canes.

"Ha, ha!" he laughed; "you cotch it dis time, sah. How you like feel de shot, eh? You no 'tick arrow froo poor lil nigger hand again, you no—Oh, Mass' George, look dah!"

For the prostrate man suddenly rolled over, half rose, darted amongst the canes, and we could see by his movements that he was rapidly getting ahead. Then another and another darted to him, and to our misery we saw that they were making for a wooded point a couple of hundred yards ahead.

"Mean to take us between two fires," said my father, who was coolly reloading, in spite of the arrows which kept on dropping down in and about the boat as the Indians sent them right up in the air.

"Morgan!" shouted my father.

"Yes, sir."

"Turn your fire in the other direction, and drive those fellows out of that clump of trees on the point."

"Yes, sir."

The next minute there was a sharp report, and then another.

"That's right, boy," said my father to Pomp, who was eagerly watching him reloading, and handing the ammunition. "Why, George— Ah, that arrow was near; did it hurt you?"

"Only scratched me, father," I said, as I winced a little, for one of the Indians' missiles had fallen, ploughed my leg a little, and pinned the fold of my breeches to the thwart on which I sat.

Pomp crept to my side and pulled out the arrow, examining the hole in the thwart, and saying merrily—

"I no 'tink you want lil bit rag round you, sah."

"No, Pomp; go back and help to load."

Bang—bang! Was heard again from the foremost boat; but arrows came now fast from the wooded point we were approaching.

"How does Morgan manage to load so quickly?" said my father, who kept on talking calmly, as I believe now to encourage us.

"I think Morgan is—I mean I think Sarah is loading for him," I replied, rather confusedly, as the trees and the wooded bank began to grow misty and dim.

"Ah, very likely. Great—"

The one word came in a very different tone of voice, as a wild shriek rang out from the foremost boat, followed by a momentary silence.

"What is it?" said my father, sternly.

His demand was almost accompanied by a couple more shots in close succession.

"One down, sir," said Morgan, coolly; but his voice sounded to me distant and strange.

"Pull hard, George, my lad—your right. We must give that point as wide a berth as we can."

I obeyed as well as I could, and half wondered at the singing noise in my ears.

Bang! Came from the foremost boat, and I seemed to know that Morgan had no one to load for him now, and that poor Sarah had uttered that shriek we had heard. Then I saw that my father was resting his gun on the foremost part of the boat, and he too fired at the woody point, from which arrow after arrow came in quick succession.

And still I rowed hard, with the perspiration streaming down to soak me.

Whizz—thud—whizz—whizz, and an angry ejaculation from my father; I did not know why, nor yet why Pomp uttered a shrill ejaculation, for I was pulling with all my might like one in a dream. I felt once as if I should like to look back and see how near we were to the point that I knew must be close at hand; but everything was getting dark, and a horrible sensation of sickness was coming on. Then the sharp report of my father's piece made me start and pull harder, as I thought, and I tried to look toward the shore, where a wild yelling had arisen; but Pomp's words uttered close to me took my attention, and in a dreamy way I supposed that another Indian had been killed.

Then the boy spoke again in a low whimpering way—

"Massa—massa—look at de blood. Oh, Mass' George! Mass' George!"

Chapter Thirty Two

"Better, my lad?"

I did not answer, but looked in my father's face, wondering what was the matter—why I felt so deathly sick, as I lay back feeling water splashed in my face, and seeing a black hand going and coming from somewhere at my side.

"Come: try and hold up," said my father.

"Yes," I said. "What's the matter?"

"Nothing very serious for you, my lad. We have been playing at soldiers in earnest, that's all, and you have been wounded."

"I, father—I? Ah yes, I remember," I said, essaying to sit up. "But I did try hard to bear it."

"I know—I know, my lad. I didn't know you were hurt like that."

"But—but the Indians?" I said, struggling up, and then catching at my father's hand, for I felt a burning pain run through my leg, and the sick sensation returned.

"We have left them behind," he said, "and are out of their reach for the present. Now sit still, and the faintness will go off. I must go to the other boat."

I looked sharply round, and found that the wooded point was far behind, and also that we were well out of our stream, and floating steadily down the big river toward the settlement, whose flagstaff and houses stood out in the sunshine on our left about a mile away. I saw too that a rope had been made fast to the end of the other boat, and that we were being towed, but by whom, or what was going on there, I could not see for the great bundle in the white sheet which filled up the stern, and was still bristling with arrows.

"Hold hard!" shouted my father, and our boat began to glide alongside of the other. "Can you sit up, my lad?"

"Yes, father," I said.

"Pomp take car' of him, massa."

"Yes, but you are wounded too," said my father.

"Oh, dat nuffum," said the boy contemptuously.

My attention was riveted now on Sarah, whom I could see as the boats were alongside lying crouched back in the bottom, looking deathly white as Morgan knelt by her, holding a handkerchief pressed to her shoulder.

"Now let me come," said my father. "Are both your pieces loaded?"

"I have that charged, sir," he said aloud. Then I heard him whisper, "You don't think she's very bad, do you, sir?"

My father made no reply, but took Morgan's place.

"Go and take an oar," he said then. "Help Hannibal; and try and get us to the fort if you can. Yes," he continued, after shading his eyes with his hand, "the flag is still flying; the Indians cannot be there yet."

"Boat coming," cried Pomp; and to our great delight, we saw a well-manned boat shoot out from the shore, and begin to head in our direction.

My father uttered a sigh of relief, and I heard him mutter "Thank God!" as he proceeded to bandage the poor woman's shoulder as well as he could; and in a momentary glance I saw that an arrow, with the shaft sticking out, broken short off, was still in the wound.

I wondered why my father did not draw it out, but of course said nothing, only sat gazing from the coming boat to the shore, which all seemed peaceful and calm now, there being no sign of Indians or trace of the trouble, save on board our boats.

Just then, as I was reviving more and more, and fully learning the fact that I had received what might have proved a dangerous wound had not the bleeding been stopped, a hail came from the approaching boat, which proved to be Colonel Preston's.

"Anything the matter? What's all that firing about?" cried the colonel, as his boat's way was checked.

"Indians!—attacked!" said my father, speaking excitedly as he waved his hand toward his wounded; and then, "Don't lose a moment. Help us ashore, and there must not be a soul out of the fort in half an hour's time."

There was a disposition in Colonel Preston's manner to make light of the matter, but the sight of the arrows bristling about the defences checked him; and ordering a couple of men out of his own boat to help row ours, he stayed with us to hear the narrative of our fight.

"They are good marksmen too," he said; and then, turning to my father, I heard him whisper, "That woman—wound dangerous?"

"I am afraid so," my father replied. "She must have better attention than I can give her."

I turned to gaze on the poor sufferer lying there close beneath the bundle which she had insisted upon bringing—the great pile of soft things which had been a protection to those with her, but had not saved her from the Indians' arrow; and as I watched her I forgot my own pain and suffering, and thought of how good and kind she had always been to me in spite of her quaint, rather harsh ways; and the great hot tears came into my eyes, to make things look dim and misty again, as I thought of my father's words.

A sharp look-out was kept, and the colonel and his men armed themselves with some of the pieces we had in the boats; but the Indians were in the forest right at the back of the settlement, and had not kept along the bank when we reached the great river.

Quite a little crowd was awaiting our coming at the wharf, and as soon as the news spread, the excitement was tremendous; but almost before poor Sarah had been carried up to the great block-house, and I had limped there, resting on Hannibal, a bugle had, rung out, and having been drilled by the General in case of such emergency, men, women, and children, followed by the black slaves, ran scurrying to the entrance-gates, carrying such little household treasures as they could snatch up in the hurry.

As the women and children took refuge inside the strong palisades, the able-bodied men formed up ready outside, all well-armed; and looking a thoroughly determined set, as they were marched in, guard set, and ammunition served out.

The military training of many of the settlers stood them in good stead, while the General, who the last time I saw him was superintending his slaves in the cotton-field, was hurrying about now giving his orders; and in an amazingly short time scouts were sent out, arrangements were made for barricading the gates, and every musket that could be procured was stood ready to battle with the savage foe.

Colonel Preston and my father were, I soon saw, the General's right-hand men, and each had his particular duty to do, my father's being the defence of the gates, just outside which I was standing in spite of my wound, Pomp being close at hand, ready, with several other of the black boys, to fetch ammunition, to carry messages, and, with the guarding force outside the gates at the present, being sent to first one and then another of the abandoned houses, to bring out valued articles, such as could be hurriedly saved.

I was in a good deal of pain, but everything was so exciting that I could not find it in my heart to go into the great barrack-like wooden fort in the centre of the palisaded enclosure, but stood watching the preparations, and thinking how rapidly the settlement had increased since we came.

One thing I heard over and over again, and that was the people bemoaning their fate at having to leave their comfortable houses just as everything had been made homely and nice, to be pillaged and burned by the Indians.

"And they'll pillage and burn our place," I thought, "perhaps the first." And I was thinking bitterly of all this, and that we had far more right to complain than the rest, when Pomp came strutting up with his arm in the loose sling, of which he seemed to be very proud.

He stopped short as he came quickly up, having been summoned away a few minutes before; and now he pointed at me, and turned to a quiet, keen-looking youngish man, who wore a sword, but had his pockets stuffed full of bandages and bottles, for I heard them chink.

"Dat Mass' George, sah," he cried.

"Ah, that's right. Your father wished me to examine your wound."

"Are you a doctor?" I said eagerly.

"Well, yes—a surgeon."

"Come with me, then," I cried. "There's some one who was wounded in one of our boats."

"The woman? Yes, I have seen her and attended to her. Now then, quick, my lad. Lean on me, and let's see about you."

I limped beside him to the part of the block-house set apart for such troubles, and after giving me no little pain, he said—

"There, you can sit somewhere and load guns. You will not hurt now."

"It's not dangerous then?" I said.

"Not at all; but if it had not been sharply attended to by your father you would have bled to death."

"And how is our Sarah?" I said, eagerly.

"If you mean Captain Bruton's housekeeper, she is badly wounded, but I have removed the arrow-head, and I think she will do. I suppose you are Master George?"

"Yes."

"Then as soon as you can you must go and see the poor woman. She was talking constantly of you, and begged me to send you if we met."

I thanked him, and left him emptying his pockets of strips of linen, threads, a box of something that made me think about pistols in the case at home, and then of some bottles, all of which he laid about in the most orderly manner, and I left him with a shudder, as I thought of what they were for.

As soon as I got outside I was accosted by Pomp, who came up to me, saying—

"Leg quite well now?"

"No; nor likely to be, Pomp."

"Mass' George better wear um in fling like Pomp arm. Missie Sarah want Mass' George."

He took me to where the poor woman lay, very white and exhausted, but she brightened up as soon as she saw me approach, and the black nurse who was attending to her drew back.

"Ah, Sarah," I exclaimed, as I went to her side, "I am sorry to see you like this."

She paid no heed to my words of condolence, but caught me by the wrist.

"Where is that box?" she said eagerly.

"The box? The one Hannibal carried down?"

"Yes; where is it?"

"I don't know," I said.

"What? You don't know? Oh, Master George!"

"It was brought up from the boat, and put in the enclosure somewhere."

"Thank goodness," she said with a sigh.

"And the bundle?" she suddenly exclaimed.

"Ought you to worry about such things now?" I asked. "What does it matter?"

"Matter?" she gasped.

"Yes. Do you know your waiting to get those things made us nearly caught by the Indians?"

"If it did, they saved you all from being shot by them as I was with that dreadful arrow."

"Well—yes, they did keep off the arrows; but if you had been quicker we should not have been shot at. You shouldn't have stopped to worry about your clothes. My father would have paid for more."

"And me so weak and ill, Master George, and you to reproach me like that," she said, with the tears brimming over on to her cheeks.

"Nonsense!" I said, taking her hand, to feel her cling to mine affectionately. "I was not reproaching you, and we are all safe, and nothing to mind."

"Nothing to mind? Ah, my dear, think of what our poor house will be like when we get back."

"I don't think I will," I said dryly; but she did not heed, and went on—

"It was bad enough after that dreadful flood. What will it be now? And so much pride as I took in it, and such a home as it had become. And then, my dear, for you to go and think that I should keep those two waiting while I got together things of my own."

"Well, you know you did," I said, laughing.

"For shame, Master George! That box has got everything in that I knew you would like to save."

"Oh, Sarah!"

"And in that bundle is all the best of the linen, and right in the middle, your poor dear father's uniform."

I did not know which to do—to laugh at the poor woman for her kindly but mistaken thoughts, or to feel affected, so I did neither, but pressed her hand gently, told her she must sleep, and rose to go; but she clung to my hand.

"You'll take care, and not go into danger," she said. "You have been hurt enough."

"I'll try not," I said, as she still clung to my hand, looking wistfully at me. I seemed to understand what she meant, stooped over and kissed her, and made her cry.

"Poor old nurse!" I said to myself as I limped out, and across the enclosure, where the people were gathered in knots discussing the possibility of an attack. In one part all the blacks were together—the women and the younger boys; in another part the ladies with their children; while on the rough platforms erected at the corners of the great palisade sentries were stationed, keeping a vigilant look-out; and I now saw that to every white man there were two armed blacks, and I could not help thinking that we should all be massacred if the blacks sided with the savages against those who had made them their slaves.

At one of these corners I saw that our Hannibal was placed, his great bulk and height making him stand out prominently from his companions; and feebly enough, and with no little pain, I went towards him, thinking very little of my injury in my boyish excitement, though had I been older, and more given to thought, I suppose I should have lain up at once in the temporary hospital.

I signed to Hannibal to come to me, and the gentleman mounting guard with him giving permission, I took him aside.

"Well, Han," I said, as he smiled at me in his quiet, grave way, "you've got a gun, and are going to fight then?"

"Yes, Mass' George, going to fight."

"And will the other people fight too?"

"Yes; all going to fight," he said. "Capen say must fight for us, Hannibal, and Hannibal going to fight for capen and Mass' George."

"But—" I checked myself, for it seemed to come to me like a flash that it would be foolish to ask the question I intended about the blacks being faithful. "It would be like putting it into their heads to be false," I said to myself; and then, as the great fellow looked at me inquiringly, I continued aloud—

"Try and protect my father if you can, Han."

He gave me a quick look, and the tears stood in his eyes.

"Han die for capen and Mass' George," he said.

At that moment there was a bustle and excitement at the gate, and I tried as quickly as my injury would allow to join the group who were hurrying that way.

Chapter Thirty Three

It was the scouts coming back from different directions, with the same report that no enemy was in sight, though they had penetrated in one or two instances right to the forest.

"Isn't a false alarm, is it, Captain Bruton?" said one of the newer settlers. "Two of us went right to your little plantation."

"Well?" said my father, eagerly.

"Well, sir, you were not at home, so we did what I hope you approve of—treated ourselves as you in your hospitality would have treated us. We sat down, ate and drank, and after we were refreshed we came back, but we saw no enemy."

I felt hot and cold with indignation as I listened to this man's cavalier treatment of my father, and to see that many of those present were ready to join this scout in believing it to be a false alarm.

"I am glad, sir, that you have returned in safety to make your report," said my father, coldly.

"Oh, come, Winters," said Colonel Preston, warmly, "if you had seen those boats bristling with arrows you would not think our friend Bruton had been crying wolf."

"And if he will go into our temporary hospital he will see one of the wounded lying there seriously injured."

"But I do not want to cast doubts on Captain Bruton's report."

"Then why did you try, sir?" I said hotly. "Ask the doctor if it was a sham wound from an arrow that I got in my leg."

"George!" said my father, sternly, "remember what you are."

"I do, father," I said vehemently; "but this man seemed to think you had not spoken the truth."

"No, no," said the settler, flushing up, "only that he might have been deceived."

"I only wish you had been tied up for hours to a tree as I was, sir," I said, "expecting to be killed by the Indians. I believe even now you can't believe it is true."

"Hush!" said my father, sternly. "I'm afraid, gentlemen, that though nothing has been seen of them, the Indians are hiding in the forest, ready to descend upon us at what they consider a favourable opportunity, and I beg, I implore, for your own sakes—for the sake of all whom you hold dear, not to treat what I have said as being exaggerated."

"We shall not, Bruton," said the General firmly, after standing listening in silence all through. "I have plenty of faith in my young friend, your son, and you may rest assured that I am not going to treat what has taken place as a false alarm. Gentlemen, to your posts. Colonel Preston, the gate must be closed at once, and every other man will remain under arms till ten to-night, when the second half will relieve them. Gentlemen, I consider that the siege has begun."

The evening came in dark and gloomy, and night fell as if almost at once. All was still but the faintly-heard lapping of the water on the strand, and the customary croaking and hollow bellowing from the forest; and it seemed to me, feverish and ill at ease now, that a feeling of awe had come upon the occupants of the enclosure, who were seated about in groups of families, discussing their strange positions in whispers, and waiting at the first alarm to obey the General's command, and take shelter in the great block of wooden buildings constituting the fort—a building which had been gradually enlarged as the settlement had increased, so that, in addition to shelter and protection, there might be ample room for magazines, armoury, and stores.

I was seated with Pomp and my father, where we had partaken of the food that had been served out, thinking of my bed at home, and of how dearly I would have liked to be lying there instead of upon the hard ground, when an alarm was given, and the officers, my father amongst them, hurried up to the fort to ascend to the roof, and watch the glow which had suddenly begun to appear in the southwest.

I had followed my father and stood by him, as I heard the General say sharply, in answer to a remark made by some one of those present, upon whose faces the faint glow was reflected—

"Forest fire, sir? No; I am afraid it is—"

"My house, gentlemen," said my father, calmly. "The attack has begun."

A dead silence followed my father's words, and it was almost a minute before the General said gravely—

"Yes, Bruton, the attack has begun, and in a way I dreaded. Well, we must beat it off. I am sorry that your pleasant home should be one of the first to fall a victim to the enemy; but as it was built up, so it can be built up again. There will be plenty of willing hands to help one of our most trusty brothers."

A murmur of warm assent followed this remark, and then the General spoke again.

"Is Mr Winters here?" he said.

"Yes, General."

"What have you to say, sir, now?"

"That I beg Captain Bruton's pardon, sir; and that I will be one of the first to help restore his house, if it please God I live through the trouble that is to come."

"Thank you, Mr Winters," said my father, quietly. "If we are staunch to each other I have no fear for the result."

"Look—look!" came in a low murmur, and my heart sank, for it seemed so piteous to see the bright glare rising over the forest, as the poor house over which so much pains had been taken seemed, in spite of the distance, to be sending up wreath after wreath of golden smoke, while for a short time there was a ruddy light spreading high up into the sky.

But it all faded out as rapidly as it had arisen, and I went down into the enclosure, to stumble soon after upon Morgan, who said grimly—

"Didn't think after that soaking, look you, she would have burnt out so quick, Master George."

"Oh, don't talk about it, Morgan," I said. "There, I must lie down now; I am too weak and tired to stand."

"Come this way then, my lad, and lean on me," he said gently; and he helped me to where I could see something white lying on the ground.

It was the great bundle Sarah had made, and close by it lay Pomp fast asleep.

"Burned so quickly after the soaking it had had," seemed to be buzzing in my brain, and the ruddy glow flashed up before my eyes once more; but only in imagination, for I believe that as my head touched that great soft bundle, regardless of danger from tomahawk or arrow, I went off fast asleep, and slept on hour after hour, nor opened my eyes again till it was broad day.

Chapter Thirty Four

It was a miserable scene upon which I gazed, in spite of its being a bright clear morning; but as I grasped where I was, and shook off the drowsy confusion, there was a feeling of thankfulness in my heart, for the dark night had passed away, and we had not been attacked by the Indians.

But the moment I had felt more cheerful, down came a depressing cloud, as I remembered our row for life, our narrow escape, and the reflection of the fire I had seen.

"Poor old house!" I sighed to myself, for it was so terrible that the beautiful little home should have been utterly destroyed; and it all seemed to come up before me with its high-pitched gable ends, the rough pine porch, the lead-paned windows that came over from England; and as I saw it all in imagination once more, I fancied how the passion-flowers and other creepers must have looked crisping and curling up as the flames reached them; and what with my miserable thoughts, the stiffness I felt from my previous day's exertions, and the pain from my little wound, if ever I had felt horribly depressed, I did then.

"Mass' George hungly?" said a familiar voice; and there was Pomp's contented face before me, as he came up hugging to him some slices of bread.

"No," I said, ill-humouredly, "I can't eat; my leg hurts me so."

"Pomp can," he said; "and him hand hurt too. Missie Morgan want to see Mass' George."

I took one of the pieces of bread Pomp gave me, and began to eat mechanically as I walked across the enclosure by the various little groups of settlers and their families, to where my father was busy with the other officers superintending the construction of a barricade outside the gate, so as to divide the Indians in case of an attack, and force them to come up to the entrance one by one.

"Ah, my boy," said my father, quickly, "how is the leg?"

"Hurts," I said, in an ill-used tone.

"Naturally," he cried with a laugh. "There, don't be down-hearted about a little pain. I came and had a look at you, but you were asleep. There, do you see how we are getting ready for your Indian friends? We hope to give them such a severe lesson that they will leave us alone in future."

"Then you think they will attack us, father?" I said. "Some one just now told me that all was quiet, and that the Indians had gone."

"That is the very reason why I think they will attack us, my boy, and the sooner the better, George. It must come, and I should like them to get their sharp lesson and go; for I want to hang this up for an ornament or to turn it into a pruning-hook."

He touched his sword as he spoke, and turned to Morgan, who came up.

"How is she?"

"Doctor says she's very feverish, sir, but he thinks she is going on all right."

"I am very, very sorry, Morgan," said my father, sadly. "I feel as if I were to blame for bringing you people out to this wilderness."

"I teclare to cootness, sir," began Morgan, in a high-pitched Welsh fashion; but he checked himself and smiled. "There, sir, don't you talk like that. Wilderness? Why, it's a pleasure to do a bit of gardening here. See what rich deep soil it is, and how the things rush up into growth."

"Very poor consolation for your wife, Morgan," said my father, dryly. "All that does not make her wound the more bearable."

"Bah! Nonsense, sir! She don't mind. Why, as she said to me just now, she wouldn't have got a wound from an Indian's arrow if she had stopped at home, but the knife might have slipped, and she might have cut herself, or upset a pot of boiling water over her, or failed down the cellar steps and broken a dish and run a piece into her side."

"Well, that's good philosophy, Morgan, and very comforting to me. What do you say, George, are you sorry you came?"

"No, father, not at all," I replied, for unwittingly I had finished the big slice of bread, and felt all the better for the food. "I only wish I were a man, and could fight."

"Don't wish that, my lad," he said quickly. "There is nothing more glorious in life than being a boy. But there, I have no time to waste in preaching to you about that," he said, laughing. "It would be labour thrown away. No boy can believe it. He has to grow into a man, and look back: then he does. There, don't worry yourself till your leg is better, but do any little thing to be useful, and if an attack is made, keep with Morgan. You can load."

"Yes, I can load," I said to myself, as I limped off with Pomp following me, looking very proud of his hand being in a sling, and we went into the part of the block-house where poor Sarah was lying.

As I crossed the enclosure I seemed to understand now why it had been contrived as it was to form an outer defence, which, if taken, only meant that the enemy had a more formidable place to attack, for the block-house seemed to my inexperienced eyes to be impregnable.

As I quietly entered the place, I encountered the doctor.

"Ha!" he said; "come to see me?"

I explained that I had come to see our housekeeper.

"Asleep," he said. "Don't disturb her. Let's have a look at your wound."

He drew me into his rough room, and gave me no little pain as he rebandaged my leg, Pomp standing by and looking on.

"Oh, that's all right, my lad," said the doctor. "Smarts, of course, but you'll soon mend up. Very different if it had gone into your chest. Now, Ebony, let's look at your hand."

"Pomp, sah," said the boy with dignity, "not Eb'ny."

"Oh, well then, Pomp. Now then. How's the hand?"

"On'y got lil hole in um, sah. Hurt lil bit. Oh! Hurt big bit, you do dat."

"Yes, I suppose so," said the doctor, examining and rebandaging the wound. "There, that will soon be well if you do not use it. Well, young Bruton, so they burnt you out, did they, last night?"

"Yes," I said, bitterly.

"Oh, never mind. You heard what was said. Well, let's go and see what they are doing. We're non-combatants, eh?"

We walked out into the open square, after the young doctor had admonished the black woman who had been appointed the first nurse to be watchful and attentive to her patient.

There was something going on down by the gate, and I forgot all about the pain in my leg as I accompanied the doctor there, continuing my breakfast on the second slice of bread Pomp handed to me.

We soon learned what caused the bustle. A strong party of well-armed scouts was out in the direction of the forest, which lay some distance back from the block-house now, as clearing after clearing had been made, and turned into plantations; and these scouts, with a second line in support, were ready to give the alarm and arrest the first attack, their orders being to fall back slowly to the gate, so that ample time would be given at the alarm of the first shot for the busy party now being sent out to retreat and get under cover. For now that every one was safe, it had been decided to try and bring in, as far as was practicable, the most valuable things from the nearest houses.

I was not long in mounting to a good place inside the great palisade, where I could command a view of what was going on, and soon saw that a couple of lines of men had been made with military precision, extending from the gate to the General's house, which had been voted the first to be cleared; and between these lines, under the command of Colonel Preston, a strong body of the slaves—men only at first, but as the work went on women too—were soon going and coming, bearing the most valuable of the household chattels, and these were so stacked in the centre of the enclosure that they would be safe so long as the palisade kept the enemy at bay, and would afterwards act as a line of defence.

In little over half an hour another house was treated in the same way, and all through that day the work went on, till a goodly stack of the best of the things had been brought in, along with stores of provisions, that in the first hurry had been left behind. As this went on the people who had been sick at heart and despondent began to look more hopeful, and family after family had their goods arranged so that they were able to make comfortable bivouacs out in the middle of the square; but these were all arranged under the orders of the General and his officers, so as to form places of defence, to which the defenders of the palisade could flee and be under cover, the whole of the new barricade being arranged so that a way was left leading up to the main entrance of the block-house.

I grasped all this from my position of looker-on, Pomp never leaving my side, and asking questions which I tried to answer, so that he could understand.

And he did comprehend too, much better than I should have expected, for toward evening, after the day had passed, with the scouts relieved twice over without having seen the slightest token of Indians being near, all at once he said to me—

"When Injum come an' shoot an' get over de big fence, all dat make great big fire."

My father's words about the great enemy we had to fear came back to me at this, and it was with a curiously uncomfortable feeling that I left my look-out place for the second time to go and partake of the food that had been prepared.

For the garrison of the fort were rapidly settling down to make the best of their position, and all was being done as to the serving out of food with military precision, the General having drilled his followers in the past, so that they might be prepared for such an emergency as this; and it was quite wonderful how soon the confusion and disorder of the first hours had changed to regular ways.

And now the night would soon be here—a time looked forward to with the greatest of anxiety by all.

The scouts were called in by sound of bugle, and at sundown the gates were barricaded, and sentries placed all round our defences. Fires were put out, and as darkness fell, and the customary chorus of the reptiles arose from the forest and distant swamps, a curious feeling of awe came over me where I sat watching by my father, who, after a long and arduous day's work was sleeping heavily, Morgan close at hand, with Pomp and Hannibal too.

I could not sleep, for there was a dull, gnawing pain in my wound; and so I sat in discomfort and misery, thinking that though the sentries were all on the watch, the place would not be so safe now that my father was asleep.

The moon was hidden, but the stars shone down brightly, and I sat back, leaning against Sarah's big bundle, in which some of the arrows were still sticking, gazing up at the spangled heavens, listening to the bull-frogs, and thinking how far off they sounded as compared to when I had heard them at home.

I was listening and wondering whether the Indians would come, when I heard a rustling sound close by, and directly after a low muttering. But I did not pay any heed, thinking that Morgan or one of the blacks had turned in his sleep; but the noise came again and again, and then there was a loud ejaculation, and directly after I heard a familiar voice exclaim—

"Bodder de ole han'! Oh, how um do hurt!"

"Can't you sleep, Pomp?" I whispered, as I crept softly to his side.

"Dat you, Mass' George?"

"Yes; I say, can't you sleep?"

"Yes, Mass' George. Pomp can't sleep ebber so, but dis 'tupid han' won't let um."

"Does it hurt?"

"Yes. Big hot fly in um keep goin' froo. Pomp goin' take off de rag."

"No, no; let it be; it will soon be better. Go to sleep."

"Han' say no go sleep. Let's go an' try find de coon."

"No, no; we are not at home now. We can't go out of the fort."

"Out ob de fort?"

"Well, outside of the big fence."

Pomp gave a little laugh.

"Why, Pomp go over easy 'nuff."

"But it's against orders," I said. "Here, I can't sleep either. Let's go and have a talk to the sentries."

Pomp jumped up at once, and without waking the others, we walked slowly to the gate, where one of the sentries challenged us and let us go on, after recognising me, the man saying with a laugh—

"That anybody with you, sir?"

"Yes," I said; "our boy Pompey."

"Oh! Shouldn't hardly have thought it. Looks like a bit o' the black night out for a walk in a pair o' white cotton drawers."

"Him laugh at Pomp," said the boy, as we went on.

"Yes; it was only his fun."

"But what um mean 'bout de dark night in cottum drawer?"

"Oh, nothing. Nonsense!"

"Yes, nonsense; Pomp know better. Night can't wear cottum drawer. All 'tuff."

"Hush! Don't talk so loud."

"Den why say dat, an' make fun ob poor lil nigger? I know dat man. Wait bit; I make fun ob him, an' Mass' George an' me laugh den."

"Will you be quiet, Pomp?"

"Yes; Pomp be ebber so quiet. Wait till laugh at him."

"Who goes there?" came from just ahead, out of the darkness.

"Mass' George an' me," said Pomp, promptly.

I hastened to give the word, and we were allowed to pass on, to be challenged again and again, till we reached the part of the palisade on the farther side of the block-house.

Here the sentry proved to be one of the men who had rowed out to us in Colonel Preston's boat; and as he asked about my wound and Pomp's hand, we stopped by him where upon the raised platform he stood, firelock in hand, gazing over the great fence toward the forest.

"So your hurts wouldn't let you sleep, eh?" he said. "Well, we must pay the Indians off for it if they come nigh; but it's my belief that they won't."

Then he fell to questioning me in a low tone about my adventures, and I had to tell him how Pomp and I escaped.

"I should have liked to have been with you, my lad," he said. "I'm not fond of fighting; had too much along with Colonel Preston; but I should have liked to have been with you when the arrows were flying."

"I wish you had been," I said.

"Do you? Well, come, I like that; it sounds friendly. Yes, I wish I'd been there. The cowards, shooting at people who've been soldiers, but who want to settle down into peaceable folk, and wouldn't interfere with them a bit. I only wish they'd come; I don't think they'd want to come any more."

"That's what my father says," I observed. "He thinks the Indians want a good lesson."

"So they do, my lad, so they do. Let's take, for instance, your place, which they burned down last night. Now what for, but out of sheer nasty mischief! There's plenty of room for them, and there's plenty of room for us. If they think they're going to frighten us away they're mistaken. They don't know what Englishmen are, do they, little nigger?"

"How Pomp know what de Injum tink?" said the boy, promptly.

The man turned to me and gave me a nudge, as he laughingly continued, in the whisper in which the conversation was carried on—

"Ah, well, they don't know, but if they'd come, I think we should teach them, for every one here's fighting for his home, without thinking about those who are fighting for their wives and children as well. You don't understand that yet, squire."

"I think I do," I said. "I suppose a man would fight for his wife and children in the same way as I would try and fight for my father."

"Well, suppose it is about the same. You'll have to fight some day, perhaps."

"Mass' George fight dreffle," put in Pomp. "Shoot lot of Injum."

"Nonsense, Pomp!" I said, hurriedly.

"Not nonsense. Pomp see um tummle down when. Mass' George shoot um."

"Why, you didn't fire on the Indians, did you, squire?" said the man.

"Lot o' times," said Pomp, quickly.

The man let his firelock go into the hollow of his left arm, and he shook my hand warmly, as Pomp stood staring over the fence into the darkness.

"I like that," he said, as I felt very uncomfortable and shrinking. "But then I might have known it. Your father and Colonel Preston didn't hit it very well together, but the colonel always said your father was a very brave officer, quiet as he seemed—and like father, like son. Feel chilly?"

"No," I said.

"Well, it isn't cold, but after being so hot all day it feels a bit different. Heigho! I shouldn't at all mind having a good sleep. One gets tired of watching for nothing."

"Sit down and have a sleep," I said. "I'll hold your gun and keep guard."

"Will you, my lad?" he said, eagerly.

"Yes; I can't sleep, and I'll wake you directly if there is anything wrong."

"Come, that's friendly," said the man. "I like that, and I'd give anything for an hour's sleep. Catch hold; I'll lie down here. You'll be sure and call me?"

"You may trust me."

"Bah!" cried the man in an ill-used tone, and snatching back his firelock, "that's done it."

"What is the matter?" I said, wonderingly.

"You said you may trust me."

"Yes; I did."

"That did it. It's just what I said to the colonel when he asked me if I could keep on sentry without going to sleep."

"But you would not go to sleep without leaving some one else to watch."

"No," he said, sternly, "and I won't skulk. I've been digging and planting so long that I've forgotten my soldiering. No, sir, a man who goes to sleep at his post when facing the enemy ought to be shot, and," he added with emphasis, "he deserves it."

"Here um come, Mass' George," whispered Pomp just at that moment.

"What—to relieve guard?" I said, quickly, as I thought of the sentry's mistake.

"No, Mass' George, de Injum."

Chapter Thirty Five

The sentry craned his neck forward over the great fence staring out into the gloom, and I followed his example, my heart beating heavily the while, the regular throbs seeming to rise right up to my throat in a way that was painful; but I could see nothing. There was the great star-specked sky reaching down towards earth, and ending suddenly in a clearly defined line which I knew was the edge of the forest beyond the plantations, which all lay in darkness that was almost black.

I strained my eyes, and held my breath, looking and listening, but could make out nothing, and at last I placed my lips close to Pomp's ear.

"Where are they?" I said.

"Dah!"

As he uttered that one word he stretched out his black hand, pointing straight away toward the forest; but still I could see nothing, and there was not a sound.

At that moment the sentry laid his hand upon my shoulder, and said softly, "Is he playing tricks with us?"

"No," I answered; "he thinks he sees them. His eyes are wonderful by night."

"Well, mine are not, for I can see nothing or hear anything either."

"Are you sure, Pomp?" I whispered.

"Yes; sure," he said. "Big lot of Injum coming to fight."

"Hadn't you better give the alarm?" I said to the sentry.

"I can't give the alarm till I'm certain there's danger coming," he said, rather sulkily. "I haven't got eyes like a cat, and I don't know that he can see them yet."

I could not help sympathising with the man as he continued—

"'Spose I fire," he said, "and the enemy don't come on; nobody has seen them, and nice and stupid I should look."

"But Pomp says he's sure."

"I'm not," said the man, gruffly.

"Be ready then, and fire the moment they begin to make a rush," I said, excitedly. Then, turning to the boy, I whispered, "Now then; tell me once more, can you see the Indians?"

"Yes, dah," he said, quietly.

"You are sure?"

"Yes, suah. Dey come now. Let Pomp shoot."

"No, no; come with me," I said, catching hold of his arm. "Let's run to my father."

The boy was so accustomed to obey me, that he left the place directly, and hurried with me across the enclosure in and out among the camping groups, to where our few poor belongings lay, and I at once awakened my father.

"Pomp has seen the Indians coming on," I said.

He started up, and so dull and heavy had been his sleep that he did not understand me for the time.

"The Indians, father," I said.

He sprang up on the instant then, and felt for his sword.

"You say the boy saw them?"

"Yes, coming on. We were with one of the sentries."

"But he has not fired. I should have heard."

"No, father, he would not believe Pomp could see them."

"Pomp could see um—big lots," said the boy.

"That is enough," said my father. "Tell the bugler—no; we will not show them that we know," he said. "Come with me."

We followed him to where the General was lying on a blanket or two in the midst of his possessions, and he was on his feet in an instant giving his orders, which were conveyed here and there to the various officers, from whence they spread to the men so rapidly and silently that in a few minutes, almost without a sound, a hundred well-armed defenders of the fort were on their way to the fence in twenty little squads, each of which reinforced the sentries, and stood waiting for the attack.

So silent and unchanged was everything when I played the part of guide, and led my father and the General to where we had been watching, that my heart sank, and I felt guilty of raising a false alarm. Then I half shrank away as I heard the General question the sentry, and he replied that he had neither seen nor heard anything. Just then my father turned to me.

"Where's the boy?"

"Here, Pomp," I whispered; but I looked round in vain, and after a few minutes' search I was fain to confess that he had gone.

"It is some trick," whispered my father, with suppressed anger. "I cannot hear a sound."

"No; I feel sure he was in earnest. He certainly believed he saw the Indians."

My father turned to the General, and they conversed together in a low voice for some minutes, during which I stood there feeling as if I were wrong, and forgetting that even if I were it was only a case of being over anxious in our cause.

"No, no," I heard the General say quietly; "don't blame the boys. Of course it is vexatious, and seems like harassing the men for nothing; but it has its good side, for it proves how quickly we can man our defences. Well, what do you say—shall we go back to our beds? There seems to be no danger. Ah, here is Preston. Well, have you been all round?"

"Right round, sir, and there does not seem to be anything moving. A false alarm, I think."

"Yes," said the General, "a false alarm, and— What is it?"

My father had caught his arm in a strong grip, and pointed over the palisade.

"I don't know what it is," he whispered; "but something is moving out yonder, a hundred yards away."

Amidst a dead silence every eye was fixed in the direction pointed to by my father; but no one else could make anything out, and the General said—

"No; I cannot see it."

"Are you sure?" whispered my father. "George, are you there?"

I replied in a whisper too, and crept to his side.

"Look. Can you make out anything?" he said.

I looked long and intently, and was obliged to answer—

"No."

"Quick! Try and find that boy," said my father, angrily now. "He ought to have been here."

Bang! bang! Then report after report, followed by a volley quite from the other side of the enclosure; and, horrible as it seemed, followed as it was by a burst of yells, I felt my heart leap with satisfaction.

There was a rush being made for the spot whence the firing had come; but my father's voice rang out, calling upon the men to stand fast, and it was well that his order was promptly obeyed, for almost immediately after there was a whizzing sound that I well knew, accompanied by a sharp series of pats as of arrows striking wood, and we knew that the Indians were attacking on our side too.

Then followed the quick firm command, and the darkness was cut by the flashes of a dozen fire-locks, whose reports went rolling away, to be echoed by the great trees of the forest beyond the clearings.

Then nothing was heard but the quick beating and hissing of the iron ramrods in the guns, while I stood close under the shelter of the fence, listening intently in the terrible silence, and trying to make out whether the Indians were near.

Again came the report of a firelock, and a volley from nearer the gate, followed by a burst of yells; and a minute later a fresh volley, and the same defiant shouting, just as if the Indians had made their attack in four different places, but had been checked by the watchfulness of our men, who had been thoroughly prepared for the attacks.

I was wondering to myself whether the Indians were in a body, and had come on in one place, and then hurried on to the others, or were in four different bodies; but my wonderings soon ceased, for I quite started at hearing a voice close to my ear.

"No got arrow 'tick in um dis time, Mass' George. Tell um Injum coming again."

"Where? Where?" I whispered.

"Pomp see um crawl 'long de groun' like 'gator," he said. "Dah—one, two, tick, nineteen, twenty."

I gazed intently over the fence, but could only see the dark ground; but Pomp's warning was too valuable to be trifled with. He had proved himself now, and I hurried to where my father stood ready with twenty of our men, and told him.

He gave orders, and half the men fired slowly, one after the other, the instructions being to those who held their fire, that if they could make out the bodies of the crawling Indians by the flashing of their comrades' pieces, they were to fire too.

The rapid scattered reports were followed by a furious burst of yells; there was the rush of feet, sounds as of blows struck against the stout poles, and directly after, dimly-seen against the starlit sky, dark grotesque-looking heads appeared as at least a dozen of the Indians gained the top of the defence, but only to be beaten back by the butt-ends of the men's fire-locks, all save two who dropped over in our midst, and fought desperately for a time before they were despatched.

As silence—an ominous silence full of danger and portent—fell upon us again here, we could tell that quite as desperate a struggle was going on at other points of the palisading. Flash was succeeded by report and yell, so loud and continuous that we knew now that the Indians were delivering their attack in four different places; and more than once I shuddered as I felt how terrible it would be should one of these bands gain an entry. I knew enough of such matters from old conversations with my father, to be able to grasp that if a party did get in over the stockade they would desperately attack one of our defending companies in the rear, and the others in response to their yells would come on at the same moment, when our numbers and discipline would be of little value in a hand-to-hand attack with the lithe savages, whose axes and knives would be deadly weapons at close quarters.

For quite half an hour the firing and yelling continued. Then it ceased as quickly as it had begun, and the Indians seemed to have retreated.

But there was no relaxation of our watchfulness, for we could not tell but that in their silent furtive way the enemy were preparing for a fresh assault, or perhaps merely resting and gathering together to come on in one spot all at once.

"More likely to make a feint somewhere," I heard the General say to my father. "If they do it will be to make a big attack somewhere else, and that is where the supports must be ready to flock down."

"You will see to that, sir?" said my father.

"Yes. You and Preston cannot do better service," continued the General, "so keep your places."

"Pomp," I whispered; "where are you?"

"Here, Mass' George."

"Let's go all round, and you can tell me where the Indians are gathering now."

"Pomp go outside," he said, softly. "Climb over."

"No, no; they would see and kill you."

Mass' George: A Boy's Adventures in the Old Savannah | 261

"No. Dey too 'tupid. I go ober. You gib leg lil hyste up."

"I tell you no. Come along with me, and let's try and find out where they are."

"Much too dark, Mass' George, but I look all de same, try and fine em."

"Quick then; come!"

We started off, creeping along silently close inside the great palisade, and stopping to listen from time to time.

We had left one of the parties that defended the palisade close to the far side of the gate behind for about twenty yards, when Pomp, who was first, suddenly stopped short, caught me by the wrist, and said softly—

"You listum. Injum dah."

I placed my ear close to the paling, and stood for a few moments unable to make sure that the dull heavy rustling I heard meant anything; but at last I felt at one with my companion, for I felt convinced that a strong party was once more creeping up to the attack, and just to a spot where the sentries had not been placed.

Chapter Thirty Six

Certainly there was a body of our defenders five-and-twenty yards away in one direction, and sixty in another; but while the alarm was spreading a dozen active Indians would be able to scale the fence.

At least so it seemed to me, as without hesitation I uttered a wild cry for help, Pomp raising his voice to supplement mine.

"Here! This way! Here! Indians!" I shouted; and I heard the sound of hurrying feet, and a sharp decisive order or two being given; but at the same moment there was a peculiar scraping sound on the rough fence which told me that the Indians were climbing over, and I stood hesitating, puzzled as to whether it was my duty to run or stop where I was, so as to keep up the alarm and guide our people through the darkness to the exact spot.

All this was a matter of moments, and I hesitated too long. I was conscious of our people being close at hand; then of feeling Pomp dragging at me, and saying something excitedly. Then it was as if a big mass had fallen from above, and I lay crushed down and senseless in a darkness far greater than that of the night.

When I came to my senses again, I found that I was lying on my face with something heavy across me, from beneath which I managed to creep at last, shuddering the while, as I felt that it was the body of a dead or wounded man. Everything about me was still, but I could hear voices at a distance, and I wondered what had taken place, and why I was left there like that.

It was very puzzling, for my head was so confused that I could not recollect what had taken place before, so as to understand why it was that I was lying out there in the darkness, close to this wounded man.

At last I concluded to shout for help, and my lips parted, but no sound came. This startled me, and I began to tremble, for it was all so new and strange.

But by degrees my brain grew clearer, and I began to have faint rays of understanding penetrate my darkened mind. These grew brighter and brighter, till at last I was able to understand that I had been struck down by a tremendous blow on the head, the very realisation of that fact being accompanied by such acute pain, that I was glad to lie there perfectly inert without thinking at all.

But this fit did not last long, and I could see now the matter in its true light, and it all came back about how I gave the alarm, and must have been standing there as the Indians came over, and I was struck down at once.

Then as I lay there in the darkness, I began to recall how I had been lying with some one across me, and half suffocating me.

I had crawled away a few yards in my half insensible condition, but now a shuddering desire came over me to creep back, and find out who it was that lay there dead or dying.

It was terrible, that feeling, for I felt that I must go, and as I crept back, it was with the idea that it was probably one of those who would be the first to rush to the defence of the palisade, and in a confused, half-dreamy way, I found myself combating the fancy that it might be my father.

I paused when about half-way back, afraid to go farther, but the intense desire to know the worst came over me again, and I crept on and then stopped with my hand raised, and held suspended over the prostrate figure, afraid to move it and touch the body.

At last, and I uttered a faint sigh full of relief, for my hand had fallen upon the bare breast of a man, and I knew that it must be one of the Indians. It was puzzling that he and I should be there, and no one near, for I could not detect the presence of either of the sentries. Where was everybody? Some one was coming, though, the next minute, for I heard soft footsteps, and then the murmur of voices, which came nearer and nearer till I heard a familiar voice say—

"Oh, Mass' George, do 'peak."

I tried to obey, but no sound would come, even now that I felt a vast sense of relief, for I knew that I must have been hurt, and the two blacks were in search of me.

"Ah, here him are," suddenly cried Pomp, and I next felt two great hands lifting me gently, and I was carried through the darkness to what I knew must be the block-house, where I had some recollection of being laid down. Then I directly went off to sleep, and did not awake till nearly day, to see a black face close to the rough pallet on which I lay, and as the day grew broader, I made out that it was Pomp watching by my side.

"Mass' George better now?"

"Better? Yes; I am not ill," I said, and I tried to get up, but lay still again, for the effort seemed to give me a violent pain in the head which made me groan.

"Mass' George not seem very better."

"But I am. I'll get up directly. But tell me, Pomp, how was it all?"

"How was?"

"Yes; how did it happen?"

"Done know, Mass' George. 'Pose Injum come over big fence and jump on and knock poor lil nigger and Mass' George down. Den um hab big fight an kill de Injum, an noder big fight by de gate an kill more Injum, and den Injum say good-night, time go to bed, an dat's all."

"The Indians gone?"

"Yes; all gone."

"Then we have beaten them. Hurrah! Oh, my head!"

"Hurrah—oh my head!" cried Pomp, in imitation. "Why say 'Hurrah! Oh, my head'?"

"Oh, don't, Pomp. You make me laugh."

"Dat right; glad see Mass' George laugh. Mass' George couldn't laugh lil bit when Pomp fess um fader carry um."

"No; I remember now. I had forgotten."

"Mass' Dockor say good job Mass' George got tick head, or kill um."

"Did the doctor say that, Pomp?"

"Yes, Mass' Dockor say dat. Injum hit um wif um lil chopper, same time some one shoot and kill Injum; den Pomp knock down, and all jump on um, and dey pick um up, and take um 'way, and bring um here."

"Then were you hurt too?"

"Yes, hurt dreffle, and dockor laugh, and say nuffum matter wif um, and send um 'way 'gain. Den Pomp go an' fine um fader, and come an' fine Mass' George, and bring um here. Dockor no laugh at Mass' George, ony say, 'Poor fellow!' and 'Put um to bed,' an' 'Good job um got such tick head,' and put plaster on um."

I raised my hand to my head, and sure enough there was some sticking-plaster there.

"Does my father know?" I said, as a sudden thought occurred to me.

"Pomp done know, Mass' George. Haben see Mass' Capen long time."

Our conversation was checked by the entrance of the doctor, who smiled as he saw me sitting up on the rude bed.

"Well, squire," he said, "you seem determined to be a patient. How are you now?"

"My head aches a good deal."

"No wonder, my lad, you got an ugly crack with the flat of a tomahawk. The man must have slipped as he was leaping from the fence. A narrow escape for you."

"But the Indians are beaten off," I said, eagerly.

"For the present at all events. But they may attack again to-night, and I am beginning to be busy."

"Must I stop here, sir?"

"Certainly not, if you feel well enough to get up."

At that moment a shadow darkened the door, and my father came in quickly, followed by Hannibal.

"George? Hurt?" he exclaimed, huskily.

"Not much, father," I said, "and the doctor says I may get up."

"Thank Heaven!" muttered my father. Then aloud, "I have only just heard from Hannibal here. You gave me a terrible fright."

My father took hold of my hands to hold them in his for a few moments, as he looked full in my eyes; and I wondered at it, for I was not old enough then to understand his emotion, nor to think I was bad enough to stop in bed.

Ten minutes later I was out in the enclosure, and learned a little more about what had taken place after I was knocked down insensible. How there had been several hand-to-hand encounters where the Indians had determinedly climbed over and gained a footing, from which they were dislodged directly, with the result that several were killed and wounded—four of our party also having ugly wounds.

As I was going across the enclosure, hearing how the enemy had been finally beaten off, and had retreated into the forest, where it was not considered safe to follow them, Colonel Preston met us, looking jaded and anxious, but his face brightened up as he saw me, and he came up and shook hands.

"Why, George Bruton, you are a lucky fellow," he cried, laughingly. "Two wounds. This is grand. Of course he must be promoted, Bruton, as soon as peace is proclaimed."

"Why, George," said my father, as we went on, "what's the matter?"

"I don't like to be laughed at, father," I said; "and Colonel Preston was making fun of me, as if I were a little child."

"He did not mean it unkindly. There, come and have some light breakfast, and you must keep out of the sun."

Chapter Thirty Seven

That day passed quietly enough, with scouts going and coming to report that the Indians' trail was plainly to be seen going along the north bank of our little stream, as if they were making right away for their own country, and after the scouts had gone as far as they dared, they had returned with their good news. This was quickly debated in a little council, and the result was a firm determination not to put any faith in appearances, but to keep everything on a war footing, scouting carefully so as not to be surprised by an enemy full of cunning and treachery; and though there was some little demur amongst those whose houses and plantations were farthest from the fort, all soon settled down to what resolved itself during the next week into a pleasant kind of camping out.

Rough tents were rigged up, and the different parties vied with each other in their efforts to make their homes attractive. Fresh things were brought in by the help of the slaves from the most outlying of the houses, and when lights were lit in the evening the place looked pretty in the extreme, so that more than once I found myself thinking that we were to be the only sufferers from the Indian attack, and wondered, now that the enemy had had so severe a lesson read them, how long it would be before my father decided to go back and get our neighbours' help to rebuild the house.

A fortnight glided by—fourteen days of uninterruptedly fine weather. I had almost forgotten my injuries. Pomp had taken his wounded limb out of the sling, and only remembered the injury when he tried to move his hand, when he would utter a cry and begin softly rubbing the place.

Sarah too was recovering fast, and I knew no reason now why we should still go on living such a military life, with the General and his officers seeming to take delight in drilling, practising the men in the use of their weapons, and setting guards by night, and sending out scouts by day, with the gates closed rigorously at a certain time.

There was another thing done too, the idea being suggested by my father—a lesson taught by our own misfortune—and this was that every tub and cask that could be obtained in the settlement should be put about in handy places, and kept well filled with water always, these being supplemented by pails and buckets, which every one was bound to set outside his place full of water every night, while the men were all well practised in the extremely simple art of passing and refilling buckets—so as to be ready in case of fire.

"There's some talk of giving up all this here playing at soldiers, Master George," said Morgan to me one day.

"Is there?" I said, eagerly.

"Yes, and if you ar'n't tired of it, I am. Never so much as had a chance to go out and scout like the others have."

"Well, I haven't either, nor Hannibal, nor Pomp."

"No, my lad; but if you don't tie down that jockey or chain him by the leg, he'll be off one of these days. I'm always finding him sitting a-top of the fence like a crow with his wing cut, thinking he wished he could fly."

"Looking out for the Indians," I said.

"Not him, sir; he's thinking about games in the woods; hunting snakes, catching 'gators, or killing 'coons. He's getting a nice howdacious one, he is. If it wasn't for his black skin, you might think he was a reg'lar boy."

"So he is," I said; "what difference does his skin make? I like old Pomp."

"Well, sir," said Morgan, thoughtfully, "I like old Hannibal—old Vanity, as you call him; but you know he is black."

"Of course."

"Very black, Master George. Why, I should say he's got the blackest skin and the whitest teeth of any one I ever did see."

"And I dare say he thinks you've got the whitest skin and the blackest teeth he ever saw."

"Now—now—now—now—Master George; gently there, if you please. My skin's getting redder and browner every day, so as I don't half know myself when I shaves; and as to my teeth, just wait till you've used yours five-and-forty year, and had to eat such beef as I've had to eat in the army, and you won't be quite so proud of them bits o' ivory of yours, look you."

"Why don't you leave off saying 'Look you,' Morgan? It's always 'Look you,' or 'Teclare to cootness,' and it does sound so stupid."

"Not it, my lad," said Morgan, proudly. "It's that which shows I belong to the Ancient British."

"Nonsense! You're a Welshman."

"Ah, you call me so, my lad, but I belong to the genuwyne old British stock. You ask the captain if I don't. And as to my teeth, why, when we was out with the army, I believe they used to buy all the old bulls, and the older and harder they were the better they used to like 'em."

"Why?"

"Because they used to go the further. Ah, we did a lot of fighting on it though, and I thought I'd come to the end of that sort of thing; but it don't seem like it. Oh, how I do long to have a spade or a hoe in my hand again. I say, Master George."

"Well?" I said, as I lay in the sun enjoying my returning strength, for it came back fast.

"Think the master really means to go back and build up the house again?"

"Yes, I'm sure of it," I said.

"That's a good job, my lad, for it would be heartbreaking to know that all we've done out there, planting fruit-trees and getting the place in such nice trim, should be 'lowed to go back again to ruin, and grow over into forest wilds, as it would in a year or two."

"Ah, that would be a pity, Morgan," I said, eagerly, as I thought of the fruit-trees and the vines.

"I say, look here, Master George, I'm 'bout heart-broke over that garden. I want to see what it's like. We all might go for a day and torment some of them weeds, and keep things from getting worse, and see what mischief the Indians did."

"Yes; I should like to go and see that," I said, thoughtfully.

"Should you, my lad? Then let's go."

I shook my head, for I saw a lot of difficulties in the way.

"Nay, nay; now don't do that, lad. I teclare to coot—"

"Morgan!" I shouted.

"Well, look you, dear boy—"

"Morgan!"

"Oh, dear me, how is a man to speak! I was going to say, I did ask some of them who went scouting, and they'd got it all pat enough about how the house was a heap of ashes, but I don't believe one of 'em so much as looked at the garden, and I know there's things ready in those beds as would be a blessing to us now."

"A heap of ashes!" I said, sadly.

"Yes, Master George; but think of the barrow-loads there'll be, and they'll be worth anything for the garden nicely spread about."

"I should like to go and see the old place," I said, thoughtfully.

"Then ask the captain, lad. Do. He's just over yonder talking to the colonel. Hist! Here he comes. Ask him—do."

"Well, George," said my father, coming up. "Ah, Morgan. Want to speak to me?"

"Well, sir, I—er—that is, I think Master George does."

"No, father; it's Morgan, only he's afraid."

"Nay, nay, not afraid, Master George. Don't say that. On'y a bit okkard over it. But I will speak if you're afraid to."

"What is it?" said my father.

"Well, father, it's this; Morgan—"

"Oh, Master George!"

"—And I think we should like to go over to the old place and see what it looks like."

"And take a tool or two, sir; and go early and tidy up the garden a bit."

"Well," said my father, thoughtfully, "I don't see why you should not. I was thinking of something of the kind, now that the Indians seem to be gone for good."

"Then when may we go, father?"

"I'll speak to the General, and if he sees no objection you shall go to-morrow morning, first thing, if you feel well enough."

"Oh, father!" I exclaimed, with a thrill of delight running through me, for it was as if I was to be freed from prison.

"You will not be able to do much, Morgan," said my father, thoughtfully; "but you might take a billhook and cut back a little of the overgrowth, for we must not be beaten. George, my boy, we must go back and make the place more beautiful than it was before; for it is a beautiful land, if man would not blot it with his cruelties and evil deeds."

I saw that his eyes were fixed upon the corner of the enclosure, where the blacks were gathered.

"Then we may go, father?" I said.

"If the General approves. No one can stir outside the gates without his orders now."

He turned and walked to the central part where the General's furniture was piled up, and he had been living as humbly as the rest; and in less than half an hour he was back, just in fact as Morgan was saying, grumblingly—

"It's all over, my lad; the governor won't let us go."

"The General gives his consent," said my father, "provided that you are very careful; so the next thing is, how do you propose to go?"

"Walk across," I said.

"No; decidedly not. You will take the boat. There she lies safe enough with the others. You can have Hannibal and Pompey to row, and Morgan and the black can be both well-armed, for that man is very trustworthy. But of course you will all be very cautious. You can send out that boy in different directions to scout; not that there is any danger, but we must treat this as an enemy's country, and be prepared."

"Yes, father, we'll be very careful; and we may go soon in the morning?"

"As soon as you like. Get your bag of provisions ready to-night. Morgan, you can be passed through the gates now. Have the boy with you, and see that the boat is baled out and cleaned."

"Yes, sir," said Morgan; and as soon as my father had gone we two shook hands in our delight, for Morgan was as excited as I.

"Hurrah, Master George!" he cried. "What a day we will have! I'm off to find Pomp. You go and tell old Han. Won't they be just pleased too!"

We parted on the instant, and five minutes later I found father and son together, and told them my news, with the result that Hannibal smiled with pleasure, and Pomp threw himself down on the ground to writhe and twist and worm about till he heard Morgan's voice summoning him to go and help to bale out the boat.

Chapter Thirty Eight

I lay down to sleep that night quite satisfied of my ability to wake up in good time; but it was still dark when Pomp was shaking my arm.

"Make hase, Mass' George," he cried, with his lips to my ear, "um gettin' so dreffle late."

"Eh? Now, no tricks," I said, in that irritable state of sleepiness when one wants just an hour longer. "Why, I have only just lain down."

"Why, you've been seep all de night. You call me laze lil nigger if I say dat. Get up!"

"But is it nearly morning, Pomp?" I said, with my eyes closely shut.

"Ah, you do dat 'gain! You roll ober de oder side for? You tink um dis week when it morrow morning."

"But it isn't really morning."

"Yes; bror daylight. Able see dreckly."

"It isn't," I said, opening my eyes and looking from under the boat-sail that made our tent, and seeing the stars burning brightly.

"I neb see such dreffle man," whispered Pomp, for fear of rousing my father. "Get late. Sun get up soon 'fore we get dah. Mass' Morgan an' Pomp fader gone down to de boat, and carry big bag somefin to eat. Pomp got de fishum-line, and dey say you'n me bring free guns and de powder shot."

"Eh! Gone down to the boat?" I said, rising hurriedly, for this was suggestive of being left behind; and hurrying my preparations—my dressing-room being outside the tent—I was soon ready, took the pouches and the three guns I had undertaken to have ready, and in a very few minutes we two were marching toward the gate, I carrying one firelock under my arm, and Pomp stepping out proudly with one on each shoulder.

"How long is it since Morgan and our man Hannibal went through?" I said to the guard at the gate.

"'Bout half an hour," said the man, rather sourly. "Nice to be you, young gentleman, going out like that instead of keeping watch here."

"Oh, that will soon be over," I said. "Come along, Pomp."

It was for the sake of saying something, for Pomp was already outside, waiting. But I wanted to get down to the boat, and not stop to be questioned by the guard as to what we were going to do.

As we went on down toward the wharf, the stars were still making their reflections glimmer in the smooth water of the big river, and a sculling sound and the rattle of an oar being heard, told me where the boat lay.

"That you, Master George?" said a familiar voice.

"Yes; but isn't it too early?"

"Not a bit, sir. But it'll be daybreak directly, to be sure. See there?"

I could see a very pale streak right away down and over the big river in what I knew to be the east, but I was still too drowsy to feel much interest in our excursion, and consequently replied rather gruffly to Hannibal's good-natured—

"Morn', Mass' George."

Just then the boat's keel grated on the pebbles, Hannibal jumped out, took the guns which Pomp parted with unwillingly, and passed them to Morgan, who stowed them in the stern. Then mine was passed in, and Hannibal bent down.

"Jump on, Mass' George, no get foot wet."

I leaped on his great broad back, thinking that he was getting his feet wet, but that it did not matter as they were bare; then wash, wash went the water on both sides as the great black and his boy waded out. I was dropped into the boat, the two blacks ran it out a little and stepped in, Morgan came aft to me, and the others backed water a while, and after turning, rowed out a little but kept pretty close, so as to be out of the swift current running down toward the sea.

"Talk about early," said Morgan, pointing to the increasing pallor of the sky; "why, it will soon be broad daylight, and I want to get to the mouth of the stream by that time."

They rowed on, and the freshness of the air, the motion of the boat, and the thorough feeling of change soon made me forget my discomfort, and as the pale dawn spread and showed the thick mist hanging over the low growth at the edge of the river, the memory of the last time I came by there started to my mind, and I looked eagerly at the near shore, thinking of hidden Indians ready to send flying their keenly-pointed arrows.

Morgan saw the direction of my glance, and said with a laugh—

"No; not this time."

"What?" I said sharply.

"Indians. That was a nice row we had that day, though, Master George."

"Mass' George going have fishum-line?" said Pomp, suddenly, as the dark line of forest began to look green, and higher up there was a tiny point of orange mist.

"No," I said; "we'll get right on home."

Pomp seemed so disappointed that I added, "Perhaps we will fish later on."

Vague as the promise was it sufficed to raise Pomp's spirits, and he tugged well at his oar, while I watched the splashing of fish in the river, heard the low, floundering noise made by the alligators, and listened to the fresh, clear song of the birds which were welcoming the coming of another day.

Then slowly the sun rose to glorify the dripping reeds and canes, and fringe them as if with precious stones; the different kinds of ducks and cranes disturbed by our boat fled at our approach with much flapping of wings and many a discordant cry. And before I could fully realise it, and think of anything else, it was bright, beautiful morning; all glorious, free, fresh, and delicious, with the moss draping the sunlit trees, the water sparkling, and the sensation growing upon me that I had just escaped from prison, and was going home.

"Not sorry you got up so soon, are you, sir?" said Morgan, smiling, as he saw how eager and excited I had grown.

"Sorry? No," I cried. "Here, you two, are you tired? Morgan and I will row."

"No, no," said Hannibal, showing his white teeth. "We row Mass' George boat all away."

"Look, Mass' George," cried Pomp, as there was a scuffle, a splash, and a good-sized alligator startled by our coming hurried into the river. "You like shoot um?"

"No, no. Let's get right away home first."

"All the same, sir, we'll load the guns," said Morgan. "I don't think we shall want to use 'em, but there's a few marks about this boat to show that sometimes it is necessary."

He pointed laughingly to the holes left where the arrows stuck in the sides and thwarts.

"I broke out an arrow-head this morning," he said; and he picked it up from where it lay.

Pomp watched us eagerly as we charged all three pieces, and laid them down in the stern, after which I sat thoroughly enjoying the scene, which was all as fresh to me as if I had never been there before. But at the same time, as we went on, I recognised the different spots where the Indians had made their stand to harass us during our memorable escape down the river, notably at the wooded point we passed round just before reaching the mouth of our stream, and leaving the main river behind.

Then, as the space contracted and the banks seemed to draw gradually closer together, we soon began to get into more familiar parts, and at last the higher trees and points and bends were all memorable, known as they were to Pomp and myself in connection with fishing excursions or hunts for squirrel or nest.

The stream here ran swiftly, and swirled round some of the bends, at times well open, at others so close did the forest come that we seemed to be going along between two huge walls of verdure; and I don't know whether they would have noticed it, but just before we turned into our lesser river, something induced me to begin talking rather rapidly to both Pomp and Hannibal, for we were passing the place where the slaver had lain, and as we came by, it seemed to me that the poor fellows must begin thinking of the horrors of that day when we brought them up in that very boat, one dying, the other as wild as any savage creature of the forest.

"Here we are at last," I cried, as we came close up to the cut-down trees on the bank which served as posts to our landing-place.

"Yes. Take your piece, Master George," said Morgan, "and don't shout aloud. Let's have a good look round first."

It was good advice, and we made our rowers take the boat up a couple of hundred yards past the landing-place, and then let her drift back. But all was still. There were two or three busy squirrels, and some birds, but no sign of lurking enemy.

"It's quite safe, I think," I said.

"Yes, sir, safe enough. No Indian here, or we should have had an arrow at us before now."

"We may fasten the boat there, and leave it?" I said.

Morgan hesitated.

"Well, yes," he said; "we had better keep all together. It would not be fair to leave those two alone to mind her in case the Indians did come."

"If they do," I said, "we must retreat overland if we can't get to the boat."

"Or they get it first," said Morgan, grimly.

So we landed at the familiar place, the boat was made fast, and with Hannibal carrying one of the guns, we started for the old home, all eager and excited except Pomp, whose brow puckered up, and I knew the reason why—he had no gun to carry.

"Here, Pomp," I said; "you keep close to me, and carry my gun."

The sun was shining brilliantly over the river; now it began to shine in the wood all over Pomp's smooth black skin, out of his dark eyes, and off his white teeth, as he shouldered the piece, now the very embodiment of pride.

We had not far to go, and as we went on and found everything as we had left it, and no signs of enemy, the shrinking feeling which had haunted me, and made me fancy I saw a living savage behind every great tree, passed away, and I strode on till we reached the clearing where Morgan and I killed the rattlesnake, and there the same shrinking feeling attacked me again, for it was here that we had long back made our first acquaintance with the enemy.

My eyes met Morgan's, and he was evidently thinking the same thing as he gave me a nod.

"No rattlesnakes here to-day, sir," he said, and he smiled meaningly, "not of any sort. Shall I go first?"

"No," I said, rather unwillingly, for I felt that I ought to lead; and, taking the firelock now from Pomp, I went toward the path leading through the forest trees to our larger clearing where the house and garden stood.

"Mass' George let Pomp go firs and see if any-boddy dah," whispered the boy.

"No," I said; but Morgan turned to me quickly, as Pomp looked disappointed.

"Why not let him go on? He'll creep through the trees like a snake, and get there and back unseen if there's danger."

"Nobody see Pomp if him hide."

"Go then," I said; and the boy darted off at once through the densest part, while we followed cautiously, for there was the possibility of some of the Indians lurking about still.

But in a few minutes Pomp was back, looking very serious, but ready to tell us at once that no one was there.

Upon this we pushed on rapidly, and soon stood in the midst of our lovely clearing, framed in by the forest, where everything seemed more beautiful than ever, except in one place, where, with the strands of creepers already beginning to encroach on the blackened ruins, lay a heap of ashes, with here and there some half-burned timbers and ends of boards.

I felt a choking sensation as I looked at the ruins, and thought of how many pleasant hours I had passed there with my father, and now I could only just trace out where the rooms had been, so complete was the destruction the fire had made.

Not that it was surprising, the whole place having been built solidly of the finest pine from the sandy tract between us and the little river—wood that I knew would blaze up when dry and burn with a fierce resinous flame.

But it seemed so pitiful that the delightful little home, with all the pleasant surroundings, over which my father had toiled to make it as much as possible like an English country home, should have been entirely destroyed. And for what?

Ah, it was a hard question to answer. But I supposed then that as we had come into the land the savages looked upon as their special hunting-ground, they considered that they had a right to destroy.

I tore myself away from the heap of black and grey ashes, and rejoined Morgan, who said nothing, but accompanied me then around the garden, which to our great surprise we found untouched. It was weedy, and beginning to show a great want of the master's hand, but otherwise it looked delightful after the desolation I had just left.

"Seems hard as my part should have escaped, and your part be all burnt up, Master George," said Morgan, slowly. "But it ar'n't my fault. I'd almost rather they'd ragged the garden to pieces, and cut down the trees, than have burnt the house."

"It can't be helped," I said, thankful for the sympathetic way in which the man spoke, and at the same time a little amused at his considering the garden his part, and the house wherein he always lived too as being ours.

We went all round and were on the way to the hut where the blacks slept, when I suddenly noticed that Pomp was not with us, and I drew Morgan's attention to the fact.

"He was here just now, because I saw him stoop down and pick up something to throw at a bird."

"No, no: don't shout," I said. "I dare say he'll be here directly, and one don't know how near the enemy may be."

But Hannibal did not seem satisfied, and he began looking round the garden and peering about close up to the trees in search of the boy, though without success.

I had taken little notice of this, for I had been talking in a low voice to Morgan about the garden, and whether it was worth while to do anything, seeing that beyond a little weeding nothing hardly was required.

"I thought the fences would all be down, and the place trampled, and that I should have to cut rails and stakes to save the place from desolation."

So said Morgan, and I agreed that as far as the garden was concerned we had met with a pleasant surprise.

"We'll have a good meal now," I said. "Let's sit down under the big cypress," and I pointed to the great tree which had proved so good a friend during the flood, and unslinging the bag which he had been carrying, Morgan led the way toward the resting-place.

"Why, Hannibal's gone now," I said, looking round wonderingly. "Oh, I know," I added, laughing; "he heard me say we would have something to eat, and he has gone to look for Pomp."

We were soon comfortably seated with the food spread before us, and as I cut some of the bread and salt pork we had brought, I said—

"It's of no use to go looking out for Indians, I suppose. We must chance their being near."

"If we go looking for them, Master George, we shall have to spend all our time over it. I'm beginning to hope we shan't see them any more."

Then Morgan's mouth became too full for him to talk with comfort, and I'm afraid mine was in a similar condition, for the long row, the fresh air, and the absence of breakfast before starting had had a great effect upon my appetite.

"I wish they'd come now," I said, as I half turned to Morgan, who was leaning forward with his head thrown back in the act of drinking from a bottle, when I felt as if turned to ice—frozen—motionless—gazing up at a great muscular brown arm raised to strike; and I don't know how to explain it, for the space of time must have been short as that taken up by the flashing of lightning; but all the same, the time seemed prolonged to me sufficiently for me to see that the owner of that arm was half concealed behind the tree; that the hand belonging to that arm held one of the keen little axes used by the Indians; that the blow was intended for my head; and I knew that before I could utter a word to alarm my companion, all would be over.

A good deal to think in that moment of time, but people do see and think a great deal instantaneously, just as they have quite long dreams in a few instants of time; and as I tell you, I thought all that as I saw the raised axe, and I could not stir, though it was in motion to strike me down.

A loud report set me free, the sound of a shot from the forest, and the Indian sprang forward between me and Morgan, turned half round, struck at the air with his tomahawk, then twisted back so that I had a full view of his hideous, distorted face, and then it was hidden from me, for the little axe escaped from his hand, and he fell clutching and tearing at the grass and leaves.

By this time Morgan and I had seized the fire-locks we had stood against the trunk of the tree, and stooped down to shelter ourselves with its trunk, as we presented the barrels at where we heard some one crashing through the bushes. But it was Han.

"Mass' George not hurt?"

"No, no," I said. "Did you fire?"

He nodded shortly, and gave me the piece to reload as he picked up the axe the Indian had let fall, and took the savage's knife from his belt to stick it in his own.

"If there's one Indian there's more," said Morgan, excitedly. "Quick, sir, ram the bullet well down. We must make for the boat. Where's that boy Pomp?"

"No," said Hannibal, shaking his head; "gone, gone. Han look for him; saw Indian and Mass' George."

"And you fired and saved my life," I cried, catching his hand, as I gave him back the reloaded piece.

He smiled at me, and shook his head sadly as I exclaimed—

"Now then to find Pomp, and get back to the boat."

I had hardly uttered the words when there was a yell, and four savages dashed out of the forest toward us, knife in one hand, axe in the other. They were not twenty yards away, and I raised my heavy piece to my shoulder as I saw Morgan let his barrel fall into one hand and fire.

A hideous yell followed, and one of the Indians leaped in the air. I saw no more for the smoke, but I drew trigger too, and staggered back with the violent concussion of the piece.

Then I stood aghast at what followed, for as the smoke lifted I saw an Indian spring on Morgan, and Hannibal drop the gun he held as the other two Indians rushed at him axe in hand, yelling horribly.

Then in what seemed to me was a nightmare dream, I saw Morgan seize the Indian's hand, and they closed in a desperate struggle, while on my other side Hannibal was battling with two, and I was helpless to assist either, and—well, I was a boy of sixteen or so, and how could I at close quarters like that try to shed blood?

True, in the excitement of the flight in the boat, I had loaded and fired again and again as the Indians kept sending their arrows at us; but all I could do now was to drop my own piece and run to pick up the one Hannibal had dropped.

But I did not fire it. I could only stand and gaze first at one, and then at the other, as I saw the great calm black now frenzied with rage and the thirst for battle. He was bleeding from blows given by the knife of one Indian and the axe of the other, but his wounds only seemed to have made him furious, and he stood there now looking like a giant, holding one of his enemies by the throat, the other by the wrist, in spite of their writhings and desperate efforts to strike him some deadly blow. He looked to me then like a giant in strength; but the Indians were strong too, and though he was rapidly subduing the one whose throat he grasped, the other was gradually wriggling himself free, when, seizing my opportunity, rendered desperate by the position, I raised the heavy piece I held as if it were a club, and brought the barrel down with all my might upon the Indian's head.

I stepped back sickened by what I had done, as his arm relaxed and he fell prone, while, freed now from one adversary whose axe would the next moment have brained him, Hannibal grasped his remaining enemy with both hands, raised him up, and dashed him heavily upon the earth.

It was time, for Morgan was down, the Indian upon him, his knife raised high to plunge into the poor fellow's throat, but held back by Morgan's hand, which was yielding fast.

I stood paralysed and watching, when, with a roar like a wild beast, Hannibal dashed at this last man, and with the axe he had at his waist struck him full in the temple, and he dropped down sidewise quivering in death.

I remember thinking it very horrible as I saw all this bloodshed, but I knew it would have been far more horrible if the savage wretches had killed us. Then every other thought was driven out of my head by the appearance of Hannibal, who was quite transformed. As a rule he was the quiet, gentle-looking black, always ready to obey the slightest command; now he seemed to tower up a ferocious-looking being, with wild glaring eyes looking about for something else to destroy, and had I not caught hold of his arm he would have used the axe he held on the fallen men.

"Under cover, my lad," said Morgan, who was panting heavily. "Don't leave that gun. Now Hannibal, quick!"

He led the way in among the trees, where we quickly loaded the discharged pieces, crouching down under bushes, while Hannibal knelt beside us keeping watch, his wild eyes glaring round in every direction for some fresh enemy to attack.

"Nice—narrow—escape that! Master George," said Morgan, in a low voice, as he gave the ramrod a thud between every two words. "Pretty object I should have looked if I'd had to go back to your father and say you were killed by the Indians. Oh dear! Oh dear! I did hope I'd done killing people to the end of my days, and now look yonder."

"It was forced upon you, Morgan," I whispered, as I finished charging one of the pieces.

"Upon me!" cried Morgan. "Oh, come now, Master George, play fair. Don't get putting on all down to my account. My word! Who'd have thought old Hannibal here could fight like that?"

The great black looked fiercely round, but smiled sadly as Morgan held out his hand and said—

"Thank you, old lad."

"Yes! Thank you, Hannibal, for saving my life," I whispered.

"Mass' George save Han's life," was the reply in deep tones. Then the smile passed from the great fellow's face, and a terrible expression came over it again as his eyes rolled round, and he said in a deep, low, muttering voice—

"Come—quick find Pomp."

"And I was just going to say, let's make a run now for the boat," said Morgan. "But we can't leave the boy, Master George."

"No," I said. "Here, take your gun, Han."

I passed the firelock to him, and followed his gaze as he glared round among the trees from behind whose trunks I expected to see the enemy peering, ready to take revenge for the death of their companions. But there was no one near as far as I could see, and we rose cautiously to get a better view round through the clustering boughs whose heavy foliage cut off the light, so that we were gazing down glorious vistas that ended far away in the deepest shade.

"Might hide an army there, and no one could see 'em," muttered Morgan.

"Find Pomp?" said Hannibal, looking at me inquiringly.

"Yes," I said; "try and find him. Go on."

The great fellow drew a deep breath, and led off at once with the firelock in his left hand, the axe in his right; and I knew that if we had a fresh encounter, the modern weapon would be useless in his hands, while the axe would be terrible.

To my great horror, the course he chose was out by where the desperate struggle had taken place, and my first instinct was to close my eyes and not look at the dead Indians; but I told myself I was a soldier's son, and that these men had fallen as we were fighting for our lives. But it was very terrible to see them lying there as they had fallen, two of them still grasping their weapons, and with a look of savage hatred in their faces.

Hannibal led on, Morgan followed, and I was last, and I was beginning to feel glad that we were leaving the dead behind, where they lay beneath the great cypress, when Hannibal turned round and raised his axe to point as it seemed to me in the direction of the forest beyond the garden, and to my horror it appeared as if the man had been seized with a fresh desire to shed blood, for his great lips were drawn away from his glistening teeth, his eyes opened widely showing broad rings of white round the dark irides, and throwing up the axe ready to strike, he dropped the gun and literally bounded at me.

With a faint cry of horror as I saw the awful-looking object leaping at me, the firelock dropping from his left hand, and the blood glistening on his great arms, I dropped sidewise just as a knife flashed by my cheek and over my left shoulder.

It was then that I realised the truth, and drew my breath hard, as I saw Hannibal's axe descend; there was a terrible crashing sound and a heavy fall, and as, sick and seeing dimly, I looked down to my left, the great figure of the black was bending over a grinning object in the bushes at the forest edge, his foot was pressing back one of our enemies, and he dragged the axe free.

"Is he dead now?" Morgan whispered, hoarsely, and his face looked ghastly as he caught me by the arm.

Hannibal uttered a low deep sound, and drew himself up to his full height. Then he bent down again, and I saw him tear a glittering knife out of a brown hand, which with its arm rose above the bushes and was clinging still to the haft.

"Morgan," I said, faintly, as the great black strode back toward where we had had the struggle first, "stop him. What is he going to do?"

"I want to stop him, lad," whispered the faithful fellow, in low, awe-stricken tones; "but I can't try; I daren't. It must be done."

"But that was another Indian," I whispered, as I saw Hannibal bend down, rise up, take a step or two, and bend down again, and then everything swam before my eyes. I could hear Morgan's voice though as he went on—

"It was horribly near, sir," he said. "It wasn't another Indian, but one of those shamming dead, and as soon as we'd got by he must have crawled after us, and old Han turned just in time, and went at him as he was striking at you with his knife. It's very horrid, my lad, but these savages don't understand fair fighting and giving quarter to the wounded. There, come away, and don't look angry at the black when he comes back. He has just saved your life again, and what he is doing now is to make sure you are not attacked again."

I stood speechless, resting on the piece I held in my hand till the great negro came back with the knife stuck in his waist-belt, to stoop and pick up the gun he had dropped; and then he pointed again with the axe toward the forest beyond the garden.

"Come," he said, quietly. "Find Pomp."

He looked at me once more with so grave and kindly an aspect that I tried to smother the horror I felt, and taking a step or two forward, I drew out a handkerchief and pointed to his bleeding arms, which were gashed by two blows of axe and knife.

He smiled and nodded half contemptuously as I tore the handkerchief in two, and he held out his arms one by one for me to bind them tightly.

"Now," he said, "find Pomp."

I held up my hand and we listened to a low, hoarse, gurgling noise, which seemed to come from a distance in the forest, and I shuddered as I fancied for a moment that it must be one of the Indians dying; but I knew that the sound came from a different direction.

We listened intently as we stooped under cover and kept a watchful gaze in every direction for danger. But the sound had ceased and for the moment we were safe, for no leaf was stirring, and the deep shadowy wood appeared to be untenanted. Hannibal shook his head, and was in the act of turning when the curious hoarse gurgling sound came again.

It was like nothing I had ever heard before, and what was more strange, it was impossible to make out whence it came, for it rose and fell, rose again, and then died out.

"What is it?" I said to Morgan. "An Indian cry?"

"No," he replied. "Hark! There it is again."

Yes; there it was again, but appeared to be from a fresh direction.

"Is it something down amongst the bushes—a frog or a young 'gator?"

"No; I don't think it can be that, sir. I've heard nearly every sound they make, and it isn't anything like that."

All was still again, and we moved on slowly farther into the forest, going cautiously in and out among the trees, our weapons ready, and a strict look-out kept for the enemy. For it seemed to me that the main body could not be far off, our encounter having been with a skirmishing party.

"There again," I whispered. "What is it, Hannibal?"

He was kneeling down now listening; and as he looked up at me, I could see that he was puzzled, for he shook his head.

"Han done know," he said.

Again the sound came—a hoarse, gurgling, faint noise, as from a great distance, but somehow we were as far off from understanding what it meant as ever.

"Never mind," said Morgan. "It isn't what we are looking for. Go on, Han; we must find that boy, and escape for our lives."

The great black nodded and started off at once, Morgan and I going to right and left of him, and we searched through the great trees, working away round the opening cleared from the forest for our house, but though the sound continued, we could find no trace of the cause nor yet of the poor boy, who had dropped completely out of sight.

My heart sank as I felt sure that the Indians must have surprised him, and moment by moment, as we started again into the forest, making now toward the rattlesnake clearing and the path leading to the landing-place, I expected to come upon him lying dead where he had been struck down.

But we examined the place again and again in every direction without success, and we were neither of us sufficiently skilled to attempt in the gloom beneath the trees to find him by his tracks.

The sound had nearly ceased now, only occurring faintly at intervals, and still it was as confusing as ever, for we could not make out whence it came.

At last we stopped at the edge of the rattlesnake clearing, near where the path struck out leading to the water-side.

"What are we to do, Master George?" said Morgan. "I want to find that boy, and at any moment we may be attacked by enemies, and it seems to be our duty to get down to the boat, row back as fast as we can, and give warning that the Indians are still near at hand."

"Yes, go," said Hannibal, who had been listening intently to Morgan's words. "Boat. Injum. Han 'top find um boy."

Morgan looked at me, but I shook my head.

"No," I said; "we will not go—we cannot, and leave him here. Will you come, Hannibal?"

"To find um boy," he said, frowning.

"And we'll stop too, Morgan," I said. "We may find him at any moment, and it is impossible to go and leave the poor boy like this."

Hannibal did not speak, but I saw his eyes fixed on me as Morgan spoke.

"I don't want to go and leave him, Master George," he said, "because it's like leaving a comrade, and old soldiers don't do that. But soldiers has their duty to do, and duty says— Go and let them know at the settlement. Besides, my duty to your father seems to say, Get you out of this as quick as you can."

"Yes, I know that, Morgan," I said.

"And the Indians may be on us at any moment."

"Yes, but we can't leave him," I said; "and— Ah, there's that noise again. I'm sure it came from right in there."

I pointed back toward the other side of the clearing, toward which spot Hannibal immediately rushed, and we followed as quickly as we could, for something seemed to tell us that a discovery was at hand.

It was close by the part of the forest through which Morgan and I had made our way cautiously and silently when we were going to kill the rattlesnake; and as we reached the edge, and passed in amongst the densely growing trees, all was silent, dark, and mysterious-looking; but there was nothing to be seen but tree-trunks, and we crept up to where the great black stood bending down and listening.

All was silent. Then there was a faint rap as a squirrel dropped a fir-cone from high up somewhere invisible to us. As far as we could see there were the gloomy aisles of great growing pillars, and we knew that we had passed through this portion of the forest again and again, though it was quite possible that we might have missed parts.

"Well, do you hear it?" I said, in a whisper.

Hannibal shook his head despondently, and then his face lit up as we heard from our right, and quite close at hand, the same faint, gurgling sound, now evidently a cry.

The black rushed on in and out among the trees, a gleam of sunshine catching his black skin once, just as we were passing the gloomiest part; and then, as I was close behind him, he disappeared beyond a group of great pillar-like pine-trees, and when I reached them I came upon him suddenly in a hollow, deep with fir-needles—a natural hole formed by the fall of a monstrous tree, whose root still lay as it had been wrenched out when the tree fell, but the trunk itself had gradually mouldered into dust.

And there was Hannibal busily cutting the hide thongs which bound Pomp, who was lying helpless at the bottom of the hole, with a blanket and a rough skin garment close by him, and beside these five bows and their arrows.

It was evidently the lurking-place of the Indian scouting party, who had suddenly pounced upon the boy, gagged and bound him, for his jaws were forced wide apart, a piece of ragged blanket was thrust into his mouth, and this was kept in by another hide thong tied round and round his face and neck, passing between his jaws as if he were bridled with a leather bit, while his arms and wrists and legs were so securely tied that the poor fellow was perfectly helpless.

"Can't say he's black in the face, in the way we mean," said Morgan, sympathetically, "because, poor lad, it is his nature to be so, look you, but he's half dead."

I was already down on my knees chafing the wrists set at liberty, after the hide had been cut away from the boy's cheeks and the gag taken out, but he made no sign whatever, and we were still rubbing him, and trying to restore the circulation, when Morgan said quickly—

"We can do that in the boat. Up with him, Han, I'll carry your gun. There must be more Indians near. These were on the advance, I'll lay, and I wouldn't say we don't have a fresh attack to-night."

Without a word Hannibal handed the gun, took Pomp by the arms, gently swung him on his back, and tore off a strip of blanket with which he tightly bound the boy's wrists together upon his own chest, so that it left the black's hands at liberty should he want to use them.

"Go on now," he said; and he held out his hand for his gun.

It was only a short distance from where we were to the boat, but it was really to be the most anxious part of all, and as we approached rattlesnake clearing, I involuntarily checked the others to look out cautiously before we left the dark pine-shade.

But all was still, the beautiful young growth glistening in the hot sunshine; and striking the path on the other side, gazing watchfully as we could, ready for attack, and fully expecting to see the Indians in possession of the boat, we finally reached the landing-place, where Pomp was laid in the stern, the weapons were placed ready, and faint and dripping with perspiration, I sank down beside Pomp as the rope was cast off.

Chapter Thirty Nine

My eyes were for ever running from tree to bush, and plunged into the windings of the path, as Hannibal and Morgan seized the oars, sat down, and, after the head had been pushed off into the current, began to pull a heavy stroke that sent the boat rapidly along and out into the middle of the stream. For after my old experiences of starting from that landing-place, in addition to that which I had gone through that day, the nervous tension was so great that my imagination ran riot at first, and I saw dark faces peering out from among the canes, bronzed arms holding bows, while others drew arrows to the heads, and the loud yells of the Indians seemed to ring through my dizzy brain. But as, after we had reached the farther side of the stream, the boat surged on through the water with no sound really heard but the splash of the oars, I began to grow more calm, the more so that we passed clump after clump, and patch after patch of undergrowth, from which arrows came whizzing last time, to strike into the sides of the boat, or fix themselves in the box with a hollow sounding rap.

As soon as I could collect myself a little, I plunged my hands over the side and bathed my face, and drank. Then hurriedly turning to poor Pomp, I placed his head more easily, Hannibal's great dark eyes watching me the while, and then took the tin baler, filled it with the cold, clear water, and began to bathe the boy's temples, pausing again and again to trickle water between his closely-set teeth.

But for a long time he gave no sign of recovery, but lay back breathing faintly, and with his eyes tightly closed.

"Coming to, Master George?" said Morgan.

"No," I had to reply again and again. And each time at my response I heard the boy's father utter a sigh.

But Hannibal did not cease to row a steady stroke, though I saw his forehead wrinkle up, and there was a wild look of misery in his eyes.

We had passed round the wooded point in safety, and soon after were well out of our stream and in the big river, when, seeing that we were beyond the reach of arrows, the rowing was slackened a little, just as, to the great delight of all, Pomp showed signs of recovery.

I was bending over him after dipping the tin full of water once more, and began to trickle a little water on his forehead, when *flip*, the tin went flying, the water sparkling in the sun, and a quantity of it sprinkling Hannibal where he sat, while it was all so sudden that I burst out laughing, for Pomp's familiar voice rang out sharply and angrily—

"Don't do dat."

Then memory must have come back like a flash, for the boy's hands seized me as I bent over and touched him, his eyes opened and glared at me, he showed his teeth viciously, and then let his hands drop, and he sank back.

"Mass' George!" he said, feebly. "Ah, Pomp know all de time. Mass' George play trick. Pash water, and—" Then with a sudden fierce change of manner—"Run, Mass' George—run—quick—what gone long dem Injum?"

He looked round wildly.

"They are gone, Pomp," I said; and I shivered a little as I spoke. "We're quite safe now. Drink a little water."

I raised his head, and held the refilled water-can to his lips, when he drank with avidity.

"Are you better?"

"Eh? Better, Mass' George? Injum cotch Pomp, and 'tuff mouf full. Couldn't holler. Tie um all up tightum. No move, no breve, no do nuffum."

"Yes; don't talk now. We found you. No; lie still. What do you want?"

"Go kill all de Injum."

"Sit still," I said, with another little shiver, as I recalled the scene of the struggle.

"No; Pomp won't sit 'till."

He rose to a sitting position and began rubbing his wrists, staring at his father the while, as the latter rowed steadily on with his arms bandaged and showing stains.

"What matter wif yo' arm?"

Hannibal said something to the boy in his own tongue, and Pomp leaned forward, still rubbing his numbed wrists softly, and evidently listening intently till his father had done, when he clapped his hands together and uttered a harsh laugh.

"Ah," he cried; "dat a way. Dey no come try kill Mass' George 'gain."

Then reverting to his own injuries, he felt all his teeth gently with thumb and finger, as if to try whether they were loose.

"'Tick 'tuff, great big dirty bit blank in Pomp mouf," he said, angrily. "No couldn't breve."

He gave himself another rub or two, worked his head about, rubbed behind his back, and opened and shut his jaws softly. Then giving himself a final shake, he exclaimed—

"Pomp quite well 'gain."

"Want something to eat?" I said, smiling.

"Yes, Mass' George. Pomp dreffle hungly now."

"Oh well, we'll soon settle that," I said; and I looked round for the food, much of which was then lying under the big cypress, close to the heap of ashes I had once called home.

"I'm afraid there is nothing left, Pomp," I said, apologetically.

"Eh?"

"I'm afraid there is nothing to give you," I said.

"What? No go eat all dat and hab not bit for poor Pomp! Oh!"

He swung himself round, threw himself down on his face, and groaned.

Hannibal said a few words in a deep stern voice, and the boy moaned out—

"But poor Pomp so dreffle hungly."

There was something so childishly absurd in his anger that I could not help laughing, the effect being that in his excitable state he turned upon me with a fierce gesture that reminded me of the day he was landed from the slaver.

But at that moment Hannibal's deep firm voice rose in so stern a tone that the boy shrank down again in the boat.

Hannibal spoke again as he continued rowing, and as I listened to the curious sweet-sounding barbarous tongue, I felt as if I would have given anything to have been able to understand what was said.

But though I did not comprehend the words, I did their sense, for Pomp came crawling up closer to me like a beaten dog, and held up one hand deprecatingly.

"Pomp dreffle sorry," he said. "Don't Mass' George flog lil nigger for get in pashum. Pomp so dreffle hungly."

"Oh, I'm not cross," I said, good-temperedly.

"And Mass' George not flog poor lil nigger?"

"I will if you ever say so again," I cried.

"Oh!"

"When were you ever flogged? Did I ever flog you?"

"No, Mass' George."

"Then why did you say that?"

"Mass' George often look going flog lil nigger."

"Then don't say it again, and you shall soon have something to eat. We are close to the wharf."

For there in full view was the flag flying on its pine-tree staff, and the boats lay off anchored in the river. But the place looked singularly deserted, and it seemed very strange for there to be no one visible idling about, boating, or at work in the plantations; not a single person being in sight till we got some distance farther on, and the block-house and palisade seemed to come out from behind the trees, when the sentries could be plainly seen, and the group by the open gates, while the interior of the enclosure looked like a busy camp, so crowded was it with people and their household goods.

We left the two blacks to moor the boat, after telling Pomp to make haste up and have some dinner, and Morgan and I hurried up to my father's quarters. He was not there, and we learned that he was with the General.

Under the circumstances we did not hesitate to go to the latter's tent, where we found that a little council was being held, and that Colonel Preston and the principal part of the other gentlemen of the expedition were there.

"Well, sir," I heard Colonel Preston say, "my opinion is that further inaction would be cowardly."

"I am sorry to go against my friend, Colonel Preston," said my father, his voice coming clearly to me from under the looped-up sail which made the tent, "but I feel convinced that in spite of the lesson they have received, the Indians will attack again, and it would be extremely unwise to leave our strong quarters and go to our homes until we are satisfied that we can be safe."

"I must say, gentlemen," said the General, gravely, "that in spite of the adverse opinions I have heard—some of which sounded to me rather rash—I agree with Captain Bruton."

There was a loud murmur here.

"We have our women and children to think of."

"Of course, sir," said Colonel Preston; "and I think of mine as seriously as any man here. But our close confinement is getting painful for them all. We shall be having another enemy in our midst—fever—if we do not mind. Now with all respect for Captain Bruton, I must say he is carrying caution too far. At the slightest alarm we can again take refuge in the fort."

There was a chorus of approval here.

"Our scouts have been out in every direction, and I am convinced that there has not been for many days past an Indian within a hundred miles."

"You are wrong, sir," I said excitedly, as I stepped forward with Morgan close behind me; and at the sight of us both, and what I had not thought of till then, our blood-stained garments, there was a loud buzz of excitement.

"What? Speak out. Are you wounded, boy?" cried my father, excitedly.

"No, father; I have escaped."

"But the Indians; you have seen them?"

"Yes," I said; and in the midst of a breathless silence, Morgan and I told of our terrible adventures that day.

Chapter Forty

"I am wrong, Bruton," said Colonel Preston, as I finished my narrative, and the last question had been answered—"quite wrong, gentlemen all. I was longing to get back to my comfortable home. Come along. I suppose we may have a fresh visit at any time."

The meeting broke up, and my father led me back to our quarters.

"I ought not to have let you go," he said. "The risk was too great, but I was influenced by the general opinion. Ah!" he continued, as he saw Hannibal standing by our rough tent, "why, my good fellow, you are wounded."

He laid his hand upon the black's arm, and said something in a low voice, but I could not catch his words. I saw Hannibal's eyes brighten, though, and a look of pleasure in his face as he suffered himself to be led to the temporary hospital; and I followed, to find our Sarah sitting up and ready to welcome me with a few sharp snappish words, after her fashion. I have often laughed since at the way in which she showed her affection for me; for that she was fond of me she often proved.

"You've come back then?" she said, as I seated myself upon a box.

"Yes; and I'm as bad as Pomp now," I replied.

"Oh, I don't doubt that a bit, Master George. What new mischief has he been at now?"

"Getting himself taken by the Indians, and nearly killed."

"And you have too?"

"Not taken, but nearly killed."

"Well, it serves you both right," she cried, with her lips working. "It was bad enough to come to this terrible place without you two boys going and running into all kinds of risks, and getting yourselves nearly killed. I don't know what the captain has been about, I'm sure."

"About here," I said, good-humouredly.

"But tell me at once, sir. What do you mean about being as bad as that impudent black boy?"

"Oh, only that I'm dreffle hungry," I said, laughing.

"Hungry? Then why didn't you have some food as soon as you got back?"

"Because I had to go and tell them my news; and then I wanted to see how you were. How is your wound?"

"Oh, it don't matter about me a bit. I'm in hospital, and being attended to, so of course my husband can go on pleasure-trips, and leave his poor wife to die if so inclined."

"Curious sort of pleasure-trip, Sarah," I said. "I say, you should see how Morgan can fight."

"Fight? Did he have to fight?"

"Yes;" and I told her what he had done.

"Oh, what a foolish, foolish man! How could he go leading you into danger like that?"

"He didn't. I led him."

"Then you ought to be ashamed of yourself, Master George. But tell me; why did you go back home?"

"To see what the place was like, and whether it could be built up again."

"Built up? Why, it hasn't been blown down."

"No; burnt down."

"Burnt! What, our house?"

"Yes."

"But not my kitchen? Oh, Master George, don't say that my kitchen has been burned too."

"There's nothing left of the place but a little firewood and a few scuttles of ashes."

Sarah wrung her hands. "Oh dear—oh dear!" she cried, "why wasn't I told before?"

"Never mind; you'll soon be well again. You were not told for fear of worrying you; and as soon as we have got rid of the Indians my father will have the place all built up again, and it will be better than ever."

Mass' George: A Boy's Adventures in the Old Savannah | 295

"Never!" said Sarah, emphatically. "But you were not hurt, my dear, were you?"

"No," I said, "only horribly frightened."

"No," said Sarah, emphatically, "you may have been startled, my dear, but I'm not going to believe that you were frightened. And you are hungry, too, and me not able to get about and cook you a bit of food."

"Oh, never mind. Now I know you are better I'll go and get something to eat."

"Yes, do, my dear, do," she cried, "and make haste. It was very kind of you to come. But do, please, do take care of yourself, my dear, and don't go running any more of these dreadful risks. Then you killed all the Indians?"

"They did," I said.

"That's a comfort," said Sarah. "I'm sorry for the poor savages, but it's their own fault. They should leave us alone. The cowards too—shooting a poor woman like me. Well, there's an end of them now."

"Of that party," I said. "We are afraid that there will be another attack to-night."

"What? Oh dear me! Now I ask you, Master George, how can I get well with such goings-on as this?"

I did what I could to cheer her up, and went out to find Hannibal just leaving the doctor, and ready to laugh at the wounds upon his arms as being too trifling to be worthy of notice. In fact the pains he suffered did not prevent him from partaking of a hearty meal, at which Pomp stood looking on regretfully. I happened to catch his eye just as I was eating rather voraciously, the excitement and exertion having given me a tremendous appetite.

"Have some, Pomp?" I said, feeling half guilty at sitting there eating, while the poor boy who had suffered so much in our service should be only looking on.

"What Mass' George say?" he replied, coming nearer.

"I say, will you have something to eat?"

Pomp sighed.

"What's the matter?" I asked.

"Poor Pomp can't."

"Can't? Why not? If I like to give you some now, no one will say anything."

"Poor fellow," I added to myself, "how he remembers that he is a slave!"

All the time I was cutting him one of the solid slices of bread in which I knew from old experience he delighted so much, and then carved off a couple of good, pink-striped pieces of cold salt pork. But he drew away with a sigh.

"Why, what's the matter, Pomp?"

"Eat much, too much now," he said, quaintly. "Pomp can't eat no more."

The mournful way in which he said this was comical in the extreme, for he accompanied it with a sigh of regret, and shook his head as he turned away, unable to bear longer the sight of the good food of which he was unable to partake.

I had hardly finished my meal, and begun to feel a little rested and refreshed, before I was attracted out into the enclosure where the ladies and children, whom I had seen only the day before looking cheerful and merry, were wearing a wild, scared look as they were being hurried into the block-house, while the most vigorous preparations were carried on.

"They don't mean to be taken by surprise, Morgan," I said, as I ran against him, watching. "The Indians may not come after all."

"Not come?" he said. "What! Haven't you heard?"

"I—heard?"

"The message brought in by one of the scouts?"

I had not heard that any had been sent out, and I said so.

"The General sent them out directly, and one has come back to say that they had found signs of Indians having been about, and that they had been round by our clearing."

"Yes! Well?" I said.

"The dead Indians were gone."

I started at the news.

"Perhaps they did not go to the right place."

"Oh, yes, they did," said Morgan, seriously, "because two men told me about finding the marks close beside the big tree where we had our fight."

"Marks?" I said.

"Yes; you know. Well, they are keeping a good look-out, spread all round, and keeping touch with each other. So you may be sure that the enemy is not far off, and we expect them down upon us before long."

The thought of all this made the evening look gloomy and strange, though it was a glorious sunset, for the clouds that gathered in the west were to me like the smoke of burning houses touched with fire, and the deep rich red glow like blood. And as I watched the changes, it seemed that the softened reflections had turned into one fierce fiery glow that told of the destruction of the fort and the houses of the settlement, till, as it all died out, the light growing paler and paler, there was nothing at last but the cold grey ashes to tell of where the houses had been.

Chapter Forty One

I quite started as a hand was laid upon my shoulder.

"Thinking, George?" said my father. I told him I had been watching the sunset. Shame kept me from saying more.

"Ah, yes," he said, sadly. "It was very glorious. What a pity that the beautiful land over which such a sun shines should be spoiled by bloodshed!"

"Do you think the Indians will come to-night?" I said, a little huskily.

He was silent for a few moments, and stood gazing in my face.

"Afraid?" he said, with a smile.

"Yes, father," I said, frankly. "It makes me feel afraid. But when all the fighting and excitement is going on I don't feel to mind it half so much."

"That is human nature, my boy," he said, smiling. "No doubt there are men who never know what fear is, but they must be very rare. I have known very few."

"But you, father?" I said, excitedly. "You never knew what it was to be afraid?"

He laughed as he pressed my shoulder with his hand.

"Always, my boy, when I am going to encounter danger, and from the General downward, I think I may say we all feel fear. It is no disgrace to a brave man to shrink from that which he has to encounter. Why, my experience teaches me that those men who think and feel in this way do the bravest deeds."

"Then I needn't be ashamed of feeling a little alarm—I mean being a bit of a coward now, father?"

"No," he said, with a peculiar smile. "But as it is highly probable that we shall be attacked to-night, it would be as well to be careful. The women and children are all in the block-house now; the men will be strongly posted at the gates and palisade, while the reserves will be in front of the block-house, in our rough outer works, ready to go to any menaced point or to cover their comrades if they have to retreat, and we are compelled to take to the block-house as a last resource.—There: I must go. You are tired, boy.

You have had a long and perilous day. I'll excuse you from everything to-night, and you had better get to the block-house and have a good night's rest."

"Oh, don't say that, father," I cried, dolefully. "Go and be shut up there with the women and children!"

"What do you wish to do, then?" he said, still smiling in a peculiar way.

"Be about here, and go round to the different sentries."

"With arrows flying, perhaps."

"But it will be dark, and they are not likely to hit," I said. "Besides, I might be useful fetching ammunition and helping to load."

"You can stay about," he said, clapping both hands on my shoulders, and laughing. "I don't think you need be ashamed of your cowardice, my boy."

He walked away, leaving me feeling puzzled, for I hardly knew what he meant, whether he was joking me or laughing at me for what I said. But it was all put out of my head directly by a little bustle at the gate, where the men who had been scouting were beginning to return, so as to be well in shelter before it grew dark; and as I followed them up, the report they made to the officers soon reached my ears.

It was very brief: they had seen no Indians, but had followed the track of those who had fetched away the bodies of their dead, and traced them to a portion of the forest some six miles away, when, not feeling it wise to follow farther, they had come straight across country home.

There was neither moon nor star that night, as, with every light carefully extinguished in camp, patient watch was kept, and every eye fixed from three of the sides upon the edge of the forest beyond the plantations. So still was everything that, save when a faint whisper rose when an officer went round, the place might have been unoccupied.

But the hours glided by with nothing to occasion the slightest alarm, as we all listened to the faint sounds which came from distant forest and swamp. So still was it that even the splash of some great fish in the river reached our ears as we leaned over the great fence by the gateway.

I had been round the enclosure with my father twice in the course of the evening, for though tired I was too much excited to sleep. Then I had been and had a chat with our Sarah, in the hospital-room, and after that gone to the little side shelter by our tent, where Hannibal and Pomp were both sleeping as peaceably as if there were no danger in the air.

As I stood looking down at them, it was with something like a feeling of envy, for I was terribly heavy, and would gladly have lain down to sleep, but it was impossible then; and as I left them and crossed the great enclosure, I heard a low whispered conversation going on just in front, and as I stopped short a hand caught mine, and said sternly—

"Who is this? Oh, it's you, young Bruton. No alarm, is there?"

It was Colonel Preston who spoke, and after telling him that all seemed quiet I passed on, and in an uneasy way went from sentry to sentry to say a word or two to each, as I inquired whether my father had been by.

He had not, so I went on till I came to the corner of the enclosure farthest from the forest, where I could dimly see the man on duty straining himself over the great fence; and so occupied was he in gazing into the distance that he did not notice my presence till I spoke. "You, Master George?"

"You, Morgan?"

"Why, I thought you'd ha' been asleep."

"No; I could not go," I said. "But why were you looking out there?"

"I don't know, my lad," he whispered. "This sort of work puts one all on the screw and fidget. I do nothing else but fancy all sorts of things, and keep finding out I'm wrong."

"But the Indians are not likely to come this way," I said. "It is too far from the forest."

"Then the more likely, my lad. But speak lower. Now look straight out there, and try if you can see anything."

I looked out in the gloom in the direction indicated, and said softly—

"Yes, I am looking."

"Well, what can you see?"

"A house."

"Yes, that's right; just dimly showing against the sky."

"Well, what of it? It is Colonel Preston's."

"I didn't know for certain, but I thought it was his. Well, look again; can you see anything about it?"

I looked, making a telescope of my hands, and then laughed to myself.

"As I watched it, Master George, it seemed to me as if there was some one moving about it. I'm sure I saw men against the sky."

Mass' George: A Boy's Adventures in the Old Savannah | 301

"Why, Morgan," I said, "what you see is those tall, thin cypress trees standing up at the ends. They do look something like people, but they would be folks twenty feet high."

"Nonsense, sir! Look again."

I did look again, and, very dimly-seen against the sky, I fancied I could see something moving, and I had no doubt now about its being the colonel's house, for it was the only one standing on raised ground.

"Well," whispered Morgan, "what do you make of it now?"

"Nothing. One's eyes get dizzy and misty with looking so long. I believe it is only fancy."

Morgan gazed long and eagerly for quite a minute before he said in a low, excited whisper—

"Then fancy's precious busy to-night, Master George. I got to be wonderful powerful in the sight during the wars, being out on vidette duty. I say there's something wrong there."

I looked again, but I could not distinguish anything, and I said so.

"Look here, sir," whispered Morgan, "I don't like to give an alarm for nothing, but I can't rest over this. Will you ask the captain to come?"

"Tell you what," I said; "I'll fetch Pomp first. He has eyes like a cat."

"The very thing, sir. Fetch him," whispered Morgan, and I hurried back to our quarters, roused up Pomp, who was ill-tempered at being disturbed, and taking him by the wrist I led him to Morgan's post, telling him in whispers the while what I wanted of him.

"But it all dark," he said, peevishly. "How Pomp go to see in um dark? Wait till a-morrow morning."

"Come, Pomp," I said; "don't be foolish. You have such good eyes, and we want you to see."

"No; not good eyes," he said. "All seepy now out ob 'em."

"Hush! Don't talk," I said, gently.

"How Pomp see which way um go if don't talk lil bit? I tink you berry cross on poor lil nigger, Mass' George."

"Hist! Here we are."

"Hah! Now we shall see," said Morgan, eagerly. "Come, Pomp, look over yonder—straight away beneath that tall tree that goes to a point. Now then, what can you see?"

"House," replied the boy, shortly.

"Well, what else?"

"Lot man coming and going way 'gain."

"There!" said Morgan, triumphantly. "Now, Master George, was I right?"

"Who are they, Pomp?" I whispered. "Look, quick!"

"Pomp can't look, so 'leepy."

"But you must."

"Pomp go back—go 'leep."

"No, on, please look again. Oh, Pomp!"

"Mass' George want Pomp look?"

"Yes, yes."

"Mass' George won't call Pomp 'tupid lil nigger 'gain?"

"I'll promise anything, only pray look."

The boy rested his chin on the fence, and gazed again, while I could hear my heart going *thump, thump* with excitement.

"Lot men. All black dark."

"Black?" I said, eagerly. "You don't mean the slaves?"

"Pomp nebber say dey nigger. Pomp say all black."

"Don't talk so loudly," whispered Morgan, eagerly.

"Pomp no want talk loud. Pomp go back 'leep."

"No, no, pray look again and tell me, Pomp," I whispered.

"Mass' Morgan talk sabbage. Want to flog Pomp."

"No, no, he does not, and I want you to look and tell me."

"Pomp look and tell Mass' George, but now too 'leepy, an' eye all 'tick togedder much, tell Mass' Morgan."

"Then tell me," I whispered.

He looked again, then seemed suddenly to grow interested, and as excited as we were, as he caught my arm.

"Dem Injum!"

"There, Master George. Quick! Fetch the captain."

"No, no, fire and give the alarm," I said.

"No. Better not. It will alarm them too. Go and fetch the captain."

I hurried away, closely followed by Pomp, and luckily found my father on his way to go the rounds in company with Colonel Preston.

I told them what we had seen, and they hurried with us to the spot where Morgan was on duty.

"It can only mean one thing," said the colonel, excitedly. "They would not trouble much about plunder."

"What do you mean then?" said my father; "a point from which to attack?"

"No," said the colonel, hoarsely. "That!"

As he said the words, there was a faint gleam of light in the direction of the house, a flash, then quite a burst of ruddy flame; and by the time we reached Morgan, his face was lit up by the glow as the wooden structure blazed away rapidly, and the flames like great golden tongues licked at porch and veranda; while from one window, which showed quite plainly, so great a volume rushed out that it showed where the house had been fired.

There was no need to sound an alarm, the great golden fire-flag which floated in the darkness of the night brought every man out to gaze; and as the flames mounted higher, illuminating the settlement far and near, the other houses stood forth plainly, the trees seemed turned to gold, and the wavy corn and cane came into sight and died out again in a way wonderful to behold.

"Preston! Bruton!" said a firm voice, "round to the men. Every one on his guard. Reserves in the centre ready. This is a ruse to take our attention prior to an attack."

I looked up admiringly at the stern old man, who gave his orders so promptly, and then saw my father and the colonel hurry off, while the General shaded his eyes, and looked keenly over the place.

"No," he said, as if to himself, as he drew back. "Ah, you boys! Your eyes are young and sharp. Try if you can see the Indians crossing along by the edges of either of the plantations, or coming this way."

"No, sir," I said, quickly. "I have been trying to see them."

"Injum gone round dah," said Pomp, pointing.

"Ah!" cried the general; "you saw them?"

"Yes; gone dat big house."

"Mine," said the General, with a quick catching of the breath. "Yes; there is no doubt about that."

For as we were speaking, a tiny tongue of fire began to creep up one of the pine-tree supports of the porch, which, quite invisible before, now stood out plainly, and in a very few minutes was blazing furiously, while a light from the back showed that it had been fired there as well.

"Watch for the men who are doing this, my boy," said the General. "Here, sentry, can you use that piece of yours?"

"Middlin', sir, middlin'," replied Morgan.

"Then wait till you see one of the wretches, and try and bring him down. No," he said, directly after, "it would be useless. It would have no good effect."

The Indians who had fired the General's house must have stolen off by the back, for Pomp did not see them go; and we were not long in learning that they were busy still, for at intervals of only a few minutes, six more of the best of the settlers' houses were blazing furiously, lighting up the whole of the clearings, while the sparks ascended in great clouds, and floated gently away as if a fall of snow had been suddenly turned into gold.

Overhead a cloud of wreathing smoke rolled over and over, turned ruddy by the burning homes, as if a second fire were in the heavens, and reflecting the light so that the block-house and the encumbered enclosure, with its piles of boxes and rough furniture, with here and there a tent, rapidly grew lighter and lighter, but with shadows of intense blackness marked out where the light did not fall.

So clearly did the defenders' faces show now, as they sheltered behind the defences, that had there been high ground near that the enemy could have held, our position would have been bad, so excellent a mark should we have made for the Indian arrows. But, fortunately for us, save where Colonel Preston's house stood, the land round the fort was absolutely flat, and the Indians could not very well get into position for attack without exposing themselves to a rain of bullets.

Our officers were soon fairly well satisfied that if an attack were coming it would be from the dark side, and there our forces were concentrated to stand waiting, while scarcely any one but the sentries stood at the fence nearest the house and watched the flames.

Had the houses been together, the whole place would have been rapidly burned down; but, fortunately for us, each little house stood in the middle of its own plot, fifty, a hundred, and sometimes several hundred yards apart, so that they burned as so many separate fires, others springing up in various directions till twelve were blazing, and no effort could be made to check the flames.

"It would only be sending men to their death," I heard my father say as I stood near, hot with impotent rage.

"Yes. It is impossible to do anything," replied the General. "If we were free to act, our whole force could not save the houses; and I cannot set the men to work with their buckets in the blazing light, to be shot down by the arrows of the Indians hidden somewhere in the darkness."

As the twelfth house blazed up, with the Indians still cunningly keeping out of sight and crawling among the trees or crops, we all stood watching the houses left, wondering which would be the next to burst out into flame; but now we waited in vain, for the destruction had ceased as far as fresh additions were concerned. But the doomed dwellings crackled and flashed, and every time a beam or a ceiling fell in, the heavens were brilliant with the great bursts of sparks, which eddied and rose higher and higher, to join the great cloud floating quietly toward the now golden river.

Still there was no sign of Indians; and at last my father walked round to the other side to join the most keen-sighted of our men in the look-out for the enemy, who was momentarily expected to be detected creeping up.

From where I now stood I could hear the buzz of voices in the block-house, where the whole of the occupants were watching the destruction—in twelve of the cases this being the sweeping away of a treasured and peaceful home.

By degrees the exclamations and words of sorrow—more than once mingled with sobs—grew fainter, and there was a terrible silence, through which came the sharp hissing and crackling of the burning wood, with again and again a dull thud as some beam went down. At such times the flames seemed to glow with twofold brilliancy, and the sparks were doubled in size, while after a few minutes the fire, that had been temporarily damped, blazed up higher than ever.

"If we only had the orders to shoot," I heard one man say to another, "I wouldn't care then."

"But there's nothing to shoot at," was the reply. "I say, though, I've been thinking."

"What?"

"Suppose that they could manage to set fire to the block-house here."

"Don't talk about it, man. What? With those women and children there! No; we must shelter them from that, even if we die for it."

I was standing with my father when Colonel Preston's house had been reduced to a glowing heap of embers, and he came up to my father to say in a light, cheerful way—

"Ah, I've been looking for you, Bruton. I wanted to tell you that I thoroughly understand now what your feelings must have been like the other night."

"Don't talk about it," said my father.

"Oh, I don't know," said the colonel. "It's painful, but one knows the worst."

"No," said my father, sadly; "unfortunately we do not know the worst."

"What do you mean? We can soon set to work and rebuild. The ground is clear. We cannot be so badly off as when we first landed."

"I was thinking," said my father, in a low voice, "that the enemy has achieved his work for the night, but to-morrow they will continue this horrible destruction, and the next night and the next night, till the palisade and the block-house only remain. Then the worst will come."

"They will try and fire that?" said the colonel, in a whisper.

"Yes. We have a deadly foe to combat, and one full of cunning."

"But we must never let him and his fire-fiends approach the place,—we must make an outer palisade."

"Of brave men?" said my father. "Yes; I had thought of that; but the danger cannot be stopped that way. They will fire the place without coming close."

"How?" cried the colonel.

"With winged messengers," said my father; and I felt what he was going to say before he spoke.

"Fiery arrows? I see what you mean. Pray heaven they may not think of such a hideous plan. But if they do, Bruton, we are Englishmen, and know how to die."

"Yes," said my father, sadly. "If the worst comes to the worst, we know how to die. Well, there will be no attack to-night," he continued; and he turned round and seemed to realise the fact that I was there, having forgotten my presence in the earnestness of his conversation with the colonel.

"Ah, George," he said, "I did not think that you were there to hear what I said. Did you catch it?"

"Yes, father," I said in a hoarse voice.

"What did I say?"

"That we should know how to die."

There was silence then, and the ruddy glow in the smoke-clouds began to die away, leaving everything dark, and cold, and depressing; so that the cheerful words of the various officers now, as they talked encouragingly to the men, appeared to have lost their power.

Chapter Forty Two

Morning at last, after the horrors of that eventful night. Every one looked jaded and despondent; but as the sun rose, and the women and children were allowed to leave the confinement of the prison-like block-house to return to their larger tents and shelters, a good deal of the misery and discomfort was forgotten.

For as soon as it was day a couple of scouting parties issued from the gate and advanced cautiously through the plantations, tracing the course of the Indians easily enough, and following it up to the forest.

The advance was made with the greatest precaution, the men stealing from garden to plantation, and from fence to fence, expecting to receive arrows at any moment, and with their fire-locks ready to reply to the first inimical shot.

But no arrow sped toward them as they scouted on past the ruined houses; and the men's countenances grew sadder as they passed the smouldering heaps of ashes, and grasped their pieces more firmly, longing for an opportunity to punish the wretches who were destroying our homes.

My father took command of one of these scouting parties, and after a little persuasion he gave me his consent that we two boys should accompany it. He refused at first, but on my pointing out how keen Pomp's sight and sense of hearing were, he reluctantly said yes, and we went slowly on.

We stopped at each burned home we passed, to see how complete the destruction was; and, though I said nothing to my father, I could not help comparing the piles of newly-charred wood, and ashes to what I had seen at our own clearing.

It was exciting work as we went on, with our eyes fixed upon every spot likely to afford shelter to an Indian. The men spread out, and worked round clump of trees or patch of cane. But no Indian was seen, and at last we approached the forest.

Here Pomp was invaluable. He seemed to have no sense of fear, in spite of the experiences he had gone through; and again and again he had to be checked and kept from rushing among the trees, where the enemies might have been lying waiting in force.

He was not long in pointing out the place where the Indians had left the shelter of the forest, and soon after he found out another spot where it was quite as plain that they had returned—evidently working in a regularly organised way; and at first sight, as we gazed down at the footprints, one might have thought that only one man had passed, but my father explained to me how one seemed to have stepped in another's track, which had grown deeper and broader, till it was plainly marked wherever the soil was soft.

As soon as Pomp had pointed this out, he was for diving in among the densely-clustered trees, which began directly cultivation ended, just beyond where their fellows had been levelled and dragged away, leaving the stumps in many cases standing out of the ground with the crops between. But my father sternly called him back, and, satisfied that the enemy was not within touch, as proved by the fact that no arrow had sped towards us, the word was passed along the widespread line from our centre to the extreme ends, and we retreated, leaving three videttes under shelter in commanding positions, where they could at once see if any Indian scouts left the edge of the forest, and so give the alarm.

As we marched back toward the fort through the plantations, which were already displaying the effects of neglect, I asked my father if he did not think it possible that the Indians might be watching us all the time.

"They were watching Morgan and me that day when we killed the rattlesnake," I said.

"It is quite possible," he replied, turning to me directly; "but we could do no more. My orders were to search the ground, and make sure that no Indians were lurking in the plantations. I have done that. To have attempted to enter the forest with the few men under my orders would have been to invite destruction without doing any good."

"Yes, I see, father," I replied.

"They may have been lying in hiding only a short distance in, but I scarcely think so. The temptation to destroy from their lurking-places, whence they could shoot at us unseen, would have been too great."

By this time we had reached the gate, and we filed in for my father to go and make his report of what he had done to our commanding officer, while I went with Pomp to where Hannibal was playing the part of cook, and waiting our return.

"What's the matter?" I said to my companion, who was looking disturbed and sulky.

"Why come back?" he said. "Why not go shoot all um Injum, and—"

Pomp stopped short and gave a loud sniff.

He had smelt food, and nothing else had the smallest interest for him now till his wants had been supplied.

A busy day was spent in perfecting our means of defence against the enemy we dreaded now the most. Blankets were laid ready by twos, and men were drilled in the use to which they were to be put if the block-house was fired. For they were to be rapidly spread here and there and deluged with water, scouting parties being sent out to each of the uninjured homes in turn to collect any tubs or barrels that had been overlooked before.

The men worked well, and a cheer was sent up whenever some barrel was rolled in from one of the farther dwellings and carried up to the block-house roof, and filled ready. But at last there was nothing more to be done in this direction, and we rested from our labours.

So great had been the stress of the previous night, that the men were ordered to lie down to sleep in turns, so as to be prepared for a fresh alarm; but it was a long time before I could close my eyes as I lay under the canvas.

I was weary, of course, but too weary, and though I closed my eyes tightly, and said I would go to sleep, there was always something to battle against it. At one time, just as I fancied I was dozing off, there was the sound of footsteps and a burst of laughter from some of the children, who raced about in the hot sunshine untroubled by the dangers that threatened.

As I lay listening, and recognising the sport in which they were engaged, I could not help wishing that I was a child, and not mixed up with all these terrors just as if I were a man.

"If we could only be at peace again!" I thought; and I lay wakeful, still thinking of the garden, the growing fruit, the humming-birds that whirred about like great insects among the flowers, and emitted a bright flash every now and then as the sun glanced from their scale-like feathers.

Then I pictured the orioles too, that pale yellow one with the black back and wings, and the gay orange and black fellow I so often saw among the trees. "How beautiful it all used to be!" I sighed. "Why can't the Indians leave us alone?"

At last I grew drowsy, and lay dreamily fancying it was a hot, still night at home with the window open, and the cry of the whip-poor-will—that curious night-jar—coming from out of the trees of the swamp far beyond the stream where the alligators bellowed and the frogs kept up their monotonous, croaking roar.

Buzz—oooz—oooz!

"Bother the flies!"

I was wide-awake with the sun glaring on the canvas, and a great fly banging against it, knocking and butting its head and wings, when all the time there was the wide opening through which it had come ready for it to fly out.

"Ugh! You stupid thing," I muttered, pettishly, as I lay watching it hardly awake, thinking I would get up and catch it, or try to drive it out; but feeling that if I did I should only kill it or damage it so that its life would be a misery to it, make myself hotter than I was, and perhaps not get rid of the fly after all.

"Well," I cried, pettishly, "that's too bad!"

For there was a fresh buzzing. Another fly had dashed in, and the two were playing a duet that was maddening to my overwrought senses.

"Now, what can be the use of flies?" I said, pettishly. "They are insufferable: buzzing, teasing, and stinging, making the whole place miserable."

I was in such an overstrung state from want of rest and excitement that I found myself thinking all kinds of nonsense, but there was some common-sense mixed up with it, like a few grains of oats amongst a great deal of the rough tares in which they grew, and I began to look at the state of affairs from the other point of view, as I watched those two flies darting here and there in zigzag, or sailing round and round, to every now and then encounter with a louder buzz, and dart off again. And in spite of my vexation, I found myself studying them, and thinking that small as they were their strength was immense. Compared to mine it was astounding. I walked a few miles and I was weary, but here were they apparently never tiring, darting here and there with their wings vibrating at such an astounding rate that they were invisible. *Whizz—whuzz—dash!*—here, there, and everywhere with lightning-like rapidity.

"It's wonderful," I said at last, and I thought how strange it was that I had never thought of such a thing before.

"Now I dare say," I found myself saying, "they think that we are as great a nuisance as we think them, for putting up a rough canvas tent like this, and catching them so that they cannot get out. Stuff! I don't believe flies can think, or else they would be able to find the way out again."

Buzz—buzz! buzz—buzz!

A regular heavy, regular long-drawn breathing that grew louder now after a rustling sound, and I knew at once that it was Pomp who had turned round, got into an uncomfortable position, and was now drawing his breath in a way that closely resembled a snore.

"Oh, you tiresome wretch!" I muttered. "How dare you go and sleep soundly when I am so tired out that I can't?"

At last in utter despair I rose, pulled off my loose coat so as only to retain shirt and breeches, bathed my face in a bucket just outside, and could not resist the temptation to sprinkle a few drops on Pomp's face as he lay there fast asleep in the shade. But they had not the slightest effect, and I crept into our rough tent again, smoothed the blanket, and lay down and closed my eyes once more, while the two flies were joined by another, and the buzzing was louder than ever.

"Go on," I said; "I don't care. One can't go to sleep in the daytime, but one can rest one's legs;" and as I said this pettishly I knew it was not true, for Pomp's heavy breathing came plainly through the canvas to prove how thoroughly I was in the wrong.

So giving up all idea of going to sleep, I lay there on my back, looking up at the fabric of the canvas, through which every now and then there was a faint ray of sunshine so fine that a needle-point would have been large in comparison. Then I began to think about my father, and what a deal of care and anxiety he seemed to have; how sad he generally was; and I set his grave manner down to the real cause—my mother's death.

Then I began to think of how hot it was, and that as near as I could guess it must be two hours after noon. Then about how pleasant it would be to begin rebuilding our house, and how long it would take, and about Hannibal and Pomp, and what a gentleman the former seemed to be by nature in his stern, quiet way; always willing to do anything for us, and watching me whenever he saw me, to know if there was anything I wanted; and so big, and strong, and brave.

Then I thought of our terrible experience under the great cypress tree, and at one time it was very horrible, but directly after not at all so.

"It seems very terrible to kill any one, but Han knew that if he did not kill them they would kill us, and I do believe he would sooner be killed himself than let any one hurt either father or me. And what a rum little fellow Pomp is," I thought; "and how he gives up directly Hannibal says anything in his language.

Mass' George: A Boy's Adventures in the Old Savannah | 313

"I wonder what his language is! One can't call it black language, because it isn't black—only what black people speak. I wonder whether I could learn it. Seems to be all *ing,* and *ung,* and *ang,* and *ng,* without any letters before it. I'll make Hannibal teach me to speak like he does. He would if I asked him. S'pose I should have to learn it without books, and one couldn't write it, and— Oh, dear me! How hot, and tired, and thirsty I am!

"I wish Pomp wouldn't buzz so.

"No, I mean I wish the flies wouldn't snore so.

"No; I mean the Indians—the—"

I started up, and looked round confusedly, to see the flies darting here and there, and buzzing more loudly than ever, while Pomp had settled into a decided snore. It was hotter than before, and great drops stood on my face, and tickled as they ran together and made greater drops. The children too were still playing about, and laughing merrily, and I went on thinking that the flies must be teasing Pomp very much, and that those children would laugh and play if the Indians came and buzzed round the tent; and that one which had settled on the canvas just over my head didn't frighten them by swelling out so big, and opening and shutting his great jaws with such a loud snap. What a number of fish he must eat in a day, and how I should have liked to watch him when he beat the water with his tail, so as to stun the fish and make them easy to catch!

"And so that's where you live, is it, my fine fellow? Pomp and I will come with a stick, and thrust it down the hole, and make you bite, and drag you out. We should want a rope ready to put round your neck, and another to tie your jaws, and one of us would have to slip it on pretty quickly before you spread your wings and began to fly round the tent, and began talking in that ridiculous way. Whoever heard of an alligator imitating Morgan, and trying to deceive me like that, just as we were going to catch him on the canvas where it was so tight? Eh! What say? Why don't you bellow? What!—no, I shan't. He is very comfortable here, and— Ah!"

That alligator had crept over into the tent, planted its foot upon my chest, and was moving it heavily, as it said out of the darkness in Morgan's voice—

"Oh, Master George, do wake up, my lad, and come! Be quick, pray!"

Chapter Forty Three

Quite dark. My head confused. The alligator's foot on my chest. No; it was the butt-end of a gun pushing me.

"Here! Don't! What's the matter?"

"I thought I should never get you to wake, sir. Come along. The Indians are here."

I sprang out of the tent, with it gradually dawning upon me that I had been sleeping heavily from early afternoon right into the darkness of night, and dreaming away in a heavily confused fashion of the various objects that had just filled my eyes and ears.

"You said the Indians were here?" I said, excitedly.

"Yes, my lad. Look!"

I gazed in the direction pointed out, and saw there was a bustle going on at the block-house, where by a faint blaze men were throwing buckets of water.

"Just caught it in time, sir," continued Morgan. "They mean mischief now."

"Yes, I know. They fired arrows at it blazing."

"How did you know when you were asleep?"

"My father expected they would; I heard him say so."

"Ah, well, they won't do it again. We're going to soak blankets, and lay all over the top."

"Morgan, look—look!" I exclaimed, as three fiery long-tailed stars came swiftly sailing through the air from one direction; and as if they had been sent as a signal, three more came from the opposite quarter, and directly after two more threes, and all fell blazing on different parts of the block-house, the Indians evidently aiming for the spot where the first blaze appeared — that which was rapidly being extinguished as I crept out of our tent.

These fiery arrows had no doubt been prepared with tufts of cotton saturated with some resinous gum, which, after being lighted, burned furiously in its rapid passage through the air, and seemed to resist the efforts of those who were on the roof trying to extinguish the patches of glowing fire. In fact their efforts soon became useless, for the first twelve arrows were followed by dozens more, and then by hundreds, till at one time quite a fiery shower descended on the doomed place; while, emboldened by their success, amidst a fierce yelling, some of the Indians ran from their cover, their progress being marked by tiny specks of light which seemed to glide like fireflies over the fields. Then they made a sudden dart, blazed out, and stuck in the sides of the fort.

This was repeated again and again before sharp orders were rung out, and from that moment whenever one of these sparks was seen gliding along toward the palisades, it was met by shot after shot, sometimes by a regular volley. Twice over as I watched I saw one of these sparks drop to the ground and begin to burn, showing by it the body of an Indian; but though scores of shots were fired, these were the only two which checked the savages, who, encouraged by their success, kept on running in and shooting at the fort.

"Hard to hit a man running with a bullet," said Morgan, in answer to one of my ejaculations of impatience.

"But why are you here, Morgan?" I said, suddenly, as I felt that most of the defenders were either at work firing, or busy with buckets and water.

"Because I was sent here, sir," said Morgan, gruffly.

And though I questioned him, he said no more, but chuckled a little when I made a guess, and said that my father must have sent him to look after me.

The men on the roof of the block-house worked splendidly amidst the fiery shower, though they were checked several times by the horrible missiles taking effect, inflicting wounds and burning the poor fellows' clothing as well; but they returned to their duty as soon as their comrades were passed down below into the fort, and wherever the flames got hold they were extinguished. But that which the falling arrows sent high in air, to drop almost perpendicularly on the fort, failed to do, though shot with wondrous skill, was accomplished by the arrows sent in the ordinary way point-blank against the walls.

I was watching the progress of the attack with Morgan, and we were uttering congratulations about the admirable way in which the men on the roof worked, and how cleverly each fiery messenger was quenched now almost as soon as it fell, when there was a fresh attack.

"Yes; we've done 'em, clever as they are, this time, sir," said Morgan. "I tell you what: if I'd had the management of that affair I'd have had young Pomp up there."

"Where is he?" I said, for I had forgotten all about him.

"'Long of his father carrying water, sir. But as I was saying, I'd have had young Pomp up there with a small bucket as he could handle easy, half full o' water, and set him to catch the arrows as they fell. He's quick as lightning, and I'll be bound to say he'd have caught the arrows one by one in his bucket."

"Look—look!" I cried excitedly.

"Eh? What? Ah!" ejaculated Morgan, as evidently from behind one of the houses, quite invisible in the darkness, we saw quite a little group of specks glide out, and almost simultaneously another group—and there seemed to be about thirty in each—came out from the other side, the two parties joining with almost military precision, and gliding as it were over the fields till quite close in, when there was a perfect blaze of light as a golden cloud of trailing lights was discharged straight at the wooden wall of the fort, and in a few seconds it was wrapped in fire from top to bottom.

A tremendous yell followed this successful discharge, but it was drowned by the rapid firing which succeeded, and as I looked on excitedly, longing to go and assist, and wondering why I had received no orders, I had the satisfaction of seeing figures flitting to and fro before the blazing pine-trunks, and hearing the hiss of the water as bucketful after bucketful was discharged.

"Why, Morgan!" I exclaimed suddenly; "the women and children?"

"Well, sir, they'd be safe enough."

"What, if the fire is not put out?"

"Oh, it'll be put out, my lad. Look, they're battering it now. It aren't so fierce, but they don't happen to be there; the captain spoke to the governor this afternoon."

"To the General?"

"Yes, sir. We're getting to call him the governor now; and the captain told him, I hear, that he was afraid the main attack would be on the block-house, and it was settled to have all the women and children out; and they're all safe behind barricades in the middle there. Yonder, you see."

"See? No," I said; "how can I see through this terrible darkness?"

"Darkness?" said Morgan, in a peculiar tone. "I was just thinking that it was a bit lighter now, and yet they seem to be getting the fire a bit under."

"Yes," I said; "and now the clouds of steam are rising; you can see them quite plainly now. Perhaps they are reflecting the light down upon the building. Oh, look!"

I could hold back no longer, but started off at a run, closely followed by Morgan, so as to get to the other side and see what was going on there.

For I had suddenly grasped the meaning of the light that had puzzled me. It was plain enough now. With their customary cunning, the Indians had fired such a flight of fiery arrows that they had forced our people to combine their forces to put out the blazing side of the block-house, and then combining their own forces, the enemy had sent low down on the opposite side, after creeping close in, a tremendous discharge, which at once took hold, and the flames as I got round were already running up the building, fanned by the wind which seemed to be rising, and there was a fluttering roar which sounded like the triumphant utterances of the flames.

"That comes of using pine-logs," said Morgan, in a low voice, as amidst the shouting of orders, the tramp of men, and the hissing of the fire, volley after volley was fired from the palisades; but naturally these shots sent forth into the darkness were aimless, and in imagination I could see the enemy, after sending in their arrows, crawling away unhurt.

The progress of this last fire was rapid. Something was done to check it at first with the buckets, and the brave fellows on the roof made desperate efforts by hanging the saturated blankets over the side, but they were soon driven back by the heat and smoke; all but one, whom I saw—after working desperately, the leader evidently of the shadowy-looking, blackened band— topple forward and fall into the flames at the foot, just as a herculean black approached, bearing two buckets of water.

Then there was a rush, a deal of confusion and shouting; and as I neared I saw the black coming through the crowd bearing some one on his shoulder.

I needed no telling that the slave, whoever he was, had dashed in and dragged the fallen man away, and, roused to enthusiasm by the daring act, I was approaching the group, when I heard murmurs running from one to the other of the line of men we had approached, men whose duty it had been to pass water from the well to those whose task it was to scatter the fluid on the flames.

"What—what did they say, Morgan?" I whispered.

"Water's give out, sir."

"What! Just as it is needed most?"

"Ay, my lad, that's just when it would be sure to go. They've been too generous with it t'other side."

"But look!" I said; "the fire's getting firmer hold. Can nothing be done?"

"Not that we can do, sir," said Morgan, sadly. "It's got it tight now."

It was too true. Started by the Indians' fiercely-blazing arrows, the pine-logs were beginning to blaze well now, dispiriting those who had worked so bravely before; and, seeing that their attack hail been successful, the Indians ceased now to send in their fiery flights, for moment by moment the flames increased, completely enveloping one corner of the block-house, and displaying such fierce energy that we knew the place was doomed.

And now, not to solve a puzzle that had troubled me, but of course to strike fresh terror into their enemies, the Indians made it plain how they had managed to keep up their supply of fiery shafts. For, all at once, a house standing back in the plantation, on each of the three sides of the fort away from the river front, began to stand out clear in the darkness of the night. One of them was the place from behind which I had seen the two groups of sparks glide out, and in these they had cunningly had parties preparing the fiery arrows ready to start alight for others to discharge.

Yell after yell now arose from a distance as the three houses rapidly began to blaze and add to the lurid glare that was illumining the whole interior of the enclosure, while groups of smoke-blackened men were watching the destruction going on.

"Better seek cover, my lads," cried Colonel Preston. "Get your pieces, and be ready. We can do no more there. It must burn."

The men showed their military training by rapidly getting their piled weapons, and taking their positions behind the barricades which surrounded the temporary quarters of the women and children.

"I don't think they'll attack," said Colonel Preston to the General, who came up now.

"No," he said, calmly. "The men are standing well to their places round the palisades, but I have no fear of an assault to-night. By the way, how is Bruton?"

I heard the words, and my throat seemed to grow dry.

"Bruton? I don't know. Tired out, I suppose."

"What!" said the General; "didn't you know?"

"Nothing; only that we have all been working like slaves to put that fire out."

"Great heavens, Preston, didn't you hear?"

"Hear?" cried the colonel, excitedly; "is he wounded?"

"Not wounded, but badly hurt, I fear. Didn't you see a man fall from the roof right into the flames?"

"Yes, but—"

"It was Bruton."

"Ah!"

I felt as if I should have dropped, but at that moment, as I was trying to get over the horrible feeling of sickness, and to make my way to the place the doctor had been forced to take as his temporary hospital, I felt a thrill of delight run through me, for a voice exclaimed—

"Gentlemen, are you all mad?"

"Bruton!" exclaimed Preston, hoarsely; "then you are not badly hurt?"

"Badly enough," said my father; "but look—look! Of what are you thinking?"

"Thinking?" cried the General. "We can do no more; the place is doomed."

"But are we to be doomed too, man?" cried my father, furiously; and he looked as if he might have had the question he had first asked put to him. For his face was blackened and wild, his long hair burned, and a terrible look of excitement was in his starting eyes.

"Doomed?" exclaimed the General and the colonel in a breath, as the men gathered round.

"Yes; the women—the children. This enclosure will be swept away. Have you forgotten the powder—the magazine?"

Chapter Forty Four

There was an involuntary movement amongst those within hearing at this, and for the moment it was as if every one present was about to seek safety in flight, as my father stood pointing wildly toward the blazing fort. Then, recovering himself from the shock of my father's words, the General exclaimed, hoarsely—

"I had forgotten that." And then in his customary firm way, he said, "The reserve supply of ammunition is in the little magazine, men. Twelve volunteers to bring it out."

A deathly silence for a few minutes, only broken by the terrible crackle and roar of the flames; and then my father stepped toward the blazing building.

"I am too much hurt to carry," he said, "but I will lead. Now, my lads, for Old England!"

"Hurray!" shouted Morgan, darting to his side, "and bonny Cymrw."

A great black figure with torn and scorched cotton garments was the next to step forward, and, carried away by a strange feeling of enthusiasm which mastered the horrible dread I felt, I ran to my father's side.

"No, no, no, my boy," he groaned. "Go back!"

"With you, father," I said; and he uttered a sob as he grasped my hand.

"God be with us!" I heard him whisper; and he said no more, but halting and resting wearily on me, as a dozen men now came forward with a cheer, he led the way to the door of the blazing pile.

Twice over I felt my legs tremble beneath me, but the tremor passed away in the excitement, and with the flames seeming to roar more fiercely, as if resenting an attempt to save that which was their prey, we passed from the eye-aching blaze of light through the strong doors into the black darkness of the fort, all reeking with smoke and steam.

Chapter Forty Five

I often sit back in my chair pondering about those old days, and thinking about them in a very different way to that in which I looked upon them then. For to be quite frank, though something in me kept tugging me on, and seeming to say to me, "Be a man; go bravely on and support your poor lame, suffering father, who is going to risk his life to save the poor people around!" there was something else which would keep suggesting that I might be killed, and that I should see the bright sunshine no more; that I was bidding farewell to everything; and I know I felt as if I would have given the world to have heard him say, "Go back. It is too dangerous for you."

But he only hesitated a few moments, and then, as I have said, he grasped my shoulder as if glad of my help, and went on into the great dark place.

On thinking over these things, I often tell myself that though my father may not have been a hero—and I don't believe much in heroes myself—I know they do brave deeds sometimes; but I have often found that they have what an American friend from the North—Pennsylvania way—called a great deal of human nature in them, and that sometimes when you come to know them, you find that they are very much like looking-glasses. I do not mean because they pander to your vanity and show you your own face, but because they are all bright and shining and surrounded by gold that is not solid, and have a side, generally kept close to the wall, which is all rough wood, paint, and glue.

Let me see! Where have I got to? Ah, I remember. I said my father may not have been a hero, but he had a great deal of that sterling stuff in him which you find in really sterling people; and in addition, he performed his brave acts in a quiet, unassuming way, so that often enough they passed unnoticed; and when he had finished, he sank back into his perfectly simple life, and never marched about in metaphorical uniform with a drawn sword, and men before him beating drums, and banging cymbals, and blowing trumpets for the people to see, and hear, and say, "Oh, what a brave man!"

Some may think it was not the act of a brave, self-denying man to let his young son go with him into that awful place to try and remove the powder.

I am not going to set up as his judge. He thought as a true man thinks, as a soldier, one of the thousands of true men we have had, who, without a word, have set their teeth fast, and marched for their country's sake straight away to where cannons were belching forth their terrible contents, and it has seemed as if the next step they took must be the last.

My father no doubt thought that as he was so weak he must have help, and that it would be better for his son to die helping him to save the lives of hundreds, than to hang back at such a time as that, when we marched straight into the steam and smoke of the burning block-house.

I can remember now that, although overhead the logs were burning and splitting and hissing in the fierce fire, and I knew that almost at any moment the burning timbers might come crashing down upon us, or the fire reach the little magazine of spare powder, the feeling of cowardice gave place to a strange sensation of exaltation, and I stood by my father, supporting him as he gave his orders firmly, the men responding with a cheer, and groping their way boldly to the corner of the building beyond the roughly-made rooms, where the good-sized place, half cellar, half closet, had been formed.

It was quite dark, and the men had to feel their way, while the air we breathed was suffocating, but we had to bear it.

My father, Morgan, and I were the first to reach the place, and there and then seized the cumbrous door which was made on a slope, like a shutter, to slide sidewise, while just above was a small opening leading into a rough room beyond, between the magazine and the outer wall, in which was a sort of port-hole well closed and barred.

"Shall I get through and open that port, sir?" cried Morgan, his voice sounding muffled and hoarse. "It will give us fresh air and light."

"Yes, and perhaps flames and sparks," cried my father. "No, no, down with you and hand out the powder-kegs. Form a line, men, and pass them along to the door."

"Hurrah!" came in muffled tones; and directly after, from somewhere below, Morgan's voice cried—

"Ready there! One!"

"Ready!—right!" cried a man by me, and a quick rustling sound told that the first powder-keg was being passed along.

"Ready!—two!" cried Morgan; and I pictured in my own mind Morgan down in the half cellar, handing out keg after keg, the men working eagerly in the dark, as they passed the kegs along, and a cheer from the outside reaching our ears, as we knew that the dangerous little barrels were being seized and borne to some place of safety. Not that in my own mind I could realise any place of safety in an open enclosure where sparks might be falling from the burning building, and where, if the Indians could only guess what was going on, flaming arrows would soon come raining down.

It was a race with death within there, as I well knew; and as I stood fast with my father's hand clutching my shoulder, and counted the kegs that were handed out, my position, seemed to me the most painful of all. If I had been hard at work I should not have felt it so much, but I was forced to be inert, and the sounds I heard as I stood breathing that suffocating air half maddened me.

Hissing that grew fiercer and fiercer as the fire licked up the moisture, sharp cracking explosions as the logs split, and must, I knew, be sending off bursts of flame and spark, and above all a deep fluttering roar that grew louder and louder till all at once there was a crash, a low crackling, and then, not two yards away from where I stood, a broad opening all glowing fire.

The men nearest to us uttered a yell, and there was the rush of feet, but my father's voice rose clear above all.

"Halt!" he cried; and discipline prevailed, as through the smoke I could now see all that was going on; Morgan still in the magazine, and Hannibal standing ready to take the kegs he passed out, while the men, instead of being in line, had crowded together by the entrance.

"How many more, Morgan?" said my father, calmly, as he backed a little toward the fiery opening at the end where I could feel the fierce glow on my back.

"Three more, sir. Shall we leave them and go?"

"Leave them? Come, my men, you can see what you are doing now. Morgan—Hannibal—the next keg."

It looked to be madness to bring out that keg into a low, earthen-floored room, one end of which was blazing furiously, with great tongues of fire darting toward us. But it was done; for Morgan stooped down and reappeared directly with a keg, which he handed to the great black, who took it quietly as if there was no danger, but only to have it snatched excitedly away by the next man, who passed it along the line.

"Steady, men!" said my father. "Don't make danger by being excited and dropping one of those barrels."

Those moments seemed to me to be hours. The heat was terrific, and the back of my neck was scorching as the second and third kegs were handed out.

"Last," shouted Morgan, with a wild cry of thankfulness.

"Look again," said my father. "Stand fast all."

Morgan dropped down again, and as he did so there was another crash behind us, a shower of sparks were literally shot into the place, and one burning ember fell right into the opening of the magazine, to be followed as Morgan leaped out by a quick sputtering noise, and then the smell of powder. There was a rush for the door, and we four were alone.

"Only a little loose powder lying about," said Morgan, huskily. "That was the last. Look out, Master George—quick!"

The task was done, the place saved from hideous ruin by an explosion; and as the last man rushed from the place, the energy my father had brought to bear was ended, and I had just time, in response to Morgan's warning, to save him from falling as he lurched forward.

But there was other help at hand, and we three bore him out fainting just as a burst of flame, sparks, and burning embers filled the place where we had stood a minute before, and we emerged weak and staggering, bearing my father's insensible form out into the bright light shed by the burning building.

"Bravely done! Bravely done!" we heard on all sides; and then there was a burst of cheering.

But I hardly seemed to hear it, as I was relieved by willing hands from my share in the burden, and I only recollected then finding myself kneeling beside a blanket under the rough canvas of our extemporised tent, waiting until the surgeon had ended, when I panted forth—

"Is—is he very bad?"

"Very, my lad," said the surgeon as he rose, "but not bad enough for you to look like that. Come, cheer up; I won't let him die. We can't spare a man like your father."

Chapter Forty Six

Everybody considered it was all over then, as we stood regularly at bay behind our palisades and barricades of boxes, cases, and furniture with which the women and children were surrounded, watching the flames of the great block-house rising higher and higher in the still night air, in a way that to me was awful.

So there we were waiting for the final onslaught, gloomy, weary, and dispirited. The men were chilled, many of them, with the water, and worn out by their efforts, and as I went round from group to group silently, in search of some one I knew to talk to, I could not help seeing that they were beaten, and thinking that the Indians would have an easy task now when they came.

"It's very horrible," I thought; and I went over the past, and dwelt upon the numbers that we must have killed. I knew that there would be no mercy; that the men would all be butchered, and the women and children, if they escaped that fate, would be carried off into a horrible captivity.

Pomp seemed to have disappeared, for though I came upon group after group of black faces whose owners sat about in a stolid indifferent way, as if the affair did not concern them, and they were resting until called upon to work once more, I did not see our boy.

I could not see Colonel Preston, and Morgan had gone away from my side on being summoned by one of the men.

There were plenty of our people about, but all the same I seemed to be alone, and I was wandering along in the fitful glare of the fire, when I saw at last a group of men standing together by a pile of something wet and glistening, over which one man was scattering with his hand some water from a bucket as if to keep the surface wet, and in this man I recognised Morgan.

"What's he doing?" I asked myself; and it was some few moments before I could grasp the truth, and then in a shrinking manner, with sensations similar to those I had felt when I was going into the burning block-house, I slowly advanced toward the group.

Sparks were being hurled high in the air at every fall of beam or timber, and they rushed round and round, as if agitated by a whirlwind, to be carried far away, but every now and then flashes of fire that escaped the whirl floated softly here and there, making it seem horrible to me as I watched them drop slowly to earth, some to be extinguished and disappear just as a great pat of snow will melt away when it touches the moist ground, while others remained alight and burned for a few moments.

"If one did," I said to myself as I approached timidly, for I knew now that I was opposite to the little heap of powder-kegs that had been brought out of the magazine with so much risk, and were lying covered over with canvas and a tarpaulin, whose surface was being kept wet.

"The powder, Morgan?" I said, as I approached, just as the men were talking earnestly together, Morgan standing by and holding his empty bucket.

"Yes, sir; the powder," he replied, turning and giving me a nod before looking back at his companions and saying sadly—

"Then you do mean it, my lads?"

"I do," said one of the men, sternly; "and I think it's what we ought to do."

"Without waiting for orders from our officers?"

"I shouldn't say do it while they can lead us and help us to fight and drive these demons back. I say when all's over and we've got to the last. I mean when the Indians have got in and are butchering us."

"Yes, yes," came in a murmur from one man, "It will be quite right then, and they'll feel it too."

"Yes," said the first, "it wants doing just as they've crowded into the place, and the lad among us left living must swear he'll do it."

"Don't need any swearing," said Morgan, in a low deep voice. "I'm afraid that you're right, my lads, and for one I'll promise to do it when it's all over."

"Do what?" I said in a whisper, though I felt that I did not need telling.

Morgan looked round at the others.

"There's no harm in telling him," he said.

"Not a bit. Tell him."

Morgan coughed as if to clear his throat, and he raised the bucket and threw a few drops from the bottom on the glistening heap.

"You see, Master George," he said, "we're afraid that we're getting close to the time when the Indians will quite get the better of us, and we shall be beaten."

"Englishmen are never beaten," I said, looking round proudly.

"Ah, that's only a bit of brag, Master George," said Morgan, quietly. "That's what we all say, and perhaps we never are in spirit, but our bodies aren't much stronger than other men's bodies, and there are times when the enemy gets too strong for us. I've been beaten many a time, and I've beat many a time. This is one of the times when I've been beat."

"But we are not beaten yet," I said, excitedly. "When the Indians come and attack we shall drive them off."

"If we can, my lad—if we can. Eh, my lads?"

"Yes, yes," came in a loud murmur.

"Don't you be afraid about that. As long as our officers can lead us we shall fight, and some say we shall do our best when we haven't one left to lead us. In plain honest English, Master George, we shall fire as long as we can load; when we can't use our guns we shall use our fists, and when we can't raise an arm we shall kick."

"Yes, I know, I know," I said, excitedly. "But what you are thinking of it so dreadful."

"So's lying down beat out to let savages knock out your brains, my lad; and so we've all made up our minds that when the worst comes to the very worst, it will be an act of kindness to everybody and a big lesson to the Indians to let settlers alone, and perhaps be the means of saving the lives of hundreds of poor creatures in times to come, if one of us—"

"Yes, I know," I half groaned—"sets fire to this powder and blows everything away."

"That's it, Master George, and the right thing too."

"Oh!" I cried, with a shudder.

"Don't take on, my lad," said Morgan, gently. "It's fate, that's what it is. We shan't do it till the place is full of Indians, and they've begun their terrible work; then one touch with a spark and it'll be all over."

"Morgan!" I cried.

"Ay, my lad, it seems very horrid, and I don't want to have it to do; but when we're all half dead, and can't lift a hand, it will be a mercy to every one; and I know if your poor father was here and listening to what we say, he'd think so too."

"But—but—" I faltered, despairingly, "I don't want to die."

"More don't I, my lad," he said, taking my hand; and I saw by the light of the burning building that the tears stood in his eyes. "I'd give anything to live, and go back yonder and work like a man to put everything straight again, and see my trees and plants growing more beautiful every day in God's bright sunshine; but if it aren't to be, Master George, why, it aren't. I haven't been a man who hasn't done his duty."

"No, no," I said; "they've all fought bravely."

"Ay, that they have, and are going to fight bravely to the very end. Why, look at those poor niggers too. See how they've fought, brave lads! No one would have thought they were slaves to see the way they've gone at it, just as if this was their own place, and they'd never been sold and bought. There, my lad, once more, don't you go thinking we're all going to turn cowards, because we're not. Our officers have done their duty by us, and we've tried to do our duty by them; and if it comes to the worst, I say what's been proposed is only doing our duty still; what say you?"

"Ay, ay," came in a chorus; and I could not say a word. I felt choked as I looked round at the enclosure, all lit up by the glow, with black shadows cast here and there by the various piles of cases and the tents, and then I seemed to see beyond the great fence, and the black and pale-faced men, right away through the forest to our own bright home, close to the pleasant river, where all was sunshine, and glorious with bird and flower and tree. It was impossible to believe that I was never to see it all again, never to wander through the forest, never to ride on the stream and pause to watch the brightly-plumaged birds and the glittering insects or the gorgeously-scaled fish gliding through the clear waters, down where I had so often seen them amongst the roots of the overhanging trees.

It all came back like some bright dream—the creeper-covered house, my father seated at his window, about which the flowers bloomed, as he sat and studied some book, Morgan and Hannibal busy in their long fight with the weeds, and a magpie-like patch under some tree, where black Pomp lay asleep in his white shirt and short drawers, while from the end of the house came the busy sounds made by poor Sarah.

I think it was at that moment most of all that I quite thoroughly realised what a delightful home we had built up in the wilderness. And now it was a heap of ashes; my father, Hannibal, and poor Sarah seriously hurt; Pomp gone too for aught I could tell; and Morgan here talking so calmly and coolly of setting alight to the pile of destruction lying there by our side.

Was it all true? I asked myself, and felt ready to rub my eyes and try to rouse myself from the horrible nightmare dream from which I was suffering.

I was awakened sufficiently the next moment by Morgan's words, as he said in a quiet, decided manner—

"Yes, Master George, we've done our duty as far as we can, and there's only one more thing left to do—when the time comes, sir; when the time comes."

Just then, to my utter astonishment, there was a movement among the men, and one of them came up close to me.

"You'll shake hands, sir," he said. "I've taken a deal of notice of you, different times."

I held out my hand mechanically, felt it warmly wrung, and then had it seized in turn by the others, while I was struggling to speak words that would not come. At last though they burst forth.

"But the women and children!" I cried, as my heart seemed to stand still.

"Better than being butchered by those savages," said Morgan, gloomily. "I'd sooner see my poor wife die than fall into their hands."

His words silenced me, for I knew that they could expect no mercy. Then feeling utterly exhausted, I was munching a piece of bread, where I sat on a rough case, and sipping a little water from time to time, when just as the fire was at its height, with great waves of flame floating gently away from the great pine-wood building and illumining the wide clearing all round, I heard a familiar voice behind me say in his droll, dry fashion—

"What pity!"

"Ah, Pomp!" I cried, turning to him; "you there?"

"Iss, Mass' George. When we go home again? Pomp done like dis place 'tall."

"No, nor nobody else, boy," said Morgan, sadly. "Hark! Hear anything?"

He seized his gun as he spoke, but it was only a hissing scream made by one of the water-soaked timbers as the steam was forced out.

"Nobody come. Injum all gone away."

"How do you know?" I cried, eagerly.

"Pomp done know. Tink um all gone. No shoot arrow now."

"Wrong, boy," said Morgan. "They are hatching some fresh scheme, and they'll be down upon us directly."

There was a pause.

"And then it will be all over," muttered Morgan, as he turned towards Pomp, looked at him firmly, and then held out his hand.

"Come here, boy," he said.

"Wha' for? Pomp no do nuffum. Can't do nuffum here."

"Come and shake hands."

Pomp laughed and held out his hand, which Morgan took.

"If I don't see you again, boy, good-bye, and I'm sorry I've been so rough to you sometimes."

"Mass' Morgan go walking out in wood? Take Pomp."

Morgan heaved a deep sigh. "Ah, you don't bear any malice," he said.

Pomp shook his head, and looked at me, for it was Greek to him.

"Not so bad as that," I said. "Come, cheer up."

"Can't any more, my lad," said Morgan. "No one can't say, look you, that I haven't cheered up through thick and thin. But, look here, Master George, speaking fair now, what is the good of Injuns?"

"Injum no good," said Pomp, sharply.

"Right, boy; no good at all. Phew!" he whistled; "how them logs do burn!"

"Ah! No duck, no fis', no turkey roace on 'tick!" said Pomp, regretfully. "Shoot, shoot, shoot, lot time, an' no shoot nuffum to eat. Pomp dreffle hungly."

"There's plenty of bread," I said, smiling at the boy's utter unconcern about our position of peril.

"Yah, 'tuff! Nas' 'tuff. Pomp too dreffle hungly eat any more bread. Why no go now and kill all Injum? Pomp fine de way."

The boy looked quite vexed at his proposition being declined, and squatted down to gaze at the fire, till after a time he lay down to look at it, and at last Morgan said to me—

"Don't trouble him much, lad. Fast asleep."

It was quite true. There lay Pomp enjoying a good rest, while we watched the progress of the flames, which rose and fell and gleamed from the pieces of the watchful men dotted round the great place, then left them in shadow, while a terrible silence had now fallen upon the camp. The fierce fire crackled and roared, and the flames fluttered as a great storm of sparks kept floating far away, but no one spoke, and it was only when an officer went round to the various posts that there seemed to be the slightest motion in the camp.

"Takes a cleverer man than me to understand Injun," said Morgan at last, just before daybreak, as I returned from the tent where my father was sleeping peacefully, and Hannibal outside wrapped in a blanket quite calmly taking his rest.

"What do you mean?" I said, wearily.

"I mean I can't make out the ways of Injuns. Here have we been watching all night, expecting to have a big fight by way of finish up, and Pomp's right after all. They seem to have gone."

"If I could only think so!" I replied, with a sigh.

"Well, lad, I think they are," said Morgan. "They might have had it all their own way, and beaten us pretty easy a time back, but they've let their chance go by; and I suppose they're satisfied with the mischief they've done for one night, and have gone back to their camp to sing and dance and brag to one another about what brave fellows they all are."

It soon proved to be as Morgan had said, for the day broke, and the sun rose soon after, to shine down warm and bright upon as dejected, weary-looking, and besmirched a body of men as could have been seen. For they were all blackened with powder and smoke; some were scorched, and in every face I could read the same misery, dejection, and despair. But the General, Colonel Preston, and several of the leading gentlemen soon sent a different spirit through the camp. A few orders were given, the sentries changed, three parts being withdrawn; the women, who looked one half-hour haggard, pale, and scared, wore quite a changed aspect, as they hurriedly prepared food for their defenders; and in a very short time cries and shouts from the children helped to make some of us think that matters were not quite so desperate after all.

Chapter Forty Seven

It is astonishing what can be done in the most painful times when there are good leaders, and a spirit of discipline reigns. I remember how I noted it here that noontide; when, after food and rest, the fresher men relieved sentries, and strove to listen to the General as he pointed out that though the block-house was gone and our retreat cut off, we were in nearly as good a position of defence as ever, for our barriers were firm, and it was not certain, even in the most fierce of assaults, that the enemy could win. In addition, he pointed out that at any hour a British ship might appear in the river, whose presence alone would startle the Indians; while if the worst came to the worst, there would be a place for us to find safety.

"There, Morgan," I said, feeling quite inspirited, as I noted the change which seemed to have come over the men. "You see how mad all that was last night."

He smiled as he laid his hand on my arm. "Look you, Master George," he said, "you always forget that I only talked of that as being something to be done if it came to the worst."

"And it has not come to the worst," I said.

"And I hope it never may," he replied.

I hurried to my father's side to tell him what had gone on; and I found him in a great deal of pain, but apparently quite cheerful and grateful to the big black, who now declared himself well enough to attend to "de massa," and forgetful of his own injuries, which were serious enough, the cuts on his arms being still bad, while he had been a good deal scorched by the fire.

"I can never be grateful enough to you, Hannibal," said my father again. "You saved my life."

"Massa sabe Hannibal life," said the great negro, with a grave smile. "Can't say well, but tink great deal 'bout all massa done for us."

"Don't talk about it," said my father, quietly.

"No, sah," replied the great black, turning to me, "not talk 'bout; tink about much—much more."

"Well, Hannibal, if we live to get clear of this dreadful trouble, I will try to be fair to—" He stopped for a few moments, wincing evidently from pain.

"Better now," he said, with a smile. "I was going to say, I have never considered either you, Hannibal, or your boy as slaves."

"No, massa," said the big black, calmly.

"But you are considered to be so here; and from this day I give you both your liberty."

Hannibal smiled, and shook his head.

"Do you not understand me?"

"Massa give holiday. Han done want holiday," said the black, laboriously.

"No, no; I set you both perfectly free."

"Massa tink Pomp lazy—Hannibal no fight 'nuff?"

"My good fellow, no," said my father, drawing his breath hard. "You do not fully understand. You were brought to this place and sold for a slave."

"Yes, understand. Massa bought Hannibal."

"Then now you are quite free to go where you like."

"Where go to, sah?"

"As soon as we have beaten off these Indians, back to your own country."

The black shook his head.

"You would like to go back to your own country?"

"No," said the black, thoughtfully. "'Top fight for capen and Mass' George."

"But we shall have done fighting soon, I hope, and then you can go in peace."

"No peace in Han country."

"What?"

"Alway fight—make prisoner—sell slave. Han want Pomp here talk for um."

"Ah, well, wait till we get peace, and things are getting on smoothly again, then we can talk."

"Capen cross wif Hannibal?"

"Cross? No; grateful."

"Han stay here 'long massa and Mass' George."

"Ah, George, any good news?" said my father, turning to me. "You see I am forced to be a slave-owner."

I shook my head rather sadly as I thought of Morgan's words.

"Oh, don't despair, my boy," he said, cheerfully. "It has seemed very desperate several times, but the Indians are still at bay, and we are alive."

"Yes, father, but—"

"Well?"

"The fort is burnt down."

"Yes; the enemy got the better of us there, but we are not beaten yet. Things looked black last night; after rest and food they are as different as can be. When shall you be ready to start home to begin rebuilding?"

"You are only talking like that, father, to cheer me up," I said, sadly. "Do you think I don't know that it is all over?"

"I do not think—I am sure you don't know, my boy," he said, smiling. "How can you? A battle is never lost till it is won. Did you ever see two cocks fight?"

"Yes; once or twice, father," I said, wonderingly.

"So have I," he replied, "not in the case of so-called sport, but naturally, as such birds will fight; and I have seen one beaten down, apparently quite conquered, and the victor as he believed himself has leaped upon his fallen adversary and begun to crow."

"Yes, I know," I cried, eagerly; "and then the beaten bird has struggled and spurred the other so fiercely that he has run away in turn."

"Yes; you have finished my anecdote for me. It is too soon yet for the Indians to begin to crow. They are still outside our place, and the powder is plentiful yet."

I shivered a little at the mention of the powder, and tried to tell him what I had heard, but somehow the words would not come, and soon after as he dropped asleep I went down into the open space about the block-house.

To reach it I had to pass the powder, which still lay covered as before, and it seemed to me that some fresh place might be found for it, since if the

Indians began to send their fiery arrows into the camp again, one might fall there, and the destruction talked of befall us at once.

But a little thought told me that if arrows came now, they would be aimed at men and not at buildings. There was nothing more within for the fire to burn, so I went in and walked round the pile of smouldering ashes, and tried to recall the scene of the previous night, and the position of the magazine. But it was rather hard to do now, there being nothing left by which I could judge, and I was going on, when I caught sight of something which made me alter my course, and walk softly up behind where Pomp was busy with a shovel at the edge of a great heap of smouldering ashes.

"What are you doing?" I said.

"Eh? Mass' George 'top bit and see."

"No, I can't stop," I cried. "What are you doing with that shovel?"

"Dat to 'crape de fire up. You no see? Pomp bake cake for de capen."

"What?"

"Oh yes. Plenty cake in de hot ash. Hot bread for um. 'Top see if um done."

He looked up at me and laughed as merrily as if there was no danger near.

"Mass' George see more Injum?"

"No," I said. "They are in the forest somewhere."

"Pomp like roace all de whole lot. Come burn fellow place down like dat. Ah, you don't want come, sah! Hah, I pob you in dah lil soft wet dab ob dough, and now you got to come out nice cake all hot."

He felt about in the fine embers with the shovel, and directly after thrust it under something invisible, drew it out, blew off a quantity of glowing ash, tossed his find round and brown up in the air, caught it again on the shovel, and held just under my nose a hot, well-cooked bread-cake, showing his teeth the while, as he exclaimed triumphantly—

"Dah!"

"Bread," I said, mechanically.

"Nice hot cake, sah, for de capen, and Pomp got fibe more juss done. Dat one for capen, one for Mass' George, one for Pomp fader, one for Pomp. How many dat make?"

"Four," I said, in the same mechanical way.

"Four, and den dah two more for a-morrow mornin'."

"Oh, Pomp," I said, "how can you think of such things now!"

"Eh? Cos such boofle fire, and Pomp know where de barl ob flour. Mass' George not glad to hab nice hot cake?"

I shook my head, but the boy was too busy fetching out his loaves, and soon had the whole six, well-cooked and of a delicate creamy-brown, beside him ready to be replaced in a little heap on the shovel.

"Dah!" he said; "now go take um home ready for tea."

"Why, Pomp," I said, sadly, "suppose the Indians come, what then?"

"What den? Dey 'tupid 'nuff to come, we shoot dem all, sah. Pomp don't fink much ob Injum."

"Do you think they'll come to-night?"

"Pomp done know. 'Pose so."

"You think so, then?"

"Yes, Mass' George. Injum very 'tupid. Come be shot."

Evening was coming on so fast that it would soon, I felt, be put to the proof, and followed by the boy with his cakes balanced on the shovel held over his shoulder, I went back to our apology for a tent.

My coming in awoke my father, and he sat up wincing with pain, but trying hard directly to hide his sufferings from me.

"Give me your hand," he said. "I must get out now and help."

I gave him my hand, and he rose, but sank back with his eyes half closed.

"No," he said, sadly; "I have no strength. Go out and see what preparations are being made, and—"

"Here is Colonel Preston, father," I whispered.

It was he, but he was not alone, for the General was with him, and both exclaimed loudly against my father attempting to move, but stayed both of them some time discussing the position, and asking his candid opinion about certain things which they had done for strengthening the defences, and they ended by proposing that I should accompany them as a sort of aide-de-camp, and bear messages to and fro.

I followed them, and was soon after going with them from post to post, to see that the men were well supplied with ammunition; and I could not help noticing that in spite of all they had gone through, they looked rested and self-reliant; quite ready in fact for a fresh encounter with our hidden foe.

For as the setting sun turned the plantations and edge of the forest to ruddy gold, all was perfectly calm, and for aught we could see there was no sign of an enemy. In fact to judge from appearances the Indians might have departed finally to their home, satisfied with the harm they had done.

As night fell all fires were extinguished, and we then commenced our dreary watch, every one feeling that the attack was coming, but how soon or from what quarter it was impossible to say.

Chapter Forty Eight

I passed the early part of that night now seated in the darkness by my father, now stealing away when I believed him to be asleep, and joining Morgan, who was acting as one of the sentries, and had kept Pomp by his side so as to make use of his keen young eyes, which seemed to see farther through the darkness of the night than those of any one else in the camp.

And as I stood at Morgan's side I could not help thinking of the great change that had taken place. Only a few hours before the fort was crackling and blazing, huge logs splitting with a loud report, and wreaths of fire and smoke circling up into the lurid sky, while all within the enclosure was lit up, and glistened and glowed in the intense light. Now all was gloom, depression, and darkness—a darkness so thick that it seemed to me as if the Indians had only to come gently up and select the place to climb over and then carry all before them.

I was tired and despondent, and that made me take, I suppose, so dreary a view of my position, as I waited for the enemy's advance. And yet I think my despondency was warranted, for I felt that if the Indians attacked they would carry everything before them; and if they did I could not doubt the determination of Morgan and his companions. And there I found myself standing beside the man who was ready to put a light to the powder and send everything into chaos—for that he would do it in the emergency I felt sure.

I had been backwards and forwards several times, and was standing at last gazing over the fence in silence, trying to convince myself that some objects I saw in the distance were bushes and not Indians, when Pomp suddenly yawned very loudly.

"Hush!" whispered Morgan, sternly.

"Pomp can't help um. So dreffle tire."

"Then keep a sharp look-out, and try if you can't see the Indians."

"Pomp did, but eye got blunt now. Why not go look for Injum?"

"I wish the General would let the boy go," whispered Morgan. "He might be able to get in some news."

"Pomp nebber see noting here. May Pomp go, Mass' George?"

"Of course you can't, boy," said Morgan, shortly. "Go and ask the commanding officer, and see what he'd say to you."

Pomp yawned, put his arms over the edge of the fence, after getting his feet into a couple of notches, and drawing himself up and resting his chin upon his fists, he stared out into the darkness.

"Here de Injum," he said; and a thrill ran through me as I followed the boy's pointing finger, but could see nothing.

"Can you, Morgan?"

"See? No!" he said, pettishly; "but you'd better go and give warning, sir."

I hurried off, and found Colonel Preston with the General, who received my news, and word was passed round to the various sentries, while the colonel made for the reserves in the centre of the enclosure, where in utter silence every man seized his piece, and stood ready to march to the point threatened, while I guided the General to where Morgan was stationed.

"No, sir. Not seen anything, nor heard a sound," said the latter, on being questioned. "It was this boy who saw them."

"Yes, ober dah," said Pomp, pointing.

"Can you see them now?"

"No, sah. All gone."

This was unsatisfactory, but the General seemed to have perfect faith in the boy's declaration, and a long exciting watch followed.

The Indians' habits had grown so familiar that every eye and ear was on the strain, and finger upon trigger, as tree, shrub, and grassy clump was expected momentarily to develop into a foe. The secretive nature of these people made our position at times more painful and exciting, as we knew that at any moment they might come close to us in the darkness, and almost before the alarm could be given, dash up to the palisade and begin climbing over.

But the weary hours crept on without any fresh sign, and the opinion began to spread that it was a false alarm, while Pomp was so pressed with questions that he slunk away into the darkness.

I followed him though, just making him out by his light, white cotton clothes, and saw him at last throw himself down on his face; but he started up into a crouching position, ready to bound away as I came up to him.

"No good, Mass' George," he said, angrily. "I 'tupid lil nigger, and done know nuff talk. Nebber see no Injum; nebber see nobody. Keep ask say—'Are you suah?' 'Are you suah?' Pomp going run away and lib in de tree. Nobody b'leeve Pomp."

"Yes, some one does," I said, as I sat down beside him in the darkness; and for the first time I noticed that we were close to the tarpaulin and canvas spread over the powder-kegs.

"No. Nobody b'leeve Pomp. Um wish Injum come and kill um."

"No, you don't," I said; "because you know I believe you, and have often seen that you have wonderful eyes."

"Eh? Mass' George tink Pomp got wunful eye?"

"Yes; you can see twice as well in the dark as I can."

"No; Mass' George tink Pomp 'tupid lil nigger; no good 'tall. Pomp go run away."

"I shall call you a stupid little nigger if you talk like that," I said. "Don't be foolish. I hope the Indians will not come any more, and that we shall soon go back home."

"Injum coming; Pomp see um. Dey hide; lie flat down on um 'tummuck so; and creep and crawl um."

He illustrated his meaning, but crouched down by me again directly.

"Dat on'y Pomp fun," he whispered. "Pomp nebber run away from Mass' George, and ah!—look dah!"

He pointed away into the darkness so earnestly that I stared in that direction, but for some little time I could see nothing. Then, all at once, I made out a figure which came cautiously toward where we sat, but turned off and went round to the opposite side of the heap out of our sight, and it was evident that we were not seen.

I was going to speak, but just as the words were on my lips I recognised Morgan, who must have just been relieved; and as I fully grasped now where we were, I turned cold as ice, and a peculiar feeling of moisture came in the palms of my hands.

I wanted to speak, but I could not; I wanted to cry to him hoarsely, but no words would come; and if ever poor fellow suffered from nightmare when he was quite awake, it was I in those terrible moments, during which there was a peculiar rustling, then a loud cracking sound, as if something was being wrenched open and broken, and the tarpaulin was agitated and shaken.

My ears were strained to listen to what came next, and that would be, I felt sure, the clicking of a flint and steel; but the sounds did not come, and just as I was at last feeling as if I could bear all this no longer, there was a sound of the tarpaulin falling on the earth, and Morgan came softly round and close by again without seeing us, while I crouched there ready to faint, and fully expecting every moment to be swept away by a terrific explosion.

"What Mass' Morgan want?" said Pomp at last, as a sudden thought struck me, and mastering the feeling of paralysis which had held me there, I made a dash round to the other side to tear away the slow match which the man must have started, and which would, I supposed, burn for a few moments and then start a train.

To my surprise I could see no sparkling fuse nor smell smoke, but concluding that it must be under the tarpaulin, I raised the edge with trembling hands, when Pomp said quietly —

"Dat powder, Mass' George; Pomp know. Mass' Morgan come fess lot more; and oh! What lot tumble all about."

His quick eyes had made out that which was invisible to mine; and, after stooping, he held a handful before me.

I drew a breath full of relief. I knew now. He had not come to fire the fuse, but to tear open one of the kegs and let a portion of the powder lie loose, so that whoever came to do the terrible deed would only have to discharge his firelock down amongst it, when a spark would explode the whole.

"Only to be quite ready," I thought, as the desire for life thrilled through my veins.

"Pomp 'crape it up and put in Mass' George pocket," said Pomp; and then we both stood away, for there was a flash and the sharp report of a gun.

"Pomp did see Injum, Mass' George," said the boy; "and here dey come."

Another shot, and another, and my heart seemed to leap as I felt that Morgan's plan might not be long before execution after all, if the Indians made a desperate assault.

One minute before, the great enclosure was perfectly still, now it was all excitement; orders rang out; there was the tramp of armed men, as they hurried toward the spot from whence the firing had come.

Then came a shot from quite the opposite side, fresh orders were shouted, and there was a tramp of feet in that direction, the enemy evidently attacking in two places at once so as to divide our little force.

Flash after flash now cut the darkness to right and left, and we both stood listening to the quick orders and the curious ringing sound made by the ramrods as the men reloaded.

The firing was not rapid, our men seeming to have had instructions to be very careful and only fire when they saw a good chance; but it was kept up steadily, and it was evident that the Indians had not succeeded in gaining a footing as yet.

"Let's run and tell my father what's going on," I said. "He'll be so anxious."

I made for the tent, with Pomp following, and found my father standing at the entrance, supporting himself on Hannibal's arm.

"Ah, George, my boy," he said, excitedly. "It's hard not to be able to help. Who is at the front?"

"At the front?" I said, wonderingly.

"Yes. Is any one protecting the palisade between the two points attacked? Go and see how many are there; and if few, tell Colonel Preston to draw the General's attention to the fact. If there are people there, ask his forgiveness for my interference. It is solely from anxiety for our safety."

I ran off, followed by Pomp, and soon found Colonel Preston and gave him my father's message, as he was leading some more men to where the firing was fiercest.

"Yes, yes, of course," he said, angrily. "It is not likely it has been forgotten."

I drew back at his words, and felt that I should like the General to have heard my father's message; and just then I came upon Morgan running, loaded with ammunition, to the other side.

"Where is the General?" I asked.

"Over here, lad, where I'm going. Don't stop me."

But I did stop him to tell him my father's words.

"Of course it is!" replied Morgan, as sharply as the Colonel had spoken. And I have often thought about it since—that such a slip should have been made by two gentlemen, both of whom had had great experience in military matters. But, of course, in the excitement of the double advance, and with so few men at their call, it was easy to think of nothing but repelling that attack, the more especially as there were men posted all round.

My answers were so unsatisfactory for taking back to where my father was, that I determined to go over to the part in question, and see how it was for myself.

As I hurried on, my course lay round the heap of ashes and burnt wood which had formed the block-house; and curiously weird it all seemed to be, with the flashes and heavy reports of the pieces to right, and left, mingled with the savage yells of the attacking Indians, who, as far as I could tell, seemed to be striving to beat back our men from the fence.

It was darker than ever as I got round the remains of the fort, and knowing that the ground there was free from impediment, I was in the act of breaking into a trot, when there was a curious stifled sound in front—a noise as of an axe falling on wood; and my companion sprang at me and dragged me back.

"Mass' George," he whispered, "Injum dah. Come ober big fence."

I was too late, and yet not too late to give warning.

"Run and tell Colonel Preston," I said in a whisper. "Quick."

Pomp was too well accustomed to obey to hesitate, and he ran off in one direction round the ruins to where the colonel was defending the palisade, while I darted off in the other, rushed right up to where the General was standing calmly enough giving directions.

As I reached him I heard him utter the word, "Forward!" and about twenty men moving round, and were evidently going up to the part from which I had come.

My news resulted in their recall, and that of the men defending the palisade, orders being given to fall back toward the rough defence made in the centre of the enclosure, which we reached in safety, just as we found that Colonel Preston's men were falling back towards us, firing as they came, but toward the direction from which the new danger threatened.

The way in which the defence had been planned stood us in good stead now, for as our party was halted, waiting for the colonel's men, a loud yelling came from behind the block-house ruins, and the rapid beat of feet told plainly enough that a large body of the enemy had clambered in and were coming on.

Any want of promptitude would have resulted in the Indians getting between our two little forces; but a sharp order was given, and a volley rattled out—the flashing of the pieces showing in a dimly-seen line the fierce faces of our enemies, who appeared to be thrown into confusion, but who still came on, when a second volley was poured into them, and that was followed by one from the Colonel's men, the last checking them so effectually that we had time to get well behind the breastwork and reload.

I say we, though I was unarmed, but still I had played my part; and as soon as I could get through the men crowded behind our last defence, I hurried to where my father was anxiously awaiting my return, and the report which I had to make.

Chapter Forty Nine

"It was a mistake—a mistake," said my father, excitedly; "but I might have made it if I had been in the hurry and excitement there. Resting here I had plenty of time to think."

At that moment the firing began to be fiercer, and my father groaned aloud.

"Oh, it is pitiable!" he said, "obliged to lie by here, and not able to help. Here, George, go to the front; don't get into danger. Keep well under cover. I want you to take pity on me, my boy. Do you hear?"

"Yes, father; but I don't understand."

"Can't you see my position? I am helpless, and my friends and companions are fighting for our lives. I want you to keep running to and fro so as to let me know what is going on, and—mind this—keep nothing back."

"Nothing, father?" I said.

"Nothing."

I hesitated a few moments, and then with the reality of the horror impressed more and more by the shouting, yelling, and rapid firing going on, I told him about Morgan and the other men, even to finding the opened keg and loose powder.

"Great heavens!" he muttered as I finished; and I looked at him to hear what more he would say, but he remained silent.

"Shall I send Morgan to you, father?" I said.

He remained silent for a few moments, and then said softly—

"No."

There was another pause, during which the firing grew more fierce.

"George."

"Yes, father."

"Go to and fro, as I told you, and keep me well informed till you think matters are growing desperate. Then seize your chance, run down to the water's edge, swim to one of the boats, and try and escape."

"Without you, father?"

He caught my hand.

"You could not escape with me, my boy," he said. "There, do as I command. I can give you no farther advice, only use your own judgment as to where you will go."

"But, father—"

"Silence! Is Hannibal there?" he said, raising his voice.

"Yes, massa."

"Here, my man," continued my father, as the great black came to him. "You will try and serve me, will you not?"

"Massa want Han do somefin?"

"Yes. There is great danger from the Indians. I want you to stay with and help my son; when the time comes, you will swim with him to a boat, and try and get away."

"And carry massa down to the boat?"

"No. Save my son. Now go with him at once." His words were so imperative that we both left him, and I went back toward where the fighting was going on, with Han following me like a great black shadow, till, all at once, he touched me on the arm.

"Yes," I said.

"Mass' George won't go 'way an' leave his fader?"

"No," I replied, fiercely. "We must get him away too, Han, and Pomp."

"Suah, suah," said the great fellow, quietly. "Could carry de capen down to de boat. Find Pomp and make him swim out for boat all ready."

"Yes," I cried, eagerly, "we must save them both."

The next minute we were close to where our men fought bravely, driving back the Indians, who were close up now, avoiding the firing by crawling right in, and then leaping up suddenly out of the darkness to seize the barrels of the men's pieces, and strike at them with their tomahawks.

But they were always beaten back, and twice over I was able to go and tell my father of the success on our side, Hannibal following close behind me; but these checks were only temporary. The Indians literally swarmed about the frail stronghold, and as fast as they were driven back in one place, they seemed to run along the sides of our defences and begin a fresh attack somewhere else, while our men's firing, being necessarily very ineffective in the darkness, began to lose its effect; the savages, finding how few of them dropped from the discharges, beginning to look upon the guns with contempt.

Their attacks grew so bold at last, that twice over, as I saw dimly one of our poor fellows go down, I felt that all was over, and that the time had come for me to go and try whether I could get my father away before the last terrible catastrophe, though how it was to be contrived, with the place surrounded as it was by Indians, I could not tell.

Can you think out what my position was, with all this firing and desperate fighting going on, our men striking desperately at the Indians to keep them out as they swarmed and leaped up at us; and all the time there were the women, children, and wounded huddled up together in the inner shelter formed of barrels, boxes, and half-burned planks?

It was horrible.

Minute after minute crept by, and I began to blame myself for not going. Then a lull would make me determine to wait a little longer, just perhaps as some louder burst of firing made me believe that it was the first keg of powder gone, till a round of cheering told me that it was not, and I was able to go and report that our men were still holding their own.

I was returning from one of these visits to my father, picking my way in the darkness over broken guns snapped off at the stock through being used as clubs, and in and out among groaning men over whom the doctor was busy, when all seemed to me to be unusually silent, and then I found that I was able to see a little more as I got right forward to where Colonel Preston was making his men close up together, and handing fresh ammunition. It was rapidly growing lighter, and I saw dimly enough at a short distance, just behind where the block-house stood, the misty-looking figures of a large body of Indians.

"Look, quick!" I panted.

"Ah!" exclaimed the colonel. "Good! You can see now, my men. Hold your fire till they are close in, and then let them have a volley."

A low murmur ran along the line of men, and a feeling of elation thrilled me, but only for a deathly cold chill to run through every vein. For this was evidently such a desperate season as Morgan or his confederates might choose.

I could not stir for the moment. Then, as I mastered the horrible feeling of inaction, I drew back and made my way through the confusion within our defences to where I could be opposite to the covered-in kegs, which lay not twenty yards away untouched.

The light increased rapidly as it does down south, and I caught sight of a dark figure crawling half-way between our rough works and the tarpaulin.

One moment I thought it was a dead or wounded man; the next I recognised Morgan by the back of his head, and a cry arose to my lips, but it was drowned by a deafening volley followed by a cheer.

I glanced to my left, and saw the body of fully a couple of hundred Indians checked and wavering, when a second volley was fired and they fled.

The smoke hid the rest from my eyes, and when it rose, Morgan was standing close beside me watching the Indians, who had all crowded through the palisade where a great piece was torn down, dragging with them their dead and wounded.

Chapter Fifty

"Morgan," I whispered, and he started and looked at me wildly, the morning dawn showing his face smeared with blood, and blackened with the grime of powder.

"Yes, my lad," he said, sadly; "I thought it was all over, and as soon as they were well at their work I meant to fire it."

I could not speak, and I knew it would be useless, so I shrank away, and crept back past scores of despairing faces, to where my father lay eagerly waiting for news.

As I went I saw that the officers were giving orders for restoring portions of our torn down defences, and that the day had given the men fresh energy, for they were working eagerly with their loaded pieces laid ready, while food and drink were being rapidly passed along the front.

"Only a temporary check, I'm afraid," said my father, as I described everything. "Brave fellows! What a defence! But you have waited too long," he said. "Where is that man?"

"Hannibal?" I exclaimed; "I had forgotten him." For he had evidently glided away in the dark; but almost as I spoke he came up.

"Boat ready, Mass' George," he said. "Pomp swam out and got him. Waiting to take Mass' George and capen."

A warning cry just then rang out, and my father caught my arm. "Go and see," he whispered; "don't keep me waiting so long."

I hurried to the front again, seeing Morgan and another man in earnest conversation, but they separated before I reached them, and as Morgan went in the direction from whence he would pass out from our piled-up defence to get to the powder, I followed him, seeing now clearly enough he had his gun in his hand.

I forgot about my own escape—the coming on of the Indians, of whom I had a glimpse outside the palisades—everything, in my intense desire to stop this man from carrying out his terrible plan. I was very near him now, and should have caught him up had I not stumbled over a poor fellow lying in my way, and nearly fallen. As I recovered I could hear a fearful yelling, and saw Morgan's hard-set face as he climbed backward down from the boxes, one of the men, whom I recognised as his confederate, helping him by holding his gun.

In a wild fit of despair, as I saw Morgan's hard-set face, I shouted to him to stop, but my voice was drowned by the yelling of the Indians now coming on again with a rush, brandishing their axes, and evidently bent on carrying all before them.

As I reached the edge, Morgan was half-way to the powder, crawling on his chest, the Indians to our left, and the men I was trying to pass firing over Morgan's head.

They shouted to me, but I glided between two of them; and as they tried to pull me back, Han pressed them apart, and the next moment I was creeping after Morgan.

The firing went on over us, and the Indians dashed forward on our left, yelling more loudly than ever. Then I heard a volley, and just caught a glimpse of the half-naked figures passing through the smoke. It was but a glance, for my attention was fixed upon Morgan, who had now reached the tarpaulin and canvas, thrown it partly aside, examined the priming of his gun, and I thought he was about to fire right into the midst of the powder-kegs, but he turned first to see whether the fight had yet reached the most desperate stage.

That was my time, and I leaped upon him, and tried to wrench the gun away, as his wildly desperate face looked into mine.

"No, no, Morgan," I cried. "You must not; you shall not do that."

"Let go!" he cried, roughly; and the eyes that glared at mine seemed almost those of a madman.

"No," I cried, "I will not."

"Don't you hear, Master George? Hark at them; the wretches have begun their work."

I still clung to the gun, and turned my head as a wild burst of shrieks rose from behind—the firing had ceased, but the shouting and yelling were blood-curdling, as in that horrible moment I felt sure that our men were beaten, and a massacre had begun.

But my father was there, and it seemed too horrible for such a deed as this to be done. If we were to die by the Indians' hands, I felt that we must. But quietly stand by and let Morgan do this thing I would not, and I clung to the gun.

"Let go before it's too late, boy," panted Morgan, tugging fiercely now to get the gun from me.

"No," I panted; "you shall not."

"I must, boy. There: hark at them. I shall be too late. Look, boy; run for your life. I'll wait till I see you over the big fence first."

"No," I panted again; "you shall not."

"Will you run for your life?"

"No!" I cried, as I seemed to see my helpless father stretching out his hands to me.

"Then I must have it," cried Morgan, fiercely, and as we knelt together, he twisted the gun in one direction, then in the other; and, boy as I was in strength, in another moment he would have torn it from my grasp, when a great black hand darted from just behind me, caught Morgan by the throat, forced him back, and with a cry of triumph I dragged away the piece, and fired it right away from the powder.

"Hold him, Han," I panted; "he is mad."

As if my shot had been the signal, a tremendous volley rang out from beyond the palisade; then another, and another; and the Indians, who the moment before were battling desperately, and surmounting our defences as a wild hand-to-hand fight went on, began to give way; then they turned and fled for the gap they had made, while, led by Colonel Preston, our men dashed after them.

"Look," I cried. "Morgan, we've won!" We all gazed wonderingly as the Indians disappeared through the gap in the great fence, when another sharp volley rang out, but the smoke rose from outside.

"Help has come!" I shouted, and feeling no fear now of Morgan putting his desperate plan into action, I ran to join our men and learn what it meant, closely followed by Hannibal, Morgan coming last.

Chapter Fifty One

Our party was cheering loudly as I got up in time to see the Indians in full flight toward the forest, and a strong force of men in pursuit, stopping and kneeling from time to time to fire on the retreating savages, who did not attempt to make a stand.

For some minutes I could not understand what it meant, nor who our rescuers were, but directly after the word ran round from mouth to mouth—"Spaniards—Spaniards!" and I turned to see a large ship lying in the river as I ran back to our defences, and past the dead and wounded, to bear my father the news.

"One enemy to save us from the other," said my father. "Well, better to fall into the hands of civilised people than savages. In this case it will be prison, in the other it would have been death."

"But shall we have to give up to them?" I said.

"In our helpless state I am afraid so, unless the General and Preston hold that we are Englishmen still. Oh, if I could only get to their side, and join in the council!"

"Hannibal carry capen," said the great black, who in strict obedience to his orders was at my back.

"Can you?" cried my father, eagerly.

Hannibal smiled and took my father up as easily as if he had been a child, starting to carry him just as Morgan came up.

"Stop!" said my father; "let me go in a more dignified way if I can. Here, Morgan, pick up one of these fire-locks. Hannibal, my man, set me down again;" and, after giving his orders, Morgan and the black each took hold of one end of the firelock, holding it across him, and my father sat upon it, supporting himself by passing his arms through those of his bearers, and in this fashion he reached the group at the gap in the fence. Here an earnest conversation was going on, while the Spaniards were still in full pursuit of the Indians, chasing them right into the forest, and their shots growing more and more distant.

Mass' George: A Boy's Adventures in the Old Savannah | 353

"Ah," cried the General, as my father reached the group, "I am glad you have come, Bruton. I feel bound in our present strait to take the opinion of all. We are terribly shaken in our position; there are many wounded, and the question we debate is, whether now we surrender quietly to the Spaniards, or make one more bold stand."

"What does Colonel Preston say?" said my father, quietly.

"Fight, sir," cried the colonel, fiercely, "as long as we can fire shot or lift an arm; but the majority are for giving up. What does Captain Bruton say?"

My father was so weak that he could not stand alone, but his eyes were bright still, and he drew back his head as he looked round.

"First let me hear what others have to say." One of the settlers took a step forward. "That we have fought like men, sir, but it is too much to attempt more. We have failed in our attempt to establish this colony, so now let us make the best terms we can with the Spaniards, and try to get back home. Come, Captain Bruton, you are terribly hurt; you have done all you can. Speak out now, sir, like a brave man, who wishes to save further slaughter. You agree with me?"

Every eye was turned on my father, who, in spite of his quiet ways, had gained enormous influence, and even the General seemed to look at him anxiously as he spoke.

"I quite agree with you, sir, that we want peace, and to return home; but this is home—this country that we chose and obtained the King's charter to hold, and to defend against all comers. The Spaniards' descent has been most fortunate; but when they come back and arrogantly order us to surrender, there is not surely an Englishman here who will give up? I say No. We have our defences nearly perfect still, and half an hour to repair this breach. Ammunition in plenty; provisions still for quite a siege. Who says surrender? Not I."

There was a cheer at this, and the General laid his hand on my father's shoulder, crying—

"No one says surrender. Quick, men! Work!"

He issued his orders sharply; they were readily obeyed, and in a very short space of time the gap in the palisade was filled with board, plank, and barrel from the central defence that had been so hotly contested that morning. The barrels were stood up on end and filled with earth, and by the time the Spaniards' firing had ceased, and they were returning, our men were posted here and there; and our weakness being hidden, we presented a formidable appearance to the Spanish force, as it marched back, and without coming near our weakest part at the back, formed up at a short distance from the well-manned gates.

Quite a hopeful feeling seemed to have come over men who had been in despair a short hour before, as the ladies and women were put in the enclosure, busy, with the black people, obeying the surgeon's orders. For it was felt that if another encounter took place, it would only be after due warning, and then that we had ordinary enemies to contend against, not the savages, who had received a severe enough lesson to perhaps check further attack.

A strong desire too was manifested to make the best of things in our enemies' sight, and stores were attacked, rations served out, and every man who was wounded was disposed to treat it lightly.

I cannot explain it, but I know now that in the reaction, all felt as I did— ready to forget pain, weariness, and the peril through which we had passed. We knew that another enemy had come; but though he had driven off the savages, he did not seem at all formidable; and the blacks in their quick, childlike way, taking their tone from us, were soon laughing and chattering, as they made fires, fetched water, and busied themselves about the camp as if nothing unusual was the matter.

After seeing my father comfortably lying down and refreshed, I left him to go and find out what was going on in front of the gate, where Morgan was one of the little party on guard.

As I went up to him he stared at me curiously, and I looked at him, each of course thinking of our encounter, and it appeared to me as if it was something that had occurred a long time ago, and that I ought not to refer to such a horror—at least not till some time in the future, when we could speak of it calmly, as of some adventure of the past.

The change in his aspect was striking as I spoke, his face lighting up; and he looked like the Morgan of old, as I said, quietly—

"What are the Spaniards doing?"

"Smoking, some of 'em, Master George," he said, eagerly. "And some of 'em's eating and drinking; and, look you, the big Dons are all together yonder having a sort of confab. Think it'll come to a fight with them, sir?"

"I don't know. But hasn't any one been up to the gate or brought a message?"

"No, sir, and they don't seem to be in any hurry. Look!"

He made way for me to look over the gate at the little force, which lay about half-way between us and their boats at the river-side, while about a couple of hundred yards away lay their ship, with the Spanish flag blown well out by the breeze.

The men were standing or lying down, and, as far as I could see, no one had been hurt in their encounter; in fact it had been confined to firing upon the retreating savages. They were taking matters very coolly, all but their leaders, who were evidently holding a council before deciding on their next step.

"Strikes me, Master George," said Morgan, "that they're thinking that winning one little battle's enough work for the day, and I shouldn't be much surprised if they went back on board. They don't want to fight us, only to frighten us away."

"Think so?" I said. "They attacked the Indians very bravely."

"Don't see much bravery in a hundred men firing at a lot of savages who are running away. They never expected to find us all ready for them in a stout stockade, with every man Jack of us standing to arms, in full fighting rig, and with our war-paint on."

He said this last meaningly, and I shuddered as I thought of what I had seen.

"Well, I must go back," I said. "My father is anxious to know."

"Yes, of course sir. Then you go and tell him what you've seen, and that I say I don't think they mean fighting; but that if they do, it won't be till after they've had a good parly-parly, and asked us first whether we mean to go."

Just then there was a burst of talking close by us, and a laugh; the officer in command gave an order or two, and a couple of the men leaned over and held out a hand each. Then there was a bit of a scramble, and a curly black head appeared above the gates. The next moment its owner was over, and had dropped down, caught sight of us, and run up.

"Why, Pomp!" I said; "I had forgotten you."

"What for send Pomp out to boat and no come? Pomp dreffle tire, and come back."

"I say I had forgotten you."

"Ah, Pomp no forget Mass' George," he replied, reproachfully. "Eh? Lil fire—two lil fire—twent lil fire," he cried, excitedly. "'Mell um cook suffum. Come 'long, Mass' George, I dreffle hungly."

I led the way in and out among the busy groups, where, chattering over the fires they had lit, the blacks were making bread or cooking, and every now and then I had to catch hold of Pomp's arm and half drag him along, so great was the interest he took in what was going on; for he evidently felt no modesty or shrinking about making his presence known.

I soon had my father fully acquainted with the state of affairs, and while I was talking to him, Colonel Preston came to sit down upon an upturned barrel, and talk for a time about the state of affairs.

Chapter Fifty Two

Our officers and gentlemen made a very shabby parade that evening, when just before sundown word was passed from the sentries that a party was approaching from the Spaniards, and it was decided to go outside and meet them, so as not to show the poverty of our resources within the defences, and the sore straits to which we had been brought.

So the General and Colonel Preston, with about half a dozen gentlemen, went out to meet the new enemy, while Morgan contrived that I should, as Captain Bruton's son, be where I could see and hear all that was going on.

And, as I said, our officers and gentlemen made a very shabby parade, for their clothes were torn and stained, and there were no brave uniforms now, such as they wore the last time the Spaniards from the south came to demand that we should leave the place. But if they had no scarlet and gold to show, there was a grim sternness about our people that was very impressive, something which taught the visitors that ours were no feather-bed soldiers, but men who could face fire and use the sword.

Of that party of six who went out to meet the Spaniards, there was not one who was not injured, though slightly, while the little body-guard of eight soldiers who followed them was in similar plight.

Our numbers were hastily selected by the General, on seeing that while a larger number had come away from the main body of the Spaniards, only eight approached the gates.

Everything was done so deliberately that I noticed that the General carried his left arm in a scarf, and that the hair had been all cut away in a patch at the back of Colonel Preston's head, so as to admit of its being strapped with plaister. Another officer had a cut on his left cheek which had divided the lip; another wore a bandage in the shape of a red silk handkerchief, and another carried his injured hand in his breast.

One and all had been wounded, but there was not a man who did not seem full of fight, and ready to stand his ground come what might.

On the other hand, although they had been in an engagement that day, and had pursued the Indians, the Spaniards were smooth-looking and well-dressed; not a hair seemed to be out of place, so that they presented a remarkable contrast to our grim-looking set.

They paused at a few yards' distance, and I stood gazing over the top of the fence at their dress and weapons, all of which looked clean and well-kept, quite in keeping with the dignified, well-dressed wearers, who were looking at our people with a kind of tolerant contempt.

As they drew near, I recognised two of them as being of the party who had come before, and these two spoke to a broad-shouldered, swarthy-looking man, who nodded from time to time as if receiving his instructions. Then he stepped forward, looking from one to the other, and said, bluntly—

"Which of you is captain?"

There was a pause, every one being surprised at hearing our language so plainly spoken.

"You can address yourself to me," said the General, quietly.

"Oh, that's all right then. You see—"

"Stop a moment," said the General. "You are an Englishman?"

"I was," said the man; "but I've thrown in my lot here now, and I'm a Spaniard."

"Indeed?"

"Yes; that's it. I'm settled among them, and they're not bad sort of people, let me tell you. I just say this by way of advice to all of you, who seem to be in a tidy pickle."

"Were you instructed to say this, sir?" said the General, coldly.

"Well, no, not exactly; only having once been an Englishman, and meeting Englishmen, I wanted to do you a good turn if I could."

"Thank you. Now your message."

"Oh, that's short enough. The Don here says I'm to tell you that he is glad he arrived in time to save your lives, all of you, for if he hadn't come you'd all have been massacred."

"Go on," said the General.

"And that he supposes you see now what a mad trick it was to come and settle down here among the Indians. Let me see; what was next?" muttered the man; and he turned sharp round, and spoke to the Spanish leader for a minute or so, and then came back and went on—

"That he came once before and gave you fair warning that you were trespassing on the lands of his Majesty the King of Spain, and that he wants to know how soon you are going."

"Is that all?"

"Yes," said the man, "I think that's about all. It isn't exactly what he said, because Spanish lingo's awkward stuff to put into plain English; but that's about what it all meant; and, speaking as a friend, I should advise you to get a passage up north as soon as you can."

"Thank you."

"Shall I say you're going to sheer off?"

"Tell your leader or officer, sir," said the General, coldly, "that his message is insulting."

"Oh, come, now," said the man, "it was as civil as could be."

"That we are here in the dominion of his Majesty the King of England, upon our own lands, and that his demand is absurd. I do not wish to be insulting in return for the service he has done us and his own people by giving these savages so severe a lesson, but you may ask him what he would say if I came down with a strong party and ordered him and his people to quit the Spanish settlement."

"Am I to tell him that?" said the ambassador.

"Yes; and that we are here, and mean to stay, even to holding our homes by force of arms if it is necessary."

"Oh!" said the man, staring and looking from one to the other. "Isn't that foolish talk! You see we are very strong, while you are—"

"Not so very weak as you think for, sir."

"But I'm sure you don't want us to turn you all out by force, and burn down your settlement, though it seems to me as if there isn't much left to burn," he added, as he glanced round at the distant heaps of burned timber and ashes.

"We will build it all up ready for you, sir, against your expedition comes," said Colonel Preston, sharply.

"Oh, come, come," said the man; "that's all brag. Look here: take my advice, make friends with the Dons here, and let me say you'll pack off quietly, because they mean mischief if you do not go."

"You have had my answer, sir," said the General, haughtily. "Tell your leader that, for his own sake, I hope he will not drive us to extremities. We are prepared to fight, and fight we shall to the end."

"Oh, very well," said the man, in a grumbling tone; "I'm only a messenger. I've given our people's orders, and now I'm ready to take back yours. Only don't say, when you're all made prisoners and marched off to our plantations, that I didn't as an Englishman give you a timely hint."

The General bowed, and the man stood staring at him for a few moments, and then from one to the other, in an undecided way.

"Then you won't go?" he said at last.

The General made a sign to Colonel Preston.

"No, sir; we will not go," said the latter, firmly.

"Oh, very well. 'Tarn't my fault. I like peace, I do; but if you will have it rough, why, it's your own fault."

He turned away, and talked to the two leading Spaniards for a few moments, the elder of the two stamping his foot imperiously as he frowned and pointed to us. The man shrugged his shoulders, and came back.

"Look here," he said, roughly; "the Dons say they won't stand any nonsense, and you are to go."

"Tell him he has had his answer, Preston," said the General.

"Oh, yes, I know about that answer," said the man; "and I'm to tell you that if you do not give up at once, you will all be driven off, and you must expect no mercy then."

The colonel glanced at the General, who nodded, and the former said, half-mockingly—

"Tell your leaders we are here, and if the King of Spain wishes for this part of his Britannic Majesty's possessions, he will have to send a stronger force than you have brought, to take it; and as for you, my friend, your position as a kind of envoy protects you; but if I were you I should be careful. Your speech tells me plainly that you have been a sailor."

"Well, suppose I have," said the man, sharply.

"And I should say that you have deserted, and become a renegade."

"What?"

"I would not speak so harshly to you, but your conduct warrants it. An Englishman to come with such cowardly proposals to your fellow-countrymen! Faugh!"

Mass' George: A Boy's Adventures in the Old Savannah | 361

The man seemed to grow yellow as he gazed at the colonel; then, turning away, he spoke hurriedly to the two Spanish officers, who stood gazing at our party for a few moments, then bowed, and stalked back.

"Well, Preston," said the General; "shall we have to give up?"

"To them?" cried the colonel, sharply. "No! Do you know what Bruton will say?"

"How can I?"

"Well, sir, he will say, 'let them come, and if they drive us out of here, we will retire into the forest.' But, bah! I am not afraid. All Spanish bombast. Ah, young Bruton, what do you say to this?" he continued, as they entered the gates, and he caught sight of me.

"I'm not old enough to say anything about it," I replied; "but I think a great deal."

"And what do you think?" said the General, smiling, as he laid his hand upon my shoulder.

"That they will be afraid to fight, sir."

Chapter Fifty Three

A strict watch was kept on the Spaniards, while everything possible was done in the way of preparation for an attack, possibly a double attack for aught we knew. It was quite probable that, in spite of their defeat, the Indians would return that night, perhaps in greater strength, to come on just at the same time as the Spaniards.

"And then," said Morgan, "what the officers ought to do is to keep us all out of the way, and let 'em fight it out between them."

But that such an encounter was not likely to occur I soon saw, for the Spaniards after a long talk together slowly marched back to their boats, and rowed to the ship lying at anchor in the river; and after a night of watchfulness, the sun rose again without our being assailed either from water or land.

As soon as it was light, work was recommenced, and our defences strengthened; but it was soon found that the defenders would be much fewer in number, for many of the men who, in spite of their wounds, held up on the previous day, were unable to leave their rough couches, and had to resign themselves to the surgeon's orders, to have patience and wait.

All the same though, a fairly brave show was made, when towards midday boats were seen to leave the ship again and row to the shore. Then, after landing a strong body of well-armed men, they put back a little, cast out grapnels, and waited while those landed marched right for the enclosure.

There appeared to be no hesitation now, and as memories of the brave old deeds of the Spaniards came up, it was felt that in all probability a fiercer fight was in store for us than those which we had had with the Indians. But not a man flinched. The perils they had gone through seemed to have hardened them, and made them more determined. So that our stockade was well-manned, and in breathless silence all waited for the attack.

It was dangerous, of course, and I knew the risk, but I could not resist the temptation of trying to see the encounter, and, well down to one side of the gateway, I watched the coming on of the Spaniards.

There was no waiting for dark, or stealthy approach; they did not even spread to right and left to search for a weaker point, such as they would have found right at the back, but came boldly up toward the gate, as being the proper place to attack, halted about a hundred yards away, and then an officer and two men advanced, in one of whom I recognised the interpreter of the previous day.

They came right on, the Englishman shouting to us not to fire, and then asking, as he came close, to speak with an officer.

Colonel Preston appeared, and the messenger called upon us to surrender.

"And if we do not?" said the colonel.

"The gate will be stormed at once, and very little mercy shown," said the man, speaking dictatorially now, as if he had caught the manner of his Spanish companions.

"Very well," said the colonel. "You can storm, and we'll defend the place."

The envoys went back with our defiance, and there was a short consultation, followed by a rapid advance, a halt about fifty yards away, and then a volley was fired by about fifty men, who uttered a shout, and made a rush for the gate.

I heard the word "Fire." There was a scattering answer to the Spaniards' volley; but instead of its proving harmless, about a dozen men fell, and began to crawl or limp back, after rising, to the rear.

This checked the advance by quite half, and only half of these came on much farther, the rest dropping back rapidly till of the brave force who attacked, only one ran right up to the gate, and he, a handsome-looking young officer, struck it fiercely with his sword, shouted something in Spanish, and then began to go back, but keeping his face to us defiantly all the time.

A dozen pieces were raised to fire at him, but the colonel struck them up, and showed himself above the gate, to raise his hat to the young officer, who, half laughingly, half bitterly, returned the salute.

Morgan told me afterwards what Colonel Preston said: that if there had been fifty men like this one the stockade could not have been held.

But there were not, for when the wounded Spaniards had been carried down to the boats, and a line was formed for a fresh attack, a loud murmur arose; and, as plainly as if I had heard every word, I made out that the men would not advance, and that the officer threatened to go alone.

Then one man only ran to his side, and they two advanced together, trying to shame the Spaniards to attack.

But they were not shamed a bit, but let those two come right on, when, as they reached to within twenty yards of the gate, our men sent up a hearty cheer, for the one who accompanied the Spanish officer was the Englishman.

"Bravo!" cried Colonel Preston. "Hallo, there, you renegade; you're a brave man after all. Tell the Spanish officer I salute him as one worthy of all respect."

The officer raised his hat as this was interpreted to him.

"Now tell him," continued the colonel, "not to risk his life in another advance. An accidental shot might injure him, and I should be most grieved."

"Are you mocking him, sir? He says," shouted the man.

For answer, Colonel Preston leaped down from over the gate and advanced, Morgan following him. I saw the Spanish officer start at this, and advance sword in hand to the attack; but Colonel Preston sheathed his.

"Tell him," he said aloud,—"no, there is no need to tell him; he can understand this.—Sir, I wish to take the hand of a gallant officer in mine," and he stretched out his hand.

The Spanish officer lowered the point of his sword, and after a moment's hesitation changed it into his left hand.

"You can tell him that I do not mean treachery or trying to take prisoners," said the colonel.

His words were interpreted, and the Spanish officer said something hastily in reply.

"Says, sir, that he cannot take your hand, but respects you all the same."

At that moment the Spaniards began firing, and this roused our men into replying, a sufficiently perilous position for the group between them, till the young officer ran towards his men, holding up his sword; but before the Spaniards had ceased our fire was silenced, for I saw the General run here and there, shouting angrily.

"That was a risky proceeding of yours, Preston," said the General, as the colonel came back within the fence.

"Yes, sir; a foolish, undisciplined act," replied the colonel; "but I felt carried away by the bravery of that young fellow, deserted as he was by his cowardly crew."

"I cannot blame you," said the General, "for I felt similarly moved."

Little more was said, for every one was intent upon the proceedings of the enemy, who drew back about a hundred yards, and then formed up with military precision, apparently previous to making a determined advance together; but a full hour passed, and no advance was made. Two officers came ashore from the ship with ten more men, and we were all kept in a state of tension, momentarily expecting to have to defend ourselves against a desperate attack.

But none came, and soon after the whole force marched down to the boats and embarked, while a couple of hours later the ship was going slowly down the big river with the tide.

Now it might have been expected that on seeing this our men would have burst into a triumphant cheer, but they did not, but stood watching the ship in silence. For there seemed to be something too solemn for words or any display of exultation. Utterly worn out with fighting and watching, and feeling as if we had all been rescued from death, men moved about gravely and quietly, and I saw group after group where gentlemen and ordinary working men, old soldiers who had come out there to that pleasant land believing they had for ever turned their swords into shares and pruning-hooks, were seated holding the hands of their wives, and with their children on their knees, their heads bent, and the tears streaming down the women's faces; and I know that a heartfelt thanksgiving went silently up to heaven that night for the escape we had all had.

But still there was the feeling of insecurity afloat, which caused the greatest precautions to be taken. The forest was not far distant, and for aught we knew the Indians might again come on.

So sentries were placed, to be relieved after short watches, and I fully intended to take my turn when I lay down; but, just as it was once before, almost as I began thinking, all became blank, and the next thing I remember was waking up, feeling ashamed of my neglect, to find that once more it was broad day.

Chapter Fifty Four

Morgan and I had more than one long talk that next day about the Spaniards and the pusillanimous way in which they had behaved; but not until a good deal had been done to make our tent comfortable, and that in which poor Sarah was lying, mending fast, but still very weak. A great deal too had to be done for the wounded, who bore their sufferings with wonderful patience, and were delighted when I went and sat with them, and talked over the different phases of the fight.

Morgan was sentry once more in the afternoon, and after seeing my father comfortably asleep, I went across to him, where he was keeping a sharp look-out for the Indians; but so far there had been no sign, and we began talking about the wounded, and how long it would be before they were stirring again.

"Ah, a long time, sir," he said. "You can make a man weak with a shot or a cut with a sword. It's done in a moment, but it takes months to make one strong."

"I say, Morgan," I whispered, "don't you think the General ought to have a place dug and made for that powder?"

He turned sharply and looked me full in the eyes, but instead of answering my question, he said—

"You see, Master George, they were regularly cheated over us."

"Who were—the Indians?"

"The Indians? No; the Spanish."

"He will not talk about the powder business," I said to myself. "He always turns it off."

"You see, sir," he continued, as he softly rubbed the barrel of his piece to get rid of some of the rust that had encrusted it, "they expected to find us a set of quiet spade-and-hoe-and-wheelbarrow sort of people, quite different to them, as are looked upon as being so warlike and fierce."

"And so we are, Morgan."

Mass' George: A Boy's Adventures in the Old Savannah | 367

"And so we are, lad. We came out here to dig and live, and be at peace, with our barrows; but that doesn't mean that we haven't got the fighting stuff in us, ready for use when it's wanted. I don't want to fight, and I save my fists for digging, but they are fists all the same, sir."

"Yes, of course."

"Yes, of course, sir. But they Spanish didn't understand that. They thought that in spite of what was said last time they came, all they had to do was to make a show, and order us off, and we should go; so they made a show by shooting at the Indians; and I'll be bound to say that every time the Spanish officers cried 'fire!' they thought they were frightening us too."

"But they didn't, Morgan."

"Not a bit, sir. Wrong stuff. They made a great big mistake, and when they get back to Flori— what is it?"

"Florida."

"Ah, Florida, I should say there'll be a good bit o' trouble, for they were meant to do more than they contrived. You see, when they fired, the Indians ran, and they followed them up, and fired again, and the Indians ran faster. Then by and by they came and fired at us."

"And we did not run, Morgan."

"No, sir, not a bit; and as somebody had to run—one side must, you see—why, they did. You see we didn't look nice. We'd been at it, look you, and got the marks of battle on us to show that we could do something, and it was rather startling to men coming on to attack a place. First beginning of fighting one feels a bit squeamish; after that one don't. We'd got over our squeamishness; they hadn't, for I don't count their bit of firing as anything. Think they'll come back, sir?"

"If they do, it will be with a war-ship, and great guns," I said. "Not as they did this time."

"Then I don't think they'll come at all, sir, for bringing a war-ship means big business, and our having war-ships too to keep them off. Do you know, I begin to think that we shall have a holiday now, so as to go back home."

Day after day glided by, and in the rest and relief it seemed as if quite a new life was opening out for us. My father was mending rapidly, and Sarah was well enough to insist upon busying herself about many little matters to add to our comfort. Hannibal only seemed to me to be dull and quiet, while Pomp was at me every day about going out somewhere, and looked as if he were a prisoner chained by the leg when told that he must not stray from camp.

There had been repeated discussions, so my father told me, over the all-important question of giving up our watchful life, and beginning once more to take to that of peace; but it was still deemed advisable to wait, and another week glided away, made memorable by the deaths of two of the brave fellows who had been wounded.

It was the evening after the last of these two had been sadly laid in his resting-place, that Morgan startled me by saying suddenly—

"He's only a black, certainly, Master George, but somehow one's got to like him."

"Why, what has Pomp been doing now?" I said.

"I was talking about his father, sir."

"Hannibal? Well, what of him? I haven't seen him to-day—no; now I come to think of it, nor yesterday neither."

"No; he hasn't been up."

"Why, Morgan," I said, "I was out round the plantations yesterday with Colonel Preston, and I've been with my father and Sarah all to-day; is poor old Hannibal ill?"

"Very bad, I think, sir. I asked the doctor to go and see him."

I ran off to the rough tent he and Pomp had contrived for themselves, and to my horror I found the doctor inside, and that my father had contrived to get there by the help of a couple of sticks.

"I didn't know Han was ill," I exclaimed.

"Hush! Don't speak loud," said the doctor. "The poor fellow is in a serious condition."

I crept into the hut to find Pomp on his knees by his father's head, and with his face buried in his hands, while a startled feeling came over me as I saw how still and helpless the great broad-shouldered giant lay, his brow wrinkled up, and his cheeks hollow; but his countenance changed as he caught sight of me.

"Mass' George," he said, and he tried to raise one of his hands.

"Oh, Hannibal!" I cried. "I did not know you were so ill. Pomp, why didn't you tell me?"

The boy raised his face all wet with tears, and his eyes swollen. "How Pomp know?" he cried. "Fader nebber tell um."

"Don't talk, Hannibal, my man," said my father, gently. "We none of us knew, my boy. The poor fellow was wounded, and has been going about all this time with an arrow-head in his side, saying nothing, but patiently bearing it all. My poor brave fellow," he continued, taking the man's hand, "you have always been risking your life in our defence."

"Han belong to Mass' Capen," he said, feebly, as he smiled at us. "If arrow not hit um, hit massa."

"What!" said my father, eagerly, as if he suddenly recollected something; "was it that night when you dragged me back, as the arrows flew so fast?"

Hannibal smiled, and clung to the hand which held his.

"Yes; I remember now feeling you start," said my father. "Yes—what is it?"

He leaned over the rough bed that had been made for the wounded man, for the black's lips moved.

"Massa do somefin for Han?" he said.

"My poor fellow, only speak," said my father, who was much moved, while I felt choking.

"If Han die, massa be kind to Pomp?"

"No," cried the boy, with a passionate burst of grief, "Pomp die too."

"And Massa George be good to um."

"Oh, Han," I cried, in a broken voice, as I knelt on the opposite side to my father, and held the poor fellow's other hand.

He looked keenly in both our faces, and though neither of us spoke, he was satisfied, and half closed his eyes.

"Han sleep now," he said.

Just then the doctor bent in at the opening of the tent, and signed to us to come out, and we obeyed.

"Let him sleep, boy," he whispered to Pomp. "Don't speak to him, but if he asks for anything fetch me."

Pomp nodded; he could not answer, and we accompanied the doctor to his rough tent only a few yards away.

"Well?" he said to me as I caught his hand, and questioned him with my eyes. "Do you mean can I save him? I don't know; but I do know this—if it had been a white his case would have been hopeless. The poor fellow must have been in agony; but I have extracted the arrow-head, and these blacks have a constitution that is wonderful. He may recover."

"Please God!" I said to myself, as I walked right away to try and get somewhere quite alone to sit down and think. For I was beginning to waken to the fact of how much I cared for the great kind-hearted, patient fellow, who had all along devoted his life to our service, and in the most utter self-denial offered that life in defence of ours.

Ever since the departure of the Spaniards I had slept soundly, but that night I passed on my knees by poor old Hannibal's pillow.

It was a strange experience, for the poor fellow was delirious, and talked rapidly in a low tone. His thoughts had evidently gone back to his own land and other scenes, but I could not comprehend a word.

Pomp was there too, silent and watchful, and he whispered to me about how the doctor had cut his father's side, and it took all my powers of persuasion and insistence, upon its being right, to make the boy believe that it was to do the wounded man good.

"If Mass' George say um good," he said at last, "Pomp b'leeve um. Oh, Pomp poor fader. Pomp die too," he sobbed.

"He shan't die," I cried, passionately. "Don't talk like that."

There was silence for a time, and then the poor fellow began to mutter again.

"What does he say?" I whispered; but the boy broke down, buried his face in his hands, and sobbed. But after a time, in broken tones, he told me that his father was talking about dying down in the hold of the stifling ship, and about being brought ashore.

"Dat all Pomp hear," whispered the boy. "Talk 'tuff. Done know what."

It was a long, long, weary night, but towards morning the poor fellow slept peacefully, and soon after daylight the doctor was there, as indefatigable in his attentions as he had been over my father, for the colour of a man's skin did not trouble him.

"Less fever," he said to me. "I've got a nurse for him now, so you go and get some sleep."

I was about to protest, but just then I saw who the nurse was, for Sarah stooped down to enter the shelter, and I knew that poor old Hannibal would be safe with her.

Chapter Fifty Five

That day the embargo was taken off, and one by one the settlers began to return to their homes, those whose houses were standing sharing them with the unfortunates whose places had been burned, so that at night the camp wore a peculiarly silent and solemn aspect, one which, depressed as I felt by Hannibal's state, seemed strange indeed.

A certain number of men stayed in the enclosure, and there were ten wounded in our temporary hospital; but the doctor set others of those who had crowded the place free.

One thing struck me directly, and that was the change in Pomp, who could hardly be persuaded to leave his father's side, but sat holding his hand, or else nestled down beside him, with his black curly head just touching the great black's arm, and gently raising it whenever I went to the tent.

I can recall it all very vividly as I now write these my recollections of the early incidents in my life, and how in the days which followed I gradually found that Hannibal fully justified the doctor's words about his fine healthy state; for after the first few days, during which his life seemed to be on the balance, he rapidly began to mend, and his being out of danger was the signal for a change.

My father had been talking about it for quite a month, but our friends at the settlement persuaded him to stay in the quarters that had been rigged up for us, and nothing could have been kinder than the treatment we received.

It was always pointed out by the settlers that at any time the Indians might return, and a fresh expedition be on foot from Florida, though this was looked upon as of little consequence, every one feeling that if the block-house were rebuilt, and the enclosure strengthened, we could laugh any Spanish attack to scorn.

With this in view, and with an eye to the attack of the Indians, very little was done in the way of rebuilding houses and cottages, but the whole strength of the settlement was devoted to the rebuilding of our little fort, and the strengthening of the stockade; and so much energy was thrown into the work by the little white and black population that a stronger building was erected, and left to be finished off afterwards.

I remember well standing with Morgan one day, and seeing the powder-kegs, which had for safety been buried under a heap of sand, disinterred and borne into the new cellar-magazine prepared for them early in the making of the block-house.

Nothing was said for some time, but all at once, as our eyes encountered, Morgan exclaimed—

"There, it's of no use for you to keep looking at me like that, Master George; I know what you are thinking about."

"Do you?"

"Yes, I just do; and I teclare to cootness, I feel as if it would have been right. The only thing against it that I can see is, that I was rather in too great a hurry."

"But it was utter madness," I said, with a shudder.

"Ah, you say so now, sir, because help came, and we were saved; but how would it have been if the Indians had got the mastery, as they nearly did? There is nothing that they stop at in the way of torture and murder, and it would have been a blessing for an end to have been made of us all at once."

"Well," I said, "don't talk about it. Let's be thankful we were saved."

"Oh, I won't say another word, sir, and I wouldn't have spoken now, only you're always looking at me in an aggravating manner."

"Ah, well, Morgan," I replied; "the powder's being put out of sight now, and I will not think about it any more."

"Yes, sir," he said, as a man lifted a keg; "and if I had my way in the world, it should never be brought out again."

"And suppose the Indians came?"

"Didn't I say if I could have my own way in the world, sir? If I did the Indians wouldn't come, nor the Spaniards neither—you said it was Spaniards didn't you? I always thought it was Spaniels."

"Yes; Spaniards. And suppose they come?"

"Bah! Who cares for them? Why, I'd send them flying with a regiment of men armed with spades, and strict orders given only to use the flat side."

I burst out laughing, for somehow everything seemed bright and happy once more, and in the midst of my mirth a quick, eager voice exclaimed—

"What Mass' George laugh upon? Tell Pomp. Pomp want laugh too."

I told him, and as he could not appreciate the comicality of Morgan's remark, he looked sulky and full of doubt for a few moments, but showed his white teeth directly after.

It did not seem long after that the four largest boats of the settlement were loaded deep down with timbers and planks, to supplement those which lay just under the trees by the rattlesnake clearing, and now well seasoned and dry. Many of them had been carried here and there during the flood, but being ready cut down when the clearing was made, they were hunted up at the first thought of the return to build up our house, and dragged out of spots where they had been overgrown with the rapidly-sprung-up verdure.

Expeditions had been sent out several times toward the Indians' country, but as no signs of the savages were seen, our confidence rapidly increased, and some of my happiest hours were passed with Pomp, hunting out these logs and planks, and marking the spots with a blaze from an axe on the nearest tree.

Then a strong party came over from the settlement on the day the boats were despatched, travelled across rapidly, knocked up a shed of the planks and newly-sawn-up boards unloaded at our landing-place from the boats, and I honestly believe the two happiest people there that day among the strange party of blacks, who carried the wood along the forest path, were Pomp and Hannibal, who, though far from strong, insisted upon his being well enough to help.

So many willing bands were there who came over in a couple of boats morning by morning, that with the help of the blacks camped in the rough shed, a fortnight had not passed before the nucleus of our home was up, sufficient for shelter, the finishing and improvements being left to come by degrees.

I believe that the sight of our home slowly rising from the ruins did more to give my father back his strength than anything done by the doctor, but perhaps that is ungrateful. But be that as it may, it was a pleasure to see him.

"Only look at the captain," Morgan said to me one morning, two days after our friends had gone back. "Don't he look lovely again, sir?"

"Well, I don't know about lovely. I thought that about Sarah."

"Now, don't you make fun," said Morgan, giving a heap of wood ashes a tap with his spade, to make it lie close in his rough barrow, whose wheel was a section sawn off the end of a very round-trunked pine, and tired by nailing on the iron hooping from a cask.

"Don't you send that ash flying and smothering me," I cried, as Pomp, who was helping load and wheel the heap to the garden, began to sneeze violently.

"Then you shouldn't make fun of a woman, sir, because she's plain."

"I didn't," I said, stoutly. "I meant lovely and well. And if you say your wife's plain again, I'll go and tell her so. She's the dearest old motherly body that ever lived."

Morgan drove his spade down into the earth, took my hand, and shook it solemnly, Pomp, who had ceased sneezing, looking on wonderingly the while.

"Thankye, Master George, thankye, sir; so she is—so she is."

Pomp came forward and held out his hand.

"Well, what now?" growled Morgan.

"Tought Mass' Morgan want shake hand," said the boy.

"Get out with you, sir. Wheel that barrow right on to the bed next to the last load."

Pomp seized the handles, went off with the barrow, caught the edge against the stump of a tree, one of the many not yet grubbed up, upset the ashes, and bounded off into the forest, to stand watching us from behind a tree, as if in dread of punishment; but seeing me roaring with laughter, he came cautiously back, grinning as if it was after all an excellent joke.

"There, shovel it up again, boy," said Morgan, good-temperedly; "it was an accident."

"Iss, Mass' Morgan, all um axden," cried the boy, working away.

"One can't be very cross with him, Master George; he's such a happy young dog, and somehow, after all the trouble, I feel too happy, and so does Sarah; and to see her smile, sir, at getting a bit of a shelf put up in her new kitchen, and to hear her talk about the things the captain sent for from England—Lor', sir, it would do you good."

"Lubbly 'tuff!" cried Pomp, as he scraped up the fallen wood ashes.

"What's lovely stuff?" I said.

"All dat, Mass' George. Mass' Morgan say make um rings grow, and wish dah twenty times as much."

"Ah, that I do," cried Morgan. "Wish I had—"

"Mass' Morgan like Injum come burn down house 'gain make more?"

"No, you stupid little nigger," cried Morgan; "of course not."

Flop! Down went the spade, and Pomp began to stalk away sulkily, working his toes about—a way he had of showing his annoyance.

"Hi! Stop!" I cried; "where are you going?"

"Pomp go jump in um ribber, and let de ole 'gator eat um."

"Nonsense! What for?"

"Mass' Morgan call um 'tupid lil nigger. Allus call um 'tupid lil nigger, and hurt Pomp all over."

"No, no; come along. Morgan didn't mean it."

"Eh? You no mean it, Mass' Morgan?" cried the boy, eagerly.

"No, of course not. You're the cleverest boy I ever knew."

"Dah, Mass' George, hear dat. Now see Pomp wheel dat barrow, and neber spill lil bit ob ashums, and nex' time he go over oder place, he bring um pockets full for Mass' Morgan garden."

"He's a rum un, sir," said Morgan, "but somehow I like him. Rather like to paint him white, though. Lor', Master George, what a treat it is to be getting down the weeds again. Look at old Han, how he is giving it to 'em. I'm 'bliged to check him a bit though, sometimes; he aren't quite strong yet. Here's the captain."

"Well, Morgan," said my father, as he came up, "how soon do you think we might plant a few creepers about the house? The finishing and glazing need not interfere with them."

"Oh, we can't put in any more, sir."

"What? Why not? I particularly want two of those wild vines to be put in."

"Did put 'em in before you come out this morning, sir, and the 'suckle and passion-flowers too. They'll be up a-top of the roof before we know where we are."

My father looked pleased, and turned to examine the young plants that had been set.

"Does me good, Master George, to see the captain coming round as he is. Quite takes to the garden again. But dear, dear! It's in a melancholy state."

"Nonsense!" I cried; "why, it's wonderful how well it looks."

"Wonderful? Well, sir, I wouldn't have thought you could talk in that way of such a wilderness. Why, even old Han there, in his broken English savage way, said he was ashamed of it."

"Oh, well, I'm not," I said. "It's glorious to be able to get back once more to the dear old place. I say, though, you don't want Pomp any longer?"

"Ah, but I do, sir. Why?"

"I want to row up and have a bit of fishing. It does seem so long since I've had a turn."

"Eh? Who said go fis?" cried Pomp, sharply. "Mass' George go fish? Catch terrapum, and take de gun?"

"Morgan says he can't spare you."

"Oh!" exclaimed Pomp; but Morgan smiled one of his curious dry smiles, as he took off his hat and pointed with the corner.

"Just you go to the far end of the shed, Pomp, and you'll find in the damp place an old pot with a lot of bait in it as I put ready. On'y mind this, it's not to be all games."

"What do you mean?" I said, for Pomp had rushed off to get the bait.

"Bring us a bit o' fish. Be quite a treat."

Half an hour after Pomp and I were pulling up the river close in beneath the over-spreading boughs, ready to shout for joy as the golden sunbeams came down through the leaves and formed a lace-work of glory on the smooth deep water. Every now and then there was a familiar rustle and a splash, a flapping of wings, and a harsh cry as a heron or stork rose from his fishing-ground; then some great hawk hovered over the stream, or we caught sight of the yellow and orange of the orioles.

Pomp was for rowing on and up to a favourite spot where there was a special haunt of the fish, where the stream curved round and formed a deep pool. But I felt as if I must stop again and again to let the boat drift, and watch humming-birds, or brightly-painted butterflies and beetles, flitting here and there, so that it was quite a couple of hours before we reached the spot, and suddenly turned the curve of the river into the eddy.

As we did so silently I turned to look, and sat there petrified for a few moments, before I softly laid my hand on Pomp's arm. He turned round sharply and saw what I did—a party of six Indians on the opposite bank.

Before either of us could dip oar again we were seen; there was a deep, low exclamation, and the party turned and plunged into the forest and were gone.

With one sweep of my oar I sent the boat round into the stream, and we rowed back as rapidly as we could, expecting to hear arrows whizzing by us every moment. But we reached the landing-place in safety, secured the boat, and ran to the newly-erected house to give the alarm. I saw my father's brow contract with agony, but he was prompt in his measures.

"We will face them here," he said, "if they come." And, summoning in Morgan and Hannibal, the door and windows were barricaded, the weapons loaded, and we waited for the attack.

But we waited in vain. The severe lesson dealt to the Indians by our people and the Spaniards had had its result, and though I had not understood it then, the savages were more frightened of us than we of them; and the very next day, while we were still expecting attack, Colonel Preston came over from the settlement in company with the doctor, who wished to see his three patients once again, while the former announced a visit from some of the chiefs to make peace with our people, and to ask permission to trade.

That was the last alarm we had from the Indians, who would often come afterwards to barter skins, and some of their basket-work, with venison and fish, for knives and tobacco. And in the course of time my father and I had them for guides in many a pleasant hunting expedition, and for allies against the Spaniards, when they resumed their pretensions to the country, and carried on a feeble, desultory warfare, which kept the settlement always on the alert, but never once disturbed us, for our home lay quite out of their track and beyond them, when they came up the river upon one of their expeditions.

At such times my father always answered the call to arms; and as time went on, in addition to Morgan and the black, he had two great strapping fellows in Pomp and me—both young and loose-jointed, but able hands with a firelock.

Such calls were exciting; but after two or three, so little damage was done, that they ceased to cause us much anxiety; and after a bold attempt or two at retaliation, in which the war was carried right into the Spaniards' own land, and away up to their Floridan fort, matters gradually settled down.

For our settlement had prospered and increased, the broad savannahs grew year by year into highly-cultivated cotton land; the sugar-cane nourished; coffee was grown; and as the plantations spread, the little settlement gradually developed into a town and fort, to which big ships came with merchandise from the old country, and took back the produce of our fields. Then as the town increased, and the forest disappeared in the course of years, we found ourselves in a position to laugh at the pretensions of the Spaniards.

But over all that there seems to hang a mist, and I recall but little of the troubles of those later days. It is of the early I write—of the times when all was new and fresh; and I have only to close my eyes to see again our old home surrounded by forest, that was always trying to reclaim the portions my father had won; but the skirmishers of Nature gained nothing, and a pleasant truce ensued. For my father was too wealthy to need to turn his land into plantations and trouble himself about the produce; he loved to keep it all as he had made it at first, save that now and again pleasant little additions were made, and the comforts of civilisation were not forgotten.

But as time went on, and I grew up, my pleasant life there had to come to an end, and I was obliged to go out into the world as became a man.

It was my great delight though as the years rolled on to get down south for a month's stay at the old place, and with Hannibal and Pomp for companions, and an Indian or two for guides, to penetrate the wilds for days and days together, boating, fishing, shooting, and studying the glories of the wondrous water-ways of the forest and swamps.

Such trips seemed always fresh, and when I returned there was the delightful old home in which my father had elected to end his days; and I picture one of those scenes outside the embowered house with its broad veranda, and the pretty cottages a couple of hundred yards away beyond the noble garden, Morgan's pride. The home was simple still, for my father did not increase his establishment, save that a couple of young black girls elected to come from the settlement to place themselves under old Sarah's management.

I should not have mentioned this but for one little incident which took place two years after.

I had been in England for a long stay, and at the termination of my visit I had taken passage, landed at the settlement, made a hasty call on two old friends, and then walked across to my father's, where, after my warm welcome from within doors, including a kiss from our Sarah for the great swarthy man she always would call "My dear boy," I went out to have my hand crunched by grey-headed old Morgan, and to grasp old Hannibal's broad palm as well.

"Why, where's Pomp?" I said.

"Him heah, Mass' George," was shouted from the direction of one of the cottages. "I come, sah, but she juss like 'tupid lil nigger. Come 'long, will you; Mass' George won't eat you."

I opened my eyes a little as I recognised in the smart, pleasant-looking black girl by his side, Salome, one of the maids I had seen at the cottage before I sailed for Europe.

"Why, Pomp," I said, laughing, "what does this mean?"

"Dab juss what I tell her, Mass' George," he cried. "I know you be quite please, on'y she all ashame and foolis like."

"But, Pomp, my good fellow, you don't mean—"

"Oh yes, I do, Mass' George; and I know you be dreffle glad—dat my wife."

Yes; I can picture it all—that old plantation life started by brave-enduring Englishmen, who were ready to face stern dangers, and determined to hold their own—picture it all more vividly than perhaps I have done for you; but as far as in me lay, I have tried to place before you who read the incidents of a boy's life in those distant days; and if I have been somewhat prosy at times, and made much of trifles, which were serious matters to us, forgive my shortcomings as I lay down my pen.